Praise for *No One Aboard*

"I inhaled this book! In Emy McGuire's tense and claustrophobic debut, everyone aboard the Cameron family's yacht has a secret—and no one is safe. *No One Aboard* is the kind of compulsively readable thriller that makes you lose sleep to finish 'just one more page.'"
—**Emma C. Wells**, *USA TODAY*
bestselling author of *This Girl's a Killer*

"The killer premise is just the beginning in this twisty, claustrophobic, nautical thriller. Between the dangers of the open sea, the deliciously toxic family aboard their luxury yacht, and the mystery of how an entire family can disappear into thin air, McGuire's perfectly crafted tension will drive readers to turn pages into the wee hours—which is exactly what I did."
—**Jenna Satterthwaite**, author of
Made for You and *The New Year's Party*

"Once I picked up *No One Aboard*, I could not put it down. This taut and haunting debut will leave you gasping for breath! Twists, family drama, and so much more than just rich people behaving badly. Emy McGuire will be a name to watch."
—**Jennifer Moorhead**, Amazon
bestselling author of *Broken Bayou*

"*No One Aboard* grabbed me from the get-go with its spine-tingling opening. Expertly building suspense, Emy McGuire takes you hostage on a compelling, page-turning voyage."
—**Rick Mofina, *USA TODAY* bestselling author**

"An electrifying and page-turning thrill ride. McGuire's debut novel, with its clever plotting and sharp writing, will have you inhaling this story until the satisfying end."
—**Seraphina Nova Glass, two-time Edgar Award–nominated author** of *On a Quiet Street*

"An impressive blend of suspense and psychological depth, immersing readers in the allure of the open sea while unraveling the dark secrets of a fractured family. Emy McGuire's riveting debut will leave an indelible mark, ask if the proverbial blood *is* thicker than water, and challenge us to confront the monsters we all hold within and the lengths we'll go to survive."
—**Yasmin Angoe, bestselling author of** *Her Name Is Knight* **and** *Not What She Seems*

"A twisty voyage of family secrets and unmoored dysfunction. Will keep you on a tight rope until the very last chapter."
—**Tamara L. Miller, author of** *Into the Fall*

NO ONE ABOARD

NO
ONE
ABOARD

a novel

EMY McGUIRE

GRAYDON
HOUSE

Recycling programs for this product may not exist in your area.

ISBN-13: 978-1-525-83162-1
ISBN-13: 978-1-525-80003-0 (Hardcover Edition)

No One Aboard

Copyright © 2025 by Emy McGuire

All rights reserved. No part of this book may be used or reproduced in any manner whatsoever without written permission.

Without limiting the exclusive rights of any author, contributor or the publisher of this publication, any unauthorized use of this publication to train generative artificial intelligence (AI) technologies is expressly prohibited. Harlequin also exercises their rights under Article 4(3) of the Digital Single Market Directive 2019/790 and expressly reserves this publication from the text and data mining exception.

This is a work of fiction. Names, characters, places and incidents are either the product of the author's imagination or are used fictitiously. Any resemblance to actual persons, living or dead, businesses, companies, events or locales is entirely coincidental.

® is a trademark of Harlequin Enterprises ULC.

Graydon House
22 Adelaide St. West, 41st Floor
Toronto, Ontario M5H 4E3, Canada
www.GraydonHouseBooks.com

HarperCollins Publishers
Macken House,
39/40 Mayor Street Upper,
Dublin 1, D01 C9W8, Ireland
www.HarperCollins.com

Printed in U.S.A.

*To Mom, the reason I fell for the sea
And Dad, the reason I sailed it*

*He that would go to sea for pleasure
would go to hell for a pastime.*
—A SAILOR'S PROVERB

Chapter 1

Jerry Baugh

JERRY BAUGH DIDN'T see the ship. He didn't notice the red warning on the screen. He was, in fact, cozied up in the cockpit of his Dyer 29 lobster boat, feet propped between the rungs of the helm and hands stacked on his belly.

Jerry's day of deep-sea fishing had been successful—a sailfish bill, broken at the hilt, currently stuck out of his bomber jacket pocket—and he was thinking about whether the meat should be marinated in lemon juice or just plain old butter.

He was too distracted to detect the boat in his path—white and gleaming, suspended between the black water of the Atlantic and the starless, moonless sky with the same sinister beauty of an iceberg.

Or a ghost.

When the boat alarm went off, Jerry jolted in his seat, sending his Bass Pro Shops cap tumbling down his chest. A single drop of sailfish blood had, at some point, fallen onto the face of his watch, which read nine minutes after midnight.

He detangled his feet from the helm and peered at the radar. He was heading two hundred and fifty-eight degrees toward Hallandale Marina. The strange white sailboat blocked his way.

Jerry switched off the autopilot and eased the throttle to

slow down, his heart thumping soundly in his chest. If the alarm hadn't sounded, he might have shipwrecked them both.

This sent a surge of anger through him. Why hadn't the captain of the sailboat moved out of *his* way? *Sheila 2.0* wasn't subtle, her engine making an ugly chewing noise not unlike a trash compactor. They should have heard her coming.

Jerry allowed his boat to chug closer before he killed the engine and processed what on the devil's blue sea he was looking at.

It was a sailboat, yes, but not like the rust-laced ones that docked near *Sheila 2.0* in the Hallandale Marina.

This boat was mesmerizing.

It had twin aluminum masts, a wood-finished deck, and sunbathing mattresses laid out on the chart house. The body of the boat was a blinding white, smooth, curvaceous. The cap rails were teak and coated with a glittering crust of sea salt. No one had cleaned them in some time. Cursive lettering on the side spelled out the boat's name.

The Old Eileen.

Jerry stared, a bit starstruck. Boats like *Sheila 2.0* were made to choke marine diesel oil and seawater until they finally died twitching in a harbor like a waterlogged beetle on its back.

Boats like *The Old Eileen* were made to be beautiful.

Jerry found his radio, hooked to his waistband, and cleared his throat before speaking into it.

"Eileen, Eileen, Eileen, this is Sheila, Sheila, Sheila, over."

He waited.

There was a time when Jerry was younger (and a good bit stupider) that he wanted to buy a sailboat instead of a motorboat. It was romantic, the idea of harnessing the wind to travel the world. But in the end, it was those same winds that terrified him. Wind could overpower him, seize control of the boat and bend its course. Jerry would have had to accept that possibility. He would have had to bare his throat to the mercy of the sea.

A mercy, he had come to understand, that did not exist.

"Eileen, Eileen, Eileen!" Jerry repeated into the radio.

They must be asleep. Jerry leaned forward and sounded his horn—five short blasts to signal danger. He waited for the radio to crackle to life, for a silver-spooned captain to sputter apologies, or maybe for an underpaid deckhand to rush up top and get the boat moving once more.

There was only the sound of the luffing, useless sails, and the ever-shifting sea.

Jerry frowned and fiddled with the fish bill in his pocket. He should leave.

He fumbled in the dark to switch the engine back on. He would report what he'd seen to the coast guard, get the captain in trouble for being so reckless. He'd be back in Florida by dawn.

But Steve . . .

Jerry glanced at his dash where he had taped up a photograph of himself with his younger brother. It was the last picture taken of Steve before he died. Jerry closed his eyes for a moment. He would have traded his boat, his bait, and everything he owned if someone had stopped that night to help Steve.

"Well, shit." Jerry rubbed at his clavicle and swallowed hard. He would be in and out. Just to make sure all was well.

Jerry moved across the deck, aware of every sound his shuffling feet made. He rummaged through his fishing equipment, eyes never leaving *The Old Eileen*. His calloused, practiced hands fit right around the harpoon gun, and he felt a measure of reassurance with a weapon in his grasp. He wasn't scared, he was too old for that, but there was nothing quite like a creaking, old ship on the ocean at night to make a man into a boy again.

He tucked the harpoon gun under one arm and set to work lowering his tiny dinghy. He'd take one moment to wake whoever was on board, then get right back on his boat. Good deed done for the day. Maybe the decade.

Jerry grunted as he climbed up the *Eileen*'s porthole and over the rail. The deck was empty save for an orange life preserver tied to the stern, the boat's name written in black on the top and a slogan in italics around the bottom.

Unwind Yachting Co.
Safe to sail in any gale!

With no one in sight, Jerry located the companionway stairs that led down beneath the cockpit and gave one last scan of the deck before going below.

Downstairs, the chart house was neat and captainless, but the ship's manifest was sitting in the center of the table, open to the first page.

SHIP'S MANIFEST—THE OLD EILEEN
SKIPPER—*Captain Francis Ryan Cameron (55)*
MATE—*MJ Tuckett (67)*
CREW—*Alejandro Matamoros (54), Nicolás de la Vega (22)*
PASSENGERS—*Lila Logan Cameron (54), Francis Rylan Cameron (17), Taliea Indigo Cameron (17)*

Seven souls. Seven souls aboard *The Old Eileen*, and not a single one had answered the radio, which lay next to the manifest like an amputated limb. Jerry picked it up and felt an ice-cold trickle of sweat on the back of his neck.

The cord had been cut.

Jerry's knuckles went white against the harpoon gun. Bad things happen at sea. Storms kill and brothers drown.

But the radio cord hadn't been severed by the ocean.

Jerry crept through the luxurious salon and to a door that must lead to a cabin. He let his trigger hand slip down for a moment so he could turn his radio to *16*—the international maritime emergency channel.

Just in case.

He opened the door to the cabin.

The primary bedroom. King-size bed with an indigo comforter and cream sheets. Velvet couch molded to fit the tight corner. A woman's lipstick lay open on one bedside table, rolling back and forth as the boat rocked.

There was no one there. No sleeping captain, no apologetic deckhands, no life whatsoever. Had they just . . . left?

Jerry checked the next room. This one held two twin beds with identical navy bedspreads. One bed was unmade, with a variety of books scattered at its foot. The bedclothes on the other were tucked in, military-style. A sketchbook was half hidden by the pillowcase, open to an illustration of some kind of monster.

Jerry mopped his brow with a rag he kept in his shirt pocket, not caring that it had dried sailfish blood caking the edges. He should have motored on by and called the damn guard.

He forced himself to concentrate. He was doing the right thing. The captain could be out cold and in need of help. There were only a few more rooms.

But the last cabin was just as quiet.

Jerry peeked into the galley and the bilges, running out of places to check.

The heads. Each of the three cabins must have its own personal bathroom, and he hadn't yet tried any of them. Hands slick with sweat around the harpoon gun, Jerry retraced his steps, checking first in the crew members' head, then the primary suite's, then back to the room with the twin beds and the drawing of the monster.

He nudged open the last bathroom door and looked inside.

In the mirror, his own reflection stared back at him, interrupted only by a string of crimson words that had been written on the glass.

A weight dropped anchor inside his stomach, flooding Jerry with a kind of dread he had avoided for thirty years. The harpoon gun slipped from his hands, and he reached for his radio, unable to peel his gaze from the message on the mirror.

SAVE yOUR SELf

The Convey

OPINION: The Ocean Is Our Great Equalizer
(why the newest Atlantic disaster seems to spell K-A-R-M-A for the one percent)

MIKE GRADY

The Camerons—a family of four headed by television darling Lila Logan and business tycoon Francis Cameron—have been reported missing after their multimillion-dollar sailing yacht turned up eighty miles offshore without a single person onboard early in the morning of June 9. Authorities and reporters have leaped into extensive action. The Atlantic has already been tempestuous at the beginning of this year's hurricane season. Potential upcoming storms have given the search a dangerous time component in an investigation reminiscent of the *Titan*, the infamous submersible that imploded with five passengers aboard on its way to see the *Titanic* wreck. The world had plenty to say about the *Titan* and its affluent victims, and this latest oceanic mystery has the potential to play out the same.

Francis and Lila Cameron both had modest childhoods, but thanks to the entertainment industry, the business world, and the good old American dream, they have skyrocketed into the fraction of Americans who own multiple homes (Palm Beach villa, LA bungalow, and a sleek Aspen chalet, if anyone's wondering), not to mention the multimillion-dollar sailing yacht that came up empty in the early hours of yesterday morning. While I'm not necessarily here to say that the Atlantic Ocean is doing a better job than God or taxes to rid us of the elite, I do want to pose a big-picture question while authorities are sussing out the *how did this happen?* and *where did they go?* of it all. My question instead to you, dear reader, is this: *Why the Camerons?*

Chapter 2

```
Tia Cameron
Call sign: Thimble
The Day Before Departure
```

THE OLD EILEEN was waiting for Tia Cameron. She felt the ship's magnetic pull as she stepped onto the dock of New Haven Marina. It was the way the waves must feel, building themselves up high only to race back to shore and shatter upon the sand.

An inevitability.

Sweat spread under the arms of her school uniform as she dragged her suitcase over the wooden slats of the dock and laid eyes on her family's boat.

The Old Eileen sat like a swan among sea gulls, her body streamlined, her gold lettering immaculate. She'd been swabbed and de-fouled until she shone a brilliant white and gave off a mild scent of chemical lime. She was as stunning as she'd been the day Tia's father bought her when Tia and her twin brother, Rylan, were small. *The Old Eileen* had been a part of their lives every summer since in the same way other families had ski lodges or beach homes.

But this trip would be different from all the ones that had come before. This was no childhood day-sail hugging the coast or vacation spent inside a bay. This trip would take them out to sea for a week to celebrate that high school was now behind them and the real world loomed ahead.

For Tia Cameron, this trip marked the end of something.

"My beautiful daughter!" a soprano voice chimed out from the deck of the ship.

Tia's mother was poised at the stern on tiptoes, one hand on the back of her sun hat, the other tilting up her heart-shaped Saint Laurent sunglasses. The image made Tia think of the ship log she and Rylan used to keep, where they had given everyone onboard descriptions and call signs.

Lila Logan Cameron. Glamorous actress and mother of two.
Call sign: Cassiopeia.
Meaning: The mythic Greek queen who boasted so much that her daughter Andromeda ended up chained to a rock in monster-infested waters.

Or, as Rylan preferred, *Cassiopea: the scientific genus for upside-down jellyfish. Beautiful. Lucid. Deadly.*

The moment Tia crossed the catwalk and was in reach, Lila clasped her face, kissed her on both cheeks, and announced, "My darling girl, I am going to make you a drink. What would you like?"

"Anything but tea."

Lila laughed. "Then a pair of strawberry daiquiris, coming right up! Put your suitcase in your room."

Tia hoisted her suitcase to the ship's companionway. "Okay, Mom." She knew better than to halt the breathtaking momentum of Lila Logan.

The hatch to the companionway was open, sunshine streaming into the salon below. Tia lowered her suitcase down and climbed after it, then walked through the salon and the short hall to the center bedroom. Her brother's stuff was already unpacked neatly in his half. Even his swim trunks had been folded. There wasn't a maid onboard, but Tia couldn't imagine her unkempt, daydreamy brother taking the time to fold every article of clothing and swimwear.

And it wasn't like her mother would have done it herself.

When Tia climbed back on deck in her polka-dot two-piece, Lila was draped across the chart house in a lavender shell-scoop bikini. She sat up long enough to hand her a glass of pink, sweet-smelling liquid before they lay back side by side.

"Where's Rylan and Dad?" The ice cubes made music in her daiquiri glass.

"Off on a dive. Rylan still hasn't passed all of his rescue skills. They'll be back soon, I'm sure." Lila reached a long arm over and toasted her drink with Tia's. "But enough about them. To Tia Cameron! The newest—and finest—graduate of St. Beatrice—"

"Bernadette's."

"St. Bernadette's! Now, even if you weren't educated a bit, you at least *look* like you were on paper." Lila drained her glass.

Tia took a sip. Even though she was only two hours from her redbrick, woodsy boarding school, not nearly far enough, the sunlight, the sea, and the strawberry sweetener were enough to make her finally relax. St. Bernadette's School for Girls was behind her now. For good.

Lila wrinkled her nose and touched Tia's hair. "Did you dye the ends yourself?"

"Yup." The sink in her dorm room had still been stained red when Tia left this morning.

"Let me pay for a salon next time, hm?" Lila tossed her own corn silk hair over one shoulder.

Tia pictured for the millionth time what her life might have been like if she looked more like her mother. Lila Cameron was a classic beauty—soft hair and softer skin with a delicate frame that, like her maiden name, Lila Logan, made it seem like she was ready to soar. Tia hadn't inherited any of it. She was shorter and curvier with coarse dark hair that had taken half a dozen bleach attempts to dye the split ends red.

"My, if it isn't the dashing and daring Cameron women!"

Tia's father materialized at the swim ladder, decked out in full scuba diving apparel: skintight wet suit, half-inflated buoyancy control device, and bright orange fins under one arm that evoked some awkward avian creature.

Tia downed the rest of her daiquiri.

Captain Francis Ryan Cameron. A rags-to-riches yachting CEO and owner of The Old Eileen.

Call sign: Midas.

Meaning: The storied king whose mere touch turned everything into gold. Or, the Midas cichlid fish, known to be omnivorous, territorial, and color-changing.

Lila matched her husband's pearly grin as she leaned back on her elbows. "Ah, and the gallant, gawky Cameron men."

"Glad to see you, Tia. How was the drive?" Francis tossed his flippers aside and worked to peel off his wetsuit.

"Fine," Tia said, her focus behind her father where any moment she hoped Rylan would appear.

And he did, hauling himself over the edge effortlessly, black hair dripping beads down his face. He shed his wet suit like a selkie's coat and locked in on her with owly eyes.

Francis Rylan Cameron. Son, brother.

Call sign: Minnow.

Meaning: Small, bashful, freshwater fish. Harmless and quick. But fun fact—they have teeth in the back of their throat.

Tia stood. Rylan crossed the deck, leaned down, and crushed her in his arms. When he pulled back, his smile was electric, a current that ran from him to her and made her smile in return.

But something was different. He'd gotten tall. There was a nick on his chin where he must have cut himself shaving.

Since when does Rylan shave? And was he even thinner than last summer?

Rylan drew her in again and murmured into her hair, "Missed you."

He was definitely thinner.

"How was your dive?" she asked.

Francis answered for him. "He passed some of the rescue skills. Third time's the charm, eh, Tia?"

"Sure."

Francis strode across the deck once he was free from his equipment and planted a scratchy, stubbly kiss on his daughter's head. He did the same with his wife's cheek, and she swatted him away. "Shave. Now."

Tia set her empty daiquiri glass on the chart house. She toted Rylan to the railing, then shoved him backward into the marina water without warning. She needed to talk to him. Alone.

Rylan surfaced, spluttering. "Hey!" he shouted, whipping his head around to see if they were going to be chastised by the dockworkers. There weren't any nearby. If there had been at one point, they'd already turned a blind eye to Rylan and Francis doing a quick skill dive under the ship. Most marinas forbade scuba diving or swimming at all in case of a boating accident. But the dockworkers knew the Camerons. Francis's company, Unwind Yachting, maintained half the boats in the marina.

Tia cannonballed in after her brother, sending a soupy wave into him.

He made a face and spit. "What was that for?"

Tia swam to his side and poked his head. "Just to make sure you're still alive in there."

Rylan pushed her hand away. He treaded water, those gentle eyes of his trained on her.

Tia glanced back at their family yacht. Her parents were still flirting on deck. Alejandro Matamoros, Francis's best friend, business partner, and renowned culinary mastermind, was below, she knew, cooking up a feast. MJ, the first mate, would arrive tomorrow, along with Ernie, a longtime sailor and family friend. There would be seven of them in the end, sailing from their meet-up spot in Connecticut to the Camerons' Palm Beach home. Francis and Lila had hired a crew to charter their boat all the way to New Haven just so they could fly in and sail it back down themselves.

Tia faced her twin. "When this is over, the vacation, our birthday, all of it . . ."

She sucked in a breath. There was no going back now.

"When all of it's over, I'm leaving, Ry. I'm leaving, and I want you to come with me. We're about to turn eighteen. We graduated. We can do this."

Rylan's face drained of color. He looked as white as the hull of the ship.

Tia took him by his shoulder. "You don't have to decide now. I know it's big, but I've thought it all through and—"

"No," Rylan whispered.

Tia shook him slightly. "Rylan, just think about—"

"I can't," he murmured, and the tremor in his voice made Tia's stomach turn.

She hadn't expected this. He always went along with her plans. But he had spent more time with Francis and Lila the past year than he had with her, and leaving them behind forever was huge. Tia would need to ease him into it.

"Tia," he said, strained, in response to her silence. "You just got here. Can we talk about this later? Please."

"Fine. Of course." She let him withdraw and swim back to the ladder.

Maybe in this moment Rylan couldn't imagine the world

that Tia could outside the one built by the Cameron family. But tomorrow, *The Old Eileen* would glide out from the harbor and into open sea. One week later, she'd dock in West Palm Beach, and the seven of them would disembark. And after their birthday celebration on June 5, Tia and Rylan would be gone, and a world outside the Camerons would be far more than imagined.

Chapter 3

```
Rylan Cameron
Call sign: Minnow
The Day Before Departure
```

FRANCIS RYLAN CAMERON sat on the floor of the primary suite's bathroom, drawing in his sketchbook as his mother applied cream to her elbows and face. Rylan had his knees drawn up to his chest, one pencil in his hand and another between his teeth.

He was drawing Tia. She was underwater, hair splayed behind her, hand outstretched toward a school of powder-blue tangs.

Lila glanced down at the drawing. "It's lovely, darling," she said, and her hand, featherlight, rested for a moment on Rylan's head.

He leaned into it and kept working, pencil gliding over paper, an underwater world taking wispy shape beneath his touch.

It calmed him to draw like this, a hobby he had first taken up eight years ago when Francis purchased *The Old Eileen*. Tia encouraged him to get a coloring book so he could distract himself from seasickness, and it had worked. Now his sketchbook was filled with renderings of his family, of fish and porpoises, of white sailboats and buried treasure, and, most recently, the sister he'd been missing for the last nine months.

In this sketch, Tia was swimming ahead of him toward the blue tangs, not bothering to look back.

Running away.

Rylan pressed the pencil tip deeper into the page, his knuckles as tense and white as mountaintops.

Whenever he imagined his future, Tia was always in it, an image that had kept him steady a thousand times since he had watched her jet take off to Connecticut last August. They would be going to Pepperdine together in the fall. Rylan had gotten into five of the six schools he'd applied to, some of them Ivy Leagues, but Tia, applying to the same six in order to placate her parents, had only been accepted to Pepperdine, so that was where they were going. They would live at their Malibu beach house on the weekends, resume binging *Criminal Minds*, and go on long midnight drives when they couldn't fall asleep. They were going to have their old lives back, but better.

Except now Tia had a taste for what it was like to live away from home. Had she forgotten everything good about their family while she was gone?

The Camerons were worth staying for. Rylan had until their birthday to change her mind.

Lila let out a long whistle of a sigh. Rylan looked up at her, and she slid down beside him.

This was how things often went between Rylan and his mother. They were the quieter half of the family. The softer half. She confided in him, and he confided in her. It felt safe between them, even if Rylan did feel an occasional wash of shame for being seventeen and so attached to his mother.

"What's wrong?" Rylan asked.

"Oh. Nothing at all. Just ruminating." Lila glanced over at his sketchbook and nodded in approval. "You really are very good."

Two sharp taps came at the bedroom door, and Lila re-animated like a flower in the sun. "Come in. We're in the bathroom!"

Alejandro poked his head into the room, sleek black eyebrows quirked in a question. He was a tall man with an impressive head of black curls. His goatee was nicely oiled, and his tank top showed off a colorful kraken tattoo that snaked from his left shoulder to his wrist.

When the twins were small, Alejandro used to watch *Finding Nemo* with them, and whenever they had nightmares about the shark with the big smile, he would tuck them securely into bed and promise if they were ever attacked by such a monster, he would volunteer to be the bait.

Rylan and Tia had given him the call sign Sharkbait.

"There is a whole world out there, you know," Alejandro said, jerking a thumb behind him. "Sunsets and sailboats. But I see you two have chosen to spend the evening on the floor of a head."

Lila lifted one of her arms daintily, and the cook obliged her, pulling her to her feet. Her white cover-up streamed behind her like a sail.

"Estás radiante," Alejandro told her.

"Podría decir lo mismo de ti," Lila replied in perfect Spanish. She kissed both his cheeks. "¿Cómo va la cena?"

"Está listo." Alejandro looked at Rylan. "Before you go eat, I have questions—" he lowered his voice to a conspiratorial whisper "—about the cake."

Rylan tucked his pencils into the spiral binding of his sketchbook. Tia hadn't wanted a big party for graduation, which had fallen on the same day as Rylan's, last Saturday. When Francis had suggested either he or Lila fly to Connecticut while the other stayed back in Florida, Tia had texted in the family chat not to bother.

So instead they would give gifts tonight at dinner and have cake and champagne to christen their voyage.

Understated and elegant, Lila had called the idea (two of her favorite words).

"It is multitiered, isn't it?" Lila said, stacking her hands in the air to demonstrate the cake's imagined height. "Did you get all twelve layers? One for each year of school."

"I did indeed," Alejandro replied, seemingly amused. "I just need to decorate."

Lila barreled on. "Yes, with your homemade buttercream frosting, of course. And you have those molded chocolates, shaped like roses, I think. Or perhaps peonies?"

Alejandro chuckled, shaking his head. "Naturally. Do you have any input, Rylan?"

Rylan smiled up at the two of them. "Oh, I dunno. She likes . . . strawberries?"

Alejandro clapped his hands. "Perfecto! A twelve-layer cake with hand-whipped frosting, molded chocolate flowers, strawberries, and we might as well sprinkle edible gold on top while we're at it, yes?"

Lila tossed her head. "I don't see why not."

Alejandro shot Rylan a wink and headed for the door. "Go enjoy your first few courses, then. I'll bring it up when you are done."

Rylan thumbed through his sketchbook and stopped on his best picture of Tia. He tore it loose and folded it with great care until it could fit in the pocket of his board shorts.

"Let's feast, my darling," Lila said, clasping his upper arm and pulling him up and to the deck.

Francis and Tia were already at the table. Francis gestured grandly for Rylan to take his usual seat at his right side, between him and Tia.

The table was set with a tablecloth, glass dishes, and napkins the color of the sea. The four place settings had identical helpings of white wine lobster bisque, sugar-glazed carrots, roasted artichoke hearts, and a thick slice of almond sourdough. They each had champagne flutes with generous pours that glinted in the sun when Lila lifted hers in a toast.

"To our first full-family meal since . . . goodness . . . since August! Cheers, loves."

Francis clinked her glass and showed off all his teeth. "To the Camerons."

"Yeah, to us," Tia said, and she looked right at Rylan.

They toasted and drank.

"Rylan, tell Tia about the dives we have planned," Francis said, plunging a spoon into his bisque.

Rylan perked up. They had six dives planned so far, each of them more exciting than the last. "The first one will be in a couple days. It's off of this private cay with all these caves and rock formations. There might be tunnels we can swim through."

"Cool," Tia said around a mouthful of bread.

There was another dive in a marine sanctuary off the coast of Georgia, and another they might be able to find that was famous for nurse sharks. Rylan explained them all before realizing his family had finished with their food and moved on to second or third glasses of champagne all while he hadn't yet picked up his soup spoon.

"We have something special for dessert," Lila said to Tia. "I hope you've saved room."

Tia patted her stomach. "I got a whole wing set aside for dessert, Mom."

Lila rose from her chair. "I'll fetch Alejandro."

Rylan reached into his pocket. "I have a, uh, small present for you." He handed Tia the folded sketch.

"Aw, Ry . . ."

Tia smoothed it out on her lap, and Rylan watched for her reaction. He had sketched it based off a selfie Tia had texted him while she was at school. She was wearing her uniform, tie undone, collar unbuttoned, her hair loose around her shoulders. She had an eyebrow poised and an unlit cigarette dangling from her lips.

It was a gorgeous photo, and even more stunning in the cinematic style of the sketch. Tia looked edgy but attractive, like a movie star.

Like Lila.

Francis leaned over to get a better view of the drawing. "Is that you? What are you smoking?"

Tia flipped around the drawing so Francis could look her black-and-white self right in the face. "Cocaine. In a gum wrapper."

Rylan drowned a snicker with a mouthful of champagne. The last thing they needed was to antagonize Francis before the voyage even began.

Their father held up a finger but was interrupted by Lila breezing back to the table, Alejandro moving glacially behind her as he carried a massive, trembling cake.

"Oh, you started presents without me!" Lila looked wounded until Tia's jaw dropped at the sight of the cake.

"Holy shit, Alejandro."

Rylan stood to help him, but Alejandro had already slid his masterpiece onto the chart house.

"Sopresa!" he announced, dusting his hands together. "Twelve-layered genoise sponge cake with handmade meringue buttercream frosting, chocolate roses, edible gold, and strawberries."

The twins applauded, and Alejandro held up both hands in false modesty before he gave an extravagant bow.

"Enjoy it while you can," Francis advised as Rylan abandoned his dinner and cut himself a large slice with extra strawberries. "Once we're at sea, we won't be able to make meals as fancy as this."

Alejandro's mouth quirked. "*We?* I did not realize I had a sous-chef."

Lila giggled and placed a hand on Alejandro's kraken tattoo. "Trust me, Ale, you do not want my husband anywhere near a kitchen."

Francis nodded grimly. "Or, God forbid . . . a cake." And he reached suddenly into the frosted skyscraper of a dessert and grabbed a fistful.

Lila shrieked, but his attack wasn't meant for her.

Rylan ducked as the chunk of cake soared past him. He grabbed an empty plate to use as a shield, but then Tia was beside him, her own slice brandished above her head like the gloved fist of an army general. She sent it dangerously close to her father's face, and war was officially declared.

Lila took cover behind Alejandro, who chuckled good-naturedly as Francis and Tia tore his creation to shreds. Rylan would have apologized to him if he'd had the time, but whenever he dared glance away from the battlefield, he ended up with cake in his hair.

"Alejandro spent days on that cake!" Lila shouted.

"Oh, I'm so sorry, Mom." Tia stuck her hand into what remained of the twelve layers. "We should have saved some for you."

Lila's pupils constricted under the brim of her beautiful white sun hat. "Taliea Indigo Cameron . . ."

Tia charged, Rylan just behind her.

Rather than flee as her children bore down on her, Lila quickly shed her hat and sheer cover-up. She looked like a dandelion seed with its fluff blown off as the twins rammed into her and rubbed frosting onto her skin like it was tanning lotion. Francis whisked the hat and cover-up out of harm's way, probably guessing his wife would rather have those be rescued than herself.

Rylan couldn't stop grinning. Lila's screams had reached an operatic pitch that would have been envied by Christine Daaé. But she was also laughing, hysterically, like everyone else.

Tia and Rylan released their mother, who attempted to give them a dire that-was-a-mistake expression, though it was difficult to take her seriously with gold flakes and frosting smeared on her bikini.

"Francis, get me the hose."

Tia grabbed Rylan's arm, breathless. "Go, go, go!"

They flew down the companionway just as Francis armed their mother and she aimed the water their way.

Rylan shut the hatch behind them, and they staggered into the salon, giggling like little kids.

"We definitely won." Tia flicked crumbs off her sunglasses.

"We retreated," Rylan pointed out. He was short of breath, feeling almost giddy.

This is what you're thinking of leaving behind, he thought, watching his sister. So it didn't feel at all impulsive when he reached for her hand and said, "Stay."

Tia squeezed his hand. She looked even older and fiercer than Rylan had remembered her.

She shook her head, and his heart sank just beneath his ribs.

"Stay with *me*," she countered.

But he couldn't, not if she left, because there was something Tia didn't understand about their family. The Camerons were not a thing that could be left behind.

Chapter 4

Lila Logan Cameron
Call sign: Cassiopeia
The Day Before Departure

"WHAT A MESS," Lila declared, wiping a streak of frosting from her husband's clean-shaven chin.

Francis shrugged and sampled a bite of ruined cake with his thumb. "Never tidy with Tia."

Alejandro took the hose and started rinsing cake off the deck. "You started it, Francis."

Francis grinned and found a rag to help.

Lila smiled at the two of them as she retrieved her cover-up and sun hat.

"We didn't finish giving gifts."

"And no one ate the cake," Alejandro added.

"I'm eating it right now." Francis plucked his bisque spoon from the table and made a show of digging into what was left.

Lila picked her way over the minefield of frosting to call down to her children below deck. "Tia! Rylan! Come help Alejandro clean up your mess. Then we can do presents."

Only at the mention of presents did the twins scamper back on deck.

When most of the cake had been washed into the marina,

the twins sat at the table, and Lila produced a little velvet box too pretty to be wrapped.

Tia flipped it open to reveal a pair of earrings. "Wow," she said.

Lila had picked them out at the jeweler months ago. They were simple. Classy. Two South Sea pearl studs with solid-gold backings. Their worth totaled somewhere in the five figures. Lila hadn't examined the receipt all that closely.

"Pearls are the birthstone for June," she explained. "And I know you share your father's fondness for the sea."

She hoped this would elevate Tia's boat style from knotted T-shirts and booty shorts to something more put-together that would match a beautiful piece of jewelry. Honestly, choosing pearl studs had been rather restrained of her. She had far more extravagant items picked out for their birthday party once they reached Florida.

Lila handed Rylan a gold paper package. He took care not to tear the paper and instead slit the tape with his nail and opened the gift at the seams. Folded inside was a vicuña wool cardigan in Rylan's favorite color, navy, and a cashmere button-front raincoat from Bergdorf that Lila thought might come in handy on this particular vacation. Her son would look smart and feel warm in them both.

Rylan hugged the luxury fabrics to his chest. "Thank you," he said happily.

Lila was a master of gift-giving, in her opinion. Nobody ever seemed to understand quite what *she* wanted, but when it came to other people, she could look into their eyes, see their greatest desire, and then tweak it a bit to be as beautiful as possible.

Tia wanted to be important, which might as well be a synonym for beautiful. Rylan wanted to be taken care of. Francis wanted more of whatever he already had, and Alejandro . . .

Lila glanced sideways at the cook.

After all these years, years of being offered the same wealth and influence that Francis had painstakingly achieved for himself, all Alejandro seemed to want was a nice kitchen and a place in the Cameron family.

How many men would choose a life as a private chef when they had the option to have all their meals cooked by someone else?

"Piratey." Tia closed the box. "Thanks."

"I have one for each of you," Francis announced and stood to open one of the panels in the deck.

"Watch him have somehow stashed a Ferrari in the bilges," Tia joked to Rylan.

"After you put that dent in your Lexus, I wouldn't get too excited, young lady," said Lila as Francis lugged out a deep-sea fishing kit with a little bow tied around one of the rods.

"For you, my boy." He squatted and laid the mess of lures and tackles at Rylan's feet. "We won't even have to watch it all the time. We can set it up on the stern and whoever's manning the helm will let us know if we get a tug. How cool is that?" He stood, pleased with himself. "What do you think, Alejandro? Could you make something delicious out of a tarpon? Or a shark?"

Alejandro looked up from looping the hose. "I could make eyeballs taste like oysters."

Francis bared his teeth in a grin and raised his arms. "The ocean's your limit, my boy! Let's see what we catch."

Lila watched her son wilt in Francis's shadow. She gave him a look, but Rylan's despondence didn't change, so she reached over and poked an acrylic nail into the small of his back. He sat up straightaway.

"What about me, Daddy?" Tia crossed her ankles and tilted her saccharine expression toward what was left of the sun. "Do I get a gun to poach white rhinos in Zimbabwe?"

"Course not, sweetheart. The rhinos need a fighting chance." Francis produced something from his pocket and handed it to Tia. "To match the earrings," he said.

Lila craned her neck to see what sat in Tia's palm. It was a necklace, gold chain as thin as a thread, with a single South Sea pearl hung from a bail.

It was from the same jeweler she had gotten the earrings, part of a matched set.

But Francis hadn't been with her that day, nor had he asked where she'd gotten her gift.

Had he looked through her credit card statement?

Lila and Francis had never been the kind of couple to combine their finances. Why should they? They were each raking in millions in their thirties when they'd wed.

But, of course, they technically had the same password manager. It wouldn't be hard for Francis to access Lila's credit history if he wanted to.

But *why* did he want to?

Lila searched her husband's face, and he met her eyes with a smile. Lila returned it and pulled her cover-up tighter around her body.

What had he been looking for?

Just then her phone trilled from where she'd set it on the table. Lila scooped it up and put it to her ear without glancing at the caller ID. She hoped it was her film agent, calling about that audition coming up after the trip or maybe even about another gig she could book.

"One moment," Lila said to her family as she walked to the front of the boat, the part that pointed compass-like out of the marina and toward the open sea.

"Hello? Brett?"

"No, sorry, Lil. It's me," an older, far less exciting voice replied. Ernie Carmichael, one of Francis's old yachting employees who helped crew for *The Old Eileen* now that he was retired.

"Ernie!" Lila gushed to mask disappointment. "Are you on the jet?"

"No, uh . . ."

Something was wrong. He sounded nervous. Frightened, even. And why on earth was he calling her instead of Francis?

"What is it?" Lila cupped the phone to her ear and glanced back at Francis and the twins. They were too far to hear anything.

"I'm not coming," Ernie said at last.

"But . . . the trip is tomorrow, and everything is prepared." Lila switched the phone to her other ear. "Ernie, I don't think we can sail without you."

"Sorry. But you'll find a way. Tell Francis for me, will you?"

Before she could reply, the line went dead, and Lila was left standing on the bow alone.

"I MEAN, HE sounded really upset," Lila said to Francis later that evening, a pair of hairpins between her teeth as she set her hair in its nighttime pin curls. "I finally heard back from his wife, and she said Barbara's been living with them, Ernie's mother. She has Alzheimer's. Terrible. Anyway, she tripped over one of the mastiff puppies, and Ernie doesn't want to leave Donna to take care of his mother's broken ankle without him."

"Yes, yes, it makes perfect sense," Francis murmured, in deep concentration as he trimmed his nose hairs.

The couple was side-by-side in the primary suite's head. Lila didn't much care for ship language—how the bathrooms became *heads* and the kitchen a *galley* and so on, but then again, there were a lot of things she didn't quite care for that she put up with anyway. For her family. For Francis.

Lila made eye contact with her husband in the mirror.

"Are we still going to be able to set sail tomorrow morning? You and Alejandro and MJ will have to take on more work. I haven't even told MJ about Ernie yet. Alejandro said he'd wait up for her tonight and explain when she arrived."

"We're still going to sail." Francis set down the scissors and examined his reflection closely. "I checked to see if the crew we chartered to bring *Eileen* here was available, but they've all moved on to new assignments. So then I called a few friends and Howard—you do remember Howard, don't you? He bought a new superyacht last fall."

Lila slid another hairpin between her curls. "Of course I remember Howard, Francis. I remember all of your friends." She hadn't necessarily meant it as a jab, but it was true that Francis struggled recalling her girlfriends' first names, whereas Lila could have rattled off twenty of his closest friends at any given moment, not to mention the names of their wives, children, and designer Yorkie-poos.

Francis continued, unperturbed by (or perhaps oblivious to, in his Francis way) the remark. "Yes, well, Howard's had his fair share of incompetent deckhands. There was that one he caught sneaking around the family safe, and that kid who couldn't tell dish soap from Salt-Away . . ." Francis shook his head. "But anyway, he recommended a young man who worked for him last spring. The boy knows motorboats and sailboats alike, he was respectful and hard-working, and he should still be in the area. And best of all, Alejandro knows him."

Lila paused and glanced up at her husband. "Oh?"

"Yes, they have some kind of distant relation. Second cousins? Or maybe a long-lost nephew? Regardless, Howard gave me his number."

Lila plucked the last hairpin from the counter and found a place for it at the nape of her neck, collecting the wispy baby hairs that had escaped her improvised updo. Her days of fashionable hairstyles were numbered, she knew. As soon as they set sail, the wind would see to it that even the tightest of braids or smoothest of buns were undone in a tangled instant.

"He sounds perfect, dear. *If* he's willing to get here by eight tomorrow morning, of course."

"Of course," Francis echoed. He stepped back from the mirror and kissed Lila's cheek.

His cologne, Tom Ford's Soleil Brûlant to be exact, washed over her. Lila closed her eyes. It was black honey, amber, and wood with an edge of smoke. It was the scent of a younger man who dreamed of making riches and chasing storms. Of getting the famous Lila Logan's hand in marriage.

Lila reached up and caught his collar before he could pull away. She twisted it in her hand, enjoying the feel of it. "The children are in bed," she told him. It didn't matter if that were true or not.

Francis leaned closer again, breath against her earlobe. She wondered if she still smelled like bellflower and cherries to him, if he even thought about the way she smelled at all. His lips brushed her neck. He still hadn't shaved from when she'd told him to earlier.

Lila tilted her face to better see the two of them together in the mirror. After all these years they were still absolutely divine side by side. Some things never changed.

But the pearl necklace . . .

"So. Eisenhardt Jeweler on Worth Avenue? Doesn't seem like your kind of place, darling."

Your move.

They watched each other in the mirror. Francis lifted a hand to cup her chin. His jaw tickled her ear as he spoke at last.

"I have to make that phone call." He unwound her fingers from his shirt and stepped out of reach.

Then he was gone.

Lila gazed back at herself, alone in the mirror. Francis had been looking for something. He knew she knew that. He had *wanted* her to know.

There had been a time when Lila would have given anything to understand her husband. She still wanted to. But it had become clearer that Francis was less interested in knowing her than he was in playing these sorts of games. A decade ago when a topless photograph of Lila went viral, she had found a set of expensive bras gift-wrapped on her pillowcase. Another time, she'd gone out for a cast party at a Thai restaurant and forgot to tell Francis where she was. When she returned, he'd only asked offhandedly if there'd been scallions in the crab rangoons. But even games lost their intrigue rather quickly, in his eyes. When Lila first became famous, she had thought she'd made it, that she would forever be famous enough, be *fascinating* enough, to sustain public interest—and Francis's. Now she knew there was an unknown count limit to everything in life.

How many times can your name be in the newspaper before people get sick of reading it?

How many wrinkles can your face collect before people stop calling you beautiful?

How many kisses can you give your husband before he no longer feels the burn to kiss you back?

Lila listened to the empty room, letting her fingers dance over her filigree hand mirror and Francis's badger-hair shaving brush sitting idle on the counter. She picked up one of her favorite lipsticks—Orchid Noir—and considered putting it on. There was no real reason to do it, no event she would be attending anytime in the next eight days. But it would make her look and feel like herself.

She uncapped it just as her children's voices sounded out above. So they *weren't* in bed.

"MJ!" Tia cried, bursting with excitement. "You're early!"

Lila let out a long, movieworthy sigh and recapped the lipstick tube. Of course serious, stalwart, Southern Mary Jane Tuckett would be early. Alejandro and the twins could get her settled, Lila decided. She was going to take a long, luxurious bath on this last night where the ocean's rocking wouldn't disturb her every step.

This was the time for fine things, Lila mused as steam misted the mirrors and clouded the bathroom air. She unclasped her earrings and set them on the counter.

Lila steeped herself in the water and tried to summon enthusiasm for tomorrow instead of the dreadful understanding that clung to her skin like steam. Whatever games Francis wanted to play, Lila would play with him. It was the dance they did, the one that kept their marriage entertaining. Besides, Lila didn't have the kind of secret that would show up in a credit card statement.

Lila's secret was the kind she'd take to her grave.

Chapter 5

Jerry Baugh

FOR THE FIRST time in twenty-eight years, Jerry dreamed of his dead brother. Steve Baugh, professional sailor, champion swimmer, and Jerry's best friend, had been two weeks shy of his thirtieth birthday when he drowned.

In the dream, Jerry *was* Steve, and the ocean moved around him like a washing machine, keeping his body inside it. He could still catch glimpses of his ship—Steve's ship—as it bucked and dipped and drew farther and farther away.

Jerry had wondered his entire life how long it had taken his brother to die and the best estimation he could come up with was long. Very, very long. Steve was strapping and strong, a damn good swimmer, and an optimist to boot.

The nightmare lasted eons, all while Jerry swallowed more water and swam for his life, for his brother's life.

At some point he realized he was actually swimming deeper down.

When he opened his eyes in the morning, Jerry was comforted instantly by the familiar sight of his Bass Pro Shops cap brim. Huge sweat stains pooled under his arms, and he took off the cap to fan himself.

In the weeks after his brother's death, the nightmares had followed Jerry as if Steve himself haunted the shores that he couldn't make it back to. That was when Jerry decided he couldn't stay on land either. Aboard the beat-up lobster boat, the nightmares stopped.

Until now.

Jerry got to his feet and headed to the galley. He made a cup of joe and put a fresh-caught snapper sizzling on a pan. He waited until both sides were black before he slid them on a plate and lumbered up on deck to eat.

It was the first moment he'd had to think since the boat alarm had gone off. The events of last night came back to him in pieces: the empty sailboat, the coast guard, the lengthy drive back to port.

The message on the mirror.

It was all too much to take in, especially once a detective reminded him of the rule of salvage: If you find something at sea and no one who it belongs to, then finders keepers. It was some kind of homage to pirates and scavengers, he liked to think, to the men who risked everything to find the treasures hidden in the most dangerous parts of the world.

If the detective was right, *The Old Eileen* might now belong to *Jerry*.

He looked over his shoulder at her masts standing white against the lavender sky. Jerry could get used to that sight.

He gazed at her for so long that it took him a second to realize he was no longer alone.

A young woman, around twenty or so, in a deckhand uniform was standing on the dock. Her hair was buzzed close to her skull, and her hands were deep in her pockets. She was looking up at the sailboat with rounded almond eyes, impressed.

"Damn," the woman murmured.

"Don't have to tell me twice. I found her last night. Jus'

drifting. Can't understand it." Jerry shook his head and took a bite of snapper. "Do you work here in the shipyard?"

The woman nodded and lit a cigarette. "Yeah. I'm Lainey." She offered one to Jerry, but he waved it away. "Sorry, did you say you *found* her? As in, empty?"

Jerry fished a bone out of his mouth. "Jerry. And yep. Can't understand it . . ."

"That means you own her, right? Rule of salvage and all. Bet the press won't be able to get enough of this."

Jerry hadn't even thought of that. An empty yacht . . . a missing family . . . He set down his plate, appetite vanished, and scratched at his beard.

"I . . . I need to get some things in order," Jerry mumbled. "Before the story breaks."

But Lainey wasn't looking at him or at *The Old Eileen* anymore. She was looking down the dock where a van had pulled up. A news van. She stuck her hands back in her pockets and gave Jerry a faint smile as she walked back toward whatever yacht she crewed for.

"Better get them in order fast, Jerry. It's already broken."

NBC 6 South Florida

Is This Luxury Family Sailboat a Modern-Day Ghost Ship?

BY JENNIFER BYUN

So many stories of the sea are the stuff of legends, but ghost ships, the most famous of which is arguably the *Mary Celeste* (found empty in 1872), are unnervingly real. A ghost ship could be a phantom appearance of a ship on the horizon that isn't really there, but it can also be a seafaring vessel that is found without any crew or passengers onboard. There have been many theories as to what happened to these missing people over the centuries, but they have never been so relevant to our modern world as now.

The Old Eileen, a decadent sailing yacht owned by Captain (and Unwind Yachting Co. cofounder and CEO) Francis Cameron, was home to four crew members (including Cameron) as well as three passengers (Francis's wife and two children). Mrs. Cameron is far better known as Lila Logan, a sweetheart television actress from the '90s best known for starring in the series *Reina Gold Is Lying* (and the subsequent scandal). Before they set sail, their daughter, Taliea Indigo, had just graduated from St. Bernadette's School for Girls in Connecticut, and her twin brother, Francis Rylan (Rylan to his friends and family), had received his diploma from Oxbridge Academy.

The Camerons—wealthy and beautiful—by all accounts have a picture-perfect life.

That is, until longtime fisherman Jerry Baugh discovered *The Old Eileen* early yesterday morning, adrift and completely empty.

Authorities say it is too soon to tell what could have become of the seven people aboard *The Old Eileen*, but a massive search is being conducted in the area where the ship was found, and theories are already building to explain such a shocking and baffling occurrence.

Chapter 6

```
Tia Cameron
Call sign: Thimble
The Day Before Departure
```

ONCE TIA AND RYLAN finished settling MJ Tuckett into the crew cabin, the two of them curled up in the salon to watch reruns of *Criminal Minds*. MJ, who had arrived toting a marine-grade duffel bag and her large one-eyed Maine coon, went straight to bed, leaving the twins on the couch with the cat curled in Rylan's lap. It had been a couple years since they last saw MJ, but the cat seemed to remember them.

And it's not like the twins could ever forget MJ.

They had first met her a decade ago when Francis bought the boat. MJ had been hired as a private diving instructor for the twins and as a first mate for Francis.

They had gotten along more back then, MJ and Francis. MJ used to tell the twins she admired the motto of their father's yachting company: *Safe to sail in any gale!* MJ had seen more than her share of easily avoided maritime accidents. Later, this became a point of contention between them. MJ was the better sailor, but *The Old Eileen* was Francis's boat.

MJ Tuckett, Tia thought affectionately as she petted the cat in her brother's lap.

Called Mary Jane only under the most dire of circumstances. The self-proclaimed "last old salt" left on the "Lord's seven seas."
Call sign: Sherlock.
Meaning: Brilliant. Admirable. Takes no shit.

The Maine coon—whom MJ had christened Sir Franklin after the doomed explorer, but the twins had only ever called Pirate—arched his back and stalked to the couch's arm rest, his single black eye fixed on the porthole.

Tia couldn't wait until morning when *The Old Eileen* would set off and she could start learning more from MJ. The sailor was the kind of person Tia saw herself becoming (if she managed to get far enough away from her family to become anything). She wanted to be tough and quick-witted, the kind of woman who could find a ship's dead reckoning, adopt a stray cat, and quote the Bible and Beyoncé in the same breath.

Tia's eyes glazed from the television screen. She had already guessed the murderer, and from the cabin next door she could hear her parents' raised voices over the hum of the TV. The whole scene was familiar—her parents arguing (or maybe flirting, who was to say), the TV playing, her brother detached from the world, focused on his sketchbook. It was like Tia had never left. Only she felt outside of it all now, like a family she was watching through a window without being invited to come inside.

She turned down the volume on the TV, and her parents' conversation became clearer.

"—hasn't even shown up yet, Francis," her mother was saying. "Are we going to leave tomorrow morning anyway?"

"At oh eight hundred sharp, whether he gets here or not. This ship can be manned by one good sailor alone, Lil. And we've got two and a half."

Tia picked at the embroidery of the couch cushions. "Looks like the new crew member isn't gonna come."

"Hm?" Rylan didn't look up.

"Nothing." Tia ruffled his hair. "Whatcha drawing?"

Rylan sat back to reveal his work. She snuggled under his arm as she examined the drawing. Was it a giant squid, or maybe the creepy kraken Alejandro had tattooed on his arm?

"Sea monster?" Tia guessed.

"Yeah. The one from *20,000 Leagues Under the Sea*." Rylan pointed at the oblong head and long, winding tentacles. He really was an incredible artist.

"But there isn't a monster in that book," Tia said. "They only *think* there is. The whole thing turns out to be man-made."

"And it's even scarier than what they'd thought." Rylan pushed back his hair. "Do you like it?"

"It's terrifying." Tia elbowed him in the ribs and laid her head on his shoulder while he put the finishing touches on the monster's eyes.

"I'm sorry I missed your graduation," she said into the quiet room.

Rylan's pencil paused. "It's okay. I missed yours too."

He had, of course, but it wasn't his fault. She was the reason they had been separated in the first place, but she didn't want to say that. It felt like bad luck to bring up last summer when they were here again, on the boat. She wished more than anything that she and Rylan could have faced their senior year together. Boarding school wouldn't have been so bad if Rylan had been with her. She would have coaxed him to sneak out and wander the rose garden or skinny-dip in the pond. He could have helped her with homework and soothed her temper when the nuns got under her skin.

Without him, she'd done it all alone. Tia's classmates had been nice enough, but they existed in a world Tia had never felt home in. They were agonizing over which Ivy League to attend, debating if a career in politics or in business would be more worthwhile. Tia could smoke with them, study with them, and admire Timothée Chalamet's latest magazine cover in the dorms with them at night, but that was where their point of connection ended.

Tia didn't want any of the same things. She'd never been sure why exactly. She felt she was plenty ambitious, if ambitions could include things that wouldn't make her any money. Tia wanted to see the world, and not in the way her rich friends and family wanted to see it. She didn't want Instagram-edited photos of her wearing pastels to match the houses in Cinque Terre or captions in Google-translated French to remark on la ville de l'amour.

Tia wanted to see things nobody else had seen. She wanted to touch trees and tide pools never marred by human hands. She wanted to explore a cave no camera had ever captured. If she had lived in the Age of Exploration, Tia would have been on the first ship to the Spice Islands or the Northwest Passage. She would have charmed queens into granting her an expedition that she might or might not ever return from.

When winter break came, and all those girls went home to their families, Francis sent a brief text informing Tia she wouldn't be coming home. He had decided at the last minute.

Nothing was worse than those weeks, snowed inside a dungeon of a building with only murmuring nuns for company.

Francis and Lila hadn't just separated Tia from her twin and her best friend by sending her to Connecticut. It was like they'd severed her arm. Even with Rylan real and breathing beside her again, she still felt phantom pains.

"You didn't miss anything," she told him. "The St. Bernadette's grad party was just a bunch of nuns and sparkling cider in paper cups."

Rylan chuckled softly, a wispy sound, like drifting cobwebs. "An event of a lifetime, I bet. Did you give a speech?"

"God no. Did you?"

"Yeah. I was salutatorian. I don't know if Mom and Dad told you."

"No . . . they didn't."

And neither did you.

It shouldn't have surprised Tia. Of course Rylan achieved some ridiculous academic standard. He had always been brilliant. He'd gotten into Cornell *and* the University of Pennsylvania. He'd turned down both to stay with her.

Tia knew he could do so again.

"What did you say?" Tia tried and failed to picture her soft-spoken brother delivering a speech to hundreds of their peers.

"Not much." Rylan set the sketchbook aside. Their parents' voices had finally quieted. "I kept it brief. I was afraid I'd faint or something, so I just kinda closed my eyes and told a story. 'Plato's Cave.'"

"Now I *really* wish I had been there."

Rylan rested his head on top of Tia's. "I'm glad you're back," he murmured.

"I never wanted to go, Minnow."

Rylan shifted and withdrew. He was supposed to say *I know, Thimble* or *I never wanted you to go either.* Instead he surprised her and said, "But you want to now."

More than anything.

Here it was. The opportunity to talk about running away. Tia faced him and seized his hand. She had to get her point across. This was pivotal.

"Rylan. Listen to me. I know what life is like with our family. And now I know what it's like without them."

Rylan didn't pull away, but he dropped his gaze and twirled his pencil between his fingers. "But you hated St. Bernadette's."

"I hated it because I was lonely. But I didn't miss Mom or Dad. I missed you."

He was shaking his head, and Tia felt a twinge of desperation. She'd never had to work so hard to convince him of something.

"You were lonely, so now you want to cut off our family? How does that make sense? Where are you going to go?"

Tia sat up on her knees. "I have a million ideas. Backpacking the Swiss Alps, getting a job on a tall ship in Australia. Ry, we could go work somewhere as divers! You could work with marine animals, and I could work on boats, and we could see the whole world and be each other's home."

She leaned back on her heels, not wanting to overwhelm him with her eagerness, but he had to see it, didn't he? There was a whole world out there, waiting for them.

Rylan knit his brows. "You . . . haven't thought this through."

Tia nearly flinched. She *had* thought this through. It was all she had been thinking about for months, but Rylan continued before she could speak again.

"You want to do all these extravagant trips. Wouldn't you rather do all that with money? Mom and Dad's money? And if you leave you—what? You think they won't look for you? You haven't even picked out a specific place to go to first. And what are you going to do in a few years when your steam runs out, and you don't have a degree or a resume, and you have to come crawling back to Mom and Dad for help?"

Tia stared at him, this boy who looked and sounded like her brother but whose words hadn't been his own.

They sounded like their parents'.

She sucked in a breath. She wanted to shake him and scream, but she didn't. If she was ever going to convince him, she had to be patient. This vacation hadn't even officially begun.

"I swear, Ry, I have thought this out. I swear it's going to work. We can pick out what we want to do together, and I swear to God that no matter what happens, I won't be crawling back. Ever."

Rylan set his pencil down on the sketchbook, then straightened it so it was parallel to one of the monster's tentacles. "What if I stay? Would you . . ."

He couldn't finish his sentence, but he didn't have to. Tia understood. It was a question she had asked herself over and over, one that kept her up at night.

Would she leave him behind?

Tia detangled herself from the couch. She wasn't ready to answer that question. She would prefer to never find out. "I'm gonna go hang out on deck for a minute. Watch some stars before bed. Tomorrow's a big day."

Rylan kept his head down, leaned into the space she had vacated. "It's going to be the trip of a lifetime, T."

"Sure. Night, Rylan. Night, Pirate." She ruffled the cat's fur. "Good night."

THE OLD EILEEN was different in the dark. Tia climbed onto the deck and stretched out on one of the sunbathing mattresses where she and her mom had drunk daiquiris together earlier that day. Everything that had been warm and golden was now cool and smattered with silver moonlight. Tia couldn't wait to be out at sea where the stars would be even brighter, and the lights of the other ships in the harbor and of the buildings on land would no longer be visible. They had never sailed overnight before.

The nav lights at the top of the mast peered down at Tia, mismatched eyes in the black. Tia hugged her arms across her chest in a tight embrace, thinking about her brother belowdecks.

Would I leave him behind?

The answer was no. It had to be no. Rylan could be convinced; she was sure of that. She'd have to do it with more logic than passion. She'd have to drag him to a mirror and make him look at what he was becoming and think about what he could become.

Running away was terrifying, and Rylan sometimes let himself be ruled by fear. She'd need to be gentle.

The catwalk creaked, and Tia sat bolt upright.

Someone was boarding the ship.

She fumbled for her phone to put on the flashlight, but her fingers slipped, and she dropped it. She watched, helpless, as a tall, slim figure walked onto the deck. Were they getting robbed? Attacked?

The figure stopped dead, and Tia inhaled sharply. Had it spotted her? A scream boiled up in her throat. She wished Rylan had come with her.

Then the figure looked straight at her.

"Hey! Is this *The Old Eileen*?"

Tia blinked. She breathed out, her heart hammering. The man stepped forward into the faint pool of light from atop the mast, and Tia could see he had a guitar case strapped to his back. He was maybe a couple years older than her, early twenties, with deeply tanned skin and loose brown curls. He had a dusting of facial hair, and when he moved to adjust his pack, the light revealed little tattoos up and down his arm.

"Uh, yeah. It is. You must be the new crew member?" she asked, getting to her feet and taking a couple steadying deep breaths.

She felt stupid for having been afraid. She also felt stupid for standing there in her Snoopy pajamas, alone in the dark. Why had this guy shown up at night anyway?

He crossed the deck with his hand outstretched. His skin was warm and wide, palms lined with calluses.

"Sure am. You must be Captain Cameron's daughter."

"Tia," she told him, and the man grinned disarmingly.

"Very nice to meet you, Tia. I'm Nico de la Vega."

Chapter 7

Rylan Cameron
Call sign: Minnow
Day 1 at Sea

RYLAN KEPT OUT of the way as his father, MJ, and the new crewman strode across the deck. They shouted at one another and shuffled with the lines, preparing *The Old Eileen* to set sail. Rylan hadn't been able to sleep after talking with Tia, who was still out cold in their cabin. The anxiety had been just enough to keep him awake and exhausted at the same time. When Tia got an idea in her head, it was impossible to uproot it. At least, it had always been impossible for Rylan.

This time he had to find a way.

The day was windy already. Rylan's feathery dark hair whirled in every direction, and he closed his eyes. What would it be like to actually leave with Tia? They would live from adventure to adventure, nights in hostels, days outside. How long would it be before her passion burned out or Rylan gave up or their parents tracked them down? Because they *would* track them down.

Lila would be heartbroken.

Francis would be dismayed.

They would never trust Rylan again. Everything Francis had been working on with him would be pointless. He would finally say what everyone always seemed to be thinking about Rylan.

Coward.

"Son, come on over here."

Rylan's eyes popped open. His father was standing in the cockpit, one hand on the silver helm, the other holding out a radio to him.

"Come on," he repeated with a smile. "Wanna be mate while we pull out?"

Rylan walked over, shrinking into the collar of his linen Brunello shirt. The first mate was in charge of undoing the dock lines and maneuvering the ship out of the marina safely. Rylan would have to stand at the bow and make quick calls on how to avoid collisions.

"But, uh, MJ is your first mate," he said. He didn't want to be on lookout duty. What if they collided with something and it was all Rylan's fault?

"Baptism by fire," Francis said, a favorite of his sayings. He pushed the radio into Rylan's hand. "Go to the bow."

Rylan looked blankly at the black box. "You sure?" *You wanna risk your multimillion-dollar boat getting scratched?*

"Go on, my boy. We learn by doing," Francis said.

Rylan turned tail and headed to the front of the ship. His heart murmured its unease behind his ribs. All he'd meant to do was come up here and watch them take off from land. He should have guessed he'd be conscripted. When Rylan was nine and ten, those first couple summers day-sailing had been miserable, spent hidden below deck, vomiting into an ice bucket. He didn't get sick anymore, not like his mother anyway, but the anxiety was there, reminding him he couldn't be too careful. Better to be on deck breathing in the wind and staring at the horizon till his eyes watered.

Only, on deck was Francis Cameron's domain.

The radio crackled. "Can you hear me, Rylan? Over."

Rylan pressed the button down. "Yeah." He waited for a response, then quickly added, "Over."

MJ and the new crewmember had hopped onto the dock and were throwing the looped lines back to the deck, so the boat was no longer tethered to land. *They don't even need me*, Rylan thought with relief. *I can just stand here and wait.*

"We're pulling out now," Francis's voice sparked from the radio, and Rylan gripped the railing. "Watch out for buoys and other boats. Or unidentified *floating* objects," he said. Rylan could hear his father's smile at his own joke through the radio. "Over."

The Old Eileen moved with such graceful suddenness that Rylan didn't notice they were off the dock until he glanced back. MJ and the crewman were back onboard. They must have jumped.

But when Rylan looked back to the front, his breath caught.

They were headed toward open water, but at this angle and pace, their left side would scrape a very expensive sports yacht docked mere yards away. Rylan fumbled with the radio, but his fingers wouldn't listen. When he managed to press down the button, he froze. What was he supposed to say? Francis hadn't told him. Hadn't given him any instructions other than to go to the bow and be baptized. *Was this the fire part of the baptism, then?* Rylan thought wryly even as his fingers trembled over the button. The yacht was getting closer.

This is one of the tests, a voice hissed somewhere deep inside him. Rylan's skin crawled. *You always fail the tests.*

A warm hand plucked the radio from his grip. The new crewman. He gave Rylan a wiry smile, then pressed the button and spoke clearly. "Possible collision portside, slow and redirect, over." As he spoke, the man held his left arm in the air to give Francis a visual cue where the problem was.

"Copy," was all Francis said, and *The Old Eileen* turned with ease.

Rylan's stomach settled, the pressure relieved. He felt silly for having ever been worked up.

The man turned to him, still smiling and relaxed. He was young and strong with ropey arms, big hands, and skin well-versed with the sun. He had stacked tattoos, line after line of them up and down one arm. Like ink from a store receipt had bled onto his skin and dried there forever.

"He really threw you in it, huh?" said the man. His smile had never seen braces, teeth akimbo and an extraordinary white.

Rylan nodded, shrugged. "He does that."

"First time I was aboard a ship, my captain ordered me to raise the halyard on my own. I didn't know what a halyard was, let alone how to raise it, but I was scared shitless of asking questions, so I just grabbed a line and pulled. I ended up lifting the fucking courtesy flag. He never let me forget it."

Rylan laughed, even though he hadn't understood all the words. The man's voice was temperate, eyes penny-bright.

"I'm Nico, Mr. Cameron."

Mr. Cameron? "Oh, I, no—"

Nico broke into another easy grin. Did he ever not smile? "I'm only teasing. Anyway, if you're ever tossed to the lions again, lemme know if you need a hand taming 'em, okay?"

"Sure, yeah. Thank you."

Nico tipped an imaginary top hat and strode back to midships to help MJ with sail-raising. Rylan turned to look out front once more, in case there were more obstacles in their path, but he didn't need to worry.

The Old Eileen had glided out to open sea.

Chapter 8

Lila Logan Cameron
Call sign: Cassiopeia
Day 1 at Sea

BEAUTIFUL, SUNNY NEW HAVEN flattened into a distant smudge within minutes, it seemed to Lila. As the brown land receded, a nauseating blue replaced it, unfurling in every direction including down. Lila's stomach rocked with the boat.

She was ready to go back. Honestly, she had never understood what would make a person long for a view like this. It all looked the same: frightening and pointless. Throughout history, people had gone to sea because they had no other choice.

Lila would never understand what had possessed her husband to do the same for *fun*.

She wondered how many people had died in this water. How many broken boats and bodies lay in various forms of decomposition beneath them? There was nothing glamorous about sailing above a cemetery.

The idea was nearly as nauseating as the waves.

Lila had taken Dramamine, which she often did for daysails, but since she'd have to sleep at sea as well, she had a nausea patch behind one ear and, for extra measure, an anti-motion-sickness band, which wrapped around her wrist alongside a pair of Buccellati bracelets.

But the more she thought about vomiting, the more her body prepared to do it, and worse than that, a sensation rose in the back of her throat, altering the rhythm of her breath. She clung to the cap rails, knowing from a lifetime of experience that the way out of revealing an unmeasured heartbeat and an unsettled gut was not to fight them or to will them all away.

Lila was poised to lose control.

So she couldn't *be* Lila.

She'd be Eileen.

Lila relaxed her grip. Her old acting coach used to say that a good actor needs a moment to compose herself, to use imaginative or physical tools to place herself inside the mind of another person in another place. The moment can involve closing your eyes, dropping your head—whatever it takes to step through that door.

But the truly great actors? They needed none of that. The great actors needed only a breath.

Lila inhaled. *Eileen* exhaled.

Eileen Mavenson was left-handed. She suffered from thalassophobia, could speak Cajun French, and took her coffee with a shot of Creek Water Whiskey on mornings when she breakfasted with her husband.

But what was the plot? Why was Eileen on a boat?

It was a boat party gone wrong. Eileen and her husband had to flee out to sea after the party resulted in the death of the popular host. Was Eileen responsible? Was her husband? Eileen didn't *feel* guilty. But perhaps she was, and the feeling there instead was relief. Or pride. She would need to stew on the details, but what mattered now was that Lila's emotions were not her own. Who could blame Eileen for feeling trapped at sea? Why shouldn't Eileen be disenchanted with her circumstance? Why shouldn't she look at the ocean and see it as a monster?

Lila's heartbeat calmed. Her stomach retreated from her throat. She found herself focusing instead on the tissue-soft skin of her aging hands. She wasn't old, nowhere near it in fact, but as far as Hollywood was concerned, she was already a decade past relevant.

Even if Eileen were a real character, Lila would never be cast to play her.

Lila was far from naive. She knew that parts dried up for women as they aged—a particularly maddening fact when she also knew she'd become a better actress the older she got. Lila's career had exploded thirty years ago when she'd played a pithy detective's wife in *Herald of Mystery* (not her first movie, but the first one anyone counted). In the story, Lila's character becomes entangled in a homicide case that eventually implicates her own husband. Roger Ebert diagnosed the script as *turgid*, while Lila's performance was *inspired*. In the end, *Herald of Mystery* failed to earn out, but Lila Logan was subsequently offered a trifecta of superior roles.

Had those been the glory days? She hadn't thought so at the time, and to think so now made Lila all the more ill. She stepped back from the edge and peeked at her phone. Her agent still hadn't called about her audition last week, or even texted about the one she had coming up in mid-June. This was her last opportunity for cell service until they reached Florida.

Lila couldn't help herself.

Any word? she texted and stared at the bottom-left corner, waiting for bubbles. Instead, she witnessed the slow demise of her cell service as the bars dropped one by one to zero.

Lila tucked the phone back into her waistband, trying not to despair. But how could she not? In show business, no news was worse than bad news.

Lila would forever prefer to be a scandal than an irrelevance.

Already, her hair had unraveled from its pins, blowing in webs across her face, and she caught a wisp in her hand. Her hair was thinning, and sometimes when she twisted it into a bun as she'd done so many times through the years, it looked less like a rope of blond and more like worn and colorless string.

Lila smoothed her hands down her front to keep her linen blouse from ballooning. Sometimes the worst person in the world she could be was herself. The hunger she'd felt as a young woman to be known had only intensified over the years. But the world no longer cared to feed her.

No. Better to be Eileen right now.

And so she was Eileen, she was on the run, and yet she had absolutely nothing to lose. And whatever would poor, desperate Eileen Mavenson do when she had nothing to lose? Lila glanced around the ship. The possibilities were endless because she didn't really know Eileen, not yet. It was Lila's job to discover her.

"Lila, love!" Francis called from the back of the boat at his place on the helm.

Lila whipped her head around. Had he been there that entire time?

"Come here, you've got to try this."

Lila left Eileen at the railing, looking out to sea. She stepped into the cockpit where her husband clasped her hands and fastened them onto the helm to let her steer. He looked more alive than he had in years. Francis Cameron's love affair with the ocean was both in better standing and longer-lasting than any encounter with a woman, his wife of twenty-seven years included.

"It's magnificent, isn't it?" Francis could hardly contain himself. He was waiting for her to agree, as if the metal wheel were the most exciting thing Lila Logan had laid her hands upon.

Lila regarded the helm. She would like to understand it in order to better understand him. She would like to know what in the cold, dead ocean made his heart beat faster, his eyes shine. She turned the wheel to the right.

The Old Eileen moved. It obeyed her, and the waves were sliced to pieces in their effort to stop it. Something quivered inside her, and this time it wasn't nausea.

She almost liked it.

"It is," she said, but the wind devoured her words before they had reached her husband, and Francis was already taking the wheel back.

Still Lila returned to the railing reinvigorated. Her pale hair rippled out behind her, and she pictured herself on the filmy poster of an old movie. She'd have Veronica Lake waves, a bloodred lip, and a mink around bare shoulders. The sea would be behind her as she draped herself on a railing and looked meaningfully just past the camera. Oh, and maybe there'd be a gun placed somewhere in there so all who viewed it would know Lila had graduated from ingenue to femme fatale.

A star with incentive.

She looked around at the world, this terrible flat blue plane that thought it could erase her, and she knew without a doubt what she must do.

Make them remember me.

And in that moment, in that delicious in-between of Eileen and herself, Lila couldn't honestly say whose thought it had been.

Chapter 9

Jerry Baugh

JERRY'S PHONE VIBRATED on the dashboard in the cockpit. He had turned off his ringer two mornings ago when the press had gotten ahold of his number—God knew how—and they'd hounded him like piranhas for a statement, any statement.

What was he supposed to say? They knew everything he did. *No,* Jerry thought, *they don't want facts. They want emotions. They want me to say how scared I was that night, how unpredictable the seas are even after thirty years of me fishin' them. They want a good story.*

Just like when Steve died.

Jerry picked up his phone with half a mind to let it sit in the chum bucket for the rest of the day, but he paused when he saw the most recent text.

Come to The Old Eileen.

Jerry's heart made an uncomfortable trip to his throat. What the hell kind of ominous, cryptic shit was this?

His phone vibrated again.

This is Detective Madden.

Jerry mopped his forehead with his sleeve. He heaved himself out of his chair and made his way up top where Detective Madden was waiting, standing tall over him and *Sheila 2.0* from her vantage point on the dock.

"Could've just hollered," Jerry said, but if Madden heard him, she paid no mind.

She was a dark-skinned, trim woman with triangle earrings and a face that was achingly familiar to Jerry. In fact, now that he was no longer in the heat of discovering a ghost ship in the middle of the Atlantic, he had time to really look at her and sort out where he knew the detective from.

Cherrywood.

It was an unpleasant memory, the one of the neighborhood where Jerry and his ex-wife, Sheila, used to live. He could picture Madden perched on a barf-pink sofa with a glass of lemonade in her hand, sandwiched between other neighborhood women. But what was her first name . . . ?

"Brandy?" Jerry guessed.

The detective blinked at him. "Brenna."

"Right. Neighborhood Watch?"

"Book club," she said, and he faintly recalled being relegated to the garage while Sheila and the ladies ate key lime pie and mooned over *The Lovely Bones*.

"Book club," he repeated. "Must have been twenty damn years ago."

"Twenty-four."

Jerry scratched his head. "Guess that makes us old, then."

Brenna Madden snorted. She hadn't aged a goddamn day. "I'm younger than you. How's Sheila? We stopped talking when I moved to the city."

"We're divorced. Twenty-two years ago, I guess it was. And how's . . ." Jerry racked his brain. Was Madden married? All those ladies seemed to be, but then again he hadn't really talked to them directly. He cheated and glanced at her left hand. No ring.

"Ida," Madden offered, after allowing him to flounder for a minute.

"Yeah. Ida." Jerry found himself at a momentary loss. "How is Ida?"

Madden folded her arms. "Dead."

"Oh . . . uh . . ."

"If we can get back to work, Jerry, I'm here to update you about your new property." Madden turned on her heel and boarded *The Old Eileen*, expecting him to follow.

He did, guilty and relieved that she'd given the conversation a merciful death.

The sailboat looked untouched from when Jerry was last aboard two days ago. It was as peaceful yet unnerving as it had been that night. Jerry thought it would have looked less . . . *wrong* . . . in the light of day, docked and tied down, but he was mistaken.

In the day, it looked like a hollowed-out skull.

"Everything's been photographed and taken into evidence," Madden said as she strode across the deck. "Mostly the personal items have been removed for legal use, and unless something arises, everything else on her is in your care. And if the Camerons turn up to reclaim their property, you will still be entitled to a monetary reward for your role as salvor."

Jerry let his fingers brush against the teak wood cap rails. Was this how everybody made their fortune? Through sheer dumb luck?

Madden paused outside of the companionway to the chart house. "There is one thing we found that I want to see if you'll help me with."

"Me? Help . . . ?" He couldn't remember the last time anyone had needed his help for, well, anything.

Brenna Madden nodded sharply and turned to head down the companionway.

"Uh . . . um . . . first . . . what did they find? Wh-when they searched it all?" Jerry cleared his throat and tried again. "Did they get any closer to what happened?"

Madden eyed him, as if searching for a sign that Jerry was the type to leak to the media. She seemed to decide he wasn't.

"Not much was out of the ordinary, as you already know. The message on the mirror is of interest, as well as the ship's log that the captain kept. We found raw meat loaf in the fridge, which is of note because it likely means they were thawing it out to eat within twenty-four hours. So they couldn't have planned to leave too far in advance."

Jerry frowned. "You think they just . . . left?"

"We've searched the ship. Every cranny and bilge. There's no blood, nothing to suggest a struggle, unless you count items that fell on the ground, but that could have been from the boat rocking. We have reason to believe that some or all of the passengers could be alive."

Madden's words sounded upbeat, but her face was grim.

"What reason?" Jerry asked.

Madden ran her tongue over her teeth, taking a deep breath. "One of the ship's two expandable life rafts is missing, and there was a painter line attached to the ship that they would have used to launch it. The raft would be big enough for them to all be aboard."

They could all be alive . . .

But that was too good to be true, wasn't it?

And it didn't quite make sense to him.

"But the . . . the vessel is perfectly seaworthy." Jerry took off his cap and tossed it from hand to hand. "There was no reason for them to abandon ship. No flooding or boat malfunction or . . . or something."

"I think we should take it as a hopeful sign, Mr. Baugh. There are hundreds of coast guard members out there right now searching for that life raft. If the Camerons return safely home, you can go back to your life with a substantial reward for salvaging their property." Madden climbed down into the chart house. Jerry followed after.

"And . . . if they don't turn up?"

"Then *The Old Eileen* is yours." Madden continued, "Now for the thing that I was talking about earlier. Here he is."

"He?" Jerry came down from the last step and turned to see a large cage inside of which was an almost-as-large striped cat.

Sheila had had a cat toward the end of their marriage. Jerry had suspected that the dreadful creature was her preemptive replacement for him, and he had hated it since the moment it set its fluffy white paws on his carpet. He'd always been more of a dog person anyway and had fantasized about taking a dog with him on *Sheila 2.0*. The beloved border collie of his childhood came to mind.

"You found . . . a cat? On this ship?"

"Yes." Madden seemed almost as disgusted as Jerry. "He gave us quite the surprise. He somehow managed to hide all throughout the initial search that night, but we found him in one of the cabins under a bed during the second search yesterday."

"And you want me to . . . what?"

She faced him, lips turned down. "The rule of salvage, Mr. Baugh. This ship is yours. So far no Cameron relatives have turned up to claim it, and the legal officials who are reviewing Francis Cameron's will seem to agree that it was not intended for anyone who isn't currently MIA. So for the time being, while we conduct our search, will you keep an eye on him?" She jerked a thumb at the cat, who had paused his pacing to watch the two of them, as if aware their conversation was about him.

Jerry ran a hand through his thinning hair, then put the cap back on. "I think there's probably someone better for a job like that, Detective."

"My next person to ask is whoever owns the nearest pound," Madden said dryly. Jerry couldn't be sure if she was guilting him, but it damn well felt like it.

"Shit," he muttered. "Just a couple days, then, until you figure things out."

"That's the spirit, Jerry. I'll be in touch." Madden turned to head up the companionway.

"Wait!" Jerry called. He should say something to her. He should acknowledge this whole situation they were caught up in, acknowledge the past somehow, right? He rummaged for words for a full thirty seconds as Madden stared him down.

"I, um . . . I'm sorry. About Ida," Jerry said at last, because he was sorry. He wondered how Ida had died.

Madden didn't say a word. She gave him a curt nod, then took the steps of the companionway two at a time. Something buzzed in her pocket when she reached the top, and she fished it out.

Jerry stepped up after her. "H-hold on, now. That's it?"

Madden glanced back. "I've got roughly ten billion more things that need doing today." She waved her ringing phone in the air. "Thanks for all of your help. Oh, and there's cat food in the galley."

"Hold on!" Jerry repeated, reaching the deck. "Y-you can't just . . . I don't know how to . . . I mean, it's not like I want him put down or nothing, but . . . Detective Madden?"

Madden stopped dead, and Jerry nearly plowed into her. She turned to face him.

"Look, Jerry. We're on a major time crunch with this case.

We're looking for a nine-by-five-foot orange life raft in a search radius that spans over three hundred nautical miles, and we sure as hell better find it before hurricane season is in full force, so if you could just keep the cat alive until then, it'd be very much appreciated."

Jerry opened his mouth, then shut it again. He scratched his neck and looked down at his feet. "How . . . how long have they been out there?"

Madden blew air out from between her lips. "You located the boat just after midnight on June ninth, yes?"

Jerry still remembered the fleck of blood on the face of his watch from the sailfish. "Nine minutes after, I spotted it, yep."

"Well, the last boat check we have is dated at twenty-three thirty, just over ninety-six hours before your sighting."

Jerry worked to do the math in his head, keenly aware how his pulse beat in his own throat. "So . . . that means . . ."

"It means that half an hour before June fifth," Madden finished for him, her umber face grim, "at least one person on *The Old Eileen* was still alive."

The Tal 'n' Tea Tattler

Lila Logan and Francis Cameron Welcome Twins!

DAYNA GOSHUP

The glamorous couple has welcomed fraternal-twin newborns, Francis Rylan and Taliea Indigo. The babies were born the first hour of June 5 after what Lila describes as a "harrowing" pregnancy. Lila explained their son, Francis Rylan, was named after his father in every way except for a single letter in Rylan (as opposed to Francis's middle name, Ryan). "The *L* was my own little touch," said Lila, whose hair-care beauty brand is represented by the graphic design of a cursive *L* that loops into a woman's profile. Lila was given free rein by her husband, however, to name their daughter, Taliea, which means "dew from heaven." (Rylan means "little king.") Do twins run in the family? Apparently so! Lila revealed in an exclusive interview with *The Serrylian* that her own twin sister, Elaina, was stillborn.

"I see my children as a part of the sister I never knew," said Lila, who grew up as the only child of a Catholic-school principal and a stay-at-home mom in Goleta, California. Lila's career, which started early with child beauty pageants and teen modeling, begs the question if she will pursue a similar life for her own daughter. "While I am immensely grateful for the way my life has ended up," Lila told *The Serrylian*, "I do not see myself using dental veneers and eyelash curlers on Taliea. If she decides to be an actress, I hope she'll discover that love in a school play or community theater, as children should." Lila leaned in to joke, "Besides, I am all the star that my family can handle."

Chapter 10

Tia Cameron
Call sign: Thimble
Day 1 at Sea

WHEN THE LAST smudge of land had dissolved on the horizon and no more orange buoys or gleaming catamarans were left, Tia let her face tilt toward the sun and embraced her new home at sea. She could have been anywhere in the world, anywhere even in history. The water she sailed on at this moment had, at one point, been locked in polar glaciers or sliding through brackish streams. It had circumnavigated the globe with more completion than Magellan, and who knew if the molecules of water that now pushed up against *The Old Eileen* had once met the tallowed oak of Viking warships or the birchbark of Indigenous canoes. Here, Tia experienced insignificance with sanctity. She felt as though her understanding meant something, not in relation to the water but in concert with it.

"Nothing like it, huh?"

MJ Tuckett lumbered up beside Tia, hands clasped behind her back and shoulders set. MJ was a six-foot-tall Southern woman with spires of smoke-like gray hair and an expression lined like a rock face.

"No. There really isn't." Tia straightened her own posture. "It doesn't get old for you?"

"What?" MJ smirked at her, Carolinian drawl honeying her words. "Even as I get old, you mean?"

Tia laughed. "Pretty much."

"Think the stars get old to NASA, missy?" MJ bent to tidy a coil of lines on the deck. "You've got the bug, I see."

Tia watched MJ lift the thick rope, muscles outlined beneath her sun shirt. "The water bug?"

"Mmm-hmm." MJ deposited the rope into Tia's arms, and she nearly buckled. "Hang that on the cleat."

Tia looked where MJ gestured and managed to hook the rope to a bit of metal jutting from one of the masts. MJ nodded her approval.

Tia watched her admiringly. She had so many questions but wasn't sure how to broach them. What had MJ been doing since she saw them last? Had she gone on more great adventures? Was this trip going to bore her in comparison?

Tia opened her mouth to ask when Francis called out from his place helming in the cockpit.

"Everyone, come on over! Time for a little meeting."

MJ and Tia shared a brief glance that made Tia's chest inflate like a life raft. Tia finally had an ally. Together, they made their way to the cockpit.

Francis had set up Rylan's gift, the deep-sea fishing equipment, off the back of the stern, several translucent lines flaring out behind them as Francis himself stood at the helm.

Tia's father looked different at sea. He had spent most of Tia's childhood in ties and golf polos, bronze hair gelled to one side, and cologne pungent. He believed in impeccable impressions, and everything from the Rolex on his wrist to his brand of mouthwash had its purpose.

But when he was at sea, Francis Cameron could have been anyone.

His ungelled hair obeyed the wind, revealing iron roots and

thin spots. His cologne had been replaced by sea salt, his ties by safari button-ups. His sleeves were rolled up to his elbows, revealing a faint scar the width of a penny on his forearm.

And he was *smiling*.

"Come. Come." He motioned eagerly for everyone to make a tight circle around the helm. They were all there now. Alejandro leaned against the chart house with flour powder on his shirt. Rylan sat on the cockpit bench, chewing the inside of his cheek as Lila gripped the railing and looked in the direction of New Haven as if she were leaving for war. MJ stood beside Tia, and Nico, who stood next to Francis, gave Tia a blinding grin when they locked eyes.

Francis slapped his thigh. "Well done, everyone! We've made it to open seas. First, some business. I've posted a list of watch times on the door of the chart house and in the galley. We'll cycle through watches until we are safely docked or anchored somewhere."

Tia craned her neck to see the list, written in her father's delicate penmanship.

Captain Francis: 8 am–12 pm
MJ: 12 pm–2 pm (dogwatch)
Alejandro: 2 pm–6 pm
Nico: 6 pm–8 pm (dogwatch)
Captain Francis: 8 pm 12 am
MJ: 12 am–4 am
Nico: 4 am–8 am

"As you can see, MJ, Nico, and myself are the main crew members, so we are responsible for two watches each. Alejandro has additional responsibilities as cook, so he only has one. I thought about rotating time every day, which is more traditional . . . However," he went on, "I believe it will be easier for us to get into a routine. Furthermore, kids, Lila, you can't stand watch because you aren't licensed crew members, of course, but I really want to encourage you to take a few watches with us now and then. Trade some ghost stories. See the stars. This trip is to celebrate you, and you should get every last experience you can. And who knows?" Francis turned his smile onto Rylan. "Maybe you'll be a captain yourself someday."

Lila returned her gaze to the sea. "Is that all, darling?"

"Not quite. Everyone, please give a warm welcome to the newest member of our crew, Nicolás!"

Francis gestured to Nico so dramatically that Tia and Rylan both started to clap. Nico bowed, murmuring "Thank you, thank you," and Tia rolled her eyes to stop from laughing.

"Nico has saved us quite a bit of trouble. Not many people can drop everything they're doing to sail with six strangers for a week."

"*Five* strangers," Alejandro said, and he leaned to rub his knuckles on Nico's curly head.

"Yes, of course," Francis said.

Rylan raised his hand. "How long until we get to Florida, exactly?"

Tia looked at Francis, but it was MJ who answered.

"It's the twenty-sixth. We should make port in West Palm around June first or second."

Francis clicked his tongue. "Well, we will be stopping to dive, so it could take a bit longer . . ."

MJ stared right through him. "June third at the latest. I hear there's an eighteenth birthday party worth getting to."

Tia nodded, even though she was pretty sure the party Lila was planning was more for Lila's sake than Tia's or Rylan's. *My last birthday at home.* She looked to see if Rylan was thinking the same thing, but he had lowered his head.

"Well, then. That's all I've got. Fair winds, everyone! This is an adventure that none of us will forget." Francis glanced at his Rolex. "MJ, you have watch in thirty."

MJ grunted and turned to the twins. "Let's raise the fisherman's jib." She didn't wait for their response as she headed toward the bow.

Tia fell in step with her brother, nudging him to look at her. "Seven days till Florida," she murmured.

"Eleven till our birthday," he replied.

"And then the world." She bumped their shoulders and stopped in front of MJ before he could answer.

MJ handed Tia a line she called the *halyard*. Tia didn't quite understand how sail-raising worked, but she had figured out over the years that the halyard pulled the sail up. There was another line that needed to be eased out as the sail rose. That same line would be pulled tight (or *sweated*, as MJ said) when the sail was lowered.

"Ready to sweat, Taliea?" MJ barked, dark eyes fixed above them.

"Ready!" Tia wound her fingers around the line and pulled on MJ's command. It was exhilarating. Her biceps ached, and the skin on her palms threatened to rip. The little triangle of a sail—the fisherman's jib—unfurled and flapped noisily in the wind. The pulling became too much for Tia far faster than she would have liked, and MJ came to help. With both of them together, the sail was up in seconds.

"Make that off," MJ ordered.

"Uh . . ."

"Here." MJ's huge, strong hands closed over Tia's and showed her how to make the right knot.

Tia committed every movement to memory. Someday she would be as strong as MJ.

"Good," MJ told them when she had shown Rylan the same knot. She rested a hand on each twin's shoulder.

It was enough to make Tia burst with pride. The wind whipped her face, bright and warm and wild. Sunlight threaded between the sails as the whole ship flew and fell, and the salt-sweet scent of the ocean flooded her nostrils. The smell of adventure.

Then MJ's grip tightened. The movement was so sharp, so sudden, that Tia's breath left her all at once, her mind whirring back to what happened last summer.

Tia was kneeling on the blinding deck. Bloody teacup shards fanned out like morning glories. The hand on her shoulder was big and strong and digging into her bones. Threatening her.

Tia knew without looking that Rylan was remembering the same.

But then MJ released her grasp, and the memory was gone as soon as it had come. "He's whistling," she muttered, her eyes on the other side of the ship.

Tia swallowed as she turned in that direction. Nico was filling out a boat check sheet on a clipboard. Her mother and Alejandro had vanished belowdecks. And her father was in the cockpit, whistling merrily.

MJ patted their shoulders, then headed toward the cockpit. As she went, she put a hand over her heart and massaged as if the whistling was enough to physically pain her. "It's bad luck," she said under her breath so that Tia barely heard.

Tia rotated her shoulder to prove to herself that nothing was wrong. She wasn't hurt. Of course MJ wasn't angry at them. She was stronger than she realized, that was all.

But the memory she'd been trying to forget had been stirred all the same, and as Tia took her brother's hand, she knew it was something they would not easily escape.

Chapter 11

Rylan Cameron
Call sign: Minnow
Day 2 at Sea

RYLAN KNELT ON the carpet of the salon, sketchbook on his thighs. Lightning pulsed through his right arm, and the heel of his hand ached, but still he drew. He'd been drawing since yesterday, since they'd left land behind. It kept him calm, curious even. He was counting the hours until they would reach their first dive destination tomorrow.

"Ah, there you, Rylan!" Francis materialized, a plastic mannequin's head and torso tucked under his arm.

Rylan blanched. CPR training was one of the cornerstones of being a rescue diver, something Francis was determined both his children would be, because there was no activity or hobby in their lives that Francis did not want the Camerons to maximize. Rylan couldn't enjoy art without being prompted to research curators at museum galleries. He couldn't admire the surface of the sea without a thorough explanation of bathymetry and plate tectonics. And he certainly could not take an open water dive course without then completing Advanced, Rescue, and someday Master levels.

If only he could be like Tia, who blew through Francis's checkpoints with effortless disinterest.

Francis placed the mannequin in front of his son. He plucked the sketchbook from his hand and flung it on the sofa, leaving Rylan feeling amputated.

"Before we get started, I think it might help if you get the mannequin a name. Motivation, yes?"

Rylan nodded, but motivation wasn't what he needed. "Okay. Uh . . . Nemo," he said decisively, pocketing his pencil. He was in his third read of *20,000 Leagues Under the Sea*, and Captain Nemo was his favorite character, possibly in all of literature.

Francis clicked his tongue. "Like the clown fish? Well, whatever works for you, son. Now, do you at least remember the song that uses the right rhythm for chest compressions?"

Rylan swallowed. He had tried to explain to his father that CPR training wasn't for him, that he couldn't act under pressure to save his life, let alone someone else's.

"U-um . . . it's, um . . ."

Francis snapped his fingers. "Come on, Rylan. People could be dying. You need to know this off the top of your head."

People dying. People dying because of diving accidents or storms. People dead because he couldn't save them.

What is it? What's the song? How many chest compressions in a minute? How many, how hard, what place, what strength, what, oh God, oh God . . .

"Rylan." Francis sat across from Rylan and took his hands firmly. He placed them on Nemo's sternum. "Like this." He pushed his son's hands up and down while muttering the lyrics of "Stayin' Alive." "Got it?" he said after a minute.

Rylan didn't know how to respond. "I can try," he offered and mimicked to the best of his ability what Francis had done.

"That's fine," Francis said finally. "Now add in the breaths."

Rylan repeated the compressions. How many times until he did rescue breathing? Twenty? Thirty? And was it three breaths or four? Or maybe it was two. He squeezed his eyes shut. He wasn't stupid, but damn did he feel like it. *Oh shit.* He'd lost count of where he was. Rylan hesitated, then stopped and leaned down to give Nemo a fake rescue breath.

Francis groaned and sat back on his heels. "Congrats, son. Nemo's dead."

Rylan kept his expression neutral. Failure was familiar. He felt almost at home in Francis's random assessments followed by an unsurprised disappointment.

"You're not helping him, Francis." MJ took up the entire doorway, even slouched.

Francis made a sound in the back of the throat that was an amalgamation of a scoff and a snarl. "He needs this skill to pass the rescue diving course."

"I've certified hundreds of people as rescue divers." MJ kept talking as if Francis hadn't spoken. The air between them seemed to hum. "And if any of them was as worked up as him, I'd stop. He can't learn when he's panicking."

Francis threw up his hands. "Then he's never going to learn. Your input is appreciated but unnecessary. I can handle my kid."

MJ had Francis's full attention now. She rubbed at her chest, right below her collarbone. "Something's not right about the route you've mapped out," she said. "I came to tell you. Since you're captain and all."

Francis stood and crossed the room. "The route's fine."

MJ blinked at him. "The coordinates, they—"

Francis tossed his hands in the air. "All right, all right, I'll go take a look. Be right back."

He left, and Rylan released his own breath. He realized he'd been clenching the pencil in his pocket so tightly that it had snapped in two. He dropped the pieces on the ground and stared at them.

"How's he got you like that?" MJ asked.

"What? What do you mean?" *Keep breathing. Keep calm.*

She came and sat on the ground with him, picking up Nemo by the face and tossing him aside. "All quiet and jumpy. What'd he do to get you all worked up?"

"He's . . . my dad."

"My old man used to smack my bottom till I howled, but he never spooked me so bad as that."

Rylan tried but failed to imagine a young MJ getting spanked. "I'm not spooked."

MJ clicked her tongue and leaned forward, hands steepled in front of her. "Look. I figure you've been denying whatever's going on for so long that you don't know how not to deny it. Hard to break a habit like that. But the body doesn't lie, and you're spooked as hell. Tense and nervous, and it's got something to do with him."

Rylan's lower jaw trembled against his will. He had his arms wrapped around his knees, his eyes locked with MJ's. He opened his mouth to inhale, and it morphed into a dry sob.

MJ lingered within arm's reach, her gaze pinning him to the carpet. "Well?"

"I . . . I . . ."

She reached over, took him by the shoulder, and gave him a hearty shake. Rylan's teeth rattled, and his mind went slack.

"Tell me," she ordered.

So he did.

Rylan felt detached as he spoke, like he wasn't inside his body to make the call of what words to use, of when to breathe or where to look. He watched it from outside himself, the world on mute, and even though he knew what he must be saying, he couldn't hear it himself.

All he could concentrate on was MJ's fingers digging into his bones.

MJ absorbed what he was saying like the beach would the tide. She let it wash over her, rinse through her, rattle pebbles and erode footprints and change her coloring to a darker shade. When Rylan was done, it was her turn to speak, but she didn't. Or maybe she did and Rylan still couldn't hear.

The tinny buzz inside his ears faded just as Francis walked back into the room. MJ removed her hand and stood so fast that she looked like a wall that had risen from the carpet between Rylan and his father.

"Go up top," she ordered.

Rylan stood, unsteady on his feet, and headed to the companionway, shutting the hatch to contain the tempest he'd left behind.

He clung to the cap rail, sucked in the fresh air, swallowed and blinked and tried to reset himself, but he couldn't.

Why had he told MJ? What happened at home with his father this last year was not something meant to be shared or dislodged. It was part of him, the space between his bones, the thing that trapped his breath. It wasn't meant to be seen by anyone unless they sliced his belly open. Rylan hardly knew MJ, not really. She had sailed with them on and off over the summers, and she was friends with Tia, but she hadn't been there when it mattered. When everything fell apart.

Yet now she knew. He felt hollowed. Excavated. She had practically forced it out of him.

Rylan needed to see Tia, but she was in their cabin, and he would have to pass his father and MJ to get to her. But without Tia, he could never quite banish the ripples in his gut. Without Tia, everything went wrong. Without Tia, Rylan was in the house again, alone and abandoned and—

"Don't tell me you're getting seasick, Mr. Cameron," a voice called from the cockpit, rhythmic and warm.

Nico.

Rylan turned his back to the sea. Nico was at the helm, casually steering *The Old Eileen* through the swells. He gestured for Rylan to come sit beside him.

"If you stare at the horizon long enough, your body stops getting so confused on the motion," Nico advised.

"O-oh, no. I'm not seasick." Rylan glanced at the horizon all the same. The sun poured, half melted, over the sky. "Just . . . I get anxious. Sometimes. My dad's trying to teach me CPR stuff."

And I told MJ. I really told MJ . . .

Nico nodded knowingly. "I remember that feeling. For me it was English, though. Couldn't make sense of all the abstract stuff. Not that I fared much better at math or science." He laughed self-deprecatingly, watching the sea like a good driver watches the road.

"That's the part I don't get," Rylan said. "I understand school. I mean, it wasn't easy, but I could sort through my thoughts. With this . . . whenever he tries to teach me, my head drains."

"You can't be good at everything." Nico glanced his way, and Rylan's stomach dipped. "I heard your mom bragging about you being salutatorian. So you can't be a genius *and* a top-notch rescue diver. I mean—" he flashed a grin "—leave some stuff for the rest of us."

Rylan's face heated. "I'm not a genius."

Nico shrugged. "I dropped out of high school my junior year. I was failing all my classes, wasn't gonna make it anyway. So trust me when I say salutatorian's a big deal. At least to me."

"You dropped out of high school?"

Nico eased the helm to one side, and *The Old Eileen* adjusted. "Yeah. I was tired of everyone seeing me as stupid. The Ds and Fs were beginning to affect the person I saw when I looked in the mirror. So I dropped out, skipped town, and got hired with no experience as a deckhand a month later. I get to see the world and learn in a whole different way. Now I'm on track to get my captain's license by winter."

Rylan couldn't take his eyes off him. Nico de la Vega was like a mythic hero or world wanderer. Maybe Rylan and Tia could come up with a call sign for him that would capture something to that effect.

"You're clearly not stupid," Rylan managed. He hoped Nico could tell he was impressed. Rylan couldn't be late to first period, let alone drop out and skip town. What had made Nico so brave? Was it the opposite of what kept Rylan so scared?

"You clearly aren't either, Rylan," Nico replied.

Rylan drew his knees up to his chest.

Nico faced him, holding the wheel steady with one hand. "You wanna try steering her?"

"What? No, no, I couldn't. I can't." Rylan sunk his teeth into his upper lip.

Please don't make me.

Nico smiled. "No worries. It's scary as hell. Being in charge of something this big."

Rylan relaxed again, although he didn't believe that Nico was afraid of anything.

"How do you . . . handle it, I guess? Especially if you started being a deckhand at like sixteen. How were you not panicked all the time?"

Nico seemed to consider the question with his whole being, curving over the wheel as he let his chin fall into one hand. "You know . . . the problem was I *wasn't* scared. Not in the beginning."

"Are you scared now?" Rylan couldn't help but look up and down Nico's left arm at the longitude and latitude tattoos. Did they represent all the places he'd been? Or all the places he wanted to go?

Nico pushed back his curls. "My uncle—Alejandro—was on the same ship as me a few years back. He was cheffing, I was crewing. We weren't super close. He's my mom's distant big brother that I barely knew."

Alejandro had never told Rylan he had a nephew or even a little sister. Rylan hadn't even known Alejandro cheffed for other families. He certainly didn't need the money. Maybe he needed the space.

"But anyway, a storm was brewing, and the captain ordered us to turn the ship around and go back to port. I did what I was told, but I was complaining to Alejandro later that night. That I thought the captain was too timid, that storms are half the fun of the sea. And my uncle got all serious. He sat me down like a little boy and told me a story."

Rylan's gaze was locked on Nico's hands. He had rested his wrists on the helm and was using his hands to animate every word, punctuating the important parts. With each movement, Rylan felt himself wound tighter in the story. It wasn't the words themselves; it was the way Nico breathed life into them.

Nico continued. "Apparently he had been sailing a rich man's boat a couple decades ago. The rich guy wasn't there. He'd left them in charge of chartering the ship to a different port. But my uncle and his two best friends didn't go straight to the port. They went storm chasing. The way my uncle told it, the waves looked like tombstones, and the lightning seemed to sever pieces of the sky. The ship was out of control, and there weren't enough of them to handle that amount of weather. They were working so fast to try and trim the sails that they weren't following all the safety stuff. One of his friends got swept over the side. No life jacket."

Nico lowered his hands back to the helm. "They found his body days later. My uncle told me to always fear the sea.

It's the only way to respect her properly. So yeah. The ocean's fucking terrifying."

Rylan suppressed a shudder that slid down his spine. People died at sea all the time, he knew. But Alejandro was part of Rylan's family, and he had lost a friend. That was personal and close to home. Why hadn't Alejandro ever told him any of this? Rylan supposed he had never asked. And maybe it was too painful for Alejandro to talk about.

"Shit," he said softly.

"Yeah . . . You know, I'm kinda surprised you don't know that story," Nico said, tilting the wheel of the ship the other way.

"Why?" Rylan chewed on his upper lip.

"Because," Nico said as his eyes flickered to his, "your father was the other survivor."

Exec Monthly—Profile Watch

From Hell to the Handbasket: The Early Career of Francis Cameron

DAN GORDON III

Francis Cameron, the philanthropist and CEO/cofounder of *Prometheus Wire* and Unwind Yachting Co., has inspired a generation with his rags-to-riches career.

Raised modestly in Fontana, CA, by a single father, Cameron was an underperforming student. His grandparents sent him on a disciplinary sailing program for boys in his junior year in the hopes of inspiring more attention to his academics, but the voyage seemed to have the opposite effect, and afterward Cameron dropped out of high school.

Despite his disinterest in school, Cameron was enamored with industrial history and philosophies like Stoicism and conducted much of his own education at his local library. He worked in construction alongside his father, Bill, until Bill's death from a heart attack when Francis was nineteen. This sent Cameron into a tailspin of odd jobs from catering services to tree debarking, until he found himself working at a marina in Florida with individuals who would later pave the path for his astonishing career as an entrepreneur. Cameron told *Exec Monthly*, "I had to will it into existence. Bootstraps and such. You cannot succeed if you can't envision. It's got to already be real to you." [Profile continued pg. 39]

Chapter 12

Jerry Baugh

THE CAT WAS screaming, long, languishing yowls that made Jerry's already small cabin feel even more minuscule. Jerry slammed a pillow over his head. "Quit that, won't ya? I fed you plenty."

The cat watched him from the doorway, tail quivering like the end of a flame. Jerry lifted the pillow slowly. Had that worked?

The godforsaken creature resumed his shrieking. The cries were siren-like, hitting a pitch and frequency that Jerry truly believed could drive a man to do terrible things. Wasn't it enough that his dead brother and his worries about *The Old Eileen* were cutting his sleep hours in half? The last thing he needed was a demon cat from a ghost ship encroaching on his rest.

Jerry sat up after another minute of the screams and hurled the pillow with all his might at the cat, who easily leaped to safety.

"Damn you," Jerry growled. He stood so fast that his head hit the ceiling, and he struggled, still grumbling, into a Panthers sweat shirt.

He resisted the urge to kick the cat as he went up on deck, shutting the hatch behind him. The animal stopped screaming, as if satisfied by Jerry's absence.

"Demon cat," Jerry muttered, shuffling around his fishing gear to make himself a space to sleep in the cockpit. He was so busy lamenting his lost bed that the idea didn't strike him until he'd settled in a chair and was staring straight at *The Old Eileen*.

She's got beds, he mused to himself. *At least six of 'em. Nice ones with thick blankets and an army of pillows*. Jerry heaved himself from the chair. *Take that, cat*, he thought. *You can sleep on this dump, and I'll take a turn on your luxury yacht.*

Jerry flicked on every light switch he could find belowdecks of *The Old Eileen*, not because he was intimidated by the empty boat, just as a matter of not bumping into stuff on a vessel he barely knew. Now the question was which bed to choose. The primary suite certainly seemed to be the most sumptuous option, although even one of the crew beds would be an upgrade from Jerry's coffee-stained bunk. But why not go big? This was Jerry's ship, after all.

At least, for now.

The primary suite's king bed devoured him. Jerry sank into the eiderdown comforter like a stone in the sea. He didn't even need to pull the blankets over his body. He tilted his cap over his eyes and let himself begin to doze.

My ship. My bed. My—

Something creaked in the hallway, muffled by the closed door. Jerry didn't bother opening his eyes. Ships creak, that's what they do. He heard it again a couple minutes later, but at that point his body was heavy and drifting down deeper. The sound might as well have been the prelude to a dream.

Then something banged. Jerry snapped awake. He knew that noise, had heard it a thousand times. It was the sound of a bilge panel on the floor dropping closed. Jerry regretted not pulling the mountainous bedding over his body as a cold, creeping sweat trickled down the back of his neck.

Someone else was on the ship.

Unlike when he'd found *The Old Eileen*, there was no harpoon gun within reach. No radio hooked to his pants. There was nothing Jerry could do but walk in slow-motion horror to the door and peer outside. The hallway was dark. That couldn't be right.

He had made sure to turn on all the lights.

Nothing had appeared out of the ordinary when he'd come in. Did that mean someone had just come aboard? But no . . . the bilge panel slamming shut . . .

Someone had been *hiding*.

Jerry waited, too immobilized to do anything else. He stared into the darkness, fingernails sinking into the palm of his hand. Had the intruder come out of the bilge? Or gone inside? The thought of opening the panels to check made Jerry fiercely wish he had stayed on the *Sheila 2.0* with the scruffy cat and its siren screams.

He forced himself to uncurl his fist and dive a hand into his back pocket. He didn't want to turn on his phone. The light might reveal things in the hallway he wasn't ready to see. But someone was sneaking around his ship. He had to call for help. He had to call Madden.

Against his instincts, Jerry pressed the phone's home button. Something rushed down the hallway past him, the air from its movement hitting his face. Jerry felt around for the nearest light switch and flipped it, bathing the hallway in light.

No one was there.

He scrolled to Madden's phone number with one hand as he barreled down the hall and into the galley. He turned on every light switch, just as he had done the first time, and just like the first time, the boat looked calm and quiet.

The Old Eileen was empty.

"Hello?"

Jerry leaped out of his skin. "Jesus, hell . . ." He put the phone to his ear to confirm the voice was Madden's.

"Detective?"

"You all right?" Madden sounded distracted and muffled. There was some kind of commotion in the background of the call.

Jerry kept his back flat against the wall to steady himself. "Someone's on the boat. Or was on the boat. Just now. I heard something."

"Boats creak, Baugh. Sure it wasn't that?"

Jerry cursed. "I know what boats sound like, Detective! It was a person, okay?"

"Okay, stay put. I'll send someone over. One moment." Static thundered over the receiver before Madden's voice returned, clearer than before. "Shit, sorry, it's a madhouse over here."

Jerry continued to look up and down the hallway. He couldn't get his heart rate down. He tried to focus on their conversation instead. "Uh, what's going on?"

Madden was quiet for a moment before giving a big sigh. "Well, you might as well hear it from me. The media will be gorging themselves on it by morning."

"Tell me," Jerry murmured, wishing fervently that he had put up with the cat's screams and stayed on his own boat, that he had never gotten caught up in this mess to begin with. Maybe he even wished, deep down, that when he saw *The Old Eileen* he had just kept on motoring by.

The detective cleared her throat. "Search party finally found someone. We don't know who yet."

Some*one*? Jerry couldn't swallow. Couldn't speak. "If you don't know who, then . . ."

"All that was recovered were remains." Madden's voice was grim. "No good way to say it, Jerry. One of the seven is dead."

Chapter 13

Tia Cameron
Call sign: Thimble
Day 3 at Sea

THE SEA MONSTER from Rylan's drawing wormed its way into Tia's nightmare. Its tentacles were thick and translucent; she could see the snakelike muscles twisting beneath glossed skin as they strained for the ship. For her.

When they reached her, she was in her bed, simultaneously viewing her own perspective and that of the monster as it unlocked doors and slithered through the hall, leaving a wet trail in its wake. It wound around her foot, cold and powerful and impossible to escape.

Tia woke and yanked her foot back toward her body. Beside her, Rylan snored softly in his bed. Her watch read 4:52 a.m.

She detangled herself from her bedding and rose. She needed to refill her water bottle in the galley sink. She tiptoed out into the hallway.

A shock burst from her bare feet up through her spine.

The floor was wet.

She jumped and backed away, deeper into the hallway, but wherever she stepped, the floor was slick with water. Was it flooding? A spill? No . . . A narrow trail crept down the hall, the same exact path of the horrible creature in her dream. Tia dropped her water bottle and ran past the galley as her imagination colored monsters into every dark shadow. She hadn't grabbed her life jacket on the way up, but the sea was calm tonight. Besides, there were bigger things to worry about. Bigger, slippery, serpentine things.

The thrum of the engine gave something for Tia to focus on. Francis must have ordered the motor to run so they could keep on track without wind.

Tia locked her hands around the railing as she brought herself back to reality. She wasn't about to dismiss monsters entirely—who was she to say what was out there in the depths of the sea?—but a massive creature attacking her family's ship seemed farfetched at best. Rylan was always assuring her that the largest creatures of the sea, giant squid and blue whales, were gentle giants. They didn't have an aggressive tentacle or flipper in their bodies.

But why was the hallway wet in the middle of the night . . . *Only* the hallway?

Tia tipped back her head to examine the sky. Not a single cloud. So it couldn't have been rainwater . . .

More stars than she'd ever seen freckled the night, and she was able to calm herself even more. *How many people ever get to see stars like this?* she wondered.

"Little late for stargazing, don't you think, Miss Cameron?"

Tia spun around. Nico de la Vega stood in the cockpit, forearms resting casually on the wheel. *The Old Eileen* probably didn't require much maneuvering when the ocean was this placid.

"Hey, Nico." She joined him in the cockpit. She'd forgotten about the watch rotation. "I . . . couldn't sleep."

"Well, you came to the right place." His easy smile shone like it lived among constellations. "I'm not allowed to sleep."

"Do you get bored?"

Nico's shoulders rose and fell. "It's meditative at night in a way it wouldn't be if I had company. Like I'm out of my body and one with the ship."

"Damn, so I'm disrupting your path to nautical enlightenment?" Tia joked.

"Don't act like you don't like disrupting," he replied.

Tia laughed. "Can I try it? Steering, I mean. Dad never lets me."

Nico looked her up and down, pretending to mull it over. "You want me to shirk my responsibilities and turn command of a multimillion-dollar ship over to my boss's inexperienced daughter?"

Tia threw up her hands in defense. "Hey, I'm just trying to alleviate boredom. If I commandeer an entire ship in the process, that's just good business."

Nico chuckled, and Tia knew she wanted to hear that sound again. He gestured for her to stand next to him and put her hands on the wheel. The metal was warm from his grip.

She placed her feet shoulder-width apart to copy his stance. Nico tapped the screen in front of the wheel, which she'd never paid much attention to. "This tells you what heading you're at. We're going pretty much straight South, so you wanna keep between one ninety degrees and one seventy-five. There's nothing much to fight you right now, no wind and tiny swells, so it's really as easy as it gets."

The screen showed *The Old Eileen*, a tiny dot along a straight line that shifted direction as Tia moved the wheel. "What's that number mean?" she asked, pointing to a big black *6* in the corner of the screen.

"Six knots. It's how fast we're going," Nico replied. "We can maybe hit eleven with full sail power, but we average more at six."

"So you just stare at the numbers and try to keep on track?"

This was simpler than Tia thought. When Tia was little, Francis had let her touch the wheel, his hands over hers. *Do you feel the power?* he'd say in a low Disney-villain voice to make her laugh. It had been a long time since then. Along the way, Francis had stopped trying to teach her things.

"Yeah." Nico let his head loll back, and starlight washed over his crooked nose and full lips. The dark prickles of his five-o'clock shadow almost seemed to sparkle. He was, she had decided, extremely handsome. "But I don't use the screen anymore," Nico said conspiratorially.

"Oh yeah?" Tia glanced back at the screen to make sure she was still at the right heading. She was.

"Yeah. At night, I use the stars. I pick out a bright one, or sometimes my favorite, and I see where it falls when I'm at the perfect heading. Then if the ship ever strays, all I have to do is find my way back to her."

A thrill spread through Tia and she found herself on her tiptoes, reading the night sky to find her favorite star. "I want to do it your way," she decided.

"As you wish," he said and peeled off his windbreaker. He draped it over the screen, cutting out the only man-made light within miles aside from the red and green eyes atop the masthead.

One of the most dazzling stars shone slightly to the left of *The Old Eileen*'s main mast. There were smaller stars around it, a shimmering royal entourage. "That one," Tia whispered to herself. As long as the main mast ran along that path of stars, her heading was true.

They stood side by side in reverent quiet for many minutes. Tia wondered if Nico was as taken with this sight as he was the first time he'd seen it, if views like this ever lost their allure.

"You have a hand for this," he murmured. His voice didn't

shatter the moment, like Tia had been afraid hers would. Instead, something about this—about them, the ship, the stars, the sea—felt indestructible.

It was the sea's doing. Being out here had a way of mummifying time.

"I want to be a captain," Tia breathed. She had, just now, decided.

Nico sat on the bench to her left, arms behind his head. "You know, Tia, I think you will be. Runs in your blood."

"Right . . ."

Francis Cameron felt the draw of the sea. Hell, Tia probably inherited her fascination from him. *Do you feel the power?* his voice echoed in her head.

She did.

Tia pictured her father, strewn out on his king's mattress belowdecks. She wondered if he slept well, if five-hundred-thread-count sheets and bamboo viscose pajamas were enough to get through the night or if nightmares woke him up too.

Nightmares about monsters in the hallway.

Nightmares about hands clamping her shoulder.

Nightmares about what he feared his children wouldn't—or *would*—become.

123 News

Millionaire Ghost Ship Found in Bermuda Triangle

MIRIAM H. SHULMAN

It has been three days since *The Old Eileen* was discovered empty, and officials' only lead regarding the whereabouts of the seven people once onboard is an unidentified body reportedly recovered earlier this morning. No official statement regarding the remains has been made, and authorities have likely not confirmed whether or not the body is related to the ghost ship. We do know the empty boat was found by a local fisherman within the bounds of the Bermuda Triangle, an infamous area of ocean that has been the site of twenty plane crashes, fifty shipwrecks, and hundreds of disappearances in the last two centuries.

Also known as the Devil's Triangle, Gateway to Hell, or Limbo of the Lost, the Bermuda Triangle has confounded the scientific and public community since the days of Christopher Columbus. Theories range from rogue waves and wormholes to methane bubbles and electromagnetism from a ninth-millennium BCE comet.

But in the case of the Cameron family, perhaps it is more important to ask what the people on *The Old Eileen* were doing near the Bermuda Triangle in the first place. According to friends of the Camerons as well as first mate Mary Jane Tuckett's great-niece, the trip was supposed to end at Palm Beach Marina, near one of the Camerons' homes.

The fisherman who found the ship recorded it at over one hundred and eighty nautical miles southeast of the family's destination. Even accounting for leeward drift, the sailing yacht could only have been inside the Bermuda Triangle if something on the family's trip caused them to deviate from their route.

"It's unnerving," Coast Guard Captain James Rayes told ABC regarding the investigation. "You don't get that far off course, not with four experienced sailors onboard—you just don't. Either there was an incompetent navigator, a reason to panic, or someone had something to hide."

Chapter 14

Rylan Cameron
Call sign: Minnow
Day 3 at Sea

RYLAN KNOCKED ON his mother's bathroom door. It was the morning of their first dive. Everyone, including Francis and MJ, were up on deck preparing to dock at Icara Key. But he couldn't bring himself to join them. He was excited. At least, he had been looking forward to diving for weeks. Only now, the thought of being below water his father and the woman he'd just told everything to seemed more claustrophobic than freeing.

Lila opened the door, wrapped in a buttermilk kimono, its long bell sleeves lined with marabou trim. She smiled, wrinkleless, and pulled her son into the bathroom.

"Sit, my love. Have you put your sunscreen on?"

Rylan let her guide him to a seat on the lip of the bathtub. "Not yet." He watched her deposit a dollop of 50 SPF foundation onto her palm. She rubbed it into his face, starting with the crescent of acne along his jaw. Rylan shut his eyes. His mother's hands moved along his cheeks to his temples until his whole face felt smoothed and cold.

"Won't you come with us?" He knew the answer, but he wanted to ask just in case.

"Simply isn't for me, my sweet." Lila sat beside him and used her index finger to redefine Rylan's curls.

"I know."

Lila had only gone down with them once, the first time, when the twins had their open water certification dive with MJ eight years ago. Rylan had been astonished by his mother, always so graceful and empyrean, floundering underwater like a drowning kitten. Alejandro eventually fished her out, and from then on the extent of Lila's relationship with the sea was to sunbathe beside it. Rylan had been so young at the time that the whole thing seemed silly. The water was safe to him. But all these years later, he wondered if his mother had been having a panic attack. He wondered if his anxiety and the stomach-flipping sensation that he was always out of his depth came from her.

"I just . . . don't feel so good about it anymore."

Rylan let himself lean slightly into Lila. She took his face in her hands and ushered him down until his head lay in a cloud of marabou trim in her lap, careful not to get the sunscreen from his face on her robe. Her fingernails ran along his scalp. She smelled like cherries. And roses, maybe. He felt cocooned by her robe, her hands, the room. Steam from the bath she must have just taken misted the mirrors and made the whole space warm and sleepy.

"You've been on edge this week," Lila said. "Your sister has that effect on people."

Rylan wanted to say that she was wrong. Tia wasn't the thing that was bothering him. Well, at least, not the main thing. But her haphazard runaway plan *had* put a strain on him. How was he suddenly responsible for whether or not the Camerons remained intact?

"It's not just her," Rylan whispered, and he rotated his

shoulder reflexively. If he hadn't told MJ what she wanted to know, would she have kept shaking him? Would she have yelled?

"Your father?" Lila guessed.

"No."

Rylan turned his face and buried it into Lila's stomach. He liked feeling small like this, as if he were only his head and shoulders, tiny enough for his mother to wrap herself around him.

"MJ?" said Lila, going down the list, apparently, in order of who she deemed most inflammatory.

Rylan didn't reply.

Lila sighed. "I do wish we could have vacations with just the five of us. I tried to talk your father into an overwater villa in Bora Bora, but he insisted on this."

Of course he did. A Cameron graduation could not be celebrated with relaxation. There had to be an adventure. A rite of literal passage.

"Rylan!" Francis's voice called out from abovedeck.

"You'd better get ready, dove." Lila helped him sit up. She touched her thumb to his chin. "You'll have a ball."

She rose and steered him to the door just as Francis opened it wide.

"Ah, there you are. Going to see us off, Lil?"

"Dressed like this?" Lila said, sweeping the sheer fabric of her kimono through the air in a grand gesture. "No, I must—"

"Change first," Francis and Rylan finished for her in unison. Francis slapped Rylan's back affably. A warm feeling broke open in Rylan's chest.

"Am I that predictable?" Lila moaned as she followed the two of them up on deck.

"Yes, Mom."

"Having the proper outfit is an art," Lila said, hugging the kimono around her slim form. "Even if there's no one to see it."

"We appreciate you making an exception, Picasso." Francis looped an arm around her waist and planted a brief kiss on her scalp. "Don't we, Rylan?"

"Yeah. It's an honor," Rylan laughed.

He was getting excited again. The water was beautiful, the day was perfect. Even if MJ were coming on the dive with them, it's not like he'd have to talk with her. They could just swim and admire the sea, and when they returned Lila would be waiting for them, with drinks in hand.

Someone cleared their throat behind them, and Rylan, Lila, and Francis turned.

Tia was leaned against the chart house, arms folded. She had on her wet suit already, zipped up to the chin, and with her red-tipped hair and dark-rimmed eyes, she looked like some kind of angsty, dystopian warrior.

"We diving or what?"

"Yes, yes, go get your gear ready," Francis said, and he pulled away from Rylan and Lila.

Tia shouldered her way past Rylan, and he rolled his eyes when her back was to him. Was she really upset by them having a good time? Acting like a family? It was like she didn't *want* the Camerons to be good. He gritted his teeth.

"Suit up, Rylan!" MJ shouted from the cockpit.

"Okay, okay," he said, already irritated by Tia's tantrum.

He started to cross the deck, but Lila drew him back. "Stay safe down there. Listen to your father. And when you come back, let me attend to your hair. It always looks so good after being in salt water—"

"*Okay!*" Rylan snapped. He yanked away. "Anybody else want to order me around while we're at it?"

Lila reached up to grasp his arm. "Francis Rylan Cameron..."

Rylan shrugged her off and spun on his heel. Francis stepped in the way. The two of them were eye to eye.

"Boy," Francis said, and Rylan's spine seemed to fold. He dropped his chin to his chest and stared hard at the deck.

"What?"

Francis took him by the shoulders and spun him to face Lila, who was using her thumb to dab at the corners of her eyes.

"You upset your mother," Francis said calmly. He had Rylan's shoulders pulled so far back he was sure his shoulder blades would touch.

Rylan glanced around for Tia instinctively. She was on the other side of the ship, getting a scuba tank out of one of the bilges with Alejandro's help. MJ, however, had heard or maybe sensed the disagreement. She thundered across the deck.

"Francis!"

Francis released Rylan and stepped instead by Lila's side, arm around her once more. He looked at Rylan in profound disappointment, and every muscle in Rylan's body seized up. MJ was going to try to intervene. Or, worse, let her temper boil over and spout off everything she knew. Everything Rylan had told her.

"I'm sorry," Rylan whispered.

MJ reached them, nostrils flared. She paused when she heard Rylan apologize. He did his best not to look like a damsel, just sulky. But he couldn't ignore the way his breaths came clipped and his muscles wouldn't unclench.

Lila perked instantly. "That's my gentle boy."

Francis studied him for a moment, then gave a nod, and relief rinsed away Rylan's tension. MJ's brows gathered over narrowed eyes.

"I'll go get ready now," Rylan said, and he removed himself from the three of them before something worse could happen.

"Excellent idea, son," Francis called after him. "And once we're in the water, gird your loins. I think it's the perfect time to demonstrate your new rescue skills."

Chapter 15

Tia Cameron
Call sign: Thimble
Day 3 at Sea

TIA LUGGED HER full tank to a bare space on the bow where she could set up the regulator and BCD. When everything was connected—tubes and mouthpieces flailing about—she laid the tank on its back and hunted for her fins and mask. Rylan lagged behind her.

Tia hadn't seen her family laughing and talking like they just had been in years. It made her angry, furious even, but not because she thought they were faking it or even that it made her guilty about her plan to run away.

She was angry because they had found that sense of family after all this time *without* her.

Not that it was new for Rylan to be Lila and Francis's favorite child. They'd always had a sort of fascination with him that curdled to disgust whenever Tia tried, in vain, to get them to focus on her.

Tia tried to force herself to relax, tell herself she didn't care about her parents anymore, but she couldn't help it. It was like she was a kid all over again, desperate for attention and receiving only mild disinterest.

Francis and Lila had disappeared belowdecks, and MJ was

at the stern of the ship, muttering something to Nico, who had popped out from the chart house companionway with his guitar strapped to his back. Tia headed toward them until she almost tripped into the open dive locker. The locker was similar to the anchor one up at the bow, only it was wedged in the walk space between midships and the cockpit/stern. She knew it was there and that it was open, and she wouldn't have stumbled except that Alejandro was stooped inside, working on a tank valve.

"Alejandro?" What was he doing in the dive locker? As far as Tia remembered, he had never been on a dive with them. He wasn't certified, let alone interested.

Alejandro straightened up and nodded to her. "Tia."

"What are you doing?"

"MJ asked me to grab a tank for her while she speaks to Nicolás." Alejandro handed her the tank and hauled himself out of the locker, shutting the panel behind him. "Make sure she gets it, sí, Tia?"

"Sure." Tia glanced back at MJ and Nico who had gone their separate ways like they'd never spoken.

Tia lugged the two tanks to the stern and laid them on their sides. She had stored her mask and fins in a cabinet in the chart house, so she headed belowdecks to find them. The counter, which was usually tidy aside from the open ship's log, had been papered with maps. Tia stopped what she was doing and peered at the navigational charts spread out beneath and around the log. A protractor and a ruler were lying on top of Georgia. Someone had drawn out their sailing route from New Haven to West Palm Beach in pencil with little dots along the way marking the projected coordinates. Icara Key was roughly adjacent with Southern Virginia. There was a different set of coordinates marked in the ship's log, circled several times with a red pen. Francis's handwriting. He must have left it as a note for himself.

Tia located her mask and fins and headed back on deck where she'd left the tanks.

Rylan came up beside her. "You're pissed," he said.

"Thanks for letting me know." Tia double-checked her gear as Rylan fixed his octopus mouthpiece to his tank valve.

"Thimble . . ." He sounded more exasperated than apologetic, Tia thought.

MJ walked up behind them, wet suit bunched up at her hips. She mussed Rylan's hair, and he ducked his head sharply.

"Like old times, huh? Lord, I haven't been diving since two summers ago when we saw that eagle ray in Antigua."

Rylan avoided eye contact. "Yeah. I'm so excited."

The three of them dragged their gear to the stern of the boat where Nico had unhooked the lifeline and settled on one of the sunbathing mattresses to strum his guitar. *The Old Eileen*'s orange life preserver looked like a drop of sunshine against the deck.

Unwind Yachting Co.
Safe to sail in any gale!

Tia stood shoulder to shoulder with her father and her twin as MJ took charge.

"We're going to enter with a giant stride off the stern," she told them.

Tia couldn't help but glance at her father. Was this going to be a fight, MJ taking charge of the dive? Francis, however, seemed fine. He leaned behind Tia to yank one of Rylan's shoulder straps tighter.

"Make this signal once you pop up to the surface to show all's well." MJ tapped her fist to the top of her head. "Like so. Then we will all descend together. I'm not sure how this dive site looks, so be careful and stay with your buddy."

"I'll buddy with Rylan," Francis said silkily. Of course he would. Since they were so close now. Tia looked to see Rylan's reaction. He had his eyes on the deck. Where had all his excitement for the dive gone?

"No, you will not," MJ answered with all the flexibility of a mountain range. A muscle jumped in Francis's jaw, and Tia cleared her throat before the two could go at it again.

She would have loved to buddy with MJ, but the last thing Rylan needed was to spend this whole dive demonstrating skills for Francis. If he were paired with MJ, he could focus on the fish. He could relax. Tia wished she could just buddy with her brother, but Francis always stressed the importance of them being with a more experienced diver.

The things I do for you, Minnow.

"Dad, Rylan's gotten to be your buddy for dives all year," Tia said. "I want to go with you. Please?" She mustered her best daddy's-little-girl eyes, and Francis gave in with reluctance.

MJ patted Rylan's arm. "That leaves us, sonny. Do you have your underwater whiteboard? You can take notes on any wildlife we find."

Rylan nodded but didn't acknowledge Tia or her sacrifice. She would find a way to talk to him alone after the dive. He'd probably thank her then for taking one for the team.

"I can go in first," Tia announced. Protecting Rylan did that to her, flooded her with a strange kind of pride. She wondered sometimes if his fear made her braver, if there was only so much strength between them and she preferred being the one to have it all.

Tia inflated her BCD so that there would be enough air to keep her floating on the surface, then put her hand over her mask and the regulator in her mouth to stop them from flying off on impact. She took a huge step over the side of the boat and crashed down fifteen feet.

When they were all in the water, MJ gave a thumbs-down

to signal that they were ready to descend. Tia took a deep breath, hearing the telltale sign of the regulator's Darth Vader breathing, and slipped beneath the surface.

Bubbles crowded her mask as Tia sank and blew gently through her nose to equalize her ears. Nico's guitar-playing and the steady heat from the sun were inconsequential the moment they were underwater.

A sandy bottom was visible about sixty feet down, and to Tia's left was a cluster of huge boulders, crumbs broken off of the croissant island. A school of electric blue and black fish nibbled curiously at the dark underbelly of *The Old Eileen*. *Damselfish*, Tia remembered from her dive pamphlet. They were some of Rylan's favorites.

MJ swam in front and used a metal rod to tap on her gauge, the handheld device that told each of them how much air they had. Tia took the hint and made a mental note of her gauge, which pointed toward 2800 PSI. Plenty of air for a dive. She turned over the device to check how deep they had gone: already forty-five feet.

Francis caught up to Tia and waved to get her attention. He pointed at the rock cluster near the island. Tia signaled *okay*, creating a circle with her thumb and index finger, with her other three fingers sticking up, and stuck her ankles together and dolphin-kicked, pretending she was a mermaid. If it weren't for the steady presence of the tank on her back, she almost could have been.

Her father paused after a few minutes and gestured at something nestled in the sand, flat and seemingly made of sand itself. It was a regular fish that had been rolled out like cookie dough and now skittered over the ground, paper-thin. The ocean never ceased to surprise.

Francis swam deeper to examine the fish. He scooped up a shell inside of which a shy pink crab drew in its legs. Before pointed frantically, but what he was pointing at, Tia couldn't tell. Was there a shark? A riptide? What had terrified him so thoroughly?

Tia latched onto Rylan's shoulder straps. They needed to make a controlled emergency ascent. She signaled for him to breathe and started kicking to go up. As they ascended, she fumbled through the water and found Rylan's inflator and deflator, deflating all the air from his BCD and hers so their buoyancy wouldn't shoot them upward and tear their lungs. She didn't know where MJ or Francis were, but it didn't matter right now. They were almost there.

Their heads broke the surface after what felt like hours. Rylan ripped his mask off his head and the regulator from his mouth before Tia could stop him. Divers weren't supposed to shed their gear until they were back on land or boat. Even though the water wasn't choppy, it was still moving. He could lose his mask or choke on water or worse.

Rylan gasped and struggled to form words as tears sprung in his eyes. "We . . . w-we've gotta . . . We have to . . . Oh God, oh God . . ."

"Hey!" Tia shook him a little. She wasn't going to get anything out of him in this state. "Count with me. Just to ten, okay? One, two, three . . ."

He counted with her, stuttering over the words, until he finally found a pattern of breathing that wasn't going to cause him to faint in her arms.

"Okay," said Tia once they reached ten. "Talk to me."

He stared at her with the eyes of a wild animal.

"Something happened to MJ."

following, Tia scanned the area for Rylan and MJ. They were gone, probably exploring the rocky parts that promised to reveal more marine life.

Tia and her father continued leisurely along the ocean floor. This was the way Tia preferred her father: quiet and exploratory, like Rylan. Here, there was a temporary truce where there could be no verbal tug-of-war, no power struggle or testiness.

No . . . All human intentions were cut short at the entrance to the sea.

Tia checked her gauge: 1200 PSI. Time lilted underwater. She understood how Rylan felt, never wanting to leave, but there would be more diving to come on the trip. It was time to find the others and resurface. Tia got her father's attention and attempted charades to ask him where Rylan and MJ might be. Should they surface and meet up with the others back there? Francis signaled they should look around a little longer and then ascend.

Together they retraced their swim, weaving around rocks and even gliding through a tunnel. *The Old Eileen* came back in sight, the surface of the sea like twisted blown glass.

But not MJ or Rylan. Where could they have gone that Tia and Francis hadn't seen? Maybe they'd been carried by a current to a new location or were already back at the boat. Tia gave Francis the thumbs-up, the signal to ascend, but Francis shook his head and pointed behind her.

Rylan was swimming toward them, doing everything a diver shouldn't. His arms scrambled through water to reach them faster, his mask was half flooded, and Tia knew just by looking into his eyes that her brother was hyperventilating. Any annoyance Tia had felt toward him before the dive dissipated, and she swam hard to reach him. A panicked diver was unpredictable and needed—at all costs—to be kept from rocketing to the surface and rupturing their lungs. Rylan

Chapter 16

```
Lila Logan Cameron
Call sign: Cassiopeia
Day 3 at Sea
```

LILA SLIPPED INSIDE the crew's empty cabin, her bare feet whispering like satin over wood. She had changed out of her post-bathing kimono and instead into her featherlight cover-up and a white bikini. Alejandro, Nico, and MJ had kept their room tidy, tidier than Lila's children's, at least. It was odd. Lila had assumed that Tia's stint at boarding school would have made a bed-maker out of her daughter, but it seemed to have had the opposite effect.

Lila skimmed past Nico's bunk. The boy had pinned a couple postcards on his wall: marble columns in Athens, a vineyard in Tuscany, even a spired building in Guadalajara with faded cursive in the corner that read *Miss you, m'hijo.*

Alejandro's bed was the upper bunk. Lila poked her small nose over the mattress to see what he kept closest to him. The only scrap of decor was an old photograph of Alejandro, Francis, and another man, when they were about thirty years younger. Their arms were around each other, and they were sunburned, shirtless, and beaming. Lila felt a pang at the sight of her husband's youthful face.

At home, Lila had her own collection of pinned papers on

the wall over the old landline. They were headlines with her name in them mostly, and as the years crept by and she noticed the papers were yellowing and the dates sounded far away, she began to burn to add to it again.

MJ had her own small bed. Everything was not only in place but it also seemed prepped for a storm. Her books were tied up in a net that hung over the bed and swayed with the rocking of the boat. The only thing loose was an orange prescription bottle on the side table. Lila picked it up and ran her thumb over the label.

Verapamil.

"Señora Cameron. ¿Estás husmeando?"

Lila's heart gave a gentle flutter. She tucked the prescription bottle in her cover-up pocket on instinct before turning. Alejandro leaned in the doorway, wiping his hands on his jeans. He wasn't wearing a shirt.

"Claro que no, guapo," Lila replied.

Alejandro nodded. He never betrayed any emotion. He was the opposite of Francis in that way, Francis who projected anger or lust with a single muscle twitch. Lila could read the tension in her husband's shoulders or trace the cut of his jaw and know his longings.

Alejandro was different. His feelings, whatever they might be, never reached his body, not even his dark eyes. And she preferred it that way.

He regarded her, waiting. "My nephew is sitting surface for the divers . . ."

"Which means Francis and the others are still underwater," she finished for him.

Alejandro nodded again and closed the door behind him.

They were alone together. Nico had to watch for the divers from above as a safety precaution in case another ship came by or there was an accident. And, rest assured, Lila would hear her noisy husband and children returning long before they ever came belowdecks.

Alejandro crossed the small room until they were eye to eye.

"Nunca lo diré," he growled low and soft.

I'll never tell.

The promise he made each time before they began.

It had started seven years ago when Francis and Alejandro had had a fight and Francis left for two weeks of business meetings. The twins had been in sixth grade and were gone all day, and Alejandro had stopped by unexpectedly to bring her chouquettes.

Or maybe it had started earlier, when Lila was pregnant and cooped up at home. While Francis worked eighty-hour weeks, Lila was alone in their Palm Beach villa, which they had originally purchased for her to have a quiet space outside the limelight. Palm Beach would become their default home. She was between projects then, taking Lexapro and prenatal vitamins in lieu of the tequila that usually passed the time. Her hair-care brand was in the red and needed to be euthanized. And Alejandro didn't like working more than necessary unless it was to cook. Lila and Alejandro hadn't done anything back then, not really, but he would stop by to cook her fajitas or play a round of blackjack. He tutored her in Spanish, traded stories about growing up Catholic, and never looked away when she spoke.

Or maybe it had been penned in the stars the moment he laid eyes on her.

The day Lila met Francis Cameron, there had been a smiling man with copper hair loitering around her trailer after a shoot. And then there was the smaller boy that lingered behind.

Francis's shadow.

Lila had just made a name for herself filming *Herald of Mys-*

tery, and the two boys were day hires for a catering company, nobodies who wanted to catch a glimpse of a star. Lila had still been Catholic in those days, still a natural blonde. She hadn't yet taken up smoking (her director allowed her to film scenes with herbal cigarettes instead), and she blushed whenever someone recognized her on the street. The two boys following her had been flattering, cute even. She offered to sign her autograph on a napkin, and Francis had countered by asking her out.

You can't afford this, Lila had told him.

Francis showed off his crowded teeth. *I've been saving.*

I don't mean dinner.

She shooed him away, and the other boy stopped and asked for her autograph. It was the only time he'd spoken.

While Francis was away on business, it became a dizzying corner of her life, an affair that held the gravity of Guinevere falling for Lancelot while Camelot looked on, unwitting. If King Arthur ever knew, would he find it in him to burn his queen at the stake?

"Nunca lo diré," Lila repeated. *I'll never tell.* She moved to fit into Alejandro's arms.

The sharp blare of a horn cut between them without warning.

"Jesus!" She clapped her hands over her ears. "What on earth is that?"

The horn sounded over and over. Lila curled her head into her body. *All right, we get it. Now, make it stop.*

But the interruption seemed to tell Alejandro something that Lila had missed. He stood straight and tense like a prey animal with cocked ears.

"Five blasts," he said and then rushed from the room.

Five blasts? Lila followed after him to the companionway and up onto deck before it clicked.

The signal for danger.

Chapter 17

Rylan Cameron
Call sign: Minnow
Day 3 at Sea

RYLAN TRAILED AFTER MJ. It was hard to stay upset underwater, and there was no dive guide as dignified as MJ Tuckett. She seemed to know the sea with the intimacy of an old lover. She could coax a snow crab from its shell or point out a stonefish disguising itself as a stone. She moved through the water less like an astronaut exploring a new world and more like an appendage of the current, at one with every movement of the sea.

Rylan felt cumbersome by her side. He struggled to keep even buoyancy, releasing too much air from his BCD and falling into a cloud of sand. Or he'd add too much air, and MJ would patiently catch onto his straps and pull him level once more. Mostly, he tried not to move too much, and the two of them kept a steady, gentle pace.

MJ picked up a shell and revealed a black-and-orange sea slug underneath. She waited as Rylan drew it on his whiteboard.

She gave an approving nod at the drawing and continued ahead.

Rylan studied her as he followed. Why had MJ insisted on

being his dive buddy? Did she think she was protecting him? As if he hadn't had to live with his father his entire life. And why did she have to be so *obvious* about it? MJ was not the kind of person who was good at keeping secrets, Rylan guessed all too belatedly.

What if she confronted Francis again? What would Francis do if he knew Rylan had told someone what went on in the Cameron house?

MJ paused over a patch of coral, studying a cluster of cryptobenthic fish that huddled inside. Those fish were named literally for being *hidden on the bottom*; otherwise, bigger fish might spot them and gobble up a whole school like candy.

I'm cryptobenthic, Rylan thought. *Hiding on the seafloor, always ducking my head.* Fish could sense danger laced inside the tide. Entire schools would go darting long before Rylan ever saw the shark.

Rylan sensed something dangerous now that MJ knew the truth. Should he beg her to keep quiet? That would never work. Maybe he could keep Francis far from her until the trip was over. But what if MJ somehow prevented Rylan from returning home?

That would ruin everything. If Rylan abandoned his parents, whether he ran away or MJ took him away, it would be a failure. It would be proof that Rylan could never have handled being a Cameron in the first place. Francis would be right.

Why did I tell her? he thought to himself furiously, and an answer came to him.

Because I'm a coward.

Something caught Rylan's attention. A few yards away, a jellyfish glided around a field of rocks. It was mesmerizing, pale, translucent, and almost hypnotic in the way it moved. Rylan swam to get closer. It was a moon jellyfish, and well-named. When Rylan pictured little pieces of the moon, he saw them like this. The jellyfish was about the size of a football helmet. Its whole body rippled to propel it downward, and it slipped into an opening between the rocks. Rylan fumbled with his whiteboard and underwater pen. Drawing the jellyfish would never do it justice, but he wanted to try anyway. It calmed him, like it always did, to zero in on something beautiful and captivating. The world above the surface was miles away. He didn't need to be so scared. Here, he could just worry about sea slugs and jellyfish.

He swam over the mouth of the little cave. Inside, the jellyfish looked just like a pearl nestled in the dark. He uncapped his pen.

He concentrated everything he could into his drawing. The more details he captured now, the more he could remind himself of later when he drew it properly.

Rylan found that he was squinting to see his own work. How had it gotten so dark all of a sudden?

He looked up, and his heartbeat hammered to life. He was sinking into the little cave of rocks. He hadn't even noticed for a moment—the pull of the water was so slow and serene. He kicked to orient himself and swim upward again. He didn't ascend. He kicked harder. He might as well have been on a treadmill: the current in the cave was far stronger than he'd thought, and it worked like a conveyer belt against him.

Rylan stopped, trying to calm himself. But he only sank deeper, and that's when he realized: he was trapped.

He dropped the whiteboard and kicked with all his might, flailing his arms and struggling to gain any traction against the water that was sucking him down. He was well inside the cave now and could see a circle of blue light that marked its entrance at the top. He screamed into his regulator, and a stream of bubbles rose upward.

MJ wasn't going to get to him in time. Who knew how deep

the cave went? Could MJ even rescue him if she did know? How long until he ran out of air and suffocated? Would anyone even find his body?

Rylan's eyes burned with frantic tears. The amplified sound of his breathing in the regulator became frenzied and all-consuming. This must be the final sound astronauts heard if they died in space: only the damning noise of their own last breaths.

Rylan continued to swim, but he was already exhausted, already aching and breathless.

Until overhead, a form blocked part of the blue light.

MJ.

Her outline grew bigger as she moved closer, navigating the cave quickly and carefully. Her gloved hand found Rylan's, and he started to sob inside his mask, which had fogged up. He was saved.

They swam together. With her free hand, MJ grasped the sides of the cave and shoved Rylan upward. He seemed to fly with the strength of her push, and in a blur of blue he was out of the cave. He looked back down.

MJ was still inside.

Rylan waited for her to glide upward and out, but she didn't. She was struggling, just like he had been. Behind her mask, her eyes had rounded, and one of her long arms stretched up toward Rylan.

For help.

Chapter 18

```
Lila Logan Cameron
Call sign: Cassiopeia
Day 3 at Sea
```

LILA AND ALEJANDRO rushed across the deck. The prescription bottle rattled in her dress pocket. *Too late to put it back now.* Nico, who must have been the one to hit the horn, was leaned far over the side of the ship, shouting to someone in the water.

What could have happened? Lila found her sun hat and glasses so she could better squint at the glittering sea. *We're at anchor. Where's the danger?*

Alejandro rushed to his nephew's side and appeared to comprehend the situation instantly. "Grab your fins and snorkel, sobrino," he ordered.

Both of them scattered and reappeared with flippers and masks in hand.

"What should I do?" Lila called out.

"Get ready to pull people out of the water," Alejandro told her. He finished tugging on his fins and dove clean into the water, Nico right on his heels.

Lila was left alone on deck, white hat flapping gently in the breeze. Only then did her knees wobble beneath her.

What if Tia was hurt? Or Francis?

Or, God forbid, *Rylan*?

Lila caught herself on the railing and mustered the courage to look down.

The water was calm, marred only by Alejandro and Nico who kicked quickly in the direction of the island. They were heading toward a stream of bubbles that puckered the surface. The divers were still underwater.

They're still breathing.

She simply had no choice but to wait. Lila certainly wasn't going to do any good down there in the water with them. She paced. She fussed with her hair. She stayed by the swim ladder in case one of her family members resurfaced—bleeding or broken—and she needed to drag them onboard.

Mostly, she watched the sea. The two snorkelers shrank into specks. No . . . *Three* snorkelers.

Lila tilted down her sunglasses, then removed them from her face altogether. Yes, there were definitely three swimmers out there. Two were Nico and Alejandro, identifiable by their respective sets of purple and green flippers. The third was between them as if they'd just appeared from underwater.

Lila abandoned her post at the swim ladder and rushed to the stern. Nico and Alejandro had turned back, toting the third swimmer. Lila's heart dropped so suddenly that she almost tripped over her peach Lululemon sandals.

The person was not swimming.

They were floating. Facedown in the water, legs akimbo, arms limp.

Lila shrieked. "Oh my God!" she screamed at no one in particular. "Help!"

This couldn't be real. The sunlight, the sea, and the beautiful boat beneath her feet, *those* were real.

A body didn't fit.

Please don't be Tia. Please don't be Rylan.

Was this what people meant when they said their entire

lives flashed before their eyes? Lila saw her twin babies swaddled in white and placed on her bare chest. She held her little boy's hand while her little girl toddled wildly ahead. She cradled her son in her arms and wondered if her daughter would ever let her hold her like that again.

Lila's life wasn't in danger, but if the body in the water was her child, she would already be dead.

Nico and Alejandro reached the ship. Nico flipped the body over in the water, and MJ, slack and dead, turned upward to face the sun.

Lila released a horrible sob. "My babies, where are my babies?" She was clutching at her chest and her hair, anything to find purchase and dig her acrylic nails into. *That could have been Tia. That could have been Rylan.*

"They are okay," Alejandro shouted to be heard over her hysterics. "Nico, go get them."

Nico and Alejandro exchanged a grim look before Nico swam out again.

"They can't see this. They can't," Lila gasped for air.

But it was too late.

The twins had been out of sight, under the shadowy bow of the boat. Tia saw the body first and tore through the water.

"MJ!" Tia cried, and she fought off Nico to swim to the dead woman's side.

Rylan bobbed in the water. He looked as though he'd sink if he weren't wearing his inflated scuba belt.

Nico guided Rylan up the ladder as best he could, leaving Rylan's gear in scattered pieces, floating in the sea. Lila enveloped him the moment he was within reach, and she managed to slow his collapse to the deck.

"Get back on the boat, Tia," Alejandro said sharply, blocking Tia's path in the water.

Francis had caught up to her and hauled their daughter to the swim ladder. Lila stretched an arm out for her.

Lila held them both, tight and defensive, as Nico climbed on deck; as Francis and Alejandro pulled MJ's body to the ladder; as they passed it up to Nico and laid it to rest on the bench in the cockpit.

Rylan swiveled suddenly and vomited over the side of the boat.

Tia found her feet, but Lila stayed kneeling beside Rylan, keeping his hair out of his face as he heaved.

"What happened?" Lila asked them all. She couldn't stop herself.

The twins didn't say a word.

"An accident," Francis said. "Rylan came to get help, but it was too late. He said she got sucked into a cave."

Francis fumbled, unblinking, to remove his own tank. Nico stood as still as stone, his hands trembling at his sides. Alejandro had his eyes screwed shut as he knelt by the corpse.

MJ's corpse.

"My God . . ." Lila breathed. She ran her hand over Rylan's wet hair.

"We need to . . . we need to collect ourselves. And clean up. As captain, I will handle this . . . this tragedy as best I know how." Francis smoothed a hand over his scratchy chin and looked around at what remained of them all.

Six, Lila thought, and she wondered if she might vomit herself. She held tighter to her children, wanting to absorb her shaking son back into her body where he could be warm and still.

There are only six of us now.

Chapter 19

```
Tia Cameron
Call sign: Thimble
Day 3 at Sea
```

TIA'S PULSE THUNDERED in her head.

She couldn't wrap her head around it. MJ dragged into a cave. Rylan going for help. And then the *body* . . . Tia placed the heels of her hands on her temples, applying pressure as if she could physically keep her thoughts intact.

And then the body . . . then the body somehow moved from inside the cave to near *The Old Eileen*, near enough for Alejandro and Nico to find it.

"It doesn't make sense," Tia stated. If MJ had drowned, shouldn't she still be in that cave? How did she drown while wearing gear that allowed her to breathe underwater? Maybe she'd had to ditch the heavy tank and BCD to outswim the cave's current and had run out of air on the way up? That was the only explanation.

But MJ wouldn't have left behind her equipment unless it was the last resort. She must have seen Rylan swim away, must have known he was going for help. She would have had enough oxygen in her tank to wait down there longer. So why . . . ?

"It doesn't make sense," Tia repeated, her momentum slipping.

"I'm so sorry, lovey." Lila reached for her, teary-eyed.

"Scuba diving is dangerous," Francis said. "We take risks every time we dive."

Tia pushed her mother away. "She'd been diving for decades! She's a—was a—a-a dive instructor. A master. She wouldn't have just . . . died."

"She must have unstrapped her gear in order to outswim the current," Francis told her. "And drowned before getting to the surface."

"Why didn't she wait for Rylan to return?" Tia cried, shaking like a leaf. MJ couldn't be dead. She wasn't a normal, fragile person, she was MJ Tuckett. Sherlockian and strong and larger-than-life.

Francis inhaled deeply. "She must have panicked."

"No!" Tia hadn't meant to yell, but her body was no longer under her control. She raised a hand without knowing what she meant to do with it.

Francis winced but kept nodding. "She panicked, Tia. She was in an unfamiliar dive site, she was being sucked deeper underwater, and her buddy . . . left her."

Tia stopped, head still pounding. She looked at her brother, folded on the deck. He left her. He left his buddy. It was one of the unbreakable commandments of scuba diving, a dogma that had been drilled into the twins over and over since they'd started diving as kids.

Don't leave your buddy. *Never* leave your buddy.

Rylan tried to speak, but his breathing didn't seem to be his own. He gulped for several moments, then managed to sob, "I'm sorry. I'm so sorry."

"Oh," Lila whispered, both hands flying to cover her mouth. "Oh no."

Everyone turned toward her. Even Rylan lifted his head.

"What?" Tia asked. "What is it?"

Lila plunged her hand deep into her sundress pocket and fished out an orange canister. A prescription bottle. "Verapamil. This was on MJ's bedside table. It's heart medication."

Heart medication. Tia frowned. She placed a hand over her chest to ground herself and reassess. The movement triggered a memory of MJ doing the same, putting a hand to her heart and rubbing the area like she was in pain. Had she been having heart palpitations?

And why did Lila have it in her pocket?

Francis's eyes widened. "If she was getting treatment for her heart, she shouldn't have been in the water in the first place."

"So that's what happened," Alejandro said. It was the first time he'd spoken. He made his way over to midships where the rest of them stood, leaving MJ behind in the cockpit. He folded his arms tightly over his chest, almost in a self-embrace. "She didn't panic, exactly. She had a heart attack. The combination of the stressful circumstance and the underwater pressure was too much."

Francis nodded slowly. "Then she must have abandoned her gear and tried to swim for it. It was the only chance she had."

"But she never made it," Tia finished, her energy drained away.

No one spoke after that. Lila went back to worrying over Rylan. Francis began to pace. Tia remained motionless.

"It's . . . my fault," Rylan hiccupped, then broke down into desperate, heaving sobs.

Tia watched him cry, watched her mother smooth his hair and attempt to quiet him. She should have felt sympathy or pain as her twin brother wailed, but she didn't.

It *was* his fault.

Tia turned her face away from her brother whimpering in Lila's arms. She didn't want him to see her disgust.

Nico cleared his throat. He was standing shoulder to shoulder with his uncle, who still had his arms folded across his chest. Nico stepped forward. "I . . . I was going to radio for help when I first saw Rylan and Tia on the surface, but there was no one in range to hear it. We need to sail to the nearest port, probably a day away."

What a Cameron way to end a trip, Tia thought. *With an emergency port and a body bag.*

"No." Francis slid a hand over his wet hair and shook his head. "We aren't stopping."

"What?" Lila said.

Tia gaped at her father. Didn't they have to tell someone what happened? Didn't they have to admit this vacation was dead in the water?

"You heard me," Francis said patiently. "We will finish this trip. We only have five or so days go, and MJ has family in Florida. We have an obligation to transport her body to them."

"We have an *obligation* to report a death as soon as possible. We can worry about transportation later," Nico responded.

"We will continue to sail," Francis said, steel in his voice, and not even Tia could find the words to speak against him.

They stood there, the six of them, in an ugly silence, as the wind whispered against the sails.

At last, Alejandro unfolded his arms. "All right, then. I'll clear out the freezer."

The Convey

Body Found Has Possible Ties to Ghost Ship

RACHEL YURA

The remains that have been recovered in the search radius for the Cameron sailing yacht belong to a male body. The Hallandale Coast Guard could not confirm the identity, but they have released a statement that, due to its proximity to where the schooner was found, they suspect it to be one of the men who was aboard *The Old Eileen*: Francis Cameron, Alejandro Matamoros, Nicolás de la Vega, or Francis's teenage son, Francis Rylan Cameron.

"We do not know as much as we would like due to water damage and decomposition," Coast Guard Master Chief Petty Officer Beth Gemmel explained at a press conference. "With the absence of any Camerons to try and match DNA, we are searching for members of the Matamoros or de la Vega families to narrow down the body's identity. In cases like these where human remains are not completely intact, cause of death may never be known for sure."

Officials have reported they are no closer to finding *The Old Eileen*'s missing life raft, which seems to be the key to uncovering what happened to the remaining six people onboard.

Master Chief Gemmel concluded her statement by saying, "We have high hopes of finding the rest of the Cameron family and their crew alive and well."

Chapter 20

Jerry Baugh

JERRY FIXED THE security camera on its mount, tongue between his teeth. The ladder wobbled beneath his feet from the swells under the ship. *Storm's brewing*, Jerry thought as he climbed down the ladder and surveyed his work. The camera overlooked the hallway of *The Old Eileen*. It would catch any suspicious activity, like something sneaking out of the bilges, and send an alert to his cell phone. That had been Madden's first recommendation when he called her days ago.

Right after she'd informed him about the recovered body.

Like Madden predicted, the media published their first stories before daylight, and they had only grown more grim. News vans packed the perimeter of the marina gates, and more and more journalists became brazen enough to climb the fence to snap a photograph of *The Old Eileen* or to call out to Jerry for a comment. This continued until Madden herself came by with a couple officers to state loudly that trespassing could warrant up to sixty days in jail.

Madden's second recommendation to Jerry had been hiring help, a pair of young deckhands who were now chattering up top as they hosed down *The Old Eileen*'s deck. Jerry had hunted down Lainey and given her a job, and the other kid was a boy named Ricardo who was still in braces but knew his way around a boat. Jerry did wish that Lainey and Ricardo hadn't hit it off as well as they did so he could go back to some peace and quiet, but part of him was grateful for the company. Something had been in the bilges that night. Something he never wanted to encounter alone again.

Jerry tucked the ladder under one arm and headed to the deck. The smudged prints left by the army of coast guard and cops last week in their investigation had been wiped clean by the two deckhands. Lainey took the ladder from him as he squinted in the bright morning light.

"Camera's set up," Jerry said. He had told them about the person sneaking through the bilges in case it scared them off the job, but Lainey and Ricardo had only found the prospect of a murderer (in Ricardo's opinion) or a ghost (in Lainey's) more enticing.

"Cool. We finished with the bow and midships. All that's left is the cockpit." Lainey propped the ladder against the chart house and waved the hose toward the stern of the ship.

Ricardo sniggered. "Cock-pit." Lainey spritzed hose water at him.

Jerry walked along the bow and midships, inspecting for any missed spots. He had to look like he knew what he was doing with *The Old Eileen*, or the hired deckhands would never respect him. He couldn't find anything wrong, though, so he grunted his approval at the sparkling teak wood and white deck.

"All righ', keep working, then."

The TV in the salon was still on. Jerry had powered it up as background noise so he wouldn't have to listen to the ship creaking while he installed the security camera, but now he settled into the cushy sofa in front of it. Boy, did he feel like a rich man perusing the morning news while he paid a couple teenagers to scrub his yacht.

Jerry and Steve had grown up in a trailer park in Gainesville, knee-deep in swamp water and seventy-five miles from the sea. They'd been raised by their ma and an occasional man claiming to be their father (Ma never confirmed any of them). Growing up, the brothers associated wealth with the ocean: coastal mansions and private islands and the beautiful white sailboats that sat in wide blue backyards. Steve had dipped a toe in that life, swabbing the decks of those yachts and chartering them to wherever their owners needed them to go. *The Old Eileen* would have been Steve's dream home.

So he couldn't just sell it. The choice was extra stupid because he couldn't bring himself to sell *Sheila 2.0* either, and living off what he fished all year wasn't gonna get both boats through a summer. And Jerry damn sure wasn't getting a landlubber job. He went round and round in circles with the problem, encountering new bouts of his own stubbornness at each turn.

He wouldn't sell the boats, he wouldn't get a land job, he wouldn't work for one of the yachting idiots, he wouldn't take out a loan, he wouldn't sell the boats . . .

Something had to give. But he couldn't for the life of him decide what, so instead he turned up the volume of the television and propped his feet on the table.

". . . reminding viewers that the state is currently on hurricane watch. Hurricane Ida is expected to make landfall in three to four days," the news anchor was saying.

Hurricane Ida, huh? Poor Madden. It couldn't be easy having her dead partner's name plastered all over the news.

Jerry made a mental note to find out how to secure *The Old Eileen* against the coming storm. With *Sheila 2.0* he usually just tied a couple extra dock lines and bought beer.

Jerry surfed to another news channel.

". . . and still no sign of the passengers of *The Old Eileen*, though police are racing to uncover clues about the body of the unidentified male found in the search site. Friends and teachers of the Cameron twins have come forward to express their horror..." The reporter pointed beside her where two photographs had popped up on-screen. They were yearbook photos of the Cameron twins. Tia Cameron was in a school uniform, hiding behind a curtain of long dark hair. Rylan Cameron had a thin smile that didn't reach his large, sad eyes. They were just kids. Jerry hovered his thumb over the remote but couldn't tear himself away.

Those kids had lived here on this boat. And now . . .

The reporter continued, never seeming to take a breath. "We have heard from a family friend that Nicolás de la Vega was not meant to even be crewing for the Camerons that week, and in fact Ernie Carmichael changed his mind about the trip at the last minute. We have a brief statement from Mr. Carmichael, who was a personal friend to both Francis and Alejandro."

The screen flashed to what looked to Jerry like the outside of a miniature mansion. A pudgy man in a golf polo shook his head at the camera. "I can't even imagine what might have happened to them, to those poor kids. I just keep thinking if my mother hadn't fallen, if I'd been onboard too . . . maybe I could have stopped this from happening. Or, I—I don't know, maybe I'd be gone too."

"How long have you known the Camerons, Mr. Carmichael?" a man asked from behind the camera.

Ernie Carmichael adjusted the microphone clipped to his collar. "I was there at the beginning stages of *Prometheus Wire*. Thirty years ago, right? He was my boss, a groomsman at my wedding. Good guy. I just hope wherever they are, they are safe. I don't believe for a second that the, er, the body that was found is him. Or any of them. I think they're all still out there."

Jerry turned off the television.
I think they're all still out there.
All but one, right? Even then, the odds couldn't be good. Still, maybe he was wrong.

Maybe one of these days the coast guard would scoop a boatful of shivering millionaires out of the water, and Jerry would end up having champagne on deck with the captain who'd be more than grateful for Jerry looking after his beautiful ship. Those two kids would be home playing up top with the hose like Lainey and Ricardo were now.

As Jerry's ex-wife used to say, *Everything comes out in the wash*. And with a hurricane brewing, they were all about to get one hell of a cleanse.

Chapter 21

```
Lila Logan Cameron
Call sign: Cassiopeia
Day 3 at Sea
```

LILA DIDN'T DARE approach her husband until Alejandro was belowdecks and his nephew was at the wheel. She trailed Francis to the primary suite.

She knew what she wanted to say, had spent the last half hour getting tipsy on hibiscus tequila and rehearsing the words in her head after the twins had gone to their room.

This is madness, Francis. The longer we delay telling the authorities about the accident, the worse it looks for us. All of us.

Lila had flirted with scandal, and she'd found it to be a selfish and rather uncouth lover. Already, the untimely death of a woman who worked for the family was enough to make waves. If Lila's name could snag an entire article under suspicion she'd had undisclosed lip injections, then an experienced sailor's drowning on her family boat going unreported would certainly make nasty headlines.

Francis must see reason. Her husband might defy common maritime laws, but he was still a rational man. To ignore this hiccup and continue on their family vacation could be catastrophic down the line. Surely he knew that? She settled on reminding him in such a way that it would seem like his idea.

That was the key with powerful men; Lila knew that from decades of show business and marriage.

She parted her lips to croon his name, start the conversation out light when he turned without warning and pressed his mouth over hers.

Lila's half-baked words smoothed into a sigh. She hadn't tasted Francis's lips in ages. The scent of sea salt from the dive had replaced his carefully chosen cologne. She dissolved into him, letting his arms bear her weight and carry her to the bed. What had changed? What had made him see her? She hated to question it, but she had to because there was another flavor in his kiss, one that resurrected that boyish, ambitious man from years ago.

Triumph.

"Francis," she breathed as he loomed over her on the bed, his jaw grazing her throat. He inhaled heavily, and she imagined that he was reacquainting himself with the scent of her hair.

"Francis, wait . . ." she whispered.

He paused, one hand propping him above her, the other hand on his belt. "Why wait, Lil?"

She sat up but cupped his face. Held his focus. "I could ask you the same thing, my love."

Francis leaned into her. "You should trust your captain, Lila Logan."

She should. She did. Well, she almost did, but she knew him too well to trust him again.

"I just have to know why," Lila went on with care while he watched, unreadable. "I have to know, and I *want* to know because we're on the same team." She unspooled his fingers and threaded hers between them while he considered her words and her.

Francis sat back on his heels and broke their grip. Lila resisted the urge to yank him back again, but she was a patient woman. She waited for him to nod and explain and mostly for him to kiss her once more and paint a silver lining on this horrible day.

"No," he said without a shade of apology. Then he stood, adjusted his belt buckle, and left with a brief twist of the watertight door.

The place where he had been, heavy and burning, froze over.

No . . .

The tequila she'd already consumed was no longer enough. Lila made her way to the galley, and for once she was thankful Alejandro wasn't there. She poured herself a double shot and added a slice of lime and a rim of pink Himalayan salt.

The galley was empty, but it didn't feel like it. A net of bananas swayed over the kitchen sink, and a Florida-shaped spill of truffle sauce had congealed on the steel counter. A sweaty plastic bag of meat loaf was left defrosting next to the stain. Lila supposed Alejandro would have thrown everything from the freezer out now that they could no longer store food there. Why keep the meat loaf? Their freezer was now a coffin.

There's a dead woman in that freezer.

She knocked back the glass.

Maybe, in a beautiful and terrible way, it was better like this, she told herself. The reporters would smell a scandal. But Lila could guide it. She could massage the narrative.

MJ was like an older sister to me. A member of my own family. The ocean stole her, and I will never forgive it for that.

Lila *was* profoundly disenchanted with the ocean; no part of that was a lie.

And the death had been a rather cinematic one, hadn't it? What if it got made into a movie? But what would the overall plot be?

She pinched the lime's juice into the empty cup and poured a fresh shot. This time she didn't bother with the salt before she drank. Her body thrummed with anticipation. She couldn't hold still. She swept down the hall, alit with nervous energy, and hovered outside the twins' door.

They'd been slack and catatonic when they'd descended the companionway hours ago. They hadn't reemerged since. Her children were unraveling. Her husband wasn't listening.

No, Francis had said to her, but now she wondered what exactly he had been referring to.

No, Lila, you don't have to know.

Or maybe, *No, Lila, we're not on the same team.*

Or worst of all . . . *No, Lila Logan . . . you don't want to know.*

Chapter 22

```
Tia Cameron
Call sign: Thimble
Day 3 at Sea
```

THE ANCHOR LOCKER of *The Old Eileen* hummed with the pressure of the sea as Tia sat inside it, listening to the ship surge through the Atlantic. There was something comforting in it. At least here, the sea sounded just as dangerous as she now knew it was.

At least here she could be away from Rylan.

Rylan . . .

There was no thing or person in the world who mattered to Tia more than Rylan. But he'd left MJ in that cave. He had left her to die. Not even Rylan himself denied that the accident was his fault.

She leaned her head back against the rumbling wall. The movement of the ocean rattled through her body, between her ribs and through her veins until it felt akin to blood flow.

Tia understood what it was like to be scared. She had fumbled with her regulator and inhaled a lungful of salt water when she'd taken her open water test. She had run a red light in a friend's Bugatti convertible when neither of them was licensed. Or wearing seat belts. And she had stood at the black iron gates of St. Bernadette's School for Girls, ripped from her twin and fearing that, when she returned home, her family would have moved on without her.

So she knew it, that sick feeling when it all slips out of your control and you're left to make a momentary decision or be destroyed.

What Tia didn't understand was how Rylan could make the wrong choice over and over, if doing nothing and panicking was even much of a choice at all. How could he have faltered the one time it counted, the one time a person's life was on the line?

MJ's life.

It wasn't fair. It wasn't fair that Rylan had failed MJ, and it wasn't fair that Tia would never talk to her again because of him. MJ Tuckett was the closest thing to a mentor that Tia had ever had. She had only begun to show Tia the things she now knew she wanted to learn. Knots and wind patterns and travel stories and stars. MJ always said she was one of the last salt-blooded sailors, the last of a generation of seafarers reared on tall ships instead of engines.

She had been irreplaceable.

Now she was gone.

She drank in a couple of deep breaths, then stood, running her hand along the flaked anchor chain which sat like a human spine, each chain link a vertebra stacked on the next.

If MJ were here and Tia were the one in the freezer, MJ would have done anything in her power to radio land and end this trip. It was the right thing to do. Vacations didn't continue when people died.

Tia opened the hatch of the anchor locker and poked her head out. Her hair was crisp with dried salt, and it flapped rather than flowed in the wind.

Nico stood a few feet away, the clipboard they used for routine boat checks in his hands. He blinked in surprise at Tia.

"Miss Cameron. Hiding from something?"

My brother.

"Course not. Is the ship passing all your inspections, *Mr. de la Vega*?" She pasted on a smile.

He spun the clipboard between his fingers like a card trick. "Well, I haven't checked the anchor locker yet."

Tia was relatively certain boat checks never included the anchor locker, but he was playing with her, and she liked to play along. "Don't let me get in your way." She smiled up at him again, very much in his way.

Nico crouched down, narrowing the gap between them.

"I've gotta get down there, miss. Are you going to step aside? Or should I . . . move you myself?" He reached out a hand and rested it for just a second on her waist.

Tia wanted to feel flirtatious and coy, but her stomach was stone, and all she could think about was MJ. How could Nico stay so light when MJ lay dead belowdecks?

Tia envisioned MJ struggling deep underwater. She pictured her clutching her chest, making the split-second decision to shed her gear and swim for it. Clawing to the surface, desperate for air, only to never breathe again.

She retreated back into the locker, giving Nico the space to follow.

He did.

"Well?" Tia spread her arms, taking up half of the small, dark space. "Does this pass, Inspector?"

"Hmmm." Nico did a slow rotation, one eyebrow articulated in an arch. He knocked on the walls and glanced at Tia to see if he had made her laugh.

He hadn't, but then she felt bad that she hadn't. A handsome, playful guy distracting her sounded like the perfect thing in her head. But she almost wished he would hold still. She wished he would ask if she was okay.

"It doesn't feel right to just . . . keep going," Tia said, hugging herself.

Nico touched her elbow. "Nothing feels right after a death."

"A funeral does, right?" Tia had never really known someone who died before. Her paternal grandparents were dead long before the twins were born, and Lila had kept them from her own parents. They must have died at some point, but Tia hadn't heard about it, and no one seemed sad, so it didn't really count.

Nico tucked the clipboard under his arm. "You know, burials at sea were real common throughout history. They'd sew the deceased in cloth and put the last stitch through their nose to make sure they were really dead. Then they'd weigh down the body with cannonballs or rocks, and send it into the water as someone led a prayer and maybe a chantey."

Tia imagined MJ's body sinking into the sea, weighted with stones. "That's probably something she would have wanted," she said. "She was old-fashioned."

"I'm sure her family will have her buried at sea in some way," Nico said. "But that's not up to us."

"I know." Tia shuddered. Instead of drifting into the bottomless ocean, MJ was sitting, bunched up, at the bottom of their freezer. She deserved something of dignity at least. "Maybe we could do the other stuff, though? The prayer? Or a chantey?"

She looked to see Nico's reaction. He was nodding along.

"I can grab my guitar," he offered.

Tia smiled a little. "Yeah. You know a song we could do?"

"I got an idea. Be right back."

He bounded up the ladder to the deck, leaving Tia to sit again on the cold anchor-locker floor. She had never given much thought to an existence after death, or really death in general, but MJ had believed so strongly in heaven it must be true. At least for her. She had talked about angels like they were overworked elementary schoolteachers and God like he lived just down the street. She was with them now, Tia decided, in whatever way she could be.

Nico reappeared in the mouth of the hatch, dreadnought guitar slung over his shoulder. He climbed down and sat shoulder to shoulder with Tia, who let herself lean into him.

Nico positioned the guitar on his lap. "The man who wrote this was leaving for the navy. 1950-something."

"Ohh, a history lesson," said Tia, half teasing.

Nico smiled. "It's called 'Grey Funnel Line.'"

And he began to play.

The fingering was simple. Bittersweet. Nico sang in a threadbare voice as the strums filled the tiny locker till it burst.

Tia saw MJ Tuckett standing at the silver wheel of a ship. She heard Pirate purring as MJ found his favorite spot beneath his chin. She felt the current of water that carried MJ like a sea creature.

Tia hadn't known her as well as she would have liked or as long as she would have wanted, but she had known her, and she was grateful for that. She realized her cheeks were wet as Nico's chantey came to its end, the final notes twining as long and low as wind.

"Thank you, MJ," Tia whispered. She drew herself up with a breath that swept through her entire body and looked over at Nico. His eyes were shut, lashes beaded with tears. Tia couldn't help her surprise. Nico and MJ couldn't have spoken more than once or twice. They hardly knew each other. She placed a hand on Nico's shoulder, and he blinked so fast that the tears vanished. Like she'd imagined them.

"It's a great song," he said.

"What now?" asked Tia.

"That's up to you, I think."

Tia thought, keenly aware of how hollow the locker felt

without the sounds of the guitar. "Get off this boat. And then . . ."

And then the last thing Tia had promised to do with her family would be done. The trip would be over. She'd leave. She had a wide-open world waiting for her. She was going somewhere far—Iceland, maybe. Or Alaska. She would get a job on a boat like Nico had done and work her way up to be a captain like MJ. Maybe she'd circumnavigate, maybe she'd swim with whale sharks, maybe she'd make a whole new family, and the Camerons would be an old story she'd tell during storms.

She'd make MJ proud.

"Then this is over," she finished.

"All of it?" Nico asked. He slung his guitar back over one shoulder but made no move to push away Tia's hand. He leaned one of his tattooed arms against the wall above Tia's head so that his body made a crescent shape above her.

"Is there something you don't want to be over, Nico?"

He lowered his face to hers.

The overhead door opened and blinded them both. Nico retracted his arm, and Tia craned her head to see the silhouette of the person climbing down into the locker.

Rylan.

"Oh," Rylan said when he saw them.

The anchor locker was barely comfortable with two people and a guitar inside. With three of them, it seemed like a coffin.

"Sorry . . . didn't mean to interrupt something." Rylan smiled at Nico. His eyes were red.

"Hey, Rylan," Nico said smoothly. "Here to join?"

Tia shifted. Selfishly, she was glad she'd gotten a moment to mourn without him.

Now she just felt uncomfortable.

Rylan squatted in front of them. "What were you guys talking about?"

"Boat inspections," Tia said, as Nico answered, "Life."

"Life and boat inspections . . ." Rylan repeated.

"What is life if not one giant boat inspection?" Nico tried at a joke.

"Why'd you come here, Ry?" Tia turned to her brother, trying to sound gentle.

"Looking for you," he admitted. Rylan was taller than both Tia and Nico, but now, folded up like a tent pole, he seemed tiny. "Were you playing music?"

"Yeah," Nico said. "For MJ. We figured she'd have liked a good chantey."

"Can I hear?" Rylan asked. He looked so sad that Tia nearly felt guilty for being cold toward him.

"We can do one more, I guess," she said. Rylan's fear might have cost MJ her life, and she wasn't sure she would ever forget that. But he was her twin. He was her best friend. He was the only one who had been there since the beginning, even when Tia's parents turned away.

"Encore it is, then," Nico said, and he returned the dreadnought guitar to his lap to play.

Chapter 23

Jerry Baugh

THE LIQUOR STORE had been picked to the bones by the time the rain started. Hurricane Ida had sent every man, woman, and child to the shelter of their homes. Everyone, it seemed, besides Jerry Baugh and the pimply liquor store attendant.

Jerry scooped up a case of Bud Light, the only thing left on the shelf of refrigerated beverages. He thumbed through his slender wallet as the attendant, who Jerry could scarcely believe was old enough to *be* in this place, let alone run it, checked him out.

"Your total is seventeen dollars and seventeen cents, sir."

Jerry dropped a sweaty twenty on the counter. "Keep the change," he said, then, before he could feel too generous, added, "And stay in school."

He shouldered through the door. The wind hit him like a slap in the face as he hobbled down the empty street. The marina was a six-minute walk at most, but it took him ten just to reach the street corner opposite the sea. Palm trees bowed to the authority of the wind, and Jerry Baugh proved no exception as he found himself stumbling into a boarded-up window. He adjusted the case of beer. Last thing he needed was a massive gust to knock him over and shatter his chance at an inebriated storm watch.

The crosswalk sign told him to wait as a single truck, its bed overflowing with plywood and Coca-Cola, slid through the intersection. Jerry grunted and glanced at the window he'd run into.

Hallandale Coast Guard Station.

The lettering on the glass was visible between slats of wood. Jerry peered past the letters to where he could make out an office light deep in the belly of the building.

What kinda cop was still at work filing paperwork in a hurricane?

He knew the answer before he even saw the fist-thick braid of hair and ramrod shoulders. Brenna Madden sat at her desk, typing away.

Jerry squinted at the rain, which had started to come in sideways, then banged a hand on the door. He waited until Madden stood in the doorway, confused and displeased.

"Brenna," he touched his knuckle to his Bass Pro Shops cap.

"God's sake, Baugh." She grabbed a fistful of his flannel and pulled him inside, closing the door against the wind. "Unless one of your jackass fisher friends got themselves tussled up by this storm and needs the coast guard, I suggest you go on home."

Jerry skated over the fact that he didn't have fishing friends, jackasses or otherwise. In his mind, the whole point of fishing was to put friends and humanity in his lobster boat's rearview. All Jerry really remembered about being around other people was how loud it was.

His brother trampling through their trailer home with a BB gun.

His mother wailing as they put Steve's remains in the dirt.

His wife screaming when she told him she was done.

People were noisy and ugly. There was no such thing as graceful grief or a happy marriage. Happy was a thing that only happened to Jerry alone at sea.

"Why, um, aren't you home?" he asked the detective.

"Why aren't you?"

Jerry showed her his Bud Light. "Essentials. I just, uh, I just figured that you wouldn't like being stuck in a cubicle until Ida blows over."

Madden flinched. She crossed her arms to cover it, but Jerry had already seen. He frowned, feeling the rain dagger through his Panthers sweat shirt. *Ida.*

"I have a lotta work to do," she said eventually.

"Work on the case? Any new updates?"

"No updates. This hurricane's gonna hide any evidence we mighta found, if we'd had more time anyway."

Of course it would. Jerry was beginning to think that they might never get answers. But sometimes people drowned, and he supposed sometimes they just disappeared too, and there was nothing anyone could do to find out why. Even the man's body they found might not be connected to this case.

"Well, uh, I s'pose I'll be getting back to the dock." Jerry shifted his feet and wondered why Madden hadn't shooed him out the door yet. Could she possibly be glad he knocked? She had a funny way of showing it. Or maybe in the midst of a violent tempest named after Madden's dead partner, she was just happy to see another human face. And that's why she couldn't go home.

"Hey, so, I'm just gonna be drinking on my boat, waiting this thing out. One of my deckhand's there too. Ricardo left, but Lainey's family is out of state so she needed a place. And if you, well . . ." Jerry waved the beer case again. "You know, if beer's your thing and you wanted to stop by—"

"Can't stand the taste of that stuff," Madden cut him off.

"Oh."

"But . . . I've got an old bottle of gin in my desk."

Jerry grunted away the smile that threatened to turn his lips. "I'll see you on *Eileen* in a few, then."

Madden gave a curt nod, her hand already turning the doorknob. She paused. "Feels weird to just put my feet up and wait out the storm in an inactive crime scene."

"Feels even weirder livin' in one."

Madden clicked her tongue. "Well . . . can't argue with that. I'll get my coat."

WHILE RAIN DRUMMED against *The Old Eileen*'s portholes, Jerry claimed the corner couch in the salon, leaving Lainey and Madden to sit across from him. The cat paced the length of the room, whether disgruntled by the storm or the ship, Jerry couldn't say.

"Lainey, I, uh, hope you like beer, since Madden here seems to be more of a gin gal."

Madden tipped her entire bottle back, not bothering to retrieve one of the crystal glasses from the galley cabinets.

"Rum, sorry," Lainey said with a smile.

It registered with Jerry that Laincy was even younger than the guy in the liquor store. She shouldn't drink anyway. Not that Jerry was one to judge. He and Steve were sneaking beers before either one of them graduated high school.

Jerry popped the top on his first can and settled back. He flicked through a couple channels before deciding on the weather one. There was a strange satisfaction watching the hurricane unfold both on his television screen and outside the portholes. Jerry's gaze slid occasionally to the bilge panels, just to make sure they were all still in place.

A clap of thunder made him splash beer down the front of his sweat shirt. "Dammit." He'd meant the words to be gruff, but his voice broke.

The two women looked at him.

"It's okay, Jerry," Lainey said, not unkindly. "It's just lightning breaking the sound barrier."

"Who taught you that, kid?" Madden asked.

"My dad. He always had answers like that. He didn't say things to comfort me, though, just to point out how I misplaced my fear."

Madden unscrewed her bottle. "He dead or something?"

"To me."

Madden snorted. "My pa always said it was God's angels bowling. 'The bigger the boom, the better the score.'"

Another clap quieted them all momentarily. Madden lifted the bottle heavenward. "Strike."

Jerry set his beer on the table, then thought better of it as it careened sideways with the ship. He cocooned it between his hands and leaned forward. "I ain't scared," he insisted, though no one had said otherwise.

Storms reminded him, was all. A stormy sky had been the last one Steve had seen. Jerry wondered, if his brother had survived that night, whether booms of thunder would have sent him out of his skin for the rest of his life.

He drank deep, settling back again into the seat where the missing family used to sit.

Did the Camerons take their breakfast here? Did they watch TV and fight over the remote? Did they talk about the future like it was something inevitable? Something already belonging to them?

And, just like Steve, was a storm at sea the last thing they saw?

Chapter 24

Rylan Cameron
Call sign: Minnow
Day 4 at Sea

THE CAMERONS BREAKFASTED together in the salon, seated around the table on the cream chenille sofa built into the wall. The twins sat opposite their parents, Rylan stabbing at his potatoes but never finding the appetite to bring them to his mouth. Tia poked at her eggs, seemingly in a similar predicament.

Francis was supposed to be on watch, Rylan thought with a glance at the schedule. Of course, without MJ in the rotation, Nico, Alejandro, and Francis should have each been pulling extra weight.

But here Francis sat at the salon table with them, sawing his sausages in half and sipping freshly squeezed orange juice out of a crystal glass.

Lila—who often insisted on eating a different meal than the rest of the family—took a dainty bite of her blueberry parfait, then laid her spoon on the table. "I think . . ." She cleared her throat. "I think we should be planning our next family activity! We have—what?—three or four days left of our lovely little vacation, and it's about time we make an itinerary since diving may no longer be the highest of priorities."

Very smooth, Mom. Rylan shoved some diced potatoes in his mouth.

Lila reached over and rested a hand on Tia's arm. "I know. Why don't we plan a nice spa treatment? I have all the supplies. You could let me get one of my hair masks on you. And maybe tonight we could play some family poker?"

Tia stopped eating.

Here we go.

"Omigod, yes, and maybe while we do chemical peels and drink cucumber juice we can finally acknowledge the fact that MJ just died."

Well, there it was. Rylan leaned back in his seat as Lila rubbed her temple and all three of them turned their eyes on Francis.

Francis tilted his head to one side, then took a large bite of sausage. He chewed. Swallowed. Drank some orange juice. Swallowed.

Rylan began to think his father wouldn't answer at all and the silent meal would resume, but Francis set down his glass and smiled. He had wanted them to wait.

"I think," he said in a faint mimic of his wife, "that is a great suggestion, Lila."

Rylan, Tia, and Lila watched as Francis sliced open a fried egg. The yolk bled bright yellow over the plate. Francis dragged his potatoes through the mess and took another bite.

Rylan fiddled with his fork.

The boat hit a bump, and Lila's spoon clattered to the floor. As she hurried to pick it up and wipe the yogurt off the wood, Francis kept chewing.

"Maybe we could keep sailing, but we could send a message to shore for MJ's family," Rylan suggested, hoping for a compromise.

Francis clicked his tongue. "I think that would put unnecessary strain on our vacation."

"Unnecessary strain?" Rylan tried to make eye contact with Tia again, but she was already forging ahead. "MJ is dead. We are well beyond *unnecessary strain*." She leaned over the tablecloth, her fists making towers around her plate of untouched food. "What would you have done if it was Mom that drowned? Or Rylan?"

"Tia." Rylan stood with a start and tried to tug on one of her arms. "I'm not hungry. Let's go to our cabin."

She just had to pick at Francis, didn't she? Rylan understood she was upset about MJ—he was too—but was she *trying* to make their father snap? Was she *trying* to repeat last summer? Look how well that had turned out for her.

"It's all right, Rylan." Francis waved a hand, and Rylan let go. Francis wasn't even looking at him. He felt tiny. Like the sofa and the cushions he sat on were growing around him. Like he was being swallowed inside.

"You're quite right, Tia," Francis said, and his tone made Rylan's hackles raise. "Life at sea is dangerous. Deadly, sometimes. I couldn't have predicted an accident, but we always take into account some amount of risk."

"This isn't how normal people respond to a death!" Tia raised her voice, which wobbled ever so slightly.

"Tia, please," Lila said, resting a hand on Francis's thigh. "We understand you're upset. This situation is very painful, and I'm sure your father has a good reason for it all."

Tia blinked rapidly, looking to Francis. "Do you?"

Rylan felt the urge to lean over and grab her wrist, but he didn't. He was the reason she was in mourning at all. He wished he could collapse in on himself. But more than that, he wished Tia would stay quiet.

Francis took a huge bite of meat and potatoes. He spoke around the food in his mouth.

"It's simple, sweetheart. We'd have to go closer to land to radio the coast guard. It would stop the trip altogether and . . . well . . . I have a big surprise for all of you, and going back to land now would ruin the whole thing."

Lila clapped her hands, but the line in her forehead deepened. "Oh, a surprise! How thoughtful, love."

"Yes, I thought so too." Francis leaned backward, hands behind his head, and finally swallowed his food.

"What surprise?" Tia whispered, shoulders drooped. She just seemed sad now. Rylan's stomach lurched.

"Well, Tia . . . our destination. It's a surprise."

It was Rylan's turn to gape at their father. "Wait. Our . . . destination?"

Francis dropped his crumpled napkin onto his empty plate, lips pulled wide. "That's right, Rylan. We *aren't* going to Florida. We never were."

Francis slapped the table so suddenly Rylan flinched.

"Now! Who wants mimosas?"

Chapter 25

Tia Cameron
Call sign: Thimble
Day 4 at Sea

TIA AND RYLAN shut themselves in their cabin. Tia leaned back against the closed door and slid to the ground until her knees propped up her elbows and her head was in her hands.

"I don't understand. Where could he be taking us?"

The carpet blurred in front of Tia. She couldn't blink or cry, only stare straight ahead as her best laid plans turned to dust.

He wasn't taking them home to Florida.

But Florida was where all of Tia's things were. She had a mason jar of cash on her dresser, rain boots in the closet, a travel pack that could easily fit half a dozen outfits and a sleeping bag. She had everything she needed to run.

Tia's fingers dug into her scalp as a horrible thought took shape.

What if Dad knew about my plan?

Why else would he change their destination? He was trying to mess with her head, show her who was in control. She had to get out of here, contact the outside world, and cut off this random surprise vacation.

Tia forced herself to calm. No, he couldn't have known. He

hadn't even seen her since last August when she got on the jet for St. Bernadette's.

"I don't understand," Tia repeated.

From the end of his bed, Rylan was making swirls in the carpet with his toe, chin dropped to his chest.

Tia dropped her hands and zeroed in on her brother. "Why aren't you saying anything?"

Rylan didn't look up. "I—I don't know what to say."

"Did you . . . know about this?" Tia couldn't help the note of accusation that crept in her tone.

Rylan looked at her, shoulders scrunched to make himself small. "No."

"You're not reacting like normal."

"What's normal?"

A panic attack. Tia bit her tongue. "You just . . . You're not even upset. You hate surprises."

Rylan shifted around the bed, not meeting her eyes. "It's just more vacation. Dad seems so excited."

Tia pushed against the wall and stood. She didn't want to be angry at him, but her frustration filled every inch of her, and Rylan was in her line of sight, not even reacting to the massive wrench in her plan. He wasn't even mentioning it.

"Rylan," Tia said in an effort to keep her voice even, "you realize I can't run away until he takes us home. I can't survive any extra time with them."

They hadn't talked about running away since MJ's death, but Tia was more certain about running than ever. Rylan had to understand.

Instead, he stood, hands in his pockets and chin to his chest. "I'm going to go . . ."

Tia folded her arms. "Are you at least going to come up with an excuse?"

Rylan kept his head down and left the room without another word.

What. The. Hell.

Was he hiding something? Either he knew about Francis's surprise or . . . Or what? He wanted Tia to stay so badly that he was celebrating the change in their destination? No, that couldn't be it. He wouldn't have acted so guilty.

So why would he be guilty?

MJ.

Tia paced the cabin between the two twin beds.

He's relieved we aren't going home because MJ's death won't be reported right away. Because if MJ's death is Rylan's fault . . .

Tia sank down onto Rylan's bed. Her leg hit something tucked underneath the sheets, and she dug around to pull it out.

Rylan's notebook. The thing might as well have been her brother's diary.

Tia opened it without hesitation.

The first half of the book was everything she remembered from last summer. A prickly lobster from their dive at Alligator Reef practically bristled off the page. A rendering of the bronze Christ statue from their snorkel at a state park gazed up with sad, blank eyes. The sketches got less artistic and more clinical as she looked on. Anatomy of a pearl fish. A close-up of a lionfish's spines with notes of its venomous and invasive nature. Atlantic tarpon, giant squid, some weird-looking shark . . .

The drawings took on a different shape after a while. Straight lines grew wispy. Orderly strokes wobbled into scribbles. Tia turned another page and stopped dead.

The sketch was magnificent and out of control, jets of bubbles penciled around the perimeter as if the scene was being viewed from behind a diver's mask.

And what a scene it was.

A diver clad in svelte black, face to the side, profile sharply outlined. The diver's flippers looked less like a piece of equipment and more like an appendage that grew seamlessly from their dark legs. And they had one hand straining for the surface.

Tentacles, not thick and sucky like the ones of the giant squid, but needlelike and fine as silk, gathered around the diver's waist. They wouldn't have been so threatening if not for the sheer number of them. Thread-thin tendrils curled around the diver's legs, and a single narrow tentacle was poised to claim the diver's outstretched arm.

It was a jellyfish, Tia guessed. A fantastical, monstrous jellyfish that lived in her brother's mind.

Tia couldn't stand to look any longer. She turned the page and was met with more straggly drawings with flyaway lines and reaching people. Drowning people.

Tia placed the sketchbook back where she found it and left the room.

In the cabin next door, Nico lay draped across his bottom bunk. He must have just gotten off watch. Tia paused in the doorway. "You okay?"

Nico sat up at the sound of her voice. He drew a threadbare smile over his face. "Sure am. How you doing?"

Tia took the liberty of entering the room and sitting beside him on the bunk, glad for company that was not her family. "You're beat," she said. She'd never seen Nico look so worn-out. The bags under his eyes and the sag to his shoulders reminded her of Rylan. Like he'd been rung out on a washboard.

"The double shift may be catching up to me. Slightly." He held up his thumb and finger to demonstrate how slight this catchup had in fact been. "Even when I have the chance to sleep, I can't."

"Why not?" Tia studied the coordinates tattooed on Nico's arm and quizzed herself on their meaning. Latitude 30, longitude 81. That was above the equator, way east of them. Mediterranean, maybe? Aegean? Latitude 34, longitude 18. Was Antarctica 18? How much of the world had Nico seen? Would she get to see all those places someday?

Nico stretched, hiking up his sleeves. "Just, I dunno . . . can't sleep."

Tia touched one of his tattoos, a trio of swallows just behind his elbow. Each swallow stood for five thousand nautical miles, she knew. She couldn't wait to have a flock of her own.

"What could possibly keep someone like you up at night?"

"Someone like me?" Nico nestled back into the pillow and let her examine him. "You think I don't have regrets?"

Nico seemed to be the definition of a man without regrets. He had committed his life to a primal piece of him, a piece that Tia believed was inside everyone. It was the thing she thought made adrenaline junkies, thrill-seekers, the thing that made people leave a dead-end job or drop out of school. Or run away from home.

"Tell me the worse thing you've ever done," she said. She removed her hand from his arm and sat back against the wall, which was papered with postcards and photographs. A couple thumbtacks poked her in the back.

Nico had gone perfectly still. He reached up and touched his temple, maybe checking the little vein that throbbed just next to the ear. Was he . . . upset? Tia had no idea what to do with that possibility. Nico had never looked so much as perturbed.

But then his smile rose, quick and electric. "Only if you tell me yours."

"Huh." Checkmate. The worst thing Tia had ever done. It wasn't hard to come up with. It had been a year ago on her birthday. And she hadn't told anyone or brought it up to the people who had seen, even in those ugly, secret moments when the memory made her proud.

"Counteroffer," she said. "How about the *second*-worst thing you've ever done? And I'll say mine."

Nico's eyes were clear and bright. "You first."

Tia sifted through her history of misdemeanors and classroom crimes and settled on the most impressive. "Back when I lived in Florida, an old friend of mine and I stole her dad's Bugatti and drove out to the Keys. We went skinny-dipping and got sand all over the seats. On our way back, we ran a red. And to top it off, we left the convertible roof open, so of course it poured that night. Went from sports car to swimming pool."

Tia hadn't thought about her Florida friends in months. She had ghosted them all eventually, or maybe it had been a mutual disinterest as their lives diverged. Tia didn't have the patience to keep around people who weren't right in front of her. Except for Rylan.

Nico threw back his head. "Man, fuck you, Cameron."

Tia crossed her arms over her chest in mock offense. "What?"

"You've driven a Bugatti."

"I've *stolen* a Bugatti."

He put a pillow over his face as if the conversation physically pained him. "I don't want to hear it, princess."

Tia smirked. "What's the second-worst thing you've ever done?"

She couldn't see his face but could practically hear the air whir as he thought.

"Board this boat," he said at last.

Tia looked at him. "You mean because of what happened to MJ?"

"My uncle told me we aren't going to Florida," Nico murmured.

So Alejandro had known too. That made sense. Francis and Alejandro were partners in everything. Tia had learned that the hard way the time she asked Alejandro to keep it secret that she was in trouble at school when he had picked her and Rylan up. Francis had known less than a day later and grounded her.

"My dad just told us too. Do you know anything else?"

Nico shook his head.

Tia hesitated, then lay down beside him, letting her head rest on his tattooed upper arm. Had Francis hired Nico without telling him the real plan? It wasn't right. Nico had a life to live that didn't involve the Camerons' forever vacation.

Tia frowned to herself. If Francis had decided on this surprise from the beginning, he must have prepared the route for their alternate destination, right?

Those coordinates.

Tia sat straight up.

"What is it?" Nico stretched out his arm, inviting her to lie back again.

"I . . . I might know where we're going."

Nico propped himself up on his elbows. "Shit, really? Where?"

"Well, I know how to find out, I mean." Tia could picture the messy chart house desk. It had caught her attention days ago with all the maps, the protractor, the ruler. And the ship's log lying open with a seemingly random string of coordinates written in her father's penmanship.

"He wrote it in the log book. It has to be where we're going. And if I can find out where we're going . . ."

Then she could figure out how she could run from there instead.

"Then we'll find those coordinates." Nico reached out and rearranged a red strand of Tia's hair.

She faced him fully, blood hot beneath her skin. She was close to his face now, close enough to smell the kind of toothpaste he used. She wanted to tell him right then about her own plan, but the more rational side of her won out. She liked him, but that didn't mean she really knew him yet. What if he told Alejandro?

"Are you sure you can handle carrying out such a dangerous mission, de la Vega?"

Nico tilted his head one degree to the side. Tia could have sworn his eyes flickered to her lips.

"General, I'm at your command."

Tia let her nose brush against his, tantalizingly near his lips. "Still think boarding this ship is your second-biggest regret?"

Nico reached up to cup her chin with his large, calloused hand. "I revise my previous statement . . . I have no regrets."

Tia smirked. "Then let's get going, shall we?" And she pulled away from him.

If Nico had been affected, he didn't show it. He stretched and slipped out of bed, clicking his tongue. "Whatever would my captain think if he knew I was taking orders from his teenage daughter?"

"Doesn't matter," Tia said, opening the door for him. "When we're through, *I'll* be your captain."

Nico paused in the doorway. He smoothed a hand through her hair and gave her a little push so she was flat against the door. "Aye aye," he breathed, then stepped away and down the hall.

A bloom of heat swept through Tia as she hurried to close the door and follow behind him.

No one else was in the salon or the galley, so they reached the chart house in peace. Tia wondered where Rylan had gone—the anchor locker, maybe?

The chart house was neater than she had seen it a few days ago. The maps were folded and tucked away, the ship's log shut with a pen tucked in its spiral binding. Tia flipped it open and went through it page by page.

"It was here somewhere," she said. She could picture the coordinates written at an angle on the top of a blank page. While she searched, Nico unfolded some maps and retrieved a ruler.

Tia was getting near the back of the log. She hadn't imagined the page with the red notes. But what if someone had torn it out? If only she'd known then how important it would be.

There. She stopped on a page. Two lines of letters and numbers in Francis's handwriting.

"This is it." She showed Nico, who immediately picked out a map. Tia peeked around his arm as he traced to find where the coordinates intersected. It was a map of southern Florida, the Bahamas, and below. So they must be continuing south of West Palm. Maybe just a resort in the Bahamas?

Then Nico stepped back. He had penciled in two neat lines that lay over each other, crossing in the middle of a swath of pure ocean.

"What?" Tia leaned closer. Had Nico traced these wrong? No . . . there was something. A tiny speck, no larger than a single grain of sand. That's where Francis was taking them. Some random, minuscule, unlabeled island.

Tia grabbed a pen and copied down the coordinates on a fresh scrap of paper. She tore it from the ship log and shoved it in her shorts pocket.

They were headed somewhere isolated, uninhabited, and far from any other piece of land.

Why was Francis taking them there? What lay on that island? And why had it been so important for him to keep it secret?

Chapter 26

Lila Logan Cameron
Call sign: Cassiopeia
Day 5 at Sea

LILA'S FINGERS TRACED Alejandro's rib cage. He was dozing but would start every once and a while to cast a glance at his watch. Each time Lila soothed him. They still had over an hour until Francis was done with his shift.

The rhythm of Alejandro's breath lulled Lila into a sense of calm that she hadn't experienced since *The Old Eileen* left land. Alejandro Matamoros was sturdy. An anchor.

Her thumbnail paused over a freckle below his pectoral. She wondered if Alejandro afforded her the same amount of trust that she did him.

"Mi amor . . ." she purred, and he woke in an instant.

"You are not asleep," he pointed out.

Lila's fingers moved to his throat and the outline of his Adam's apple. "I suppose I am not all tired out."

"Mmm."

Her other hand found the soft skin behind his earlobe. "And I've been thinking hard."

Alejandro stretched and traced the curve of her leg. "Too hard . . . There is a simple solution for that, señora."

Lila clasped Alejandro's face in her hands so he could not look away. "Where is he taking us, Ale?"

Alejandro said nothing.

She tried again, this time sliding her bare thigh across his chest, so she sat perched over his boxers. "Is it a nice surprise, at least?"

She was hoping for a Bahamian resort or a new holiday home in the Caymans.

"He'd kill me if I spoiled it."

"He'd kill you if he found you here," Lila whispered in his ear, and Alejandro's entire body shivered in response. "You know I have plans for the twins' birthday. Will we at least be home by then?"

Alejandro tried to sit up, but she pinned him to the mattress. He couldn't hide. Not from her.

"Ale, I have auditions booked. Luncheons with friends. Audra Tines and I are supposed to spend a weekend at her place in the Catskills. These things might not seem important to you. Or to him. But to me . . ." Lila cleared her throat carefully. "To me, they are everything I live for."

Event to event. There was nothing as exciting, as life-giving as that. Her childhood had been a series of activities, being whisked from church to pageant, from party to play. Lila needed an existence that brimmed with exhilarating moments. Overflowed with them. It was only in the soundless in-betweens where her spirits sank. Rylan once told her she was not unlike a shark, which must keep swimming, keep passing water over its gills, or it will suffocate and die.

But how could she make Alejandro understand that, this man who was, in many ways, her opposite? He preferred to be silent rather than speaking. He preferred to be cooking than having any sort of adventure. He didn't talk about himself much, but Lila had once gotten out of him a glimpse of his childhood in his apartment kitchen in Fontana. His parents had worked two jobs each, and his abuelita watched him and his baby sister during the summers. She taught him how to cook and play cards. She taught him how to change his sister's diapers and make a healthy meal that even a picky little kid would devour. Alejandro spoke a language of slow, sunny Sundays where the only sounds were his abuelita's afternoon soaps and the sizzling of tortillas on a pan.

Alejandro shifted on the bed. "You like surprises, though, no?" He sounded less certain.

Lila lay on top of him, hoping to apply physical *and* emotional pressure.

"I like diamond necklaces, not schedule upheavals."

"Lila . . ."

She fanned her hands across his clavicles. "*Alejandro . . .*"

Alejandro caught her hands and sat up even with her entire weight against him. He propped himself against the headboard, holding onto her. "It's not that kind of surprise. It's . . . uh . . . it's not for fun, okay? That really is all I can say."

Lila sat back on her heels. "Not for fun?"

"And not . . . not really for you."

Well, of course it wasn't. This trip never had been for her, had it? Lila refrained from rolling her eyes.

"What is it for, then? Will we be home in time for my audition?"

Alejandro watched her for so long that Lila began to feel uncomfortable under his gaze, a sensation she had never felt with him before. She hated it.

"No," he answered at last, and the word might as well have been a gunshot.

"No." Lila touched her ribs. If she wasn't going to be in Florida in time for the audition, she wasn't going to be in Florida in time for the twins' birthday, the trip to New York, or a thousand other engagements.

Francis, that narcissistic bastard. Where were they going that was so important, then? And if he had to go, why drag her along with him? It's not like he enjoyed her company.

Lila's eyes smarted, and she waved her hands to keep too much heat from splotching her complexion. She wanted to slap her husband. She wanted to strangle him.

"Well, then," she whispered. "Fuck."

"I'm sorry." Alejandro attempted to recapture her hand, but she folded it in her lap instead.

Francis had lied from the beginning about their destination. Lila sucked in her cheeks, trying to remember back to the day they had boarded the ship. Had anything been off? Had there been a kind of sign she'd missed, something she should have noticed so she could turn to her husband with her finger in his face. *Aha! I know what you're up to!*

But she couldn't think of anything. Tia had arrived. They'd eaten dinner. Then the cake fight, the gifts, and . . .

The pearl necklace that matched the earrings.

The one that meant Francis had been keeping track of Lila's spending habits. And then, after that . . . the phone call.

Ernie Carmichael had called Lila—not Francis, not Alejandro, but *Lila*—to tell her he wouldn't be coming. His mother had fallen, but he didn't sound disappointed about missing the trip or upset about his mom. He sounded nervous.

"Let's talk of cleaner things, señora." Alejandro found her hand and opened it, tracing the fine lines on her palm and wrist.

"I want to talk about this." His touch sent every nerve in her arm tingling, but she held steady. She would not be as seduced as she was seductive. "Did Ernie Carmichael know about Francis's . . . surprise?"

Alejandro's lips quirked, and he tucked a piece of her hair

behind her shoulder. "What has gotten you thinking about Ernie Carmichael? You could hardly stand him. Or his wife."

Lila caught his hand before he could lower it. "Tell me if he knew, and I'll pause my interrogation."

He nodded, very serious. "Just a pause, hmm?"

Lila waved his trapped hand over his face. "Do you want this back or not?"

Alejandro didn't break her grip, though she knew he could if he wanted to. "Yes," he said finally. "Ernie knew."

And what he said next was barely audible, more mouthed than spoken, as if this particular thought of his had simply spilled out of him, unbidden.

"Ese cobarde . . ."

That coward.

Lila let his hand go and lay on Alejandro's chest, her cheek against his collarbone. His heartbeat filled her ears. The blood beneath his skin ran hot and loud. In this moment, Alejandro Matamoros was hers.

Alejandro's loyalty to Francis held no question. They had been boyhood neighbors, then best friends, then business partners, and at some point, she knew, they had become brothers.

Arthur and Lancelot indeed.

But even Lancelot chose Guinevere in the end.

"Alejandro . . ." She said his name with an echo of the accent she'd picked up learning Spanish from him.

"Sí, señora?"

She lifted her head, swirls of her silver-blond hair pooling on his throat. "Who are you here for?"

Who are you loyal to?

She let him sit in silence for a minute, wondering if his brain was grappling for a diplomatic escape to the impossible question. He served Francis, no doubt about that. But Francis wasn't here right now.

Alejandro swallowed, the only hint of nervousness Lila had ever witnessed from him.

"He is like blood," he told her.

It was an answer of sorts, and the one Lila had expected. She gave him an understanding smile and bent down so that her hair curtained around him and the tip of her nose lightly touched his. "But?" she prompted, and Alejandro was helpless in their proximity.

"But I'm yours," he breathed.

Lila's chest swelled, and she bathed him in kisses, marking her territory with each stamp of her lips. He was hers. He was in her bed, after all, keeping her warm and guarding her heart.

Alejandro dissolved at her touch, and they traded kisses for several slow minutes. At last, she settled back onto his chest and looked at his watch. Fifty-two minutes left.

She would have been content to remain quiet until the time seeped away, but Alejandro was no longer on the verge of sleep.

"I know he is your husband, and you know him very well," he said carefully. "However . . . I see him in those moments when someone wants something from him. I see how he clenches even tighter onto something when he realizes it's desirable."

A part of her knew this. Being with Francis was not at all unlike show business; she had learned that the hard way. Throwing herself into every audition and interview had only lessened her appeal. The movie stars most sought after were the unavailable ones with tragedy-ridden lives that filled up tabloids and gossip columns. She was never going to get back home to rescue her career by badgering Francis. But she was not someone who would hide from him either, like Ernie Carmichael.

She was going to get it the same way her darling husband had gotten where he was in life now.

By outsmarting everyone around her.

Alejandro cupped her chin. His hand was rough. An oil burn welted on one knuckle. "Make him come to you."

Lila smirked slowly and brushed her lips against Alejandro's cheek. "Of course, apuesto. You are right. And I just have one favor to ask . . ."

She leaned down and whispered into his ear, as if it was no more than sweet nothings between lovers. As if she hadn't just come up with a plan for the world to burn.

He was right, after all. About more things than he realized. The way to get through to her husband and resurrect the famous Lila Logan was the same.

All she needed was a touch of fire.

CelebriTEA

Partial Nude of Lila Logan Leaked

A leaked photograph has scandalized and intrigued fans of *Reina Gold Is Lying* star Lila Logan Cameron.

Lila Logan, 44, is pictured with her chest exposed with her wedding dress undone and bunched up around her waist, a cigarette in hand, and hair styled like Elizabeth Taylor. Clearly, this was a posed shot meant for, er, personal friends. *Not* the internet. But whatever. Who doesn't want to get more use out of their wedding dress? Specifically Logan's, which cost upward of FOUR HUNDRED THOUSAND DOLLARS. Or, so sorry, *euros*. (The designer's French.)

You may have noticed the window just behind Lila giving a nice view of the Malibu skyline as well as a blurred reflection of her photographer. Who is not her husband, Francis Cameron. After a flurried attempt online to identify the man (alleged to be anyone from Pedro Pascal to John Leguizamo), another fan account has posted a far juicier tidbit of information: the original photograph was leaked from an IP address in Logan's own home.

So the culprit is either a jealous husband, jilted lover, tech-savvy preteen, OR, far more likely, Lila has invoked the time-honored commandment that there's no such thing as bad press, and she has taken it upon herself to manufacture her very own scandal.

Chapter 27

Jerry Baugh

JERRY CRUMPLED HIS fifth can of beer and tossed it toward the trash bag on the floor. He missed.

"Nice one," Madden said from her place slouched in a mountain of cushions.

Lainey, who was lying on the floor with her feet on the wall, chuckled and hiccupped. *The Old Eileen* roiled beneath them, but the screaming wind didn't seem to bother any of them anymore.

Jerry looked around for more beer. They'd been trapped in the salon for hours, drinking and watching television. Now the hurricane was picking up speed, and he wondered how he had spent all those storms alone in *Sheila 2.0*'s minuscule cabin.

A sound like a whip cracked outside the porthole, and Jerry flinched. Madden raised her head to look through the boards.

"What's the damage?" Jerry asked, words running together.

"Dock line down," Madden asserted. "Should we fix it?"

Jerry thought about one of them going out on the dock right now. The wind would slam them into a tree or worse, fling them into the raging water. Better to lay low.

"Eh," he said and turned up the TV. They had surfed all the

channels, and nothing good was playing. They were lucky the TV was still running at all.

Lainey watched him. "You good, man?"

Jerry humphed and broke open his sixth beer. He was buzzed for sure, but it didn't feel like enough.

Lainey let her feet fall to the floor. "You just seem on edge."

Jerry opened his mouth to deny it, but a roll of thunder sent him to his feet. *The Old Eileen* rocked unsteadily under him.

"No, no. Just, well, maybe this wasn't such a good plan. Being in here." He threw away the crushed can on the floor to make it seem like getting up had been his idea.

"Why not?" Madden played with the lip of her empty gin bottle.

More thunder. More wind. *The Old Eileen* felt alive. Jerry scratched at his stubble and flattened himself against the back of the sofa so he could see the entire room in case anything was trying to get inside.

"Cause it's a goddamned ghost ship," Jerry heard himself say. There was something on this ship, something he wasn't convinced had left completely after that night with the bilge panel. Not that he had any proof of it.

Madden scoffed. "You tellin' me Jerry Baugh believes in ghosts?"

"Just in this damn creepy boat, and that damn dead family, and goddamned Ida who ain't shut up for a second."

It was Madden's turn to flinch, and Jerry caught himself too late.

"I didn't mean . . . I was talking about the hurricane." He laid aside the sixth beer. Six beers in and words vomited plumb out of his mouth.

Madden fiddled with the badge on her chest. "S'alright . . . She woulda gotten a kick out of it, you know. Hurricane Ida. I would have been stuck calling her that for the rest of time."

Jerry wasn't sure what to say to that.

Lainey sat up. "A friend of yours?"

Jerry wondered if Lainey was sober. She seemed to be. But Madden also seemed to be until her oak eyes overflowed, and she started to weep.

"My wife," she managed to say. "In all the ways that count."

Jerry shifted uncomfortably in his seat. He didn't like crying, especially if someone around him was doing it. The last thing he needed was to be trapped in the belly of a murder boat while the detective bawled her eyes out.

Lainey seemed to have no such discomfort. "Tell me about her," she prodded gently, zeroing in on Madden.

"Um . . . She gardened," Madden said. "Taught kids karate. Raced dinghies on the weekends. That's how we met. I, uh . . . I got hired by her sailing club after a couple of their 420s got stolen."

Jerry wished she would stop talking. He considered jamming his hands over his ears but decided against it in case either of them noticed. He didn't like remembering people like this, all rosy-lensed about their hobbies and quirks. It made a person sound unrealistic as well as dead.

Even though he fell into the same trap with Steve.

But Madden and Lainey were locked in a world all their own, with Jerry flying at the fringes.

Madden went on. "We dated for a year, then got a place in Cherrywood. Across the street from Jerry and his ex."

Jerry tasted bile in the back of his throat. *Cherrywood.* A chipped-paint town with pastel flats and palm trees. Jerry and Sheila's house had been yellow with a flea-rotten front door and a pot of Russian sage on the porch. How had he ever lived like that? Newspaper on the driveway, ants in the cabinets. The closest beach was a two-hour drive.

It had been Sheila's idea. *Let's get away from the coast. From all the bad memories.*

And at the time, it had somehow made sense. Jerry did want to get away. Just not from the sea.

"We couldn't really afford the place," Madden was saying. "But Ida's soul lived in those walls. She grew a salsa garden in the backyard and designed an office for me in the spare bedroom. We went to the neighborhood book club and painted the house tissue pink. I remember the name on the paint wheel—isn't that dumb? *Tissue Pink.* Like we were living in a box of Kleenex."

Madden's fingers unwrapped from the gin bottle and stretched ever so slightly. As if she was reaching for something. "I think I hated it. But now it's something I miss. Which is also pretty dumb, I think. If she hadn't died, I'd have gone on and hated it till the end of time. But she died, so I moved downtown, and now I miss the pink house and the book club politics. Sometimes I miss most what never happened. There's a German word for that. Anyway . . . we'd just started researching IVF when she got sick."

"Shit . . ." Jerry said, unsure when he'd gotten rolled up in the story. He couldn't recall Sheila saying anything about Ida's illness. It must have happened around the same time that Sheila threw him out. They'd both been too busy dealing with their lives to wonder what the folks across the street were going through.

Madden pushed her hand across her nose. "I thought she would make it to her fortieth birthday, one more decade, but her organs gave out the month before."

Jerry shuddered. Steve had been about to turn thirty when he died. Jerry had already picked out his present, a used guitar wrapped in the Sunday comics, when he got the call from his mother.

"I don't believe in ghosts." Madden looked from Lainey to

Jerry, and he felt as though she could tell he was squirming. "But if I did, this storm is her. And she's screaming."

Lainey got up to hug Madden, but Jerry couldn't make himself move. He didn't know how to reach out, how to comfort this woman who wasn't even exactly his friend. Lainey was hardly an adult, and yet she knew how.

Jerry stared at his shoes instead. They stunk of fish, and flecks of dried blood decorated the tired laces. The wind whined, and Madden cried, and Jerry didn't dare look up for fear of seeing the people he knew were dead.

"M-my brother drowned," he said at last. How else could he comfort Madden besides relating to her?

The women looked at him, and he was sure he'd been wrong to speak, but Madden nodded. Listening.

"My kid brother . . ." Jerry lifted his head, and his heart sank.

He was there. Steven Baugh, frozen forever at twenty-nine years old. He lived at the margins of the salon standing over the galley freezer. Blond hair dripping wet. Eyes gaping. This time Jerry didn't look away from his brother's bloated skin and blue lips. He *couldn't* look away.

"I was older by a year, but he was braver. By a long shot. He never bothered with anything less than what he wanted. And what he wanted was adventure."

Damn it, now *he* was doing the rosy-lensed thing. Jerry racked his brain for his little brother's flaws, which used to be so easy to recall. "He was a bit of a stoner. He was always knocking stuff over and not always cleaning it up. He couldn't have dark moments. Only wanted to talk about the good stuff. The fun stuff. But he was unflappable. Worked as a raft guide, an outdoor camp counselor, a sailor. Anything to keep the momentum going and spend his life outside."

Jerry blinked hard. Steve remained there staring. "And he died for it. It was in a storm like this, I think. So maybe . . . I guess I do believe in ghosts. His ghost. Maybe this hurricane is both of them tryna' get our attention."

Lainey crossed the room and hugged him too. Jerry tried to protest, but she was already there, arms around his neck. Her shaved head blocked his view, and when she pulled away, Steve was gone.

"It's all righ'," Jerry told her, patting her shoulder awkwardly. Tears welled behind his eyes. "It's all righ'," he repeated, willing them to evaporate.

They didn't. Jerry stood hurriedly. It was one thing to see Brenna Madden cry and quite another to let her see him cry. "I need to get more beer," he said.

Lainey glanced at the case which still held well over a dozen cans, but she didn't say anything, and Jerry headed into the hallway.

"Good Lord," he muttered once he had shut the watertight door. The tears threatened to fall, so he kept walking, like he could outrun them. He found himself in the crew cabin, the one with the three beds, two stacked on top of each other and the third alone. He was about to collapse on it when he realized someone was already there.

The ugly old cat crouched on the pillow. He was awake, his paws digging at the pillowcase at an intense pace. No, not digging—kneading. How did he even get over here? Lainey must have rescued him from *Sheila 2.0* before the hurricane.

The kneading was a sign of love, or so Sheila had insisted when her awful fluffy cat had done the same to Jerry. Nursing kittens did it to their mothers to get milk flowing and to show affection. *Making biscuits* Sheila called it. The stupid thing was kneading a pillow, though, not a person.

Jerry's throat felt thick. Who used to lie in this bed? Had

the cat loved them? Did he miss them? How many times had the creature come to this room and kneaded the pillow in the hopes that his person would return?

How many times had Jerry hoped the same thing for his dead little brother?

This time there was nothing he could do to stop the deluge. Jerry broke down and fell onto the bed. The cat regarded him with alarm, then slowly, cautiously crept closer. He didn't shove it away. He gathered the animal in his arms and wept in a way he hadn't done for decades.

He wept for Steve's crooked smile and sun-bleached hair. He wept for Madden's wife and their hideous, happy home in Cherrywood. And he wept for the cat and its people who'd vanished from *The Old Eileen* and left it there alone.

Chapter 28

```
Rylan Cameron
Call sign: Minnow
Day 6 at Sea
```

IT WAS JUST after four in the morning when Pirate woke Rylan up by kneading his paws on his shoulder and purring like a tractor. Rylan's heart broke for the cat, and he shifted to include him underneath his sheets. He hadn't been sleeping well anyway, for fear of dreaming up swollen, waterlogged bodies dripping salt water in the corner of his bedroom.

So instead he lay there, trying not to think about what Francis had said at breakfast. He wished that Tia hadn't pushed their father, that Francis hadn't revealed there would be a surprise destination. Rylan would have preferred to find out when they got there instead of wondering for the rest of the trip where they could be headed and why.

Pirate also seemed uneasy. The cat curled on his chest, and Rylan couldn't shake the feeling that Pirate knew something the humans didn't. Everyone said that the cat didn't understand MJ was gone, that he was waiting patiently for her return, but Rylan suspected the opposite was true. Pirate had been pawing at the freezer in the galley, and now he stared down the door.

As if someone was waiting on the other side.

Tia's watch alarm beeped. Why would she have had an alarm set at this hour? Rylan watched her. Even though the watch was pressed against her face as she slept, it still took her a solid sixty seconds to groan and switch it off. She dragged herself to an upright position, hair sticking at strange angles.

"Did I wake you?" she whispered loudly.

"Did you think you could somehow *not* wake me after all that?" Rylan replied, knuckle rubbing between Pirate's ears.

Tia sighed. "I was trying not to."

"Technically Pirate woke me. Why are you getting up?"

Tia seemed to hesitate, which drove Rylan crazy. He was desperate to regain the ease of their friendship, back when the only secrets they had were from the world, never each other.

"Tell me," Rylan pressed. He couldn't sit up, with the cat like a paperweight on his torso, but he tried to round his eyes persuasively.

Tia made a throaty, exasperated sound, and Rylan knew she'd relented.

"I'm going to the chart house. Nico and I found where we're going, and he's on watch now, so this is the best time to contact whoever's nearby and try to get off this ship."

"Oh."

"I stashed the paper with the coordinates on it in your raincoat pocket, just so you know."

Rylan frowned. "Why my coat?"

"Because I want you to be part of this too," Tia said.

Rylan heard what she didn't say. *Whether you like it or not.*

Tia's jaw popped as she yawned. "So you should come with us. Since you're already up."

Rylan wanted to be a part of things, but not if it meant sleuthing behind Francis's back.

"I don't know . . ."

It was Tia's turn to make her pupils into disks. "Come on,

Ry. I've been having a really hard time since MJ. It'll be like when we were little, playing with the ship's log. Please?"

She *had* been having a hard time since MJ's death. Rylan swallowed. Tia knew exactly how to find an exposed nerve and flick it.

"Fine," Rylan said at last. He carefully scooped Pirate into his arms as he got up, petting the cat profusely to keep him from slipping away.

He hugged him to his heart and followed Tia out into the hallway and onto the deck. Pirate shifted in his arms, on edge.

Nico waved the twins over from the cockpit, and they took their seats on the cockpit bench.

"Tia drag you into this?" Nico joked, then glanced between them. "You look like you didn't sleep a wink."

Pirate wormed out of Rylan's arms and wove between Nico's legs. Rylan watched Pirate. If he needed any more confirmation that Nico was trustworthy, it was this.

"We're good. We need to call in on that radio," Tia said.

"Probably easier if I go down there myself since neither of you know VHF. Can you take the wheel, Tia?"

Take the wheel? Tia couldn't steer the ship—she didn't know how.

"Sure I can." Tia traded places with Nico, and Rylan stared at her. Since when could his sister helm a sailboat?

Tia turned her face up toward the stars, as if she knew what they said.

Nico put a hand on Rylan's shoulder, snapping him out of it. "You can help me in the chart house. And I can show you the spot we think they're taking us to. Francis ordered our heading changed to one hundred and ten. We're officially off course now."

Rylan followed Nico to the chart house companionway.

Belowdecks, Lila and Francis were asleep. But what if they woke up?

Nico put a finger to his lips and pointed down into the chart house. Rylan looked and froze.

Alejandro was slumped on the counter, snoring. The ship's log sat by his outstretched hand. What was he doing there? Had he known Tia and Nico planned to look at the log book? No . . . no, he must have fallen asleep doing navigation work. Or something.

Nico crept into the chart house, apparently unconcerned by his uncle's presence, though he took care to be quiet as he thumbed through a stack of maps. Rylan stayed rooted to the spot, afraid of making noise if he tried to help or retreat. Nico gestured with his other hand for Rylan to come see a map.

Rylan held his breath and tiptoed closer. Nico pointed.

This is it, he mouthed.

At first, Rylan didn't understand. There was nothing on the map where Nico had indicated, just empty space that represented the ocean. But when Rylan bent closer he saw a minuscule speck that stood for land. It was far south of Florida, closer to the Bahamas than anything else, and unlabeled.

An island.

That's where Nico and Tia had found that they were going? To this dot in the center of the sea? Rylan swayed a little: he'd been holding his breath too long. He inhaled, but his breaths came shallower than he needed. He couldn't look away from the map, from the wide white space and the small black dot. Something about it stunted his breathing.

Could it still be a vacation if the place they were going was the size of a piece of dust and wasn't associated with any other place on the map?

Nico started writing, copying the coordinates in the ship's

log down on a separate scrap of paper that he placed inside his pocket before looking past his uncle's sleeping form at the wall.

Rylan followed his gaze.

The ship's radio sat in its cradle over the counter. Nico moved so he was almost touching Rylan.

"The radio is attached to a cord," Nico breathed into Rylan's ear. Rylan shivered.

Even if they managed to get the radio, the cord would keep them from sneaking back on deck to use it. There was no way they could use it without Alejandro waking up.

This is ridiculous, Rylan told himself, mouth dry. *If he wakes up, what's he going to do anyway?*

Wake up Dad . . .

Rylan balked and tried to go back up the companionway, but Nico held him steady by the hand and gestured for him to breathe.

"I *can't*," Rylan said between his teeth. "It won't work."

Nico hesitated, then released his hand and offered a kind smile. He wasn't even angry at Rylan's cowardice. It made Rylan sick. Tia should have been the one in here, but it wasn't like Rylan could steer *The Old Eileen*. He sucked in a breath. He should have stayed with Pirate in bed.

"What do you want me to do, anyway?" he whispered.

"Distract him if he wakes up. Just be casual."

Rylan whipped his head from side to side.

Nico caught his shoulders. "Okay, *I'll* distract him. You grab the radio."

"I—I don't know what to do with it even if I got it," Rylan sputtered. He glanced to make sure Alejandro was still sleeping through this.

"Just press the button on the side and start talking." Nico

tilted Rylan's chin upward and gave a heart-melting smile. "You're braver than you think, Rylan. Trust me."

Braver than you think . . . I'm braver than I think . . . Rylan filled his lungs, then snuck forward. His long arms easily reached over Alejandro's slouched form, and the radio came loose from its cradle with a gentle click that made Rylan wince. But Nico was right beside him, ready to move between Rylan and Alejandro in case he woke up.

Rylan stepped back, radio in hand. His pulse made its way into every one of his fingers.

He held his thumb over the big button on the side. Once he pressed the button, static would crackle, and Alejandro would wake up for sure.

Rylan tried to organize his thoughts. *This is* The Old Eileen. *We're being taken to some island without our consent.*

The thought of the island made Rylan's fingers buzz.

This is The Old Eileen. *We're being taken to some island without our consent. Can you help us get home?*

He had to speak quickly and articulately.

Would Nico be able to distract Alejandro long enough?

Nico signaled at him to go ahead. Rylan retreated as far from Alejandro as the radio cord would allow before he pushed down on the button.

Nothing. No static. No connection. Rylan pressed it again then looked at Nico in confusion. Only Nico wasn't looking at him. Rylan followed his gaze to the radio cord, which was uncoiling from the cradle.

But instead of stretching the distance between the radio and the wall, the cord unraveled and fell.

Cut clean through the middle.

Chapter 29

```
Tia Cameron
Call sign: Thimble
Day 6 at Sea
```

TIA FELT AS though she'd been shackled to the helm of the ship. She couldn't leave it because they'd get off course, and she wasn't close enough to the companionway of the chart house to hear what was going on inside. But they had to call out before it was too late, before they got too far from land and other ships were still within radio range, and it delayed her running away even longer.

Tia studied the stars to follow Nico's steering method. A triangle of them sat just to the right of the main mast, and she focused on keeping them there. The black velvet sea could have been any sea in the world. She was sailing solo around Cape Horn or passing through the Strait of Gibraltar. If she dove over the side, she'd swim between plate tectonics or over the Great Blue Hole. She'd dissolve in the water, hair turning to foam, skin to salt, and she'd ride ribbons of current until the ocean covered the earth and it was as intimate to the world as it already was to her.

Why hadn't she learned about MJ's travels while she'd had the chance? Tia's heart pinched, and tears welled in her eyes. Why hadn't she gotten every detailed story? Every scrap of wisdom? There was no one left to talk to now, no one who understood the raw energy she had as she steered the schooner into the stars. Maybe she would meet someone like that when she ran away.

"Tia!" Rylan's form darted from the chart house companionway. His teeth were clenched as he hissed her name once more. "Tia!"

"Did you get a response?" Tia asked.

Rylan covered his own mouth as if that could shut up his sister. "Shhh . . ." He lowered his hand slowly. "Alejandro's asleep down there."

"What?"

"Can't you whisper?" Rylan held out his other hand, wrapped around the radio with its coiled cord dangling. The end had been sliced through.

Tia reeled. Who the hell would sever their communication method, their only communication method?

"Where's Nico?" she whispered.

"Still down there, I don't know." Rylan wrung his hands. "Do you think Alejandro cut the cord so we wouldn't be able to communicate with the outside world?"

Why would he do that? So they would have to go to that island? Had Alejandro guessed they would go for the radio, so he'd slept down there to guard it from them? But if the cord was cut, he didn't need to guard it.

Maybe he slept there so he'd know if they tried.

Tia felt helpless once more, stationed at the helm. She couldn't leave Rylan to steer while she confronted Alejandro, she couldn't undo the damage to the cord, and she couldn't magically produce another way to contact anyone.

Tia looked at her hands, curled around the silver wheel.

The wheel . . .

She stared for a moment, giving the idea a couple seconds

to take shape before she put it into action and turned the wheel hard to the right.

At first nothing happened. But then *The Old Eileen* responded to the command and swung starboard, slowly at first, then picking up speed. Tia kept the wheel turning, even when Rylan yelped and grabbed onto the cockpit bench for support, even when the sails flapped like sea gulls and the triangle of stars were far to the left.

"Tia! What are you doing?"

"Getting us to land." Tia tried to steady the wheel now that they were pointing toward what she hoped was Georgia, even though they were too far from shore to see it. But the sails only got louder, rattling like bones, which never happened when MJ or Nico or Francis turned the ship.

A trench opened up in Tia's stomach, but she held the wheel still until suddenly the boom, twenty feet of horizontal aluminum, swung across the deck.

"Oh my God," Tia said in shock, just as Nico and Alejandro burst on deck with identical expressions of panic.

"Give me the wheel," Alejandro ordered, and Tia backed away as he seized it and barked to his nephew. "Trim the spinnaker, damn it!"

Nico flew across the deck, head low to avoid the boom. Rylan huddled below the cockpit bench, and Alejandro turned the wheel, hand over hand, back to the left.

It was agonizingly slow, but the sails quieted as the wind caught them in just the right place. *The Old Eileen* settled back in her heading. One hundred and ten degrees.

Nico returned to the cockpit, having secured the boom and shortened one of the sails. Alejandro handed the helm off to him wordlessly and faced Tia.

"That was a crash jibe. They are incredibly, incredibly dangerous. You could have hurt someone. Or everyone."

Tia's face burned. She had been so confident a moment before. "I'm sorry, I—"

"And you." Alejandro cuffed Nico on the back of the head. Rylan flinched as if he'd been the one hit. "Giving the helm to a landlubber? The helm of your employer's yacht, no less? You know better than that, sobrino."

"Lo siento," Nico muttered. Tia had never heard him sound so serious. Or so small.

At her side, Tia's fingers curled into fists. But she couldn't reveal to Alejandro that they knew about the island, or he would make it harder for them to end the trip. Maybe she could guilt him instead. "It wouldn't have happened if you'd let us radio into land the moment you found MJ's body. We were trying to do the right thing."

Alejandro put a hand on his hip, the other massaging his temple. "And when you couldn't radio, you thought you'd turn the whole boat round and chart your own damn course, hmm? Was that the plan?"

Tia squared her shoulders. "I saw the radio cord. That didn't happen innocently, did it? Couldn't have been an accident. So yeah, I decided to try and get help another way."

"MJ is dead," Alejandro replied. "There isn't anyone on earth who can help her now." He looked at Rylan, who was now huddled on the bench with the radio in his lap, kneading the severed cord between his thumb and forefinger.

"Why did you cut the cord, then?" One of them must have come to the chart house and cut it after MJ died, afraid her death would derail the trip they were so hell-bent on completing.

"I know how it looks," Alejandro said, and he sat down on the bench, fight drained out of him. Or maybe it was for show. "It looks like we cut the cord in order to hurt someone."

We . . .

"Did you?" Tia asked in a whisper.

Alejandro shook his head, elbows on his knees. "We cut that cord to protect someone."

Rylan reached for Tia's hand. He was shaking. Tia lowered herself beside him and let him cling to her.

"Protect who?" Tia asked.

Alejandro's tongue flickered across his lips, and he drew in a great breath through his nose. "Ourselves. It wasn't cut to prevent reporting MJ's death. Because . . . well . . . it's been cut since the beginning."

Chapter 30

Jerry Baugh

JERRY STARTLED HIMSELF awake with his own snoring as morning light spilled in through the portholes of *The Old Eileen*'s salon. He had been zonked out on the couch, his blanket long kicked aside. As he sat up, he felt a rumbling weight on his belly. It was the cat, pleased as pudding and curled up over Jerry's navel.

"Stupid cat," he mumbled, but he lifted the creature, careful not to wake it, and set it on a stray couch cushion.

Madden had left the night before when the storm started clearing up. Her empty gin bottle rolled on the ground past Jerry's feet. Lainey was still asleep, tucked behind a galley counter.

The forty-eight hours of the hurricane ran together in Jerry's mind. The drinking, crying, TV dinners, reheated fish for breakfast. It had been a storm unlike any he'd experienced in thirty years, because this time he hadn't been alone.

Jerry stooped to grab his discarded blanket and, on second thought, draped it over Lainey. The two of them had hardly gotten a wink of sleep last night after Madden left, too busy drunk and raving about dead brothers and whale songs. Jerry couldn't remember the half of it. He picked his way over the empty beer cans and crumpled paper towels to the companionway. The hatch had been spattered with rainwater that rushed to flow on deck when he pushed it open.

He blinked in the sunlight. *The Old Eileen*, always so pristine and pearly white, was littered with broken palm fronds and trash. Beside her, *Sheila 2.0* had borne the brunt of the storm, her already-battered hull showing new scars from bumping up against the dock. The loose dock line floated in the water like a dead fish.

"Hell's bells," Jerry sighed. He shuffled below deck to find a broom and returned up top to start cleaning.

Around him, the world emerged from its hibernation to do the same. The few ship owners who had stayed aboard their vessels during Ida's wrath were hosing down the decks and carrying loads of blown-around garbage to the dumpster. Jerry worked in silence, sweeping and hosing and dragging loads of wet fronds and plastic bags until *The Old Eileen* began to shine again. Outside the bars of the marina, shop owners drove up to their stores and unnailed the boarded-up windows. A stop sign arched in a permanent backbend.

Jerry fished the dock line from the water and wrung it out. He wondered if Madden was back at the station, drying the rainwater from the carpet or getting straight back to work.

He glanced out at the sea, which still shifted listlessly.

This hurricane's gonna hide any evidence we mighta found if we had more time, Madden had told him.

"Whoooa . . ." Lainey climbed out of the companionway of *The Old Eileen*, scanning the world around them.

"Never seen the aftermath before?" Jerry retrieved his broom and worked to rid the scuppers of sopping cardboard and grime.

"My family usually flies to Colorado before they hit and stays a few days after they're done." She shielded her eyes and grabbed the hose. "Need help?"

"It's mostly done. Just make sure there isn't any salt clinging to the rails."

Jerry did his best to erase the stains and scrapes, but between the stench of rotting fish and soggy garbage, she was a far cry from the beautiful, white sailboat he'd found. He heaved his cooler of fish to the dumpster and got rid of the ones that had gone bad. He rinsed the cooler and poured the bloody water into the marina.

Damn, he missed fishing. He hadn't gone since the night he found *The Old Eileen*. Maybe a quick trip to a nearby fishing spot was just the thing he needed to set his head right. Hurricane Ida would have the fish more active than usual, teeming beneath the surface and ready to be harvested.

"Hey, Lainey, you interested in going fishing?" Jerry could barely believe himself even as the question tumbled out. He hadn't invited anyone to fish with him since, well, since he'd been married to Sheila, who had agreed grudgingly and spent the entire morning complaining about her wet shoes and slurping her Starbucks drink loud enough to drive Jerry to leave her. Maybe that was an exaggeration, but between the grating iced pistachio latte straw and soaked ballet flats, Jerry had determined to never, ever go fishing with another human being again.

He was half relieved when Lainey hesitated.

"Uh, I don't know if I'm much of a fisher."

"S'alright. Forget I asked." Jerry busied himself with taking a rag to a nasty streak of something on *Eileen*'s stern. Darn thing wouldn't budge. He spit on the rag for good measure and rubbed at the spot again.

"Actually, maybe I should go with you. I've never given fishing a fair shot." Lainey looped up the hose quickly. "I think I left some clean clothes in one of the cabins."

"Sounds fine," Jerry said. "Get dressed and we'll head out?"

Lainey nodded. She disappeared down the companionway.

Jerry found himself whistling. Jerry Baugh with company on a fishing trip. Who would have thought it? He was suddenly excited, even eager, to show Lainey some of the ropes. Steve had been squeamish about fishing, and Jerry had been too young and stupid to have patience with him. But with Lainey, Jerry felt sure he could explain it all right. Hell, by the end of this, the kid would be on her way to catching her own dinner.

Jerry whistled the tune of "Wellerman" and stood to cow hitch the rag on the lifeline so it could dry. Down the dock, a few people were milling about. Deckhands scurried to aid their captains with the cleanup effort. A pair of sunglass-wearing ladies sat on a bench, soaking up the sunshine. And a man strolled down the dock toward them.

Jerry squinted. Was the guy wearing a suit?

He was. Iron-pressed white shirt, black jacket, and slacks complete with a red-striped tie. What kind of bizarre asshole went on a walk the morning after a hurricane in his finest formal wear?

Jerry snorted to himself and tied up the rag. He considered changing for the fishing expedition, but he hadn't gone to the laundromat in weeks now, and if his faded T-shirt and jeans had lasted two days in a storm, they would do the trick for a quick jet to a fishing spot. He adjusted his cap and went onto the dock to undo the remaining lines that tethered *Sheila 2.0* to land.

The man in the suit walked over, but instead of going past, he stopped in front of *The Old Eileen*, hands deep in his pants pockets.

He was Asian, lean and tall with gelled hair and dimples on both cheeks. He offered Jerry a friendly smile that Jerry did not return. Usually the people who came to gawk at *The*

Old Eileen were held back by the coded fence. You had to be a member of the marina to get inside.

"She's a lovely ship," the man said conversationally.

"Mmm-hmm." Jerry unlooped a dock line.

"Yours, I take it?" he asked.

"Why would you think that?" He didn't bother to sound polite. He knew how he looked to people like this. Why didn't the guy just go to his own yacht already? Jerry had some fishing to do.

The man pulled something—a black leather wallet—from his pocket. "Are you Jerry Baugh, sir?"

Jerry eyed the wallet, not liking where this was going one bit. "Who's asking?"

The man flipped open the wallet, and Jerry's jaw went slack.

"Special Agent Koshida, sir. I'm with the FBI." He flashed his paper-white teeth at Jerry, who was rooted in place.

"With the . . . But . . . You're here to talk about *Eileen*?" This didn't make any sense. Jerry had been holed up with Madden for days. If there was a break in the case, she would have told him. Unless even she didn't know. And since when were the feds tied up in a missing persons case?

"I'm not here about the ship, Mr. Baugh. At least, not directly." Agent Koshida slid his badge back into his pocket.

"What, then?"

The agent smiled once again, this time sympathetically, as if he knew what he was about to say was going to split Jerry's life in two.

"I'm here to talk about Steven Baugh."

Chapter 31

```
Rylan Cameron
Call sign: Minnow
Day 7 at Sea
```

SLEEP EVADED RYLAN once more, burning his eyelids and twisting just out of reach. He drew instead, sketching for hours, and underlined passages of his beat-up Jules Verne novel. Pirate slept beside him, occasionally rousing to make biscuits on Rylan's thigh. Rylan didn't want to think about what Alejandro had said, that the cord had been cut since the beginning of the trip, that it was meant to protect *ourselves*. He didn't want to think about what they needed protection from or how tiny that speck of land looked in the middle of the ocean. All he could stand to think about was his drawing.

So he drew.

"Perfume is the soul of the flower, and sea-flowers have no soul."

He drew a garden underwater, azaleas drowned and drifting.

"Steam seems to have killed all gratitude in the hearts of sailors."

He drew a steamship running over a sailboat and splintering it to pieces.

"We may brave human laws, but we cannot resist natural ones."

He drew a body folded in a freezer, barnacles blooming over its eyes and mouth, seaweed snaking its claim across the concave chest, and salt water loosening sinew until the corpse spread like unwound string.

Rylan's wrist ached in protest. He needed sleep but could not command it to come to him. He glanced at Tia, mouth agape and breathing steadily in her bed.

Rylan flipped the page of his sketchbook. He set aside *20,000 Leagues Under the Sea* and picked up a book about sea monsters through the ages. He opened to a random page and skimmed it as he sketched.

The Blue Men of Minch were blue-skinned people in Scottish myths who lurked beneath the surface in the hopes of dragging down passing ships. They were also called storm kelpies for their ability to summon tempests and were thought to be angels who'd fallen from the heavens and landed in the seas.

A blue man took shape on Rylan's paper. He was slender and ribbony, his eyes huge like the creatures in the deepest parts of the sea. He was creeping down the hallway of *The Old Eileen*, leaving a trail of salt water with each step.

There was one way to save yourself from the Blue Men of Minch, Rylan read as he shaded water droplets on the monster's skin. The creatures often called out lines of poetry to the men aboard their ships, and the captain would be tasked with completing the verse. If he could not, the creatures sank the ship.

Rylan listened for a fallen angel's poetry through the door to his cabin. The pain in his arm reminded him that the Blue Men of Minch had come to life in his sketchbook and nowhere else. He had no reason to believe in actual monsters.

Rylan snapped his sketchbook shut and forced himself out the door and to the companionway. He focused on the pain in his arm. That was real. The Blue Men of Minch were not.

The night that greeted Rylan up on deck was muggy.

He realized he'd sweated through his T-shirt, which stuck to his chest. He massaged his palm and looked to see who was steering in the cockpit.

Francis.

"Couldn't sleep, son?"

They were alone, the two of them. The rest of the family and crew were asleep. Or dead. Rylan took a deep breath. He didn't need to be scared of Francis. Francis was the person protecting them from . . . from what, exactly, Rylan didn't want to know. His father waved him over, and he approached the cockpit, cradling his drawing. "Guess not."

"Keep watch with me, then."

Rylan crouched down on the cockpit bench and watched his father steer in silence. He couldn't remember the last time he'd been somewhere this quiet. Even diving underwater had a constant sound to it.

"When I learned how to sail, it wasn't nearly this nice," Francis said.

Rylan rubbed at his tendons and let his father talk.

"It was an all-boys trip across the Atlantic, meant to whip us into shape a bit. I got into some trouble when I was around your age, and my family pooled what little they had into straightening me out. My father was a proud man, even though he didn't have a dime to back it up.

"So I worked like hell and learned to navigate and swab the deck. Felt like a sixteenth-century military draft. The food was awful, sawdust bread and dried beef. I got so seasick in the beginning, I could hardly get out of my bunk to stand watch with my team."

Rylan waited patiently for the point. Something like *but I persevered and look at me now*. Or maybe *it's a hard life at sea, so don't think you're the exception*. Or even *this is my roundabout explanation for where I'm taking you all*.

Francis was fond of pounding life lessons into his stories.

"One night I belly-crawled out on deck to vomit my dinner over the side. We didn't wear life jackets all the time, so I was just soaked and shivering, holding onto the lifeline with one hand and pushing my hair back with the other. I thought I was going to die I felt so sick. I was also a touch dramatic back then." Francis smiled, and Rylan caught what he didn't say. *Dramatic like you.*

"Anyway, when there was nothing left to hurl, I took in my surroundings. I'd been on the boat for days, but it was the first time I really looked at the water. And I saw it was glowing."

Rylan stayed still and kept eye contact whenever Francis looked over.

Francis shook his head in wonder. "The white water that broke across the bow was glowing. Found out later it was bioluminescent phytoplankton, provoked by the moving boat. From then on I made a point to look around, *really* take it all in. I still remember all the shitty stuff from that trip if I think back on it, but what comes to mind when I recall where sailing started for me, where life started for me, I see the bioluminescence. I see porpoises swimming in a lightning storm. I see how high the ocean can raise a ship, and how deep she can drag it down. I see what she's given me to make me into the man I am now."

Francis went quiet for a moment in that way older people sometimes did, as if arrested by a thing that happened long ago. Rylan wished he could meet his father when he'd been seventeen, before he was rich or successful, when he'd only been a boy on a boat.

He wondered if they could have been friends.

Francis faced him. "Power and potential. That's what I see when I look at the ocean, and it's what I see when I look at you."

Rylan met his father's eyes, blue like a Perlemoen crab's. Did he really see power or much of anything when he looked at Rylan? Rylan wanted it to be true, even if he felt like an impostor. He wanted to be what Francis imagined he was.

Francis waved a hand around in the air. "So look around, son. The sea isn't the end of the world. It's most of it."

Out of habit, Rylan obeyed. He looked around.

Sails brimmed. A fine layer of crystalized salt had encrusted the railing like tiny stalagmites on the mouth of a cave. Rylan dragged a finger through the salt, leaving a trail on plain wood.

He peered down into the water and did a double take.

Francis chuckled behind him. "Go to the bow. Take a good, long look."

Rylan laughed despite himself and rushed to the front of the boat, leaning as far out over the ocean as he dared.

Luminescent blue water pushed up against the bow. Rylan wondered for a moment if this is what the Blue Men of Minch actually looked like, if their lore about being fallen angels meant that they were actually toppled stars that had collected in the water to give *The Old Eileen* a gleaming cloak.

Of course, that was ridiculous. Like Francis said, these were phytoplankton, dinoflagellates, if Rylan remembered correctly. They shone in response to movement in case a predator was attacking. The glow was a last-ditch effort to attract an even bigger predator to scare away the first.

Rylan tried to imagine how the boat looked from above, flying on a carpet of stars. He stayed there, grinning like an idiot at the glowing water, until his eyes stung and he returned to the cockpit.

He felt . . . relieved. For a precious moment, he wasn't worrying about his father or his sister or the dead. He just thought about how nice it was that ocean water sometimes glowed.

"It's something, huh?" Francis clapped his back.

"Yeah." Rylan hesitated, feeling like he should say more but coming up empty. "Thanks."

"You're welcome."

Francis pulled him inward then, an ambush embrace. He mussed Rylan's hair and patted his back in a masculine affirmation.

"My boy," he murmured, and Rylan realized he didn't know the last time he had hugged his father.

He screwed up his face and let himself lean into Francis's chest. It was safer to be this close. It meant he was protected.

Francis's hand landed on Rylan's narrow shoulder. "I cannot wait for you to see where we're going."

"Where *are* we going, Dad?"

Francis held him at arm's length. They were the same height now, and Rylan was still growing. He'd be taller than him someday. It was a strange thought to have.

"It's going to be an adventure, Rylan. Our whole lives are about to change."

Their *whole* lives?

Rylan stiffened, his body reacting before he had the foresight to remain calm. Miraculously, Francis hadn't noticed. He kept talking. Almost . . . nervously?

"Just wait. It'll be an adjustment at first, but where we're headed is beautiful. Finally we can get away from all the noise, right? We'll dive every day, watch the sun set into the sea every night."

Francis seemed thrilled. He was still speaking, but Rylan couldn't process the words anymore because, between them, Rylan finally heard the answer to the question. Not to where they were going, exactly, but *why*. He had heard the same fanciful language from his twin when she explained her plan to leave.

"This was never a vacation. You're running away . . ." Rylan breathed, and Francis went silent. He was still holding Rylan by his shoulder, and his grip tightened, fingers into bone. Rylan inhaled sharply and struggled to remain rooted in the present moment, fighting not to trip into memory.

"I want you to understand something, son."

He's not denying it.

Rylan couldn't move. Francis looked up to the sky as if for guidance, then pushed Rylan down onto the cockpit bench. Rylan's knees buckled and he folded. Francis kept one hand on the wheel even as he trained all his focus on Rylan.

"The life we live is a privileged one. A truly unique one. How many fathers can give a world like this to their sons and wives and daughters?"

Rylan was nodding even though Francis hadn't been asking him a question. Francis placed a hand on the back of Rylan's neck, and he stopped.

"You don't get to be extraordinary if you only operate in the ordinary," Francis continued. "Simple as that."

"I know. I know, I know," Rylan said, unable to break out of a loop. He couldn't let himself be too emotional. Too dramatic. But suddenly he couldn't shut up, like something had short-circuited inside him. Francis moved his hand over Rylan's mouth.

"Shh, shh, shh. I know you do. That's why I'm telling you this. Smart kid. Ordinary people will never understand the lengths it takes to achieve the extraordinary. How can you be expected to comprehend the sun if you've only ever seen a fire in a cave?"

He's running away. He's taking us with him. He's trying to protect us from something.

That means we're never going back.

Rylan tried to nod, but Francis kept his head from moving.

"Don't be scared." He withdrew his hand, but Rylan still held his breath.

"The Cameron family is the thing I love most fiercely in this world," Francis said, holding eye contact with Rylan. "Built it with my bare hands. Ordinary people will not be the reason it falls."

He extended a hand. Rylan took it, and Francis pulled him smoothly to his feet.

"Let's get you back to bed."

Chapter 32

```
Tia Cameron
Call sign: Thimble
Day 7 at Sea
```

TIA LAY COCOONED in her sheets like a corpse wrapped up for burial at sea. She had gone through the day corpse-like as well, unsure what to do now that she knew they couldn't radio out for help. Alejandro had said cutting the cord had been meant to protect someone. *Ourselves.* But what did *ourselves* really mean? Him and Francis? Him and the Cameron family? All seven of them? Or—now—six of them? How would cutting them off from the outside world protect them? And protect them from *what*?

Or *whom*? Did her father have enemies? She supposed plenty of rich men had people who disliked them. There were other yacht companies that had rivalries with Unwind. Some had gone bankrupt. Maybe someone was jealous, wanted revenge?

Or maybe Lila was the one who'd riled up somebody. Tia's mother had a habit of attention-seeking that could border on antagonizing.

Once when Tia and Rylan were eleven, Lila's professionally photographed nudes were leaked all over the press. That week, there'd been paparazzi hiding on the beach behind their house, following Tia and her friends in the mall, eating casually at their favorite restaurant while snapping pictures of the family from behind a menu. Tia remembered feeling annoyed, even protective of her mom, but later a classmate had shown her the article that accused Lila of leaking her own nudes. Tia didn't doubt that for a second.

Lila Logan would do anything to be noticed.

Even if it meant her daughter felt uncomfortable leaving the house. Even if it meant her husband didn't speak to her for a week.

Maybe that answered her question, though. If Lila were in danger, she would run right toward it.

Which just led Tia back to Francis.

Tia peeled the sheets off her face, coming to terms with the fact that she would not be falling back asleep. A tall, skeletal man stood in the dark corner of the bedroom.

Tia slammed her hand over the lamp switch on the bedside table, and her brother's features snapped into focus.

"Jesus," she said, heart thrumming. "Why are you standing there like a psychopath? Have you been there all night?"

Rylan blinked. "Sorry." He stayed where he was. "Couldn't sleep."

That was, distinctly, not an answer. Tia checked the time—6:00 a.m.—and loosened the sheets that mummified her lower body. Over twenty-four hours since they'd found the radio cord cut. "And I'll never sleep again after that."

"Sorry," he repeated.

"What's wrong?" Tia briefly considered throwing a pillow at his face to reanimate him, but she decided against it. "Was Mom up?" She knew Lila's past fits of insomnia often involved waking Rylan up to talk with him at late hours of the night.

Rylan shook his head.

"Dad?"

A nod.

Figures. "Why were you up in the first place?"

He waved his hand at his bed. The sketchbook peered out from underneath the comforter, which had been tossed like a candy wrapper. He must have gotten out of bed in a hurry.

Maybe he'd had a bad dream. There was enough nightmare fuel to go around. Tia peeled herself from bed and guided Rylan to sit. He resisted and made his bed neatly before finally relaxing.

"You slept through every alarm I set for the first three years of high school. You think me drawing and shuffling around could wake you up?" he said.

Tia returned to her own bed. "Oh please, you were in a different room."

Rylan seemed to be in another world even as he held a conversation with her. It unnerved her.

"A room that shared a vent. And I had the volume on the loudest setting. But no, I had to wake you up myself."

Tia tossed a pillow into Rylan's chest, hoping that would hit a switch and snap him out of the cloud that encased him. "My personal alarm clock."

Rylan picked the pillow up. He seemed a bit more focused, at least. "What did you do at St. Bernadette's to get up?"

"I slept in. Then I got a nice, personal wake-up from Sister Mary Sebastian every morning. Trust me, I preferred when you did it. So . . . tell me what happened."

Rylan quieted. He fixated on picking at a loose thread in the pillowcase's stitching. Tia waited.

"Dad was on watch."

Tia waited for more, but he was agonizingly slow. "And?" she prompted at last.

"And . . . and he's running away."

What? Tia got up and plopped down beside him. "What do you mean?"

He recounted, haltingly, his conversation with their father as Tia stared at him, panic rising. Francis hadn't meant they wouldn't be going to Florida soon. He meant they wouldn't be going . . . ever? How could he do that? *Why* would he do that?

And what the hell made him think he could bring them all along?

"So we are being kidnapped." She twisted fistfuls of Rylan's sheets in her hands. "We've got to stop him, Ry, we have to turn around or . . . or . . ."

Of course Francis Cameron would thwart Tia's plans to run away by running away himself. The thought both amused and infuriated her.

Rylan snapped the limp thread from the pillowcase and let it fall. It drifted to the floor and coiled like a noose.

"Listen," she said carefully. "Whatever is going on, we shouldn't have any part in. He's maybe trying to protect us, but he's also dragging us along without consent. You saw the island, right? In the middle of absolute nowhere?"

Rylan's voice crawled up an octave. "So we're going to be trapped? That place can't have airports. Or other boats. Or people. What do we do, then?"

"Then we'll steal *The Old Eileen*," Tia said without thinking. She paused to consider the option. Nico wouldn't want to be trapped on some godforsaken island. He'd help them escape. He'd come with them. Hell, maybe he'd travel the seas alongside them and teach Tia how to properly sail. She felt giddy at the idea, her twin brother, a trusty cat, and her . . . crush? All of them could desert the world and ride waves until the end of time. Tia could be content with a life like that. They'd be pirates! Or outlaws! The whole world would endeavor to find them, but no one ever would.

"We'll steal the boat," Tia repeated, trying not to get too

far ahead of herself. "With Nico, the three of us can sail wherever we want to go."

"How? Dad, Nico, and Alejandro are barely handling the watch rotation without MJ."

Tia remembered her father's words when he was arguing with Lila, the night before they left. *This ship can be manned by one good sailor alone, Lil. And we've got two and a half.*

Tia's mind raced, but she felt hopeful. She could still make her plans work. She scooped up the sketchbook and turned to a blank page at the end. She uncapped the nearest pen. "Listen to me. We have options. And right here, right now, we'll make a backup plan that nobody beside us will know about, okay?"

"A plan . . ." Rylan watched the pen that Tia hovered over the page.

"We'll have a signal. A distress signal. If anyone else sees it, they'll think we're playing around. And it'll mean . . ." Tia thought about *The Old Eileen*. She thought about all the different safety aspects built into the ship. Life jackets, life preservers, inflatable survival suits. All of those were mere bandages if they were on their own, though. They needed a boat.

"The life raft," she said. "If one of us gives the signal, we'll inflate one of the life rafts and run before we get stuck on the island." *Or if whoever's hunting Dad catches up to us . . .*

"We'd be sitting ducks," Rylan protested. "We'd just float there and starve."

"The life rafts come with survival kits. Food, water. And flares. We would be rescued and back home before we knew it. And in a worst-case scenario, Dad stashed paddles in ours. We could row to . . . I don't know. Somewhere."

Tia was becoming more and more fond of the idea. They would figure it out as they went along. That was how adventures worked.

Rylan lay back, pillow held to his chest. "We'd have to be close to another ship. Or to land. Land that isn't Dad's island."

Tia was nodding. "We're getting close. And there are a bunch of islands in the area. I can figure out the closest inhabited one, and we can slip away the night of our birthday when everyone's asleep. That gives us a few more days."

They would be long gone by the time anyone woke up. They could do it when Nico was on watch. He'd cover for them. Maybe he'd come with them.

Rylan looked doubtful. "What would the signal even be for all this? Some boat-distress thing like the *Titanic* people used?"

Tia snapped her fingers and began to write. "That's exactly what we'll use, Ry. And when we see this signal the night after our birthday . . . if we say it, write it, mouth it, sign it . . . it means it's time to leave. Get out now."

Rylan licked his dry lips and nodded, grim. "Abandon ship."

Yes. She knew he would get behind her eventually! This was the push he needed to realize their father did not have their best interests at heart. So Francis Cameron had something to run from. What he didn't get was that they had something to run from too. Him.

Tia held out her pinkie and twisted hers with Rylan's in a promise. "Together."

He hesitated then looked her in the eye for the first time since she'd woken up. "Together."

Tia closed the sketchbook so that anyone who passed through the twins' room wouldn't see the black letters emblazoned on the page, their signal in case of the absolute worst.

SOS.

Save Our Souls.

She Talks About Shee—Blog Post #111

The Old Eileen

LAIOISE O'BRIEN

Just an Irish American lass coming in with my two cents on everything that's been happening in the news! If you have, somehow, not heard about *The Old Eileen*, a ghost ship found off the coast of southern Florida with seven people missing from it and one body recovered, you are either living rent-free under a boulder the size of Cork, or you have incredibly strange social media algorithms (what's your secret?).

Anyhow, I've seen a lot of talk about the missing people, but not too much on the boat itself, which instantly caught my attention as having a rather interesting Irish name. *Eileen* usually means *beautiful bird* or perhaps *radiance* or *life* if you're going off the old Irish name, Eiblhn. And pardon me a moment while I profusely pat my own back because I KNEW not only what *Eileen* means but exactly what *The Old Eileen* comes from (thank you, MPhil from Trinity), and I thought it might lend an interesting lens to this very strange case (don't even get me started on folks going missing in Irish mythology, that could be a blog post all its own).

The myth of *The Old Eileen* is rather rare with little to no physical text to back it up. One of those word-of-mouth stories that rarely makes it to English or paper. It was the name of a boat sent off by a queen who was certain her sailors were the finest in the world. The sails were so big and the boat so huge that she had become convinced her men could sail it right up into the stars, collect them, and bring back celestial riches that would rival anything that could be found on earth. So she sends *The Old Eileen* away and, big surprise, it never comes back. Did it fall off the earth? Did the men turn against themselves before they even got close? Or maybe, they did make it to the stars, but the sailors became too greedy to share them, and they stayed sailing through the sky forever.

An eerie and lovely name for a ghost ship to have, I would say. And the next question becomes, of course, how did the Camerons know about this myth to have given the name to their ship? *Cameron* itself is possibly Scottish Gaelic in origin (a word that means *crooked*, *bent*, or *river*). Was Francis Cameron well-versed in rare Gaelic mythology? Unlikely. But actress Lila Logan is also likely of Gaelic descent, and she is known as an actress for doing copious amounts of research into other time periods for roles.

This wouldn't be the first time a mythological name has had consequences of mythic proportions on seafaring vessels. I find that truth is often stranger than fiction. More than anything, though, whether *The Old Eileen* is a story or a ship, it can be agreed upon that it is first and foremost an omen.

Chapter 33

```
Rylan Cameron
Call sign: Minnow
Day 8 at Sea
```

RYLAN SHARPENED HIS HB pencil with one of the knives from Alejandro's galley. Wood shavings curled away and left the graphite as sharp as a blade. He was sitting on a counter in the chart house, surrounded by nautical maps and ship's logs for inspiration, even though he was careful not to let his gaze fall upon the tiny dotted island that made his spine tingle.

He had something thick at the base of his throat that he hadn't been able to swallow away since his conversation with his father last night. But until he could dislodge it, he couldn't quite breathe right. He couldn't find it in him to be either upset by being trapped or excited by the possibility of leaving. He just felt stuck.

Rylan was used to being caught up in the tide of Tia's willpower. She was infectious. Suffocating, even. Once she had an idea, it was gospel, and anyone not prepared to acknowledge it as such became obsolete. But Francis seemed to place so much faith in Rylan. He'd been tender with him last night. He'd explained himself, at least somewhat. Rylan knew it was impossible to please them both, but here he was, petrified to cross either, so the lump in his throat stubbornly remained.

Rylan flipped backward in his sketchbook, back to August of last year where he had scribbled a comic-style picture of an alarm clock in a nun habit alongside Tia's dorm room. He had drawn it from a photograph, but the drawing was half finished.

Rylan remembered exactly where he had been when that drawing had been interrupted.

The watertight door to the chart house swung wide.

"Oh hey, Rylan," Nico said. He cranked the door shut and crossed to the counter where Rylan was perched. "Mind if I . . . ?"

"Oh, yeah, sorry." Rylan scooted to the edge of the counter so Nico could grab the ship's log.

Nico wrote his name in the upper left-hand corner along with the date and time. Then he checked the ship's coordinates on a small screen above the counter and jotted those down as well.

Rylan realized he was staring. "So you do that every hour?"

"You're supposed to, but it's been more like every four hours for us since we have one-man watch teams. My uncle asked me to do it for him since he's already on the helm."

Memories of playing with the ship's log when he and Tia were little came to Rylan's mind. It had been so important at the time, like they were filing information that would be analyzed by historians to come, even though they were only on day-sails and hadn't needed to fill them out in the first place. It was the imagination of it that counted. They used to pretend to be pirates or international explorers charting their course around the globe. That's when Tia had come up with the idea for them to have secret sailor names. Call signs.

MJ's had been easy to come up with. *Sherlock*. She always seemed to know every little thing the twins had done, even if they were certain no evidence had been left behind. Their mother's and father's call signs only came about later. *Cassiopeia* and *Midas*. Grand names of mythic and scientific proportions. And Rylan had, of course, insisted on being some kind of fish.

Tia was by far the hardest to encapsulate with one word. She jumped from name to name as they grew older, which used to drive Rylan nuts. *Just pick one*, he'd beg.

I'm waiting for you to pick mine, she always infuriatingly replied.

"Whatcha working on all alone in here?" Nico asked.

"Trying to . . . I don't know. Distract myself."

Nico put his elbows on the counter. "Art's a good way to do that, so I've been told."

Rylan glanced at him. "You an artist?"

"Nohoho." Nico put his chin in his palm. "Definitely not. My uncle is, though, with his food. When his grandmother died, he left the rest of the family behind and went anywhere he could to distract himself. To sea. Culinary school."

Rylan didn't know what it was like to have a grandparent. "Her death upset him that much?"

Nico picked up one of Rylan's pencils and twirled it between his thumb and middle finger. "She raised him and my mom. It was like losing a parent. My mom told me she was the only person he was ever emotional with. She was the only one who didn't need him to be strong."

Rylan realized he didn't know a thing about Alejandro's childhood, other than he was raised in the same apartment building as Francis. He certainly hadn't given thought to the people in Alejandro's life who he might or might not have lost.

"Why did everyone need him to be strong?"

Nico balanced the pencil on his knuckles. "Machismo. People think that rich families care more about image than poor ones. I think it's the opposite. When you're poor, all you got is pride."

Rylan wasn't sure what to say to that.

Nico leaned forward to peek at Rylan's sketchbook, which he hid to his chest.

"What?" Nico asked playfully. "Don't tell me you're terrible."

"I'm not. I just . . ." There it was. That sickening feeling he'd gotten when MJ had forced an explanation out of him. Rylan wouldn't let that happen again.

"I'm not terrible. I just have to work alone."

Nico looked pensive, and Rylan was certain he would press him like MJ had, but instead he shrugged his shoulders and scooped up his clipboard.

"Fair 'nough. I'll leave you to it."

Rylan waited until the watertight door had been closed before he lowered the sketchbook and stared at the half-finished drawing in his lap.

He touched the shaded beginnings of his sister's dormitory window as he let himself remember.

Rylan had been drawing for days since Tia left. He would call her nightly, and they'd stay on the phone while he drew, asking her to describe every inch of her new school. Her new life. Sketching her dorm had been tricky—it was hardly Rylan's specialty—and Tia must have fallen asleep on the other end of the phone. His sister's deep breathing became the ambience to his art.

Then the knock at his door. Two sharp taps, which meant it was Francis. Rylan had dropped his pencil, hung up the phone.

The sketchbook was still open when his father strode inside, and he glimpsed it before Rylan could get it closed.

"You really miss her, huh?"

Francis sat on Rylan's bed. Gestured for him to join him. So he had.

"I miss her too," Francis went on. "Despite it all. House is going to be quiet this year."

Year. It was insurmountable. How was Rylan supposed to live a year without his best friend? The floor tilted, and Rylan's hands gathered to fists.

"You sent her away," he said, and in that second he really thought he could hit his own dad. "You think this will fix anything? You think it'll make her love you again? You're ruining everything!"

Francis crossed his ankles. "Are you done?"

"Not really." Rylan shot to his feet. He was scared. He always felt scared. But then he'd felt anger too, and it was rich and cataclysmic with a current strong enough to burst a dam. "Do you even realize how much damage you've done? She's my twin. We're supposed to do life together. You're so careless and . . . and cruel! The least you could have done is disowned me too."

Francis glanced at his Rolex, then back at his son. "I have no intention of disowning my daughter."

"But you—"

He raised a hand. "It is no longer your turn to speak. I do realize what I've done, and I know it is hurting you. I'm sorry for that."

Rylan faltered. Francis Cameron was sorry?

"I'm hoping that this is what it takes for you to step up."

Rylan's head swam. His anger was suddenly misplaced and misshapen. He shifted his balance and released the tension in his fingers.

"I don't understand."

Francis spread his hands. "Well, you want your sister to come home, don't you?"

"Yes," Rylan said through his teeth.

"I could make the call tomorrow for our jet to pick her up and bring her back."

Rylan teared up. It was too good to be true. Painfully so.

But he couldn't help imagining his hurricane of a sister bursting through his bedroom door, ready to take on their senior year together. He'd help her with her homework. She'd convince him to go to school events. They'd go skiing in Aspen over winter break and find out they had a crush on the same boy in psych class and talk through the vent in their closet whenever the rest of the house felt too big.

Francis patted the bed again, and Rylan sank beside him.

"How?" he whispered.

"Like I said. You'll need to step up. Put your mind to maximalizing your talents. You could be the smartest kid at that school if you wanted to be. You're interested in the ocean? Great. So become a diving instructor, get your MBA. Ocean tourism is an untapped market, and you're a goddamn Cameron."

Rylan searched his father's face. His teeth matched the whites of his eyes.

"How does this get you to bring Tia home?"

"All I want is you to be worthy of the name we share." Francis leaned closer. His aftershave smarted Rylan's eyes. "So you're going to prove yourself. I have an empire ready for you to inherit, my boy. I believe you inherit what you earn. I don't even care what you do in life as long as it is exceptional. Now. There are nine months in the school year. You'll have nine tests. When you pass one . . ." Francis snapped his fingers. "I'll bring your sister home."

"It's up to me?" Rylan croaked.

"It's up to you," Francis replied, extending a hand to seal the deal.

In his lap, Rylan's hands had begun to tremble. It'd be up to him to save Tia from her banishment. From a place she despised. It'd be up to him to get her home.

"Will Mom know?" he asked. The tests would be different if Lila was involved.

"This is between us men," Francis told him. "If you go to her crying, you've already failed."

Rylan didn't keep secrets from his mother. He didn't keep secrets from Tia. But he knew then this was a trial he'd have to endure without either of them. He could do it alone. He had to.

I'm going to get you out of there, Thimble.

"I'll do it," Rylan said, and the two clasped hands.

But he didn't do it. He couldn't. He failed nine times over, and Tia didn't even know. She hadn't even been allowed to come home for Thanksgiving or winter break. Now she wanted to get *him* out. And he had agreed to let her. Could he follow through if it came down to it?

Rylan bent his head and buried his face inside his hands.

He owed Tia his bravery. He owed Francis his legacy. But all he could think about as he curled in on himself on the chart house counter were his inabilities.

It's all my fault, it's all my fault, it's all my fault . . .

Chapter 34

Lila Logan Cameron
Call sign: Cassiopeia
Day 8 at Sea

LILA RECLINED ON one of the chart house sunbathing mattresses, her belly skyward and her sunglasses making the clouds and sails look heart-shaped. She rubbed sunscreen lotion over the fronts of her legs, her stomach, the crown of her breasts, and her collarbones. Her bikini of choice today was a push-up top with a knotted center and high-cut bottoms, both in the color the catalog had called *Persian Pastel*.

As the boat dipped and rose, Lila wondered if the motion would affect getting an even tan. She was already going to have tan lines, which was bad enough. If the twins weren't on this trip, she would have vastly preferred sunbathing in the nude, but alas.

Lila needed time like this to decompress after MJ's accident and Francis's little surprise. Her children had been quiet these past few days and her husband distracted, which allowed her the exquisite opportunity to ruminate.

After a lifetime of streaming through her days, Lila had had an inordinate amount of stillness this past year. Her momentum was dead. Her life was stagnant. Tia's absence did that to the family: made everything feel calm. Copacetic.

She hadn't missed Tia's mood swings, though.

Lila had only ever intended to have one child. With one, you were just a person with a child.

Two was what made you a mother.

That was the belief Lila's own parents had subscribed to. Patrick and Lori Logan had similarly set about to have an only child. A boy would be nice. He'd be a banker like Patrick. They weren't so arrogant to assume they wouldn't possibly have a girl, but Lila had found prayer cards in her mother's vanity that politely (and repeatedly) petitioned Saint John Bosco for a son.

Lori Logan, to her quiet dismay, had delivered not one, but two female babies in the final hour of March. The first, Elaina Maria Logan, was dead.

The second was Lila.

Lori Logan recovered admirably from her shock and her thirty-hour labor. She ordered a twenty-two-inch coffin for her firstborn, scheduled Elaina's funeral for the same weekend as Lila's baptism, and swapped her Saint John Bosco prayer cards for those of Saint Agnes of Rome.

Lori's professions included housewife and perfectionist. She collected Madame Alexander dolls and sometimes photographed her infant daughter surrounded by them, like she was a lovely little doll herself. Lila had always supposed that's where the idea for the beauty pageants came from. Lila's first memories were her mother changing her out of Mass clothes and into pageant ones: from paisley print and pressed collars to butterfly sleeves and chiffon. She remembered coughing in clouds of hair spray and squashing her little-kid feet into heels. And she remembered winning. A lot.

On the rare occasions Lila didn't bring home prize money, she'd found that, to her parents, she was worse than a disappointment.

She was an obsolete.

It became rather a talent of Lila's, understanding when and why she lost attention. Attention couldn't be maintained every single minute. It had to be prepared for and guided. When Lila's parents ran out of their ability to pay attention, Lila rotated to another source. This skill of hers did wonders onscreen. How does one become the person people look at in a room of a thousand girls who look just like her? One needed that ineffable yet scrupulously acquired quality. The kind that won pageants.

The kind that made headlines.

Lila understood that marriage and pregnancy would relinquish attention. People loved weddings, but they didn't love married people. They loved babies, but they weren't so fond of their sleep-deprived parents.

Yet she wanted to marry Francis in a château in the South of France and wake up with her head on his shoulder and hold their baby in her arms. So though it wasn't strictly career-related, Lila Logan got married. She got pregnant.

With Lila's own pregnancy, of course, she had known by her third prenatal appointment she was having twins. But—and maybe this was terrible (she'd never told anyone, not even Francis)—she had subconsciously assumed one of them would be stillborn like her sister had been. So she'd prepared herself for one baby and one death rather than for a family of four.

Rylan came first, smaller than average with a dark head of hair. *This is it*, Lila had thought when she held him. *My child*.

But then the doctor asked her to resume pushing. With the epidural, Lila couldn't feel a thing except her baby boy, who was swiftly removed from her breast.

So Lila pushed, delirious. This was the afterbirth. The placenta.

But it wasn't.

It was her daughter, Tia, who was born anything but still.

Tia screamed rather than cried, tiny tears that shone like diamonds rolling down engine-red cheeks. She was small and dark-haired too. Lila's children matched each other far more than they did the woman who delivered them.

When the blood and the shit and the war of it all had been wiped away, Lila held her two babies, one in each arm. And as Rylan slept, a tiny hand pressed to Lila's heart, Tia squirmed.

She was like that for seventeen years. Writhing to be freed from Lila's arms, twisting when she was strapped into a seat, ducking when Lila went to kiss her head, and always vocalizing her displeasure with wails and shrieks and screams.

Did you put your mother through his hell? Lila once asked her husband after four-year-old Tia had drawn blood biting a classmate's hand. Lila knew for a fact that at Tia's age she had been an orderly, convivial child who was never violent and never in trouble.

Must be why she left me, Francis joked back. Lila had wanted to ask him more. Had an elementary-aged Francis been as aggressive as his daughter? Did he bare his incisors when he raged? Was his mother's absence the reason for his poor behavior in high school?

Mostly, though, Lila wanted Francis to slide an arm around her and tell her his juvenile upheavals could never happen to their daughter. Tia had a mother, after all.

But Francis didn't say that, and Tia had resumed her fit, so the conversation never happened.

After a while, Lila disengaged with her daughter. Better to be breezy and unaffected, a sail rather than an anchor when the storm rolled in.

Meanwhile, there was not a soul on earth more endearing than her son. He was a beautiful boy, thick-lashed and slender. He flushed easily, his skin baby pink and petal-soft. He said his first word a full two months after Tia, but he was crawling and exploring weeks before her. Whenever Lila passed by, he would lift his arms above his head, exposing the full-moon of his tummy until she bent to scoop him up. His sister seemed to hoard the ability to make sound, so when Rylan cried it was silent. When he had a tantrum (which was rare), it was with his mouth sealed and wounded eyes so large he looked like one of Lori Logan's dolls.

They spent every moment together. Lila arranged for daily afternoon teas, dressing Rylan in green suspenders and pressed dress shirts, while Lila matched him in mint florals. She designed the sunroom (which she liked to think of as her *son-room*) to be a space for the two of them to set up their ceramic tea set and be waited on by Alejandro. Francis and Tia didn't understand. On the rare occasions they joined teatime, Tia would spill on the cream tablecloth. Francis would glance at his watch and ask Alejandro to mix sake in his tea. The two of them dominated conversation, arguing and raising voices.

Things were better with Lila and Rylan alone.

Lila marveled at her son. Even when everything that made him enchanting revealed him to be guarded. *Overly cautious*, a child psychiatrist told Lila. *He seems to be responding to his sister's forcefulness with wariness. He's her opposite. Try getting them in different preschool classrooms. He might find himself more without her.*

It was true. Lila had learned from the beginning that Rylan did better *away* from Tia.

Last summer had been the breaking point. Tia's rash behavior destabilized Rylan. How was he supposed to know who he was when he had his sister tugging him one way and his father the other?

Simple.

He needed someone safe and soothing in between.

It had been Lila, murmuring into her husband's ear, who

decided it was time for Tia to be sent away. There was little more they could personally do for her. Tia didn't permit any sort of parenting anyway, and that was just fine with Lila. Rylan needed all the parenting. He was receptive to it too. With Rylan, Lila got results.

And so did Francis.

He had told her about the tests long before he proposed them to their son. Francis had always been obsessed with rites of passage, the process of coming of age. His own family had obliterated their life savings to give him the chance to get his life together on an all-boys sailing trip across the Atlantic. He once told Lila that passage had changed him forever. Francis's shipmates, however, had been the wayward sons of anesthesiologists and architects. They were boys who took chances for granted.

Francis would let his entire yachting empire sink into the sea before he let Rylan do the same.

Just don't give up on him, Lila had petitioned Francis. *Promise me that no matter how many times he fails, you won't give up on our son.*

Francis promised.

And Lila turned a blind eye.

Meanwhile, as Tia's wrath zeroed in on Francis, Rylan clung ever tighter to Lila. Lila was the soft one, the safe one. From a vantage point of gentleness and motherliness, there wasn't a single string she couldn't find and pull.

Lila's phone trilled to inform her it was time to flip onto her stomach. She oiled herself down with more sunscreen and switched from supine to prone. The sunlight was an anesthetic. She hadn't been this loose, this liquid, in ages.

Francis had so many ideas for how to handle their lives. Their son. But in the end, it was always Lila who coaxed out her desired outcome, who planted seeds with whispers. This trip would end no differently. It wasn't just the sunshine that eased her in the midst of this boat with her brazen daughter and her secretive husband.

She had a new idea, one she had murmured not to Francis but to Alejandro. Once spoken, it was no longer an idea but a plan. All she had to do now was luxuriate for a few more days until her lover put it into action.

So Lila set another timer to bake the back half of her body and closed her eyes to bask.

Chapter 35

Rylan Cameron
Call sign: Minnow
Day 9 at Sea

RYLAN AND TIA sat hip to hip on the salon couch shoveling oatmeal thick with peanut butter into their mouths as they watched TV. Tia was in a good mood, probably feeling secure thanks to the escape plan she'd hatched. It was easy for Tia. All she wanted was an exciting, simple life with a few close people. She wasn't afraid of leaving behind her parents. She reveled in it.

Rylan would never be like that. He stirred his oatmeal (or as Alejandro had always called it, *boatmeal*) and ate a spoonful of the oaty, peanut buttery cement.

"Are you going to miss stuff like this? Like oatmeal and TV?"

Tia used her finger to finish off the swipes of peanut butter left in the bottom of her bowl. "You mean when we run? Oatmeal and TV exist outside the Cameron family, you know."

"I know, but . . ." Rylan set his breakfast aside. "But you never make it seem like your life is going to be normal after you leave. You're going to be living in the woods or on the side of a road, or something."

"I want adventures, yeah. But I'm not swearing off good food and television till the end of time." Tia sucked her finger and laid her bowl on the coffee table next to Rylan's. Hers was scraped clean.

"I know, it just seems like a big divide, you know? Like there's your life before you run, and your life after. And ne'er the twain shall meet."

Tia wiped her hands on her shorts and gave him a quizzical look. "Why do you keep saying when I run? Like you aren't coming with me?"

Rylan opened his mouth to respond when Francis's voice, muffled above them, rang out. "Rylan! Come up on deck!"

Rylan grimaced.

Tia grabbed his arm. "Maybe if we stay silent he'll think we're still asleep."

They waited. Francis grew louder, shouting down the companionway. "Rylan, get up here! Quick."

The blood drained from Rylan's face.

"Rylan!" Francis shouted again.

"It's okay," Tia promised now, standing and taking his hand. "I'll go with you."

She stayed in front of him all the way up to the deck, but when Francis ran over, he seemed to look right through her. Francis was giddy.

"We got a bite on the line," Francis explained, herding them to the stern. "Something big."

Not a test, then. At least, not yet.

The deep-sea fishing kit. Rylan had forgotten it was still hooked up. Nico and Alejandro were wrestling with the fishing poles. Rylan followed the fishing line with his eyes and looked down into the water.

A fish, long and powerful, fought in the waves in a desperate dance to escape the hook through its lip. It had a magnificent fin protruding from its back, blue and brilliant against the water around it, which looked gray in comparison. A blade-like bill pointed out from its face, and Rylan recognized the species as a sailfish, named for its sail-like fin that fanned out enough to catch the wind. They were the fastest fish in the sea, able to swim as quickly as a car on the highway if they wanted to. And they were huge, growing up to eleven feet.

Francis joined Nico and Alejandro. "Let's pull her up."

"Can't you cut the line?" Rylan asked, sick to his stomach. No one heard him.

"Rylan, help us out," Francis ordered, but Rylan was rooted in place. Even if he could reclaim his muscles, the last thing he wanted to do was help haul the poor fish out of the water.

Nico glanced back at him and registered his expression. "Mr. Cameron? Can we catch and release? Do a few photos and throw it back?"

Warmth spread throughout Rylan's body, and he mouthed his gratitude at Nico, who was too preoccupied with the line to see.

"Let's just get her up first," was Francis's short response.

The three men struggled to drag the sailfish onto the deck. Somewhere in his peripheral vision, Rylan realized Tia had taken the wheel and Lila was beside her.

The sailfish appeared then, wriggling and wide-eyed as it was yanked onto the deck. It was huge, easily as long as any human Rylan had ever seen, and probably longer.

Francis laughed, delighted. "Can you believe it?" he asked no one in particular.

"She's beautiful," Nico murmured.

The sailfish continued to thrash, its scales glinting like unearthed treasure in the sunlight.

"Lila! Lila, get a photo of me, darling!" Francis crouched down over the fish, who was still moving, still frantic to breathe.

Rylan found himself lost in the sailfish's eyes: glossy, marbly, and ever-staring. Its palpable fear became his own, and if he'd had the strength to lift a creature of that size, he would have thrown it back overboard.

Lila took out her phone and snapped a couple of photos of Francis, his arm around Alejandro and his hand pointing to the dying animal.

Nico hung back, out of frame. "Can we toss it back now, sir?" he asked.

"You kidding, kid? We're having this sucker for dinner." Francis waved at Alejandro, who headed to midships and came back with a mallet.

Rylan turned his head, bile rising in his throat.

"Really, Francis? A hammer?" Lila fanned herself.

"It's how it's done, Lil." Francis took the mallet from Alejandro, then turned and held it out. To Rylan. "Go on, son. I just need a couple strong hits."

Rylan's voice failed him. He shook his head.

Francis licked his lips and stepped forward, sweat gleaming from his brow. "The longer you hesitate, the longer it suffers. You want to call yourself a Cameron?"

He didn't. Not after this year. Not if it meant this. Rylan backed up, but he was against the railing. If only he and the fish could jump overboard together and swim far, far away.

"Dad, cut it out," Tia barked, but Francis didn't even spare her a glance. He held the mallet between himself and Rylan.

"I'll do it, Mr. Cameron." Nico stepped forward.

Alejandro caught his arm. Had they been planning this?

Rylan sucked in air, but it didn't seem to reach his lungs. Behind Francis, the sailfish flopped, its strength sapping.

"Come on, Rylan," Lila begged him. "It's just a fish."

"This is what it takes to survive at sea," Francis lectured, as if they didn't have weeks' worth of food stored belowdecks. As if he had ever had to survive at sea. "You either put it out of its misery or it dies gasping for air."

Like MJ.

But Rylan couldn't move. His hands did not obey. *I'm sorry*, he said to the fish. *I can't do it . . .*

"Rylan! Get down here, quickly!"

He was back in their home in Palm Beach.

His father sounded urgent. Something must be wrong. Rylan raced down the stairs. Francis was in the kitchen holding a cheese knife over the marble countertop, his sleeve rolled up to his elbow.

"What's going on?" Rylan looked around in confusion. Lila was reading a Jenna Fischer novel at the table. She hadn't even looked up.

"Think fast," Francis advised. Like a father says when he throws his son a football. Not when he plunges a cheese knife through a flap of skin in his own arm.

Francis dropped the mallet without warning, and it banged on the deck. Rylan flinched.

"What is wrong with you?" Francis spat and walked away, taking the helm from Tia and letting the sailfish flap and fight for every last second. That fish had more fight than Rylan ever had.

It happened in an instant. Tia left the wheel and scooped up the mallet. She shoved past Alejandro and raised it in the air with all her might, then brought it down.

Whack.

Rylan jumped and smacked his hands over his eyes.

Whack.

The sound of the thrashing stopped. Their mother gasped.

Whack.

When he dared look back, Tia was standing over the fish, its skull caved in with three clean hits. Blood streamed over the cockpit, flecks spattered on his sister's legs and hands. Francis, who was supposed to be steering, was watching her, stunned. Tia walked right up to him, fish blood pooling around her bare feet.

"You're what's wrong with him," she said evenly. "With all of us."

She dropped the brain-splattered mallet at his feet.

Chapter 36

Jerry Baugh

AGENT KOSHIDA SAT opposite Jerry in *The Old Eileen*'s trashed salon. Jerry nudged a beer can with his toe to hide it from view. He knew how this must appear to Koshida: a slovenly fisherman unable to keep a rich man's yacht clean. But the agent seemed unconcerned, all of his attention trained on Jerry.

"Do you want coffee?" Jerry asked. He didn't feel particularly hospitable, but anything was better than hearing whatever this man had to say about Steve. At the same time, Jerry needed to know. He needed to know, but he couldn't stomach knowing.

"I'm all right," Koshida said, but Jerry got to his feet anyway. He made himself a cup of joe, black as coal, and downed it before the steam had time to cool.

"Would you like to sit down, Mr. Baugh?" Koshida gestured at the seat Jerry had vacated.

Jerry shifted his weight from foot to foot. "No. Uh, thanks. I'd like to stand."

"You sure?" A line of concern trailed between Koshida's sleek, dark eyebrows. "I anticipate this being a difficult conversation."

Jerry slammed his cup down on the counter with more

force than he'd meant to. "I just, I, uh, I don't understand it. My brother—Steve—he died thirty years ago. And I wasn't there, so I'm not too sure what you'd like me to say to ya." He was blabbering. He shut his trap and busied his hands by making a second cup. The case of beers under the table still had a few cans left, but to get to them Jerry would have to reach right next to Agent Koshida's legs.

"Right . . . you're sure you wouldn't like to take a seat?"

Jerry shook his head.

"Very well." Agent Koshida straightened his tie and sat forward. "Mr. Baugh, due to a series of recently uncovered crimes, the police had cause to reopen your brother's case."

"Case?" Jerry interrupted. "There was no case. He drowned."

"Yes, but in situations of unnatural death, even with accidents, the police keep records. So like I was saying, Steven's case was reopened when new evidence has come to light that, well . . . Mr. Baugh, we have reason to believe Steven's death wasn't an accident. We think it was a homicide."

The coffee mug fell from Jerry's hands and shattered on the floor, black liquid seeping in every direction.

The young agent shot from his seat to guide Jerry to the bench, but Jerry was already there, sinking.

"Mr. Baugh? Mr. Baugh, can I get you a glass of water?" Koshida knelt at Jerry's side.

Jerry zeroed in on the case of beers under the table. "*Steve*," he muttered. "Not *Steven*. He hated that."

Koshida nodded in earnest. "Steve. Got it. Thank you for telling me."

"And I'm Jerry." Jerry sniffed hard, then cleared his throat even harder.

Koshida swept to the galley where he collected a wad of paper towels, sopping up the worst of the coffee and handing the rest of the roll to Jerry who blew his nose like a freight horn.

"Nice to meet you, Jerry. I'm sorry, this must be coming out of nowhere after so long without Steve."

Jerry tapped his foot underneath the table, scrubbing his nose with a rough paper towel. "Tell me what happened."

So he did.

Steve Baugh had been twenty-seven years old, wind-chapped and hungry when he'd left the world, his girlfriend, and his sales career behind to commit himself to the sea like he'd always dreamed. He'd done what Jerry, at the time, was still only dreaming about. Steve got a job at the docks for a wealthy man and ended up being best buds with the other hired crew. He must have told Jerry about those friends; he must have heard their names a hundred times. But details of people's lives weren't Jerry's specialty. Brenna Madden, Ida Graves, even Sheila's dumb cat had all slipped his memory at some point or another. Sheila was lucky her name had been memorialized in Jerry's boat in a fit of vengeance after she'd kicked Jerry out.

So of course Jerry didn't remember Alejandro Matamoros and Francis Cameron. Not from Steve, anyway.

Steve worked with them for years. Then the captain tasked his crew with chartering the boat alone from North Carolina to the Bahamas. Three young, stupid men alone on a boat with no safety regulations because the wealthy thought they were above safety regulations. The accident had been chalked up to a rich man's pride costing a poor man's life. Tale as old as time. The rich guy had settled the lawsuit filed by Jerry's mother. The settlement payment was more money than the Baughs had expected to see over a lifetime. Jerry inherited half, enough to pull a Steve and live somewhat comfortably at sea (although, he'd chosen the route of owning his own fishing boat instead of sailing other men's yachts), and his mother had gambled away her half and run herself into a well-deserved grave.

Cameron and Matamoros didn't accept a settlement. The case went to court, where the yacht-owner was ruined and the young men got away with millions to account for the danger they'd been put through and the emotional damage of losing a friend.

From there they had taken off and turned millions into more. Investments. More cons. Steve's death had only been the beginning. Francis started his own yachting company promoting safety at sea. He had sailors who worked for him, guys like Ernie Carmichael, who would sail with rival companies and catch them breaking maritime laws. At least that's what was claimed. How many of his rivals were framed? How many companies suffered financial and reputational blows because Francis Cameron knew how to pull a good con?

"The start-up capital for his yachting company, Unwind, was solely comprised of the money Cameron and Matamoros got from Steve's accident," Koshida explained.

"So you don't think it was that. An accident."

Koshida shook his head. "They had a negligent boss, a man worth millions who sent them out in an undermanned ship in unsafe waters. The dominoes were all in a row. All they had to do was push."

Jerry saw his brother, jaw set in concentration, shouting orders to his fellow crew in a storm. He watched Steve turn around to ask why they weren't listening, only to be faced with his friends looking cold and conniving. Was it premeditated? Or did one of them get a brilliant idea and act in the moment? All they had to do was push . . .

"I don't understand. How did you figure this out?" *How did it take so goddamn long?*

Koshida spread his hands. "It wasn't their last crime. For thirty years Francis Cameron has been doing whatever it takes to climb. His workers, guys like Matamoros and Carmichael, would get jobs for rival yachting companies and plant evidence they were breaking maritime laws. It's hard to keep track of legalities if you spend most of your time at sea. Suspicion alone can sink a ship. Or a company. Pretty soon Cameron's yachts got the best reputation around. He hammers his clientele with a narrative of safety. Doing everything by the book. Slaps a slogan on every ad campaign, billboard, and life preserver so people know he means it."

Jerry remembered the orange ring sitting in the stern up on deck.

"*Safe to sail in any gale*," he murmured.

Koshida continued. "Cameron sits for interviews to describe the trauma he went through working on an unsafe vessel, seeing a friend drown. He tells the public his life's mission is to prevent incidents like that from happening again."

Jerry's hands had formed fists without him realizing. "Profiting off Steve's death."

Koshida slapped the tabletop. "Exactly. Only a few months ago, someone tipped us off about his history. We looked into it, and everything started to fall apart. Right now, some of my guys have Ernie Carmichael in an interrogation room. Carmichael says he overheard Cameron and Matamoros bragging about . . . well, about how this all began. About that night in the storm with Steve. So I'm here to see how deep the bullshit goes, see if you know anything at all, and inform you your brother's death has been reopened and is being looked at as a homicide. My guess is Carmichael is more involved than he says, and soon he'll be a whistleblower. Fraud, embezzlement, murder . . . Francis Cameron's entire legacy is a sham."

"Who?" Jerry said after a moment.

"Who what?"

"Who tipped you off?"

Koshida sighed. "Not for me to say. But we no longer have contact, so we're doing our best to explore other avenues."

Jerry picked at something dark under his fingernails. "Why can't you contact them anymore? They stop talking?"

"That's one way to put it." Koshida sighed. "They were on *The Old Eileen.*"

Jerry's head spun. His tongue ached; he must have burned it on the hot coffee. He shut his eyes, willing the pain to ease as Koshida went on.

"They were supposed to be on that boat to keep an eye on things. Now everybody's missing. Somehow, Cameron guessed we were on to him, and that's when his family vacation turned into something more."

"What do you mean," Jerry said slowly and made air quotes, "family vacation?"

"I mean that it wasn't just a celebratory trip. The Camerons are on the run."

Jerry bit his tongue to stop his head from swirling. The perfectly seaworthy ship, the missing life raft, Steve facedown in the water. "On the run? You think . . ."

Koshida nodded, the intensity in his gaze unmistakable. "I think they had a plan. I think they fled never intending to return to the United States. I think Cameron and Matamoros purchased a private island outside US waters and one or both are hunkered down there now, likely with Francis's family and at least some of the crew. This is all conjecture, but if Carmichael talks . . ."

Jerry's mouth hung wide, a ringing in his ears as Agent Koshida got to his feet.

"Your brother's killers are almost certainly alive, Jerry. And I'm going to catch them."

Chapter 37

```
Tia Cameron
Call sign: Thimble
Day 9 at Sea
```

TIA GRIPPED THE counter and watched her reflection shake, not from anger or fear but from adrenaline. The squelch of the sailfish's skull rang out in her ears. The feel of such a powerful creature caving in under her blows . . . Tia turned on the sink and stuck her hands into the flow, watching the bright, slippery blood fall away into a watery swirl down the drain.

"Tia," Nico said from the doorway.

She didn't turn around. She'd had to kill that fish. It was damned either way. Francis's face when she threw the mallet down almost made the entire bloody affair worth it on its own.

"Tia," Nico said again, and she faced him, the water still running behind her.

"Close the door," she said, and he did, a question written between his brows.

"I don't—"

She seized his shoulders with both hands and kissed him with none of the tenuous gentleness of before. This was no longer about exploration as it was about the blood that coursed hot in her veins and freckled on her jean shorts.

He tasted like the sea.

They fumbled around the bathroom until Tia ended up sitting on the counter, thighs locked around Nico's waist and hands entangled in his curls. She managed to free one in order to reach behind her and switch off the faucet.

She peeled off Nico's shirt, and he did the same with hers. Hot, bare skin pushed together, blood racing. The cold counter burned her thighs.

"What are we doing?" he asked, grinning between kisses.

"I don't know." Tia matched his grin. "But just in case, lock the door."

He barely said "Aye aye" before they fell into one another again. They made out, him shirtless with his basketball shorts, her in the bloody jean shorts and a red push-up bra. Her back hit the mirror, his hands found her hips, and they kissed until her lips were raw. It was electrifying, so close to the edge but never falling.

He picked up a strand of her hair and played with the dyed ends. "Are you upset about the fish, Tia?"

Was she? She couldn't tell. She hadn't been when she hit it. Her adrenaline had kept her flying too high to make room for anything else. Was she upset now and making out was meant to distract her? Maybe.

But would she brain the fish again for Rylan's sake?

Yes.

"You were about to kill it too," she said, not in accusation. It was true. Nico had offered.

"I was."

"Have you done stuff like that before?"

"I have. That's why I thought it was cruel of your father to ask Rylan. He'd never done it, and to do it right, in the cleanest way so the fish won't suffer, you have to hit it hard and fast. I was worried Rylan would hit it softly and only cause more pain for it. And for himself."

He was right. It was cruel in more ways than one. Tia ran her tongue along her teeth, deep in thought. "Did . . . did I hit it right?"

She braced herself, sure she had caused more harm, that the fish had died in unnecessary agony because she wasn't strong enough or fast enough. After all, she'd never done that before either.

"Yes. Three hits exactly right." Nico almost looked impressed. "Like you'd done it a million times."

It was just another thing that separated her from Rylan, Tia thought. Nico, Francis, and Alejandro could have killed that fish cleanly. Rylan and Lila (who would have been terrified of ending a life and even more so of bloodying her pure white cover-up) could not.

"Do you think Rylan's weak?" She hated herself for asking. Rylan wasn't weak; he was good and kind and loved animals. So why was she always wondering?

Nico blinked, taken aback, but he seemed to give the question serious thought.

"I think he's gentle," he replied. A cop-out.

"And is that good? For him, I mean. Or is it weak?"

He stayed silent for a long time. Maybe he wouldn't answer at all, and they could continue in the blissful reality where Tia never questioned her twin, never again resented him even in the smallest, darkest way for how his behavior put more on her shoulders.

"Weak," Nico said, and the air shifted.

Tia's nod was slight, but he saw it. She had meant him to. It was an acknowledgment between them, one that perhaps spoke more about Tia and Nico than it did about Rylan, but her thoughts were irrefutable.

Rylan Cameron was weak.

Tia despised her own brain betraying her. She would die

for Rylan. But there was an ember inside her that had been fed by the confession, by Nico's agreement.

Tia brushed her lips against his throat, savoring the shudder that ran through him. He ran a finger down the curve of her side, and her skin tingled in return. There seemed to be a thread between them, connecting her heart to his, and both had the power to pull.

It was exhilarating.

She kissed up to his mouth and braided her legs with his. "I think I know what you are," she told him. His call sign. She finally knew it.

"Oh yeah? What's that?"

She breathed in the ocean scent that clung to every inch of his skin and wondered if it were him or the sea that intoxicated her. She wondered if it mattered.

Nico de la Vega. A handsome sailor whose allegiance to the sea is unmatched by any love he has for land. Or those from it.

Seductive, beautiful, magnetic, especially when he opens his mouth. Call sign . . .

She brought her lips to his ear, felt him shiver.

"Siren."

Chapter 38

Rylan Cameron
Call sign: Minnow
Day 9 at Sea

IT WAS RYLAN'S turn to hide in the anchor locker. He half hoped someone would find him, that Tia would come and lock her arms around him and listen to him rant or cry, but she didn't this time.

He longed for his sketchbook, but his hand still hadn't recovered from his past few furious drawing sessions, and the last thing he needed was to walk through the boat and face somebody. Francis's disgust, Lila's disappointment, Alejandro's blank stare . . . Rylan couldn't bear any of it. And maybe seeing Tia would be the worst of all. Maybe looking at his sister would only make him replay the image of her, bloody and angry, a mallet in her hands and something killer in her eyes.

Not for the first time Rylan fantasized about a hole yawning beneath him and dropping him into the sea. His legs would sprout into a tail, gills would slit along his neck, and he'd be where he had always belonged: underwater. Over the years of plucking oysters from their shells and hunting shadows on the sandy floor, he would grow so pale and shimmery that humans would no longer recognize him as one of their own.

He must have been under the sea inside his head for hours. He invented himself anew, the boy with a tail with iridescent scales like the feathers of a hummingbird. His name and past would be discarded, cast out with the tide. The boy with the tail needed none of that. The boy with the tail only swam and fed and took everything he wanted without a sliver of fear.

Maybe he would swim down instead of out and he'd reach a black world where the water was so cold that time could not surpass it. In the depths he'd live forever, eyes stretching huge and teeth growing sharp. A fabled monster of the deep. Beautiful, undefeatable, and most importantly, unafraid.

And one day he might deign to visit the surface, flinch in startlement at the sun. He would peek out from his realm and wonder at the mysteries of the sky and land in the same way he once had for the sea.

Trancelike, Rylan followed his daydream. He climbed the ladder of the anchor locker. He surfaced on deck and blinked at the bright light snared in the clouds.

He'd decide then that the upper world indeed held nothing for him. How could it after centuries of living among luminescent fish and colored reeds? And he'd go back down, this time for the last time, never to be seen again.

Someone caught the hatch before he could close it.

Rylan nearly lost his hold on the ladder.

It was Francis.

"Make some room for your old man," Francis said with none of the ferocity he'd had earlier that morning with the mallet in his hand.

Rylan didn't move. He couldn't move. Not until a tissue-soft hand skated over his own.

Lila.

"Let us in, lovey," she said, soft and silken.

Rylan shrank back inside the anchor locker. His parents joined him, crowded inelegantly like Tia and Nico and Rylan had been only days before.

Were they here for an explanation? An apology? How many times did Rylan need to tell them he couldn't be what they wanted him to be? He couldn't pass the tests, he couldn't endure the trials.

Lila's slender arm enrobed him, and Rylan found himself hyperventilating.

Francis patted his knee. "Deep breaths, boy."

"I don't, I don't, I don't," Rylan dry-sobbed, unable to break out of the horrible loop until his mother pinched his arm.

"I don't know what's wrong with me." He spilled open, everything chaotic and slippery, falling into himself even with his parents positioned to keep him upright.

Francis's hand rested on the back of Rylan's neck, forced him to sit up as Lila ran her fingernails through his hair.

"We're not here to yell," Lila crooned.

"We're concerned about Tia," Francis said, grasp gentle but firm. "She's been . . ."

"Brazen. And unsteady," Lila finished for him. "Since she came home. Don't you agree?"

They weren't here about him. They weren't upset. Rylan tried to reclaim his scattered thoughts. This was about Tia. Of course it was. Tia and her blood-spattered legs. Tia with the mallet raised above her head.

"Sh-she was trying to, she was trying—"

"Tell us what's been going on," Francis said. He brought Rylan's head forward, pressed their foreheads together. Lila traced swirls on Rylan's shoulders and upper back.

"I . . . I . . ." Rylan couldn't focus on anything but his parents' proximity. Their touch. The anchor locker was a safe place. The horrors with the sailfish were over. The fish was dead, Tia had gone to their room, and his parents were here to *comfort* him.

"She's been moody. These outbursts are concerning," Francis said. Rylan couldn't see his face, but he felt their skulls crushed together.

"We just want to know how to help her," Lila murmured. "Like we always try our best to help you."

Had that been *helping*, what they'd asked him to do on deck this morning?

His brain, the part of him that thought like Tia, said no. Hell no. But the rest of him wasn't so sure. He was the problem here. He was the reason MJ was dead, the reason the sailfish suffered. Even Tia wanted him to be braver so they could run away together.

Tia . . . running . . .

Was that what they were getting at? Could they sense their only daughter was ready to leave and never look back?

Francis massaged the back of Rylan's neck. "Come, now. Do we need to get her help?"

How they were going to do that when they weren't even returning to Florida was beyond Rylan, but he could hardly think.

Maybe Tia did need help. She was impulsive and aggressive. How long before she did something she was going to regret again? How long before she left him behind for good? Their plan wasn't thought out. *Nothing* Tia did was thought out. What if she was making a terrible mistake? And he was letting her?

Francis leaned back and pinched Rylan's shoulder firmly. "Tell us what's—"

"She's trying to leave," Rylan whispered, tears slipping through his closed eyelids. "She's planning to run."

If Francis and Lila were shocked, Rylan couldn't read it on

them. Francis withdrew his hand. Lila's swirls became sympathetic back rubs. She kissed his hair and tsked.

"You can't run from family. It isn't right," she said.

"No." Francis cracked a strange, wide smile. "Family's who you run *with*, right, Ry?"

Rylan sobbed. Or maybe he laughed. "Don't tell her . . . I told you . . . please . . . I don't want her to go."

"Don't worry, my son," Francis said warmly, and he gathered Rylan into his arms. "She won't."

Chapter 39

```
Lila Logan Cameron
Call sign: Cassiopeia
Day 9 at Sea
```

A WANNABE-RUNAWAY TEENAGER was such a cliché Lila could almost laugh about it.

So Tia wanted to leave it all behind, hmm? She had looked back on her childhood of flying in private jets between three houses, taking summer trips on the family yacht, attending expensive schools and red-carpet events, and she had made the decision that she could do better alone?

Lila did start laughing. Her shoulders shook, and her lips peeled back. She was out of the horrible little cave of an anchor locker, leaving behind Francis to tend to Rylan. Perhaps she should track down her daughter belowdecks and give her an idea of just how selfish, how stupid she was being.

Since when had Tia Cameron run away from anything? Since when did she give up? Lila felt even more disappointed than she did betrayed. She wasn't certain she would miss Tia if she did run. It had felt something like paradise without her this past year. But Rylan would never be the same if Tia left for good.

And Lila had tried to be a good mother.

God had she tried.

She'd read books like *Setting Limits with Your Strong-Willed Child* and *Parenting in the Spotlight*. She had found good psychologists and teachers. She left discipline up to Francis so she could be the person her children felt safe with.

Perhaps what hurt more than anything was that, in this one way, Tia was finally acting a bit like Lila, who had left behind her parents the moment she'd landed a role in her first movie.

But that was different.

Patrick and Lori Logan were indifferent to Lila's ambition. They were tedious, uninspired nobodies who had lost interest in Lila the minute she no longer looked like their doll.

Lila realized she had locked her jaw from clamping down so hard. She massaged furiously below her ear and loosened the tension until her jaw clicked. She wished there was a perfectly placed vase nearby for her to throw against a wall.

She headed belowdecks. She needed an aspirin. And something to aim her bad energy at.

Alejandro.

Lila went to his room, pressing her index fingers into the sides of her head.

She ran right into someone's chest. "Jesus!"

Lila looked up, ready to slide her hands over Alejandro's shoulders and tote him by his belt to her bed, but it wasn't Alejandro.

It was Nico holding, of all things, a packet of condoms.

"Mrs. Cameron!"

Oh God. Lila studied the young man, trying to remember if she had ever exchanged two words with him this entire trip.

"Nico. Hello."

Nico slipped his hand casually in his pocket and gave Lila a winning smile that was shaped somewhat like his uncle's. "You look lovely."

Lila let herself lean against the doorway. "And you look guilty."

She was half Nico's height but more than double his age with the nice bonus of being the wife of his boss. He didn't dare push past her. It gave Lila the chance to examine him. Closely. Was he trying to sleep with Tia? She had seen them flirting a few times. What Lila wanted to know most was whether this was the first time. Could Tia, careless and bombastic as she was, really have been able to get away with having secret sex on a sixty-foot boat? Lila doubted it. This must be the first attempt, then.

She reached up and fixed Nico's shirt collar, which stuck up on one side.

"I would put those back if I were you. Besides, my daughter is seventeen. A minor, at least for the next few days. And you're . . . let me guess. Twenty-one?"

"Twenty-two," Nico said quietly.

"Right." She patted his chest. "A bit old for a teenager, wouldn't you say?"

"Meant no disrespect," Nico murmured, keeping eye contact with Lila, which was impressive considering he'd just been caught. Most boys his age would be inspecting their feet.

"Of course not." Lila stepped to one side of the doorway to allow him to leave. "I am ecstatic, however, that you were putting safety first." She nodded at his pocket where he'd put the condom packs. "Even if those aren't yours."

Nico dropped his head, sheepish, and returned the condoms to Alejandro's sock drawer. He walked back to the doorway. Lila gave him a dazzling smile and turned to go, but Nico reached out, suddenly, and placed his arm on the doorframe, blocking her path.

"How did you know those weren't mine?"

"Excuse me?" Lila said, giving him the chance to back down.

He didn't. He leaned into his arm so his face was hovering just above Lila's. Lila looked into his eyes and no longer saw a resemblance to Alejandro. She saw Francis. She saw a litany of slimeball film directors and handsy costars and strangers watching her from the street, knowing they'd never get close enough to touch her, but if they could have, they would.

"Familiar with my uncle's condoms, Mrs. Cameron?" He tilted his head, trying to pass off this exchange as playful.

"I could get you fired, *Mr. de la Vega*," Lila replied evenly. "I could get you blacklisted from every Unwind Yachting boat in the world."

Nico was nodding, tongue between his teeth. "True, true. And I could ruin your marriage."

Lila did not consider herself an angry person. But right then, if that perfectly placed vase had been in arms' reach, she might have shattered it into Nico de la Vega's skull.

"Well, thank you," Lila said after a long moment.

The boy had the decency to look confused. "For what?"

"For showing me exactly who you are."

Lila ducked underneath Nico's arm and dusted off her cover-up. She looked back at him over her shoulder with the most girlish, unruffled expression she could muster.

"Oh, and sweetheart? Stay the fuck away from my daughter."

Chapter 40

Tia Cameron
Call sign: Thimble
Day 10 at Sea

TIA WAITED UNTIL after midnight to go see Nico. Alejandro was covering the midnight-to-four-o'clock shift, which meant Nico would be alone in his room. Tia slipped down the hall and knocked lightly on the door, trying to stay quiet in case her father was awake in the primary suite after finishing his watch.

There was no answer, but that wasn't about to stop her. It had been a dismal rest of the day with Rylan sullen and avoiding her after what happened with the sailfish. Not that she was ready to see him either, after what she'd admitted to Nico. Francis and Lila had kept their distance as well, leaving Tia to read a book, study the sails, and remember Nico's hands on her bare skin.

She knocked again before turning the handle and easing inside. Nico's back was to her in bed, but when she touched his shoulder, he startled.

"Tia? It's the middle of the night."

"Sure is. And you're wide awake." Tia sat on the edge of the bed and grinned at him. "Pining over me or something?"

He didn't laugh, only shook his head. "I'm sorry. I'm really tired."

She hid disappointment. "Oh. Then why aren't you asleep?"

He propped his head up on his hand. "Thinking. Not that you'd know much about that."

"Ha ha." She snuggled up beside him, watching his face for a reaction. "Want to talk about what's on your mind?"

Nico shifted away from her ever so slightly.

Her face grew hot. She got the message and sat up. "Sorry."

"It's okay. I'm the one who should be sorry. Really." He summoned a smile and placed a hand over hers. "Let's talk tomorrow, okay?"

"Sure." Tia pulled back and went to the door. "Till tomorrow, Siren."

"Aye aye."

She crept back into the hall and stood suspended by indecision. She sure as hell wasn't tired; she'd been waiting up for hours. Not that she would be able to sleep if she tried. Nico's rejection, no matter how slight, had stung, and she despised the feeling. She made her way up on deck, as was tradition when she couldn't sleep. The hot, pent-up air belowdecks was too much to stand—at least, that was what she told herself.

Tia wasn't exactly in the mood to have a heart-to-heart with Alejandro, who was at the helm (he'd just tell Francis anything she said anyway, and she'd decided not to confront her father about running away so he wouldn't suspect *SOS*), but she figured watching the dark waves for a while would soothe her. There was no point stressing over Nico anyway. They'd talk tomorrow.

Tomorrow . . . It was just past midnight now. That meant tomorrow was officially her and Rylan's eighteenth birthday. They should have been home in Florida days ago, wrapping presents and reclining in the sunroom. Instead they were here, imprisoned on their own boat as they headed to some island.

Tia stopped midships and craned her neck to take in the

stars, which never got old to her, especially this far out at sea. The milky way spilled across the sky, flanked by studded lights in every direction. A brilliant red one seized Tia's attention. It was huge and bright, floating just above *The Old Eileen*'s bowsprit.

Tia screwed her eyes shut and reopened them. It wasn't a star at all. It was Lila Logan Cameron standing at the front-most part of the ship, a lit cigarette balanced between her fingers. What was she doing out of bed?

Tia made her way over to her mother and leaned on the rail beside her. Lila didn't give any indication that she was surprised by her daughter's appearance.

"Isn't that a maritime violation, Mom?" *Didn't you quit smoking two years ago?*

Lila exhaled a ring of pearly smoke. "Who's going to turn me in, lovey?"

Fair point.

"Can I try?"

Lila twirled the cigarette in her fingers, then handed it over without a fight.

Tia pretended she was a movie star like her mother as she took a drag. Smoking with Lila felt very different than smoking with her classmates on Friday nights behind her dormitory. The smoke spread smooth and silklike through her.

"I'm surprised you're up here," Tia commented. It wasn't like her mother to gaze admiringly at the sea. She was dressed in a silk-thin robe with swaths of purple flowers blooming on the shoulders and hem. It clung to her body almost unnaturally, and Tia could follow the glass-shard line of her collarbones beneath the tissue-paper fabric.

Tia put the cigarette to her lips again. It stuck to her mouth, glued with remnants of her mother's designer lipstick. Smoke blew through her, and she handed it back to Lila.

"This boat is a fragile thing," Lila mused without warning or context, reclaiming the cigarette. "Fragile like a family."

Tia frowned around at *The Old Eileen*. She felt it was the opposite, the only sturdy thing in the vicinity. It was quite literally the thing that was keeping their family together. Even if it was by force.

"How do you mean, Mom?"

Lila's hair swayed in tandem with the curling smoke. "It takes so much effort just to keep it afloat. I think without us here it might simply dissolve."

"Uh-huh . . ." Tia plucked the cigarette from Lila's hand and dangled it from between her own teeth as she thought. Lila was wrong. If the world came to an end, *The Old Eileen* might sit on top of it forever. The ship didn't need the Camerons. Maybe nothing did.

"What was it like with me gone?" Tia asked, passing the cigarette.

"Hmm." Lila tapped it on the railing, and ash drifted like snow. "Rather . . . tranquil."

Tia grunted. "The three of you got weirdly close. Like, it's dysfunctional. But close. Like you could all finally connect when I was gone." Tia wanted her mother to shake her head and say *That's preposterous, lovey! We could never be a family without you.*

Lila held in a breath for a long time before blowing out a lopsided ring. "My family was supposed to have four, you know. Two parents. Two children."

Tia tilted her head. Lila didn't often speak about Tia's grandparents, let alone the sister she never had. "I remember."

Tia used to write letters to her aunt, to the little baby that never grew up. It had disturbed her as a six-year-old when she learned that her mother was missing her twin. Tia couldn't imagine until recently what it was like to miss Rylan.

"I sometimes thought my sister would have made us complete," Lila said. "But mostly, I think we were meant to be three."

What was that supposed to mean? Tia leaned more on the railing. Was Lila likening Tia to her dead twin? *We were meant to be three.*

Is that what you think of me? Tia almost asked. *Am I the thing that should have died?*

Tia hadn't considered that leaving behind her family would be ineffective, that they might not even care. She wanted to damage them in the ways she felt they damaged her. She had wanted Rylan to jump on the opportunity to leave their parents behind, wondering desperately where they went wrong. It was supposed to be revenge for a lifetime of being told she was too loud. Too angry. Too many feelings. Not the right dreams. Her every emotion was frowned upon. Her reactions were dramatic. Lila and Francis had given up on Tia long before Tia ever gave up on them. *That* was what Rylan—who Lila always doted on, who Francis always hoped would claim the world—would never understand.

"Didn't you hate your parents?" Tia asked instead, an arm's length between her and her mother.

Lila's dark eyes seemed to gloss. "Doesn't everyone?"

Maybe that was true. Tia wasn't the only one who hated Francis, though. Tia leaned forward. "Mom . . . does Dad have . . . enemies? Like business guys who hate him or something?"

Lila shook her head, which looked less like an answer and more like preening, her hair falling loose from its bun like cobwebs. She turned to Tia. "Can you believe where we are at this very moment?"

Tia slitted her eyes. "What?"

"We're sharing a Marlboro on a sailboat on the Atlantic in June. You, on the eve of your eighteenth birthday."

Tia snatched back what was apparently a Marlboro. "So?"

"So *revel* in that. Someday you'll be married and tired and working and sad, and you'll realize you will never be almost-eighteen smoking with your mother at the bow of a boat again. My beautiful girl, always in such a rush. Always longing for the next thing."

"You're always longing for a past thing," Tia pointed out, but Lila seemed beyond her now, arms outstretched as if she could marbleize and become *The Old Eileen*'s figurehead.

"Revel with me."

Tia tried. What would it be like to exist in her mother's pearlescent bubble of life? Were things really as beautiful to Lila Logan as she seemed to believe they were? Tia breathed in until her lungs were ready to pop, and she let her arms lift like wings.

Then she dropped them, feeling as stupid as her mother looked.

"Okay, can we put a pin in reveling now?"

Lila's eyes were still shut, dark lashes flush against the pink of her cheeks. Why was she wearing mascara this late anyway? No one else was even awake on the boat except Alejandro.

"I could be anyone in moments like this," Lila breathed. "Anyone in the world. Anyone in history."

She sounds almost like . . . me.

Tia held out the cigarette. "You done with this?" she asked her mom.

The orange embers had burned it to a nub.

"I have more," Lila said in answer.

Tia picked a spot in the water and aimed the cigarette at it. It fell, a tiny light spinning out of control in the dark. She squinted in the area where it had landed. Was she imagining things? Or was there something in the water? Something much, much bigger than a cigarette.

"Hey, Mom . . ." Tia tugged on Lila's silk sleeve. "Mom, do you see that?"

She pointed, and the two of them squinted down. Something paler than the sea protruded from its surface, slicing it in half as it swam.

A fin.

"Oh my God!" Tia scream-whispered in delight at the same time as Lila mouthed the same thing and clutched her chest.

It was a shark. Who knew what kind of shark it was, but the longer Tia looked, the more she could make out the massive silhouette moving alongside *The Old Eileen*.

How cool is this, she thought. Rylan would love this.

The creature stayed alongside them for several minutes before sliding out of view. Lila released a breath and retreated from the rail, leaving Tia behind.

Tia tried to estimate how big the shark had been. Nine feet? Ten? She hoped she would see it again in the morning, but in the midst of her excitement, she confronted another feeling, percolating at the very back of her mind.

It almost seemed like the shark was following them.

Chapter 41

```
Lila Logan Cameron
Call sign: Cassiopeia
Day 10 at Sea
```

LILA MADE HER way back to the cockpit and snaked her arms around Alejandro's torso from behind.

"Is it done?" she asked him.

"Almost. Waiting for the right time."

She caught his chin. "Waiting for my order?"

He never faltered. "Of course. What else? Now I need to see where I'm steering, señora."

"Of course," she repeated and released him. Both of their tasks were almost complete. Now she needed the right time. She trailed Alejandro's spine with her thumb. His shirt was almost as paper-thin as her robe.

"I should get to bed, then," she said.

"Dream of greener grass, Señora Cameron," he said calmly. He kept his gaze pointed forward, and she detached from him, leaving a single ghost of a kiss at the nape of his neck.

"Buenas noches, Alejandro."

And she did dream. Not of grass or anything green, though. No, that night, Lila Logan dreamed of fire.

"MOM AND I saw a shark last night," Tia announced at breakfast.

Alejandro had sliced the sailfish meat into delicate, salmon-like pieces that the family spread on their toast. Lila cut up her fish and toast into minuscule bites before sampling a piece. She chewed it thoughtfully. It could use some cream cheese.

"A shark?" Rylan sat up straight. He had been silent all morning as well as late to meeting in the salon. But at least he'd stopped crying, poor dear. "What kind?"

"What time last night?" Francis narrowed his eyes. "I was on watch from eight to midnight."

"A big one," Tia said with a mouthful of fish, not looking at her brother. "It was too dark to tell exactly what kind, but it was like ten or eleven feet." She held up her hands. "The fin was like this tall, I think."

"So you saw it as well, Lil?" Francis studied his wife as he sipped his orange juice.

"I did," Lila admitted. Should she have told Tia to keep quiet? No, that would have just attracted more suspicion. Her conversation with Nico had put her on edge, even more than she already was thanks to Francis's little surprise change in plans and the fact that her only daughter was plotting to escape their family and never speak to them again. "I couldn't sleep, so I went to get some fresh air. Turns out Tia couldn't sleep either."

"Yeah . . ." Francis set his glass down with a clatter. "Seems no one's been getting decent sleep around here lately."

Rylan hadn't touched his food. Did he regret confessing about Tia's plans to run away? Lila couldn't know for certain, but she saw how much the knowledge weighed on him. It was right of him to unburden himself to his parents.

As for Tia running . . . it was obsolete, as far as Lila was concerned. Once they were back home (and they *would* get back home) everything would change for the better, and if Tia still wanted to go, Lila would hold the door for her. Maybe she'd come back in a few years mellowed out and grateful. Or maybe she'd get mixed up with more boys like Nico de la Vega, and Lila would find her in a ditch someday.

Only time would be kind enough to tell.

"Rylan, darling," Lila said, "why don't you go get one of your animal books? We can try to identify the kind of shark your sister and I saw."

To her relief, Rylan got up right away to do just that.

Francis sawed at his toast. "Did Alejandro see the shark? He was on watch at that time, wasn't he?"

Lila smiled breezily. She had hoped that the lovely moment she and Francis had with Rylan in the dark little hatch would have rectified her husband's coldness toward her. Tia was planning to abandon her, abandon them all. There was nothing like having a common enemy to smooth over cracks in a family foundation.

"Alejandro was in the cockpit steering, dear. Tia and I saw the shark more toward the front of the boat."

"The bow," Francis corrected.

"Naturally."

Rylan came back in with a marine biology book clutched to his chest. He pushed aside his untouched breakfast and opened it to the sharks and rays section. Lila peered at the photographs of the dinosaur-like monsters. The dark shape in the water from last night could have been any of them, for all she knew. She hoped secretly that it had been a dolphin or a small whale. A shark following their ship was nausea-inducing. What if someone went overboard?

"A reef shark maybe. Or even a tiger!" Tia pointed at several pictures in excitement.

Lila expected Rylan to look terrified by the possibility of a tiger shark trailing after their family boat, but he instead seemed enthralled.

Guess we aren't as similar as I thought.

"I want to go see if I can spot it," Rylan said, and he bolted from the room, bringing the shark book with him.

Tia, probably loath to be left alone at the table with her parents, retreated out of sight down the hall to her cabin. It was strange that they hadn't gone together. Lila decided to take it as a good sign that Rylan was finding his own footing.

Francis dabbed at a stain on his shirt collar, then folded his napkin and replaced it in his lap. Lila drained her glass of iced lemonade.

"You weren't in bed for a while after I got off watch," he said, picking up his fork again.

Lila nodded, nibbled at the toast.

"You know, Lil, if you can't sleep, you can wake me up. I can help."

Lila stood and rifled through the refrigerator to get cream cheese. "I know, Francis. You've just been so exhausted since . . . this week."

"That's the price of being captain. Even if there were no unfortunate incidents, I wouldn't get good sleep."

Lila sat back down and spread the cheese over the fish. "You see? It isn't fair to wake you."

Francis considered this. "What kept you up?"

Lila took a bite. The cheese added a creaminess to the meal that was sorely needed. Delicious. She should tell Alejandro to add this for next time. Perhaps with a hint of lemon zest as well?

"You know I worry, Francis. About you. The twins."

"What about the twins?"

Lila scoured her brain and settled on something simple

and true. "College, if you must know. With everything so up in the air, with Tia so . . . volatile . . . I'm just agonizing over their education." She knew this was a sore spot for Francis.

Francis sat back in his chair. Then he laughed, long and belly deep with a full smile. Lila relaxed.

"Oh, Lil . . . Is that all? Lila, love, look around us. Look at me, look at you. Neither of us went anywhere near college." He opened his arms as if their multimillion-dollar boat was evidence enough that they hadn't needed college. Where had this laissez-faire attitude toward higher education been when he made Rylan cry over picking a lesser school?

Men are fickle.

"You're right," she responded.

He leaned across the table and squeezed her hand, none the wiser to what truly plagued her mind. Then his gentle squeeze turned into a vise grip.

Lila's blood ran cold.

"Tell me the truth, Lila," he commanded, his voice dropping to a baritone croon.

Her body clenched. Had Nico told Francis what he suspected? Would he betray his uncle just to kiss up to his new boss?

She gave him a carefully perplexed look. "Francis, let go."

He did. He sat back in his chair and folded his hands over his stomach. "I wouldn't worry so much about the kids, Lila. They're Camerons. They'll have it all."

He didn't know.

Her smile felt fluttery and breathless as she stood again. Her hand tingled with the memory of his strength. "Of course, love."

Francis raised a glass to her in some kind of backhanded toast. "Just as long as they learn how to take it."

Chapter 42

Jerry Baugh

JERRY DIDN'T UTTER a word the whole way to the fishing spot. Lainey sat at his side in the cockpit of *Sheila 2.0* as they bumped over the swells. She didn't speak much either.

Agent Koshida had left Jerry with his card, which Jerry now had in his pocket, the only tangible reminder that he had been there. That the FBI had really showed up on Jerry's dock step. That Steve's death had really been . . .

They jetted over the water, pushing eighty. Ninety. Jerry had to hold onto his cap to keep it from tumbling into oblivion while he steered with one hand. Lainey grabbed onto the edges of her seat, sweat shirt fluttering.

At least the cat was back in the marina on *The Old Eileen*. He wouldn't have enjoyed a ride like this.

Lainey mouthed something to him as she hugged her sweat shirt around her body.

"What?" Jerry shouted.

"Aren't we almost there?" she yelled.

Jerry realized he hadn't been paying attention. He was just going. They were a couple miles from the coast at this point, and this was as good a spot as any. He switched off the engine and regretted it immediately. This far from land, the soundscape smoothed into lapping waves and wind. It was a peacefulness that he lived for, but now he couldn't stand it.

Jerry stomped over to his fishing supplies and clattered through the various rods to find the right one. He huffed to himself as he blundered with the line and bait. And he made a back-of-the-throat primal sound as he threw the line out into the blue.

Lainey watched him, taking a seat on an overturned bucket. "You think we'll catch something out here?"

"Dunno." Jerry mounted a second rod and tossed out the line. "Don't care."

He stood still for a second before realizing there was no greater form of torture than this: quietly watching the water that killed Steve.

The water those men pushed him into.

"I need that!" Jerry barked at Lainey, who scrambled off the bucket. He picked it up, letting it scrape the deck, and grabbed fistfuls of tackle, letting it knot up like spider webs and filled the bucket, then dumped it out and did it all over again.

Lainey pursed her lips in concern. "Jerry . . . You said a guy came to talk to you."

He slammed the bucket onto the deck and hoped it left a dent.

"So what did he say? Something about the missing people?"

Something about the missing people indeed. Something about how that pretty, rich family were his little brother's killers. Something about how Jerry no longer cared whether the Camerons lived or died. It wasn't the kids' faults, he supposed. Or the wife's for that matter. But he didn't care right now. He didn't fucking care, and if the whole lot of them were feeding fish underwater, the world would be better for it.

Jerry whipped his cap off his head and twisted it into a pretzel. Wished it would snap. He let it unwind, wrinkled and frayed, then shoved it back on his head.

"Jerry . . ." Lainey pressed, and he whirled on her.

"I prefer to fish alone," he said.

She went silent. He turned his back.

It's what he'd said to Sheila, who had tried so hard to enjoy what Jerry enjoyed but had fallen so short.

I prefer to fish alone, he'd told her in a moment of pure frustration after his wife had blubbered like a baby when he'd put a spike through a red snapper's brain. They had been fighting for hours. For years, if Jerry were being honest.

Had they ever been in love? Time made it impossible to remember.

I think you prefer to live alone too, Sheila had said.

Jerry dumped out the bucket again and took a seat on it. Looking out. Open water. Quiet water. Devouring. Why shouldn't he mine the ocean for all it was worth? He'd never get back what it had stolen from him.

Sunlight dappled the sea. Jerry's head was heavy and drooped into his hands. He began to quake with heaving, angry jolts that shook his chest and belly. He raised his head and it only got worse. The light on the water was blinding. It could have been blades or diamonds. Jerry just wanted it to break.

He was on his feet then, bucket dangling from one hand.

"Goddamn it . . ." he murmured, but it wasn't loud enough. "Goddamn it!" He raised the bucket into the air—"God-*fucking*-damn it!"—and brought it down.

The plastic bounced off the deck harmlessly, and so he scooped it up again and threw it overboard. Then the snarled handful of tackle and the container of bait and the nearest rod. All of it went over and shattered the surface, but not hard enough. He searched for something bigger, something more devastating, and he found it: an ice cooler for keeping fish. He picked it up, lifting with his legs, and brought it to the edge. Raised it high.

A hand touched his shoulder. Lainey.

"That hurts the fish," she told him gently.

Jerry blinked at his equipment littering the surface, some of which was already sinking below. He swallowed a lump in his throat. "Uh, sorry . . . Shit." He set the cooler aside.

Then he jumped in.

Blue digested him, seeping past his protective layers, his T-shirt, his skin, and closing in on him. It would eat him if he stayed down here. He hadn't been submerged in decades, hadn't done a goddamn thing more with the water than fish it.

He broke the surface, no longer able to distinguish between his tears and the ocean as he gathered what he could of the gear.

Lainey scurried on deck. She lowered the swim ladder, and he climbed it, the bucket slung over one shoulder, the rod in his hand. He accepted the ragged towel she handed him and set the soaking fishing gear in a pile.

"Take us home, Lainey." His voice cracked, and his hand went to his head to adjust the Bass Pro Shops cap. It wasn't there.

Jerry peered over the side to see the twisted hat floating just beneath the surface.

"Don't you want to—" Lainey started, but he shook his head and went to put away the rods and lines.

"No, Lainey." He left puddles wherever he stepped. The ocean was unscathed, but here he stood, sopping wet.

Jerry turned on the engine, words cascading away at the sound.

"Leave it behind."

Chapter 43

```
Rylan Cameron
Call sign: Minnow
Day 10 at Sea
```

RYLAN HAD FINISHED a drawing for Tia just as the sun started setting. He hugged the sketch to his chest as he went down the hall. He felt more clearheaded than he had in days. His parents weren't angry with him. They were going to ensure they all stayed together as a family. He wasn't going to lose Tia. He wasn't going to lose anyone. He and Tia hadn't spoken, but their birthday was tomorrow, and they'd have to make up for that. She'd been trying to help him by killing the fish. She'd done it out of mercy.

Rylan paused by the door to Nico and Alejandro's bedroom. It was open, and Lila stood inside, facing the beds as if deep in thought.

"Mom?" Rylan stepped into the room. "What are you doing here?"

Lila turned and summoned a quick smile. "Looking for Alejandro."

She must have read the question in his expression. "To ask him about what desserts he could bake for your birthday, which reminds me . . ." Lila waved him into the hallway and closed the door behind her and continued. "I have some options for you to pick out your birthday dinner. Alejandro wants to do some cooking prep tonight."

Rylan tucked his drawing away, folded neatly in his pocket. "What are the options?"

"He suggested all of your favorites: pesto pasta, grilled cheese, or meat loaf. Tia said she was happy with any of them."

It was a far cry from the resplendent feast Alejandro had prepared last year: tea cakes and little sandwiches and caprese salad. By the time they had reached dinner, however, no one's appetite remained.

"Meat loaf, please," Rylan said, nauseated at the memory. It would be hearty and savory, especially with Alejandro's special herbal garnish. And it was nothing like last year.

"Meat loaf it is." Lila kissed him on both cheeks. "I'm going to go check for Alejandro on deck and let him know." She fussed with his hair. "Tomorrow you're eighteen, my love!"

"Tomorrow," Rylan repeated as Lila whisked away.

He went to the salon and folded onto the couch. Pirate, who'd been cocooned in the corner, stretched and came to make biscuits on Rylan's chest.

"Hey, boy . . ." Rylan scratched behind Pirate's ears, guilt seeping through him. He hadn't been paying the cat as much attention as he deserved in the week since MJ's death.

Pirate rubbed his face against Rylan's knuckles, then bounded away. MJ and her cat hadn't been on the ship during the twins' birthday last year. MJ would have interfered—unlike Lila, she wasn't afraid to rile Francis up—just as she would have interfered if she'd been alive when they found out Francis wasn't taking them to Florida. MJ would have been even more aggressive than Tia.

But maybe that would have just made things worse, like it did when MJ forced the truth out of him about the tests.

Rylan glanced around for Pirate, who had clambered his way to the freezer, pacing along the top of it. He saw Rylan looking at him and meowed insistently.

Rylan rose from the couch and picked up the cat. He hugged him to his chest, suddenly feeling cold. Pirate meowed again.

He's trying to tell me something.

Pirate strained in his arms to return to the freezer, but Rylan set him on the floor instead.

His heartbeat didn't consume him. In fact, it didn't seem to be beating at all, as if he was frozen himself, blood icelike in his veins.

Alejandro had suggested meat loaf for the twins' birthday dinner. Meat loaf which would need to be kept in a freezer on a voyage this long. Meat loaf which he had seen sitting on the counter in a sweaty plastic bag on the day MJ died to make room to store her body.

Only it wasn't on the counter anymore.

If Alejandro could make meat loaf for dinner, he must have been able to store it back inside the freezer. But there shouldn't be room for that, unless . . .

Rylan touched the handle of the freezer. The last thing in the universe he wanted to do was open it up. Maybe Alejandro had covered the body with a tarp and put the frozen food over it so it didn't go to waste? Maybe Rylan should go to Lila and tell her he actually wanted grilled cheese, something simple with nice, refrigerated ingredients.

He should and maybe he would, but first he had to know what was in there.

Maybe he owed it to MJ to look at what he'd done to her.

Pirate mewled and brushed up against Rylan's legs. Warning him.

"I know, boy," Rylan murmured, and he opened the lid of

the freezer. He sucked in his breath, not making sense of what he saw. The meat loaf, crusted with ice, lived in the bottom of the freezer along with a bag of peas and a plastic-wrapped lamb chop. Leftover sailfish was packaged in another corner. That was it.

The corpse was gone.

Chapter 44

Tia Cameron
Call sign: Thimble
Day 10 at Sea

TIA LEAFED THROUGH the maps in the chart house. Nico would be getting off watch at midnight, which was in two hours, and she could finally get him alone, get him to talk about why he'd been distant the past day.

Tia pilfered a ruler and a small compass from the counter drawer. Plan SOS would be enacted in less than twenty-four hours. They had to be ready.

It felt surreal that she would be eighteen tomorrow. In the midst of all of this, her birthday seemed like a fake thing from another life. Her gift for Rylan—a cone snail shell from their first-ever scuba dive that she'd strung on a leather necklace—was packed securely in her suitcase. As for herself, she had snuck into her parents' bathroom and slipped her mother's favorite lipstick into her pocket. She'd return it after she used it for her birthday tomorrow. Not for the first time, she pictured the look on Nico's face when he saw her wearing it.

The hatch from the cockpit to the companionway creaked, and Tia froze, fantasies evaporating. She couldn't be caught by Francis or Alejandro in here. She pocketed the ruler and compass and slapped the light switch to douse the chart house in darkness. There was really only one place to hide—under the counter—so that's where she crouched and held her breath.

White sneakers descended the companionway.

Alejandro.

The maps in Tia's arms crinkled softly as she shrank back farther under the counter. When Alejandro caught Rylan and Nico poking around to get the radio, he'd been none too pleased. And she didn't have backup.

The white sneakers walked by her, and she began to relax, but then they stopped in the middle of the room. Alejandro bent down, and Tia fought the instinct to attack him before he could attack her. But neither of them attacked. He hadn't seen her. He was fiddling with the bilge panel on the floor, wedging his fingers into the small hole to pry it open. His other hand supported a black duffel bag slung over his shoulder.

What the hell is he doing?

Tia held still. It was so dark that even if Alejandro faced her, there was a chance he wouldn't make out her shape under the counter, but the darkness made Tia more afraid instead of less. What reason could he have for not turning on the light?

He detached the panel from its place and set it aside, making an effort to do so quietly.

He doesn't want anyone to see this, Tia thought. What was in that bag?

Alejandro lay flat on his belly and dangled the duffel into the pitch-black hole. He waited for a moment, then let it go, and Tia heard a thump and a splash. Was there water down there? Maybe he was hiding stolen treasure, although gold or gems would have made a bigger noise. Stacks of cash, then? But then he'd be risking it getting wet down there.

Alejandro replaced the bilge panel and climbed the companionway back to the cockpit where Nico was on watch.

Quick as a cat, Alejandro vanished, leaving Tia to breathe in relief and crawl out from under the counter.

She flicked on the lights and knelt on the floor. The panel was much harder to get loose than Alejandro had made it look. It was heavy and firmly in place. The only way to pick it up was by crushing your smallest fingers into the little circle and lifting it by pure pinkie strength.

Tia almost gave up when the panel finally lifted. She leaned it against the wall and found a flashlight in one of the counter drawers to shine into the dark opening. She flicked it on, and it bathed the bilge in red light, which was the only kind of light allowed on a boat at night. It was supposed to help you see better in the dark.

A few inches of murky water flooded the bottom of the pit, which was at least a six-foot drop. The duffel bag sat in the muck, water seeping into it slowly. There was no way Tia could reach the bag, and even if she jumped down there, there was no ladder to get back up.

"Damn," she muttered and put the panel back.

Tia headed toward her room. Before she'd even reached the hallway, she bumped right into Rylan in the salon.

"Hey," she said awkwardly. Should she apologize for being distant? She searched his face, which looked blanched and sunken. "Ry? What . . . what's going on?"

He seized her shoulders. "She's not there, Tia. I don't know if she ever was."

"What? Who's not where?"

He raised a trembling finger, pointing at the freezer, and Tia's throat went dry. She crossed the salon in two strides to reach the galley and opened the freezer before she could think about what she was doing.

Empty.

Pirate, who had hopped onto the counter as if to get a better vantage point of the freezer, whined loudly. Tia scooped him up with one arm and grabbed Rylan's hand.

"Come here." She towed them to the chart house, making sure no one else was in there with them. She turned to her brother, petting Pirate to calm them both down. "I just saw Alejandro drop a black duffel bag in that bilge."

Rylan wobbled. "You think he put her in there?"

"I don't know. I don't *think* it was big enough." At least, she was pretty sure. "But why would he be putting anything in there at all? There was water at the bottom, you're not supposed to store stuff in water. What if he's hiding something?"

Rylan looked doubtful. Tia knelt by the bilge again.

"Help me with this," she ordered, and they struggled to reopen the weighty panel.

Tia stared down at the duffel bag. It definitely wasn't big enough for a body. Or heavy enough. Alejandro would have had a tougher time if a full-grown woman was zipped up in there. But then where was MJ? It's not like she got up of her own accord to wander around the ship.

Although . . .

The water in the hallways leading like a trail to their bedroom.

"What if . . . ?" Rylan whispered.

What if she's somehow still alive?

"No." Tia said with force. It was impossible. It was wishful thinking. "Keep your eyes on me, okay? I'm gonna go down there. Do you think you can pull me back out?"

Rylan pressed his hands to either side of his head, as if trying to keep his skull intact. "I don't know, I don't know . . ."

"Rylan." Tia willed herself to be patient, but now wasn't the time for his anxiety. They needed to know what was in that bag.

"I'm going down there," Tia told him. "And you're going to pull me back out. Okay?"

"Oh God . . ." Rylan moaned, shutting his eyes. "I'm gonna be sick."

Tia swallowed down frustration. They didn't have time for this.

She steeled herself and dropped into the deep, dark belly of the ship. She landed in several inches of water, caught herself on the slimy wall before she slipped more.

"I need light, Ry," she hissed up at her brother.

No answer. He was still tailspinning.

Tia inhaled and summoned her best radio announcer voice, even putting her hand over her mouth to mimic muffled static. "Ksshh, this is Thimble to Minnow. I repeat, Thimble to Minnow, come in, over."

She waited. The flashlight popped on overhead, and Rylan's face appeared above her.

"I'm here. Over," he managed to say.

Even with the distant light, the bilge remained mostly shrouded, but it was just enough to make out the dark shape in the water. The black duffel bag.

Tia bent down and found the zipper. "Move the light to the left a little," she called up. The light cast a gentle reflection on the shiny zipper teeth. The bag was brand-new.

"Ready?" she said, more to herself than to Rylan. She set her jaw. No matter what was in the bag, she was not going to scream. Unless it was tarantulas or something. Then maybe she'd let out a modest shriek.

"Ready," she repeated and slid the zipper open.

She blinked and tried to make sense of what she saw. The bag was full to the brim of cooking oil. Bottle after bottle of cooking oil, some of it uncapped and oozing amber fluid over plastic.

"It's just oil," Tia called up to her brother. Did cooking oil expire? Had Alejandro just been doing his duties as head chef, squirreling away their trash until they could properly dispose of it on land? She felt stupid but mostly relieved.

"Cooking oil?"

Tia rummaged through the bottles. They were almost all full, which was odd, but nothing else was in the bag except for an oily pack of matches buried at the bottom. She wiped her hand on her shorts. "Yeah. Hang on . . . Shine the light around for me?"

Rylan reached his arm down to light up the rest of the bilge, and Tia looked around in renewed horror as the red light illuminated the small room. This wasn't the bilge where the dive equipment was kept, yet here she was surrounded by oxygen tanks. Stacks and stacks of metal cylinders filled the space around the duffel bag.

Oxidizer. Fuel. Fire.

Tia was standing inside a bomb.

She zipped the duffel closed, surprised that her finger muscles still functioned. "Rylan, get me out of here," she said with as much calm as she could muster.

"What is it?"

"Just get me out."

Rylan's voice ramped up an octave. "Just tell me. Is it MJ? Is she down there? Why would they move her? She's already been through enough—"

"Rylan, get me the hell out!"

She didn't mean to let fear get to her, but it had. It tore through her carefully gritted teeth and slammed into her brother, whose outstretched hand began to shake. Tia fought against her rising heart rate. She was standing in a bomb. What if Alejandro was about to set it off somehow? What if she accidentally set it off herself?

Tia jumped to grab Rylan's hand, but it was too sweaty and her grip slipped.

"Rylan!" she cried, knowing full well she wasn't helping him keep calm, but she couldn't keep calm herself. She needed him to pull her out for once, goddamn it.

"I'm trying!" he snapped back, but he was shaking too badly to be of any help.

Tia battled the anger that spread in her, seeded by terror. "It's not a body, Ry," she assured him. "Okay? MJ isn't in here. Just please, please get me out."

Rylan withdrew his hand, wiped it on his shirt and stuck it back in. Tia jumped for it, and this time her grip held.

"I . . . can't . . . pull you . . . up," Rylan grunted between clenched teeth as he heaved.

I knew he'd gotten too thin.

"Just . . . hold on." Tia pulled herself into a half chin-up and managed to grab the lip of the opening. The ship lurched, and her knees crashed into the wall.

She let go of Rylan's hand, and he helped her up by her waist once her upper body gained purchase. The two of them fell back in a heap on the chart house floor, which moved beneath them.

Sea must be rough tonight.

Rylan switched off the red flashlight. His frightened face searched hers. For a single split second, Tia wanted to shake him and scream.

Why are you so helpless?

Instead she drank in deep breaths and pulled the bilge panel over the dark opening in the ground. "The oxygen tanks are in there. Maybe he moved them, or maybe there have been extra all along." Her skin felt poisoned where she'd touched the bag. She dragged her greasy hands over her shorts. "With the cooking oil, all you have to do is drop a lit match, and it'll blow right through the hull."

"Holy shit." Rylan snatched Pirate into his arms like a stuffed animal.

"Holy shit," Tia agreed, pieces falling into place. She knew who Alejandro Matamoros took orders from. "We have to get out of here."

Rylan looked at her, clutching the cat.

Tia's lower lip trembled. "Someone's going to sink the ship."

Chapter 45

Jerry Baugh

JERRY SLOUCHED ON the deck of *Sheila 2.0*, beer in hand. Lainey was propped up against the back of the cockpit bench beside him, nursing her own can. Apparently her preference for rum was no match for the weight of the day on her shoulders.

After their aborted fishing attempt, Jerry had driven them back to the marina, only to grab the case of beer from *The Old Eileen* and take *Sheila* back out to watch the sunset over the harbor.

Behind them, *The Old Eileen* sat unassumingly at the edge of the dock, bathed in orange light. From here, Jerry could see her two masthead lights winking in the twilight. From here, she looked normal. Beautiful, even.

"That thing's cursed," he slurred, waving the beer toward the sailboat. "All o' 'em are."

"What? Sailboats?"

"Yup." Jerry drank. Why was Lainey even still there? She could have gotten off when he made the beer stop. Although she was being paid by the hour. Christ, he was gonna owe this kid a small fortune.

But it would be worse to be alone.

"We weren't meant to cross oceans. S'why people get seasick." He hiccupped. "And drown."

"What about boats like *Sheila*?" Lainey countered, patting a hand on the deck of the lobster boat.

"Ehhh. My brother woulda called this thing a *stinkpot*." Jerry dragged out the word, popping the *T* at the end extra loud. "Not lika real boat, he'd say. Defies the wind."

Lainey let her bald, prickly head fall back. "All boats defy the water."

"Mmm, and the sailors defy their fears. Like Steve." Jerry hoisted his beer can in the air.

Lainey followed suit. "To Steve, then," she said and drank.

"To all the poor bastards who tried to defy." Jerry clattered his can against Lainey's, then knocked it back into his mouth. There wasn't a drop left.

"You know, I coulda been just like him," Jerry informed the bottom of the empty container. He cranked his arm back to toss the thing into the sea, then hesitated. Something about Lainey's gentle hand on his shoulder earlier that morning stopped him.

That hurts the fish.

He grumbled and searched the case for a fresh beer. He should have invited Madden to join them. He'd enjoy hearing her sour take on Koshida's information bomb about the Camerons.

"Just like Steve?" Lainey prompted.

"Always looked up to him." Jerry bent back the can's tab. "Always admired what he did with his life. Coulda been me on the boat in the storm."

It could have been, but it wasn't. Jerry was the practical one. He'd traded his life for a nice, motor-powered stinkpot, not a fantasy-fueled sailboat. Look at all he had to show for choosing *Sheila 2.0*. An empty cooler for dead fish. A lifetime of quiet moments on an uncaring sea that still scared him half to death. Jack shit, essentially.

"I'm gonna sell her," Jerry murmured to himself.

Lainey looked his way. *"Sheila?"*

"No. *Eileen.*" That was that. He'd made up his mind at last. It was the practical thing to do after all; it always had been.

"Oh." Lainey took a swig of her beer, grimaced at the taste. "Then what?"

"With the money?" He hadn't thought that far. There weren't enough things in the world, it seemed, to spend a million dollars on. "Hell if I know." He squinted to focus. "Maybe buy a nice cat bed or something."

Lainey laughed. "Million-dollar cat bed, huh? For a cat you haven't even named?"

Jerry scowled at her. "I'll fix *Sheila* up a bit. Lord knows she could use it."

"I meant in your life, old man. Or what's left of it," Lainey teased. "So you sell the sailboat. You fix up *Sheila*, buy all the little things you can think of. Then what? What do you do with the rest of your life?"

She'd struck a chord, but he didn't want her to see that. He was old. Not as old as this twentysomething might think, but old enough to know he wasn't gonna last forever. What would he do with the time he had left?

"Fish," he answered, but for once it didn't sit right with his gut. Though, maybe his stomach had turned because of the beer. He hadn't eaten since breakfast, a snapper and black coffee. Same thing he'd had for thirty years.

"What would you do?" he asked slowly, the sentiment foreign on his tongue. "With the money, I mean. If it was yours."

Lainey set her beer aside and leaned back, hands behind her head. "I'd buy a boat. Leave everything behind."

Jerry swallowed. "Like Steve."

"Like you." Lainey's eyes were full of the sunset sky. "I'd bet it all. Sell my soul, whatever I gotta do, you know?"

Jerry snorted and scratched at his stomach, uneasy. "Risk joining ranks with all the poor bastards in their watery graves?"

Lainey's fist tightened around the can. "Yes."

Jerry shut his eyes hard. He opened them again, but the blurry sunset scenery remained unchanged. He shifted around and watched the last tendrils of daylight recede on the horizon. "Well." He took a swallow of beer, realized he couldn't stand the taste, and spat it back out. "You're braver than me, then."

Lainey reached over and plucked the drink from his hands. "Let's get you back to the marina, Jerry."

"Arigh'," he whispered and grabbed the can back from her, but this time not to drink. Jerry leaned out over the side of his boat with a sense of finality and poured the beer out into the sea.

Just in case all those bastards got thirsty.

The Goss's Day in the Life: How Celebs Spiff Up Family Events

Double Trouble: The Cameron Twins' Sweet Sixteen

M. EMMIX

For the most part, Rylan and Taliea, the teenage twins of movie star Lila Logan and Unwind Yachting Co. CEO Francis Cameron, have kept out of the spotlight. Even so, the family of four lives stylishly, splitting their time between several homes across the States (and even taking day trips occasionally on their family yacht)! On June 5, the twins turned sixteen, and Lila Logan found a fabulous way to celebrate them outside their ski home in Aspen, Colorado.

Lila penned personal invitations to a "black-tie Alpine ball" in honor of her son and daughter. What does *black-tie Alpine* mean? For the Camerons, it means Brioni tuxedos, cocktail dresses, private catering, and seventy of their closest family friends (from A-list celebrities to tech founders), all partying in front of a gorgeous summer Rocky Mountain backdrop! Taliea posted a glamorous photo of her and her brother wearing matching suits on her Instagram account (@tiacamspam) with the caption "No one can tell us apart."

Lila and Francis gifted their teens not one but TWO brand-new silver Lexus IS cars, which are pictured with the twins on Lila's Instagram (@lilalogancameron). (Compare this to my sweet sixteen where we ordered sheet cake and watched Robin Williams movies on a box TV in my basement.) It sure does pay to be American royalty, huh? But it makes you wonder, if this is what the Cameron twins get for their sixteenth birthday bash, how're they going to top it when they turn seventeen? Eighteen? The years only get crueler, my friends.

Chapter 46

Lila Logan Cameron
Call sign: Cassiopeia
Day 10 at Sea

LILA BURST INTO the chart house. She couldn't help her excitement: it might as well have been Christmas Eve. First, Tia and Rylan's birthday was tomorrow. And second, Lila knew that this would be her last night on this godforsaken ship.

"There you two are!" she gushed. The twins were kneeling on the floor of the chart house, staring at each other with faces as white as ghosts. "Why the long faces, my loves? It's your birthday eve."

The twins got to their feet, moving a little too quickly for it to be normal. Must be birthday nerves, Lila decided. Big things seemed to happen to the Camerons on June 5.

"So sorry to interrupt, but you're going to need to move this party to your cabin."

Tia blinked. "Why? It's not even midnight yet."

Lila clasped her hands. "Because it's your birthday tomorrow, and the birthday fairy doesn't like it when prying children see her setting up. Plus, the weather has soured a bit, so best to hunker down for the evening."

"Mom . . ." Tia's embarrassed-by-her-mom voice was way

more toned down than usual. She didn't even add a whine when she said *Mom*.

Rylan's head dropped to give him a wonderful view of his bare feet.

"Time for bed," Lila said in a singsong voice.

"You seem awfully cheerful," Tia eyed her with suspicion.

"I got a good night's sleep for once. First night in a week I didn't dream about Nico flipping MJ's dead body faceup in the water." The description got the desired effect from Tia, whose eyes went huge. She didn't question any more as Lila ushered them out of the chart house, through the salon, and down the hall to the cabins.

Francis materialized from the primary suite and roped his arm around Lila's waist. "Locking up the prisoners for the night, Lil?"

Tia rounded on him. "That supposed to be funny, Dad?"

Oh God. Lila just needed to keep the peace a few more hours. She already felt herself on edge now that Nico de la Vega knew about her affair.

"Go get your pajamas on," Lila snapped, but her daughter didn't spare her a glance.

"No, really. I'm curious. You think you're funny?"

Francis smiled, all too pleased. "Categorically."

"Right, I get it," said Tia. "We're prisoners because you kidnapped us, right? Hilarious."

Rylan had gone gray, and Lila almost smacked her daughter across the face. Couldn't she see how this was affecting her brother?

"Tia. Bed. Now."

Again, Tia didn't look her way.

"Listen to your mom," Francis said like he was playing a father on television. Like he had a paunch and beard and a waggling finger. *Listen to your mother, now.*

"My love," Lila said, stepping right into her daughter's view. "Go lie down. The birthday fairy—"

"What is going on, Dad?" Tia shouted over Lila's head. "What have you been ordering Alejandro around to do? What's happening in the bilges?"

Francis's brows pinched. "The bilges?"

Lila clapped her hands in Tia's face, and Tia startled. "Young lady. I want you in bed. Now."

"Tia . . ." Rylan pleaded.

Finally, Tia looked at Lila, and the battle shifted to center on them.

"Why are you always defending him?"

Just a few more hours, Lila thought, her core clenched. *Everyone needs to remain calm for just a few more hours.*

"Darling, I'm de-escalating. There is no point in this right now."

Tia whipped her head back and forth furiously. "It's not about there being a point. The point is that we don't let him get away with this. He's taking us somewhere! And either you're a victim too and you're standing by, or you're part of it! Either way you're letting it happen."

Lila wished she could see some of herself in this fierce and fiery young woman. Maybe their eyes were the same shape and shade (almond and black-cherry soap). Maybe their complexion was similar enough to be a gradient in a paint catalog (natural linen to sand dollar). But if Lila hadn't been there when the doctor pulled a slippery infant out of Lila's body, she'd be hard-pressed to find evidence that this girl was her own.

Tia was right that Lila didn't know anything about a plan. But she was wrong to think her mother was standing by, that she ever just stood by. Tia didn't know a thing about her. She'd never bothered to.

"Bed," Lila said. "I am no longer asking."

Tia snorted, nostrils flared like some beast's while Rylan cowered behind her. Lila felt momentarily ill looking at the two of them, at the things she'd created.

"You're letting him ruin this family," Tia spat as her closing remark, before turning on her heel with Rylan. They crossed the threshold of their bedroom.

Lila stepped after them. She was so very sick of letting other people get the final word.

"Better than *leaving* this family, isn't it? It takes a certain commitment to ruin a thing, don't you think, lovey? Takes nothing at all to leave it behind."

Rylan stared at Lila in openmouthed horror. Even Francis had the decency to blink back his surprise. Lila took off her sun hat and fanned herself free of the heat that bloomed in her face.

"Sleep tight," she told her children before reaching out and closing their door for them.

Francis followed behind her as she stalked to the safety of the salon.

"Some birthday surprise," he commented.

Lila wasn't having it. She would put him in his place too, if necessary.

"You know I had plans, Francis. I had gifts and guests lined up for the twins' birthday. I had a hair appointment scheduled for this morning, an audition next week, and a trip with a friend."

Francis leaned against the wall, his full attention fixed on her. Had he taken that as an accusation? She hoped so. It was.

Lila inhaled and calmed. She rarely, if ever, snapped at him.

"Anyways . . ." She took another deep breath to clear her head. "Alejandro just put the meat loaf in the fridge to defrost it for tomorrow. And I was hoping you would help me slap together some decorations so the twins can at least get the sense of a normal birthday."

Best to keep everyone busy and the momentum moving forward until midnight.

"That's a great idea." Francis let his arms drop. He stepped toward her. Alarm bells went off in Lila's head. What was this about the bilges? Had he caught that comment? What exactly did Tia know? "How about a poster with their names on it?"

"Well, we don't really have poster board . . ."

"We could cut out little fish and hang them around the salon. Have Rylan pretend he's living underwater."

It wasn't a bad plan, albeit a rather juvenile one for a pair of teenagers, but Lila didn't say so. She couldn't find her voice.

Francis backed her into the couch until her knees buckled and she fell onto the cushions. "Or—I know—how about another tea party? We can set out sugar cubes and teacups."

"Francis—"

"We can tell our children how brilliant and beautiful and strong they both are."

Lila's hands twisted her silk robe, which pooled in her lap. "Francis, don't—"

"We can ask them what drives them, what burns in them, what makes them *Camerons*." He leered at her. "What makes us Camerons, Lil?"

He knew.

She didn't know how, but she knew he did. He knew about her and Alejandro. He had been monitoring her; the matching jewelry gift to Tia at the beginning of the trip had been evidence of that, had been his way of sending a message that he was watching. But she could have sworn they'd been careful . . .

"Well?" he asked, and she reached up for his face. It seemed to surprise him.

"We take," she answered simply. She couldn't reach his cheek without standing, and she couldn't stand unless he backed away. So she waited, arm outstretched.

Francis regarded her, shoulders rife with tension. Then he took her hand. Pulled her to her feet as daintily as if she were a ballerina or a cherry blossom. She leaned her weight into him.

He wanted to be the one taking, that's all. He couldn't stand being taken from. It was disloyalty that upset him most.

"You're right." The fight seemed to drain from him. Or perhaps his anger repositioned itself.

He trailed a finger through her hair, caught a small knot, broke it loose. The finger found Lila's jawbone and ran down the line of her face, snagged on her chin. He tilted her head up.

"We take," he echoed.

Then he climbed up the companionway of the salon. Lila followed. Wind hummed on deck, a requiem. Or maybe the beginnings of a hymn. Lila wore nothing but silk panties beneath her robe, and the wind found its way underneath, nipping at the softer parts of her skin. She shouldn't have been cold on this part of the Atlantic in June, but clouds bruised the southern sky.

They were sailing into a storm.

"Nico, you're relieved of watch duty early," Francis snapped at Nico, who was at the helm with Alejandro.

Alejandro's eyes met Lila's. She wondered what she looked like to him. Frightened and fragile? Desperate to warn him? She commanded herself to do so, but her body didn't listen.

"Relieved? I thought you wanted me to take your whole shift tonight," Nico said.

"Storm's brewing. I want to take charge. Go on."

They traded places. Nico nodded to his uncle and disappeared belowdecks.

"How bad's the storm?" Alejandro asked.

But he wasn't looking at Francis. He kept his gaze trained on Lila. How could she answer him? She had been crossing her fingers for a tranquil night. Her plan would be smoother that way.

Francis studied the screen, then his friend, both with the same calculating scrutiny. "Looks big. Could be devastating."

Alejandro nodded as if the news were a death sentence. Lila's heartbeat set a tempo for the wind's song. It quickened, and her tension took on a rhythm like a metronome. Lyrical even.

How does Francis know? What will he do? Is everything in place? Who is Alejandro more loyal to?

"¿Está hecho?" she asked, unable to stop herself. She had to know.

Alejandro inclined his head. "Medianoche."

Francis nodded along as if he understood, though she knew he didn't. He hadn't figured out that part, at least. Francis reached out to clasp his friend's shoulder. "How did this happen to us?"

Lila tightened her robe around her waist, her teeth gritted. How did this affair happen to them? Last she checked, *she* was the one in the center of it all. She was the person they both wanted.

"Too much love, I guess, hermano," Alejandro replied flatly.

"Ah." Francis's fingers dug into Alejandro's skin. He didn't flinch. "What about loyalty, *brother*? Where does loyalty fit in?"

Lila watched Alejandro closely. She had asked him earlier, and he had been unwavering in his sentiment. But would he say it to Francis's face? Did he know how dangerous that would be? Not that Alejandro could lie to save his life.

"She was lonely. You left her lonely," Alejandro said.

"Not her loyalty!" Francis said. Lightning speared the sky, and Lila's hair flew loose of its ribbon. "Yours, Matamoros! Who are *you* loyal to?"

He drove Alejandro backward, just as he had done minutes ago to Lila in the salon. Only this time, that left the helm unhandled. *The Old Eileen* dipped to one side. Lila cried out and grabbed at the wheel. She didn't know how to work it, not even a little bit, but holding it still seemed to right the ship temporarily.

"Francis, steer your goddamned ship!" she yelled, curls unraveling in silvery-blond swirls around her face.

Alejandro had his back to the ocean. It had started to rain. The whole scene played so familiar to Lila, like last summer, only with a stormy backdrop. With Alejandro instead of Tia. Could she let go of the wheel just for a moment?

"Well, Alejandro?" Francis raised his voice to be heard above the wind. "I just want to know who. Not out of love. Not out of fear. Which of us are you loyal to?"

Don't answer that, Alejandro, Lila thought furiously. *Make up a lie. Dance out of reach.* The truth would send her husband flying into a rage that would leave no survivors.

But unlike Francis, Alejandro Matamoros wasn't a salesman. Unlike Lila, he wasn't an actor. So he held his best friend's gaze and gave him the truth.

Lila knew it was the truth because Alejandro had worn the same look of sincerity the night they were alone together in her bed when she told him she wanted the world to burn.

It just wasn't the truth Lila expected.

"I'm loyal to you," Alejandro said without so much as a glance her way.

Francis tilted his head. "Huh." He chuckled, placed his hand on Alejandro's other shoulder in a masculine kind of embrace. "I believe you," Francis affirmed with a smile.

Then he looked over his shoulder, straight at Lila. The storm was creeping in around them, and the wind still toyed with Lila's robe, but she herself remained motionless in the eye of it all.

Alejandro was loyal to Francis. That was his simple truth after all this time? How many card games and meals and nights had they shared in giddy secrecy over the years? How many times had Alejandro said *I'll never tell*, while Lila heard *I love you, Lila. I choose you.* How could she have gotten it so wrong?

I'm yours, Alejandro had told her that night. Even then she had wondered if he would still be hers after he left her bed. Her hold over him was ephemeral.

What he should have said was, *I'm yours tonight. Yours for now. Yours until Francis says otherwise.*

So this wasn't a love story. Had Alejandro coveted whatever Francis had, and Lila was just another piece of his empire to be enjoyed? The tears that found Lila's cheeks were hot compared to the chilly drops of rain. How did everything that she held dear belong more to Francis than to her?

Her breath came heavy. She felt ill. She felt filthy. This great, unrivaled romance that had propelled her through the darkest of times was shallower than love, uglier than lust.

Francis held her eye, his gaze clear and relaxed. As if he'd always known. He understood the reality of the affair, despite having learned about it only recently, understood it more than Lila had ever grasped in seven years.

You see? he seemed to be saying. *Everything you have is fleeting.*

Lila moved forward through the rain, past the two of them until her lover's back was to her, facing her husband.

She clutched the railing for a brief moment, remembering Eileen. Had Eileen been guilty, after all?

Was it better to be guilty than inconsequential?

Lila turned, grabbed Alejandro by his shoulders, and pushed. Or perhaps Francis pulled. Perhaps her weight was enough on its own with the slippery deck. Alejandro fell forward, and on his way down his head hit one of the poles that held up the lifelines.

The sound of the impact was lost in the storm.

Alejandro lay half lidded on the deck, Lila and Francis standing over him.

She'd done it to hurt Francis, Lila told herself. But Francis hadn't flinched, and he didn't so much as wrinkle his nose as he bent down and eased his fallen friend to the edge of the deck. Alejandro's body slipped over the side, unconscious, and hit the waves.

Lila looked at her husband. Then at the blank space between them. Francis dusted off his hands, kissed her on the cheek, and returned to the helm of the ship.

Her heartbeat stuttered. She exhaled.

She wiped the tears from her cheeks, unable to unglaze her eyes as she dragged her hands over and over down the front of her robe. Alejandro had made his choice.

She left her remorse to be swallowed by the storm and climbed back belowdecks to draw a bath.

Chapter 47

```
Tia Cameron
Call sign: Thimble
Day 10 at Sea
```

"TIA, I'M SORRY . . ." Rylan whispered into the empty air between them the moment Lila had shut them in their cabin.

Tia pinched the bridge of her nose. "Don't," she said, not because he shouldn't be apologizing but because if she heard his whimpering voice one more time in the next minute she feared she'd snap.

So Rylan had told them. He'd told Lila, maybe Francis too, about Tia's plan to run away. He knew Tia was gutted over the idea she might no longer be able to leave. He knew she wouldn't stop trying, even if Francis took them to the end of the world.

And still, he'd betrayed her.

"Why?" Tia asked him.

She heard Rylan shift from foot to foot. He sniffed. Started to answer.

She cut him short. "I guess I don't really need to ask, do I? It's probably the same reason you do everything. Or don't do anything, more like."

"T-Tia . . ."

Tia opened her eyes. Her brother stood before her, withered

in on himself in that way of his that always looked delicate and doll-like.

But now he just looked pathetic.

"You got too scared. Just like you got too scared to pull me out of a goddamn *bomb*."

He started to cry, and she hated him. She couldn't help it; it wasn't fair. She couldn't even express her feelings without Rylan buckling.

"Stop crying!" Tia told him, trying not to cry herself. She wasn't the bad guy here. *He* had betrayed *her*. *He* had failed MJ.

To Tia's bewilderment, Rylan did stop crying. He sat back on his bed as if the weight of his own shortcomings were too much for him to bear. He had his palms open to the ceiling, waving helplessly.

I'm sick of apologizing, he mouthed.

Tia wasn't sure she'd understood him. "What?"

His palms curled to fists, and he raised his head. "I'm. Sick. Of. Apologizing."

Tia laughed and shoved her hair out of her eyes. "What a time to grow a spine, Ry." Her stomach felt like one of MJ's sailing knots, but she didn't care. She was done letting him get away with everything.

"I can't be who any of you want me to be," Rylan replied.

"You can be fucking loyal. It's not that hard to keep your mouth shut," Tia barked.

Rylan sprang to his feet.

He was taller and just as angry as she was—two things Tia hadn't given any thought to.

"I'm trying so hard to keep our family together. I try to be soft for Mom and successful for Dad and adventurous and exciting for you, but I end up not able to do any of it for any of you. And all of you are so . . . so selfish! You don't even *try* to fix things."

"Not when Dad makes a point to break everything!" Tia shot back.

He was going to crack at some point. He'd fall back into his bed and spool up like a cinnamon roll.

"So do you! God, Tia, you're just like him. Mom knows. That's why she treads so lightly around you. She's *scared* of you."

"That's not true—she's jealous of me. She resents me for being young and speaking my mind. She hates that I get to be exactly who I am while she just smiles and pretends all the time like she's still on camera!"

Tia snatched a pillow from her bed and balled it up in her hands so she wouldn't be tempted to throttle him. "Rylan, they sent me away. I was trapped at a boarding school. With nuns. And blizzards. There were spikes on the fence, and everybody ate the same cereal. They might as well have locked me in a 1920s asylum! So why should I try to keep the family together? They're the ones who preferred us apart."

"Because *I* needed you," Rylan retorted. "I tried so hard to get you home. Tia, please. I . . . I'm so—"

She didn't let him finish. "Tell me why it was so bad, then, Ry. Tell me why it was so horrible but not horrible enough to run away with me. What did they do to make you hand over my secrets like a goddamn spy?"

That clammed him up. He backed away and bent his head. Tia waited one second. Then another. Then she blew all the air in her lungs out her nose and faced away from him.

"What a great way to find out we don't trust each other anymore," she said, and she went and locked herself in the bathroom.

She had brought the pillow with her, and she pressed it to her face and screamed.

It didn't really matter where they were going now, did it? Francis and Lila wouldn't take their eyes off Tia. She wouldn't get the chance to run away. They might even punish her for planning it. Her last birthday had been one of the worst days of her life. Why shouldn't this next one top it?

Thunder, soft and foreboding, rumbled in the distance like a monster underwater. Tia lowered the pillow and combed the part back into her hair with her fingers.

Why would Francis and Alejandro sink the ship? The coordinates in the Bahamas were close, sure, but were they really planning on getting there via life raft? Or even if they planned to wait until they arrived to blow it up, they'd be trapped on the island for good with no way out.

Or maybe that was the point.

To get rid of the thing everyone would be looking for when the world realized the Camerons were missing.

The Old Eileen.

And now Francis knew Tia had been planning to run. He knew if even one of them didn't end up on that island, they risked telling everyone where it was. The bomb in the bilges was already set. He could pack them all on a life raft and blow the ship at any time, trapping Tia with him for good.

She wouldn't let that happen.

She had to leave tonight.

Tia listened to the waves outside. Was she imagining that they sounded bigger? It seemed to be raining lightly too. Tia wished she understood exactly what was going on. She wished she knew what her father was running from and why MJ's body was no longer in the freezer and if she could ever trust her twin again. But she didn't know any of that, and if she didn't act tonight, she might be too late.

Tia rested her hands on the bathroom counter, needing it to take her weight.

The bathroom was tidy and quiet. Rylan's toiletries were packed away in a drawer, and Tia's toothbrush sat alone by the sink. There was a jewelry box by the coiled hand towel. Tia opened it to look at the South Sea pearl earrings and necklace inside. They were the gifts her parents had given her for graduation, which now seemed like it had happened to a different girl on a different ship.

Tia had still never worn them.

She shut the box and set it back in place, then listened at the door. Rylan's sniffling had smoothed into deep breathing. He was asleep.

How could he sleep after seeing what lay stacked inside the chart house bilge? Did he trust their family so readily he believed without a doubt he was safe?

Tia stepped back.

They had promised to leave the ship together, but that was before Rylan showed his loyalty to their parents instead of to her. She had wanted to see the world with him, but Rylan was never one who could handle an adventure anyway. Why should she save him again like she had a thousand times before?

If he loved the Cameron legacy so much, he could inherit it alone.

Tia plunged her hand into her pocket and fished out her mother's lipstick. Only an hour ago she had planned on wearing it for her birthday tomorrow, planned on leaving the shape of her lips on Nico's cheek. Now, it would serve as a warning. A goodbye.

Let Rylan save himself this time.

Tia slipped on her brother's raincoat, which was hanging on a shower hook, and uncapped the stick.

Her face in the mirror was, as always, half hidden by her long, dark hair. Her cheeks were sun-kissed, her nose freckled from hours on deck.

Tia leaned over the cold counter and touched the lipstick to the glass.

Chapter 48

```
Lila Logan Cameron
Call sign: Cassiopeia
Day 10 at Sea
```

LILA LOCKED HERSELF inside the primary suite's bathroom. Her husband steered the ship overhead, leaving her to move about *The Old Eileen* on her own.

Lila grazed her fingers over the golden bathtub faucet. The floor beneath her slanted, a victim to the storm that sang outside. Was that storm killing Alejandro at this very moment? Or was he already dead?

She switched on the water, watched it stream into the porcelain tub. As the bath filled, she drifted to the porthole and unlatched it. Rain daggered its way inside the room. Lila reached past the length of her silk robe sleeve and found a bottle of bath oil on the sink counter: English Pear and Freesia. She unscrewed the cap and poured the entire thing into the tub. She wanted to reek of it.

The bathwater sloshed over the lip of the tub and spread its fingers across the ivory tiles. It seeped underneath the door. Lila lifted one foot over the tub. The movement nearly sent her toppling with the motion of the ship, but she sank into the water without bothering to shed her robe. Once submerged, nothing could touch her. The silk swirled—

rendered almost ethereal beneath the surface. Lila let her head slip underwater.

When Francis first asked her out and she'd said no, he had returned months later driving a Porsche. Alejandro had been with him again. He was always with him. And though Francis seemed to tire of Lila once he won her, Alejandro remained in awe.

Was Lila only desirable when she was out of reach?

She screamed underwater, the sound disembodied from her.

Lila's face broke the surface, and she reached her long arm to the counter where she found her pack of cigarettes and lighter. She smoked in the bath in the storm, the perfume of oils intoxicating enough to make her believe she was liquid herself.

Lila blew smoke through peony lips and let it skitter like water striders over the surface. Alejandro had looked Francis in the eye and vowed his undying loyalty. He'd said it to the wrong person.

Now he was dead or would be within the hour.

She floated, unblinking, in a veil of milk-white smoke and moonlight hair that dripped diamonds down her shoulder blades.

Maybe his loyalty hadn't been so cut-and-dried after all. She'd know for certain when the clock struck twelve.

Thirty-five minutes to go.

The Old Eileen hit a large swell without warning, and bathwater cascaded over the sides, flooding the bathroom floor even more. Lila braced herself on the sides of the tub, beads of rainwater falling onto her nose and cheekbones.

She inhaled enough smoke to cloud her doubts for good, then dragged herself out of the bathtub. The silk robe hugged her body in a downward curve, longing to plunge her back from where she had come. Her breasts and hips bloomed beneath the fabric, threadbare centimeters from being exposed.

She stepped onto the floor, and her feet sent delicate ripples out, like rose petals falling on the surface of a lake. She walked into her bedroom and opened wide the door to the hallway.

A blast of lightning outlined the space and everything in it with a purple glow.

She had been walking this hallway almost nightly after her bath. Francis must have noticed, he must have stepped in the trail of water, but he hadn't said a word about it. She wondered if he kept quiet out of kindness or discretion. Perhaps both.

But it didn't matter. By morning, if Alejandro had kept to his word, she'd be back on land, her children safe, her career secure. Her family's faces would be splashed across every tabloid in the country as survivors of the merciless sea and its terrible storm. She'd be famous again. Free. And fueled with enough aesthetic nightmares to last a lifetime of acting.

Lila walked the halls of *The Old Eileen*, drenched and ghostly. There was something feminine about the walk, she decided. She was a widow pacing the shore for her wayward sailor-love's return. She was a sea witch enchanting a curse with the pattern of her footfalls. She was a goddess built of sea-foam, a huntress tracking enemies through snow.

The water overflowing from her bathtub raced over the teak wood floor and poured into the small holes in the bilge panels. Filling up the sailboat one inch at a time. Lila's robe trailed in dripping tentacles around her as though she were some ocean beast with only one thought to drive her forward.

I'm about to sink this ship.

Chapter 49

```
Rylan Cameron
Call sign: Minnow
Day 10 at Sea
```

RYLAN FLEW OUT of bed as *The Old Eileen* tipped to one side. His water bottle and sketchbook slid off the bedside table, and he scrambled to his feet, tripping over the sheets tangled around his body. The dull thud of *The Old Eileen* slapping against another wave sounded around him, and Rylan, along with anything loose in his cabin, toppled to the other side. He managed to grab the edge of his bed and steady himself, fingers trembling.

Rylan looked to Tia's bed in the dark for comfort.

Empty.

Rylan buried his head in his hands. He had thought, stupidly, telling his parents Tia's secret would keep her in the family. Instead, he was now sure that even if they stayed together, she would be oceans apart from him. He felt tricked and tired, and more than anything, guilty.

He was so sick of feeling guilty.

Something warm trickled past his bare feet. Rylan dropped his hands. Water ran across the floor of his bedroom. He followed it with his eyes, frozen in terror, and looked up at the dark corner of his bedroom.

Someone else was inside.

A monster with a head like a translucent veil and elastic tentacles as delicate as strands of hair loomed from the shadows. The tentacles stretched out, reaching for him. Then she smiled.

Rylan screamed and jerked awake. He was still in bed. He grabbed a fistful of blanket to shield him from the creature that lurked in the corner. There was nothing there. He almost relaxed, but the sheen of the wet floor caught his attention.

The flooding was real.

"Tia!" Rylan called, not bothering to keep his voice low. He struggled to stay calm. No answer. He looked over at her bed, tearing his gaze away from the corner just for a second. She still wasn't there.

He stood, hands shaking out of control. He smoothed them over his sheets and made his bed, counting to ten.

He picked his way across the wet room, making the mistake of glancing through the porthole. He'd never seen the ocean like this, mountainous and sinister. It was an ocean that had sired the monster stories in Rylan's books. If *The Old Eileen* found herself under the hand of even one of those waves, she might spiral into oblivion.

The shaking had become unbearable, throwing Rylan off-balance to the point that he slipped and fell to his knees. Where the hell was his sister? He considered going out into the hall to find her. Maybe up on deck?

On deck where the waves could pluck him from the boat and devour him without a second thought? No one would even find his body.

Rylan clambered to the bathroom and splashed water on his face.

One, two, three, four . . .

Tia had probably gone on deck to help handle the sails against the storm.

Thirteen, fourteen, fifteen, sixteen . . .

They were all up there, wearing life jackets and working together.

Twenty-nine, thirty, thirty-one, thirty-two . . .

No one would let anyone go overboard. Rylan concentrated on things that kept him calm. Tia's laugh. Nico's warmth. Tiny fish flitting through a tranquil reef. His sister would forgive him. The bomb would not go off. The storm would pass them by.

Rylan's iron grip on the counter loosened. He breathed in the way Tia had taught him.

It's just a storm.

And if he had gone back to bed right then without looking up, maybe it would have been just a storm. Maybe he would have woken up on his birthday morning, happy and well rested. Maybe he wouldn't have seen the first ugly thing the storm had revealed.

But Rylan did look up, and any chance of *maybe*s washed away like sand in the surf, rattling against the two halves of a broken shell. He looked up and into the bathroom mirror which held his own frightened face staring back at him.

And his sister's message:

SAVE YOUR SELF

SOS. Rylan fell back, as if he could physically remove himself from the meaning behind the words. And God . . . was it *blood*? What the hell had happened in the time since he'd fallen asleep? Why hadn't Tia woken him up?

Because she hated him.

Because she wanted him to leave. Alone.

But Rylan didn't want to believe it because believing it meant leaving the cabin and venturing out into the storm to ready the last-ditch escape. He hadn't signed up for that on his own, he couldn't do it on his own, but the message was clear, a sickening edit to their original plan, their *promise*, to leave together.

He had severed any chance of *together* when he told their parents she meant to run. Or maybe it had been even earlier, when he failed to bring her home. He could have prevented her from ever wanting to leave in the first place. He should have fallen to his knees and begged for her forgiveness.

Stupid, stupid, stupid . . .

Rylan stood paralyzed against the wall. Maybe he would never move and let the world dissolve around him.

Then he heard the scream.

Chapter 50

Tia Cameron
Call sign: Thimble
Day 10 at Sea

TIA WASN'T ALONE in the hallway. For half a second, she thought what she was seeing was a ghost, pale white and dripping wet, but it was Lila. Her robe was soaked to the bone, giving her silhouette an eerie skeletal shape, and she was watching the door to the twins' cabin so intently she hardly noticed when Tia emerged from it.

"Mom?"

Was she humming? What the hell? Tia approached her and shook her by the shoulders. "Mom! What's going on? Why are you wet?"

Lila touched Tia's face with cold fingers, and the water droplets that rolled down Tia's cheek made her shudder. She could hear running water faintly inside her parents' room. Tia pushed past her mother.

Has she been doing this every night when Dad's on watch? Is this why the hall floor has been wet?

The bath was running, pouring over the side, and Tia slammed the handle to turn it off.

She ran back to the hallway, glancing behind her at the bed to make sure she hadn't woken her father.

Only he wasn't there.

Wasn't it Alejandro's watch? Where was Francis?

Lila was still standing in front of the twins' cabin door. Tia slipped past her and peered into the crew's cabin.

Every bed lay empty.

What the hell . . .

Tia backed away just as her mother murmured, almost to herself.

"Your brother is still asleep?"

"Don't wake him," Tia said. Something was very, very wrong.

"I would never." Lila had one hand clasped over her heart. She seemed to stare at the door to her children's room forever.

"Go back to bed," Tia tried to urge her, but Lila didn't seem to have heard.

Tia stepped closer. She still had Lila's lipstick in her pocket, and she took it out and pressed it into her palm. "Here. I borrowed this. Sorry."

Lila looked down at her for the first time. "My beautiful daughter," she breathed.

Tia felt a strange, sudden urge to say goodbye to her, to this woman who existed a million miles away but had somehow brought Tia into the world. But Lila wasn't in her right mind. Maybe she was overmedicated to hide her anxiety. Maybe she was drunk. Her eyes looked unfocused. She held the tube of lipstick to her heart.

It takes a certain commitment to ruin a thing, don't you think, lovey? Takes nothing at all to leave it behind.

Lila was wrong about that. It did take something for Tia leave her family behind.

Tia turned and left her there.

All the men must be up on deck or in the chart house.

Red crept into Tia's peripheral vision. Her hand levitated

over the handle to the chart house. She had no idea who she'd become when she burst through the door.

She turned the handle.

The space looked empty. Tia turned on the lights and jumped a little. Pirate was perched in the middle of the floor, viridian eyes watching her as his tail flicked back and forth. It wasn't the cat that had startled her, however. It was what he sat on.

The black duffel bag had been placed in the center of the chart house, its zipper partially undone to reveal a hint of its contents.

"Pirate, get off that!" Tia scooped the cat from the bag, holding her breath as she half expected the room to spontaneously combust. It didn't, of course. The bomb would need to be lit. But who had taken it out of the bilge? Alejandro?

Tia took Pirate to the salon couch where he'd be more comfortable, then headed back to the chart house and lifted the duffel bag, cringing at her proximity to what could so easily explode. She climbed the companionway with it awkwardly. It didn't help that the storm kept sending *The Old Eileen* tailspinning through towering waves.

How the hell was she going to get the life raft ready in these conditions? Maybe all she needed to do was throw the duffel into the sea. Then she could wait till the water was calm again to escape. *If* she could afford to wait.

Tia tossed the duffel bag up onto the deck and heaved herself after. She got to her feet, only raising her head when she had steadied herself on the railing near the cockpit.

The storm had masked the sounds of the chaos that unfolded before her. Francis was at the helm, one hand locked around the metal, the other clenched around Nico's shirt collar. The two were arguing, shouting into each other's faces, but rain poured around them and dampened the sound.

What the hell? Tia forgot everything else.

"Dad! Nico!"

Nico glanced her way momentarily, and when he did, Francis seized his opportunity. He released the wheel of the ship and punched Nico full in the face. Tia felt the blow as if it had been her who was hit. Because it had been her before. A wave slammed into *The Old Eileen*'s portside, and Tia buckled. Her chest caught on the railing, and she looked down at the seething sea. She should have put on her life jacket.

In the cockpit, Nico's fingers had found Francis's throat. He drove him backward so Francis's body hit the wheel. "Tell me, you son of a bitch!"

Tia barely made out his words through the wind.

"Where is my uncle?"

Francis kneed Nico hard in the groin, dropping the younger man like a weight. Francis punched his face again, and Tia fought to reach them. She couldn't let Francis hurt Nico again. The duffel bag skittered across the deck, but it didn't matter now.

"Stop fighting!" Tia called.

Francis kicked Nico in the throat, and he fell backward. Another wave pummeled them, and the ship bucked. Tia pushed past her father and took the helm, righting *The Old Eileen*. She focused on the night sky, which wavered overhead as they rattled around the sea. She couldn't look at the waves. She'd lose her nerve in a second, and her hands on the steering wheel were all that was keeping her from flying overboard.

She shot a glance over her shoulder. Nico had gotten to his hands and knees, Francis looming above him.

"Dad!"

He didn't turn.

"Dad, you have to steer!" she roared, and at last he looked over.

To her surprise, he nodded and changed places with her. Tia reached Nico's side. He had a bad black eye, and blood streamed from his nose. He struggled to his feet, holding onto one of the metal shrouds for support.

"I can't find my uncle." He clamped a hand over his nose.

Tia faced Francis. "Where's Alejandro? He wasn't in his room. Why isn't he on watch?"

Francis rolled his shoulders back, seemingly unconcerned by the way the waves slammed the ship. "Alejandro's dead."

Behind Tia, Nico's breathing sounded choked.

"Dead," Tia repeated, like she didn't know the word. If Alejandro was really dead, her father would be overcome. Alejandro was his best friend. His brother.

"Dead," Francis confirmed. "Your mother killed him."

Tia's T-shirt stuck to her chest. She grew colder with every raindrop on her skin. She saw her mother, wandering belowdecks like a ghost, staring at something only she could see. "I don't . . . She . . . What?"

Nico shot out a hand and grabbed the wheel. "Did you watch her do it?" His voice was deeper than Tia had ever heard it, his chin slanted down as blood poured from his nose. "Did you help?"

Francis's gaze flicked between Nico and Tia.

Nico's going to kill him, Tia realized. *Wouldn't be hard to do in a storm like this. He's not even wearing a life jacket.*

"Did you?" Nico shouted, grabbing at Francis wildly, the wheel the only thing between them.

Francis didn't flinch. He answered Nico while looking directly at Tia.

"I helped Lila kill him as much as you helped your uncle kill MJ."

What?

The rain slowed around Tia. It spiraled through the air and

burst in tiny explosions as it hit the deck. Nico's eyes rounded, and he whipped to face her.

"Tia, I . . . I'm sorry."

No.

MJ. The drowning hadn't been an accident. Nico had never been on her side.

Nico was talking, tripping over his words. He clasped Tia's hand, Francis behind them both and forgotten.

"I didn't know ahead of time, I swear. She wasn't telling you everything either. She wasn't here just to help with sailing."

Tia stared up at him, wet hair hiding half her face. A wave hit them hard, and Nico stumbled and held onto one of the metal shrouds, keeping them both upright. She didn't say anything, but she didn't have to. Nico kept talking.

"She was working against them this whole time, Tia. She wanted to get your father and my uncle thrown in prison for the rest of their lives. She was with the fucking feds."

"The feds?" Tia heard herself say. "Why would she . . . ?"

Francis and Alejandro were running from something. She'd assumed they had business enemies, rivals who were jealous of their company's success. Bad guys who wanted to hurt them.

But didn't this make so much more sense? If they were running from the federal government, that meant they'd committed a crime. Or many crimes. It meant that the people they were trying to *protect*, like Alejandro said, were just themselves from consequences. But consequences of what exactly?

Dad, what did you do?

"And you knew?" The rain was faster now, louder too. "You knew that MJ was trying to get your uncle caught? You knew, and then three days into our trip, she ends up dead?"

Alejandro had handed Tia MJ's tank. MJ and Nico had spoken minutes before the dive.

"What did she say to you before she died?" Tia stepped forward. Nico was still holding onto the shroud. With his other hand, he cupped his nose. Blood threaded between his fingers and ran down his arms. "You spoke to her. You were the last one to speak to her. What did she say?"

Nico cringed. "She warned me about my uncle and your dad."

Tia watched his blood drip onto the deck. "She didn't know you already knew."

"Tia—"

"And you went right to Alejandro and told him she was on to them."

Tia could picture it all. MJ, a woman who had the strongest moral compass of anyone she'd known, discovering the truth about Francis's business dealings, not being able to keep quiet. Offering her services to the FBI, she was going to ensure he got caught. And then they killed her before she got the chance.

But if the air mixture of the diving tank had been altered, it meant Alejandro meant to kill MJ *before* Nico even told him about her warning. Had they found out she'd betrayed them to the police and meant to kill her from the beginning? Is that what happened to someone who tried to double-cross one of Tia's parents?

MJ was dead. Alejandro was dead. But their bodies . . .

"What happened to her body? Why isn't she in the freezer?"

Nico winced and touched his black eye. He was weakening, adrenaline draining out of him while Tia only felt herself grow stronger, her fingertips starting to buzz.

"Your father had me throw her overboard. Just in case." Nico's Adam's apple bobbed in his throat. "Tia, listen to me."

Tia barreled ahead. She felt like she was twice her height, the storm a loyal soldier at her back. "So you found her in the water, already drowning. Maybe you held her there."

What was it Lila had said? She had been dreaming about Nico *flipping MJ's dead body faceup?*

"Or maybe you didn't even have to kill her yourself. Maybe all you did was not save her."

Nico lifted a finger at Francis. "He's trying to turn you against me! My uncle's dead." His voice broke on the last word, and he let his hand drop. The blood from his nose flowed freely. "I'm not your enemy."

He was right. Francis was just as culpable and far more dangerous than Nico. But her father was a threat Tia understood. She'd been raised by him. Hit by him. She didn't place her faith in Francis because there was nothing in him worth believing in.

But Tia had believed in Nico. She had liked him, had cared about him. She'd told him things that not even Rylan knew.

And he had killed the person she admired most.

The world had gone white-hot at the edges of Tia's vision. She vaguely felt her nails sink into the palms of her hands. "If you knew from the beginning where we were going, then you knew about the severed radio cord. You knew about the island on the map. You knew when you played sea chanteys to honor MJ that you were part of the reason she was gone. And you put your hands on me and kissed me, *knowing* you had lied to me about all of it from the start."

The whites of Nico's eyes shone, reflecting lightning. "I don't have any place to go back to, Tia. You think I want to go home to my mother and work behind a cash register till I die? You think I want to take care of other men's boats forever and never have my own? I didn't get the chances you got. I didn't get fancy schools or a high-school diploma or friends with Bugattis or the option to be anybody. You romanticize my life and think my choices are so simple, but you've never scrubbed bird shit off a deck that isn't yours or opened the fridge to eat food that isn't there. Do you know how many people would kill to live on a private island the rest of their lives?"

Tia stared at him, something spreading like rot in her chest. "Seems I know at least three."

Everybody chose Francis and Lila Cameron in the end. Even Rylan had spilled his guts to them. Who could resist aligning themselves with people who offered them the world?

"I'm sorry," Nico said in a small voice. He wiped his nose again in a futile effort to stanch the flow. "I didn't come here intending to hurt anyone, least of all you—"

"Stop," Tia said.

He did.

"Tia," Francis called her name, and she didn't need to look over to know what he was trying to say.

She watched a drop of Nico's blood hit the white deck and run away with the rain where just days ago the sailfish's blood had spilled. The mallet had weighed heavily in her hands but seemed to soar when she'd let it fall. The hook through the sailfish's lip gleamed like the shine of the black eye forming on Nico's skin.

The ship rolled again, sending them both off-balance. Nico grabbed at the railing, but his bloody hands were slippery against the smooth wood. He teetered at the edge, arms spread in wild wheel spokes to stop his fall.

"Tia!" he screamed, whether in a plea or an accusation, she would never know.

Was it a mercy? Was the sailfish really damned either way . . . ?

Tia tightened her grip on the shroud and extended an arm toward Nico, her mind made up.

Yes.

Her hand found his chest. She hardly needed to push. And the handsome siren tumbled over the side, swallowed by hungry waves.

Chapter 51

Rylan Cameron
Call sign: Minnow
Day 10 at Sea

RYLAN'S FINGERS QUAKED as he buckled himself into a life jacket, unable to believe he was really going up in that storm.

But the scream . . . It sounded like Nico.

He didn't bother to shut the watertight doors behind him as he flew through the hallway and up the companionway. He heard someone, his mother, climbing up after him. The rain drenched his hair within seconds and plastered it to his forehead as he tried to make sense of the chaos before him.

And why it looked so incredibly familiar.

For Rylan and Tia's seventeenth birthday, Tia had asked to go Jet-Skiing. They'd spent an adrenaline-racing morning on the water, riding at unnatural speeds that had left Rylan's heart hanging by a thread and his hair standing on end. The whole family had been breathless and wiped out by the time they returned to the boat, changed into dry clothes, and prepared for what Rylan had asked for.

A tea party.

Tia's hair had been shorter then, in dark waves just at her collarbones. She hadn't dyed it yet, and the oaky brown made the lemons on her sundress pop. Lila's outfit was periwinkle and lace with a cream hat and ribbon to match. Even Francis had traded out his golf polo for a baby-blue button-up to humor his son's request.

Rylan loved them fiercely in that moment, all three of them, and he knew this birthday would be one to remember.

He'd set the table himself, unfolding it on the deck of *The Old Eileen* so they could overlook the sunny sea. The teacups were Lila's, ceramic and white with carnation-rimmed plates to hold them.

"No, I insist, my boy. Sit at the head of the table," Francis had said with a smile.

So Rylan had, Tia at his right side. Alejandro poured the tea, the porcelain teapot out of place in his calloused hands. Rylan could have been fooled into thinking the whole family was gathered there just for him, that it was his day alone, if everyone hadn't smelled like sunscreen and salt from their hour coasting over waves. Not that he would want a birthday alone. He couldn't imagine his life without Tia, different though they were.

You wouldn't understand, he thought toward no one in particular as Tia lumped sugar cubes into her cup. *It's a twin thing.*

Rylan and Lila drank honeysuckle tea. Tia and Francis drank oolong. Alejandro went below deck to take a call. That's when Francis set down his cup and spread his hands.

"You're seventeen years old today, Rylan."

Rylan beamed and stirred cream into his drink.

"So what now? What's next?"

"Uhh . . ." He took a sip, warm and soothing. A rundown of Rylan's future wasn't an uncommon topic. "I mean, senior year of high school. Then after that, college, studying marine bio, maybe environmentalism and—"

"Not that," Francis interrupted. "Tell me what you *want*. Your wildest dreams."

"Okay. Uh, I want to work with animals. Maybe be a scientist and learn how to protect coral reefs."

Francis set his cup down hard enough to clang against the plate. His tea sloshed a bit over the side, but he didn't seem to notice. Or care. "Rylan, I want to know what keeps you up at night. What you burn to achieve or possess. What you would do anything to get. That's what makes a man or a woman. That's what makes a Cameron."

Lila fluffed up her bangs. "Rylan, darling, we mean your *passions*. We know you love ocean animals, but—"

"But hobbies don't always make careers," Francis stated. "Unless you're willing to do whatever it takes."

Rylan had looked between them, his perfect birthday tea party dissipating like water down the drain. "It's not like I'm going into acting like you, Mom. Or business like you, Dad. What I want isn't like that. It's more . . ." He wanted to give voice to the word *chill*, a word that seemed never to have entered his parents' vocabularies.

That hadn't stopped Tia, though. "Chill out, guys," she instructed them, pinching a tiny cucumber sandwich between her fingers. She swallowed it in one bite, and Rylan wondered for the thousandth time why neither of his parents interrogated Tia. God knew *she* would have an answer.

Francis pressed on, unperturbed. "When I was your age, I had nothing. I was put on a ship with boys who had everything. They didn't even have to fight for it. No one was going to hand me a life like that, so I made one. Now you will be weaned off my success in order to make your own. So answer me, Rylan. What would you do anything for?"

Getting out of this conversation. "I—I don't know, Dad." He wanted to melt into his chair.

"It's time to know," Francis snapped, his voice serrated.

Rylan froze up, muscles stiff and disobedient.

"Leave him alone." Tia slammed her fist on the table. The teacups rattled on their plates.

"Tia!" Lila rushed to dab at a blot of tea that marred the pristine table.

"This doesn't concern you, Tia." Francis's eyes bored into Rylan.

He squirmed, tears pricking. An awful feeling slithered on the back of his neck.

"Bullshit." Tia stood, banging the table. Rylan's honeysuckle tea shuddered. He couldn't bring himself to drink anymore. "You're obsessed with him. It's grooming and it's manipulative."

"Sit down, young lady," Francis ordered, and she shook her head before he could get the words fully out.

"Are you so invested in getting us to respect you for the money you made because you know we'll never respect you for the person you are?"

The air left Rylan's lungs, and he groped to grab Tia's hand and pull her down before she could keep talking.

But he couldn't reach her.

"Well guess what, *Dad*?" she continued. Rylan felt faint. "We're almost adults. And if you think we're sticking around after all the shit you've pulled, then you're even stupider than—"

Francis flipped the table, casually with a flick of his wrists, but the damage was catastrophic. Ceramic and silver poured into Rylan's lap and shattered on the deck. The tea burned his skin and he leaped backward only to slip on the deck and fell onto his knees. Shards embedded in his hands and legs.

Francis crossed to Tia and slapped her hard across the face. Rylan had never seen him go that far before. But he'd never seen Tia fight him like that either. She stumbled, and he grabbed her shoulder and Rylan's, pinching them hard. Rylan could still feel the pressure.

"You have no idea what I've done," he had told them, relaxed. "And you have no idea what you're capable of because of me."

Rylan shook violently, fighting off vomit. Tia lifted her face, hair hiding one eye.

"I think I'm starting to get a clue." She lunged forward without warning. She hit Francis at his waist, which hinged. He stumbled backward, enough time for Tia to stand and push him with all of her force backward over the railing. Into the sea.

Francis had narrowly avoided being crushed to death by his own ship. He hadn't had a life jacket on, and he told Lila and Rylan later that it had, ironically, saved his life. He'd been able to dive as deep as he could manage until the ship had passed. When he swam back up to the surface, Alejandro had already ordered a man-overboard rescue.

Later, Rylan would wonder if his twin had meant to kill Francis just like he wondered now as he and Lila stared through the sheets of rain at Tia Cameron and the man who'd just plummeted overboard.

Why am I the one you're always pushing, Dad? Rylan had sobbed to Francis after his father had been pulled back onboard. Tia had been locked in her cabin, Lila had gone to lie down, leaving Rylan on the deck with his father, shivering under a towel.

Why are you trying to force this with me, this killer instinct? Why not Tia? Because she's a girl? Because she's ninety seconds younger?

He had never forgotten Francis's reply, not when he stood by as his sister was shipped off to boarding school, not when he'd seen her raise the metal mallet above her head, and least of all now as the storm swallowed Nico de la Vega in one gulp.

Because, Rylan, Francis had said.

She already has it.

Chapter 52

Tia Cameron
Call sign: Thimble
Day 10 at Sea

TIA SAW RYLAN too late, his mouth ajar, pupils dilated. He'd seen her. She looked at the spot Nico had occupied seconds before. She looked at her mother who had come up beside Rylan, even though she had said she wouldn't wake him. She looked down at the sea which heaved, unmarred by the man it had consumed.

Tia stood still amid the storm, drenched and anchored only by the steel shroud clenched in her fists and her brother across the deck, screaming her name in silence. The ocean seemed to have no laws in the way it moved, bucking and writhing and sending them in every direction. The black duffel bag was nowhere to be seen. If Tia had been any less pumped with adrenaline, she would have sobbed with terror.

At the helm, her father smiled.

The storm seemed to mute. Rylan had looked at Tia once before in the way he did now, like she was a monster. It was after she'd pushed their father overboard. No one in the family had ever viewed her the same since. Tia hadn't given a second thought to what happens to people when you push them into the ocean, even in calm waters in broad daylight, to the fact that she might have killed her father. She'd just wanted to hurt him. Her face had been aching from where he'd hit her, and she needed her father to know that she would always strike back.

"I—I think I know what your call sign is, Tia," Rylan had said as they knelt on the floor of their room after Francis had been pulled from the sea coughing up water. "Shield. You're my shield."

Tia had shaken her head. "I'm not big enough."

She thought of her father's look of terror as he crashed into the water. The image filled her with adrenaline. And pride.

"Maybe I'm more of a sword."

Rylan frowned. "No. No." He said it like he wanted to convince himself. "You were on defense. Not offense."

Tia wondered if that was true. She wondered if Rylan believed that. She looked around at *The Old Eileen*, the flash of Atlantic through the portholes, and then at her brother and his bandaged hands.

"How about something else unbreakable?" Rylan had said. He thought for a minute, touching a bubble of blood that seeped from underneath the gauze around one thumb. "Thimble."

Tia looped her pinkie with his, careful not to brush up against any of his wounded fingers.

"Thimble," she echoed.

FRANCIS WAS LAUGHING NOW, openmouthed against the rain as he gripped the helm.

Tia found herself in front of him, the wheel between them. Rylan and Lila had retreated to midships, maybe to take shelter. Alejandro was gone, and now so was Nico.

Francis turned them portside, but the waves didn't let up.

The ship was ready to splinter into shards, ceramic pieces to be ground into sand.

"You know, Tia, you really should be wearing a life jacket up here. It isn't safe."

Tia seized the wheel, her fists against his. Rain slashed his face into fractions, a series of broken glass.

Francis wrenched it back, and she stumbled away. "You're not a captain yet, kiddo. Your day will come. Although, it was a night like this thirty years ago when I started my own path. A storm like this."

Water broke over the bowsprit and rushed across the deck. It surged around Tia's ankles. Overhead, stars swung like crystals in a falling chandelier. This ocean would eat them all alive.

"What did you do to make the feds come after you?"

Francis turned the helm. "Look at the life you've had, Tia. I didn't have that, but why should that mean I didn't deserve it? I wanted the kind of life most people never get, so I had to be willing to do things most people wouldn't do. Building an empire isn't pretty."

"By *pretty*, you mean *legal*?"

He didn't answer, just looked smug as he steered his ship. Tia wanted to rip his yacht right out from under his feet.

She moved closer again. Some things still weren't adding up. "Why would you hire MJ if you knew she was working against you?"

"That's exactly *why* I hired her."

He had always planned on killing her. Tia's hands trembled at her sides.

"And what about Mom and Alejandro?" Did Lila really kill him? Did she push him into the storm like Tia had Nico?

Francis showed his teeth in a garish grin. "Too much love, I guess."

"Well, good." She stopped within arm's length of him and bared a smile right back, unsure if the noise in her eardrums was battering thunder or the blood that beat in her veins. "I don't have that problem."

She knocked back a fist and caught him right in his perfect teeth. Pain exploded up her hand, but God it felt good to hit him hard in the face like he had hit her. Francis howled and staggered away from the wheel, which she snatched control of. She searched in vain for a marker in the sky to find her heading, but *The Old Eileen* might as well have been a stray sock in a washing machine.

That's why she couldn't be sure if the thing that ripped her from the helm was the storm or her father. Either way, Tia toppled backward and smacked painfully into the cockpit bench. She strained to right herself, but Francis was there, and he swept her legs out from under her.

She hit the deck, and her right hand shot bolts of pain through her arm once more, mimicking the lightning that fragmented the night. Francis lunged to reach the wheel, but she caught his ankle and yanked him backward. It was her turn to take control. They weren't going to his island.

"All this trouble to captain a ship you're about to sink?" she screamed.

Francis faced her, eyes burned out like cigarettes in the dark.

"What?" he called, and she claimed the opportunity to army-crawl past him and heave herself up on the wheel.

She scanned the deck for the black duffel bag, praying it had been swept overboard. Instead she saw Rylan and Lila, arguing from the looks of their gesturing hands. There was something on the deck between them, but between the chart house and the downpour, she couldn't make it out. It wasn't the bag. It was bright orange with reflective strips of silver that shone under the mast lights.

The life raft.

"You think you can steer us through a storm, Tia?" Behind her, Francis was propped against the cockpit bench. "Aren't you afraid? That sea will tear this ship in two if you let it."

He was wrong. She tightened her grip on *The Old Eileen*'s helm. She was made for this.

Francis didn't let up. He had made it to his feet once more, balanced by one hand on the bench. The rain made it hard to hear anything, but he raised his voice above it. "Being a captain means everyone's lives are in your hands. It's already too late for some."

MJ. Alejandro. Nico.

He was behind her now, but she couldn't leave the helm. "Not for Rylan, though. Do you really trust yourself with his life?"

Rylan betrayed me, she thought.

But what if he went overboard like Nico? Tia's breath caught when she imagined her brother in the water, struggling to get air, living his final moments riddled with the panic he'd felt most of his life.

She wanted him to be brave, not dead.

Tia remembered the crash jibe she had almost caused a few days ago. She had never seen Alejandro look scared. Maybe she didn't have what it took to captain this ship.

"Just let me get us through another storm," Francis urged.

Tia loosened her grasp on the helm. Francis reached for it. And for a moment, her father's eyes were that of the storm, a breath of temporary calm.

Then *The Old Eileen* hit a wall of water, and Tia careered backward, sliding over the deck and the angled railing. She spiraled down, down, down.

Right into the ocean's open mouth.

Chapter 53

Rylan Cameron
Call sign: Minnow
Day 10 at Sea

"OH MY GOD, oh my God," Lila repeated over and over in a frantic loop as she and Rylan fought their way to midships. If Rylan had the power to speak, he would have sounded similar, but as it was, his shock replayed images inside his mind instead of words.

Tia pushed Nico.
Tia killed Nico.
Tia left the message to run.

The inflatable life raft was packaged and stored by the hatch to the salon. Rylan stared at it, unable to move, even though he knew he had to get out. Tia was still in the cockpit, yelling, it seemed, at Francis as they wrestled for control of the wheel. What did Tia know that he didn't?

To Rylan's surprise, Lila dropped down on deck and started to unlash the life raft and lower it into the water. She yanked on a line with surprising strength, and an orange octagonal boat unfolded beneath them. Rylan lost his nerve immediately. Already the mammoth waves around them were sending *The Old Eileen* soaring. He couldn't imagine facing this storm in a tiny tent-like raft that looked more like an inner tube than a safety vessel.

"We have to hurry," Lila urged Rylan, heaving the raft toward the side of the ship.

"What's going on?" he said, but not loudly enough to be heard over the tempest. He shouted again, "Mom! What's going on?"

Lila clenched her fingers around his wrist and looked at his watch. "Six minutes to midnight, Rylan."

Six minutes to his birthday. But what did that matter now?

"We can't go out in this storm!" he cried. Water sprayed into his face, and he wiped his eyes madly to regain his vision. "We'll die!"

"We can't stay here!" she yelled back, dragging the raft to the railing. "The ship is going to sink!"

How did Lila know about the bomb? His seasickness waxed, and Rylan grabbed the railing and vomited over the side of the ship. Here at the edge, he could feel just how much she was dipping and bucking. His whole body quaked.

Lila yelled for him to get ready. But he wasn't ready. How could he be? Everything was happening so fast.

"No," he muttered, then raised his voice. "No! We can't leave Tia and Dad!"

Lila's hair dripped in pale tendrils around her face. She shook her head. "After everything he's done to you?"

Rylan winced at a deafening crack of thunder. "I won't leave Tia!"

Lila reached out to Rylan and cupped his face in her clammy hands, her fingers like tentacles.

"Oh, my love," Lila pressed her forehead against his. "Didn't you see? They're the same."

She was holding the tether that connected the raft to the ship. She pulled it taut, as close as she could get it.

"Jump, Rylan!" she told him, but he couldn't. Even if he wanted to, he couldn't.

Didn't you see? They're the same . . .

Tia had pushed Nico over the side of the ship. She knew he couldn't survive in this storm. And a year ago she had pushed Francis as well. But it had been to protect *Rylan*. And that's all she was doing now. Protecting him. She must have had a good reason for Nico . . .

Tears and rain flowed down Rylan's cheeks, and he hiccupped back a sob.

Why are you trying to force this with me, this killer instinct? Why not Tia?

Because . . . she already has it.

"Rylan!" Lila tugged at his arm. "Three minutes!"

Was Alejandro going to light the bomb at midnight? Maybe there was some kind of timer that would set it off? Rylan didn't know how it worked. He didn't know anything apparently, couldn't make sense of his sister or his mother or his father or this storm.

He looked to the cockpit, wishing his weak voice could carry to Tia and warn her what he was about to do.

She'd been the one to tell him to do it, though, hadn't she? *Save yOur Self.*

Though maybe she'd meant it more like *Save yourself, Rylan. For once.*

In the cockpit, Tia and Francis were facing off at the wheel. Francis reached for it, Tia stepped back from it, and it seemed momentarily that they had reached some kind of accord. But then a sudden gigantic swell pointed *The Old Eileen*'s bowsprit straight up at the sky, upending Rylan and knocking Lila overboard. She landed in the life raft, while Rylan was flattened against the railing he clung to, the wind slammed out of him. When he looked back at the cockpit, the helm spun free of its captain. He searched wildly for his father, for Tia.

They must have been swept overboard too.

Below, Lila waved at Rylan and mouthed pleas that he couldn't hear. He wanted to whimper and curl into the fetal position and wait for the nightmare to end, but his family was down in that water.

So Rylan held his breath and jumped.

He landed in the trough of a wave. His life jacket rocketed him to the surface. From the raft, Lila strained to grab onto the straps. She pulled him aboard, bellowing a very unladylike cry at the effort. They fell back together, and Rylan popped back up, scanning the surface for his twin.

"Tia! Tia!" Even if her head were above water, there was no way she'd hear him. All of Rylan's rescue-diver training came back to him in fragments. Unresponsive diver at the surface . . . rescue breaths . . . CPR . . .

But none of it mattered if he couldn't *find* them.

"Rylan! We have one minute. We need to move!" Lila unhooked the tether to the raft and picked up a paddle. She plunged it in the water, trying to get them away from *The Old Eileen*.

"Wait!" Rylan's heart dropped into his toes. His breathing came quick and ragged. He turned to his mother, pure panic in his voice. "Pirate's still onboard!"

He stood to dive back into the water. The poor cat was belowdecks, probably terrified of the noise and feel of the storm. He *had* to go back for him.

"It's too late." Lila yanked him down and dropped the paddle. She held Rylan to her chest and covered her ears as best she could. "Hold on!"

Through his desperate sobs, Rylan managed to glance at his watch.

11.59.58
11.59.59
12.00.00

Rylan braced himself for the explosion.

It didn't come.

Lila's hands dropped to her lap, and she gaped at the ship, openmouthed. Rylan sobbed in relief. His cat was still okay.

It didn't go off . . . Lila must have said—at least that's what he read on her lips.

Suddenly Rylan felt very cold.

"Mom," he said, a numb sensation crawling across his skin even beneath the life jacket. "Mom, how did you know the ship was going to sink at midnight? Why weren't you worried about Alejandro getting killed in the blast?"

Lila rocked, her silk robe soaked. The rain between them made her pale face look cracked. "He's dead," she said. The storm made her sound shrill. "And he didn't love me."

"Wh-what?"

The tent-like apparatus of the life raft was keeping some of the rain off them, but it also blocked their view of the water. Not that they needed a view. Rylan could feel the ocean roiling under them.

Lila's lower lip quivered. "I told him to set the explosives. I knew we had the supplies we needed. I gave him the midnight deadline. So you don't have to spend your birthday on that boat, see? It's okay! We're going to be rescued, lovey. We're going to be rescued, and this will be all over the news."

Rylan's jaw hung loose. He should never have gotten into the raft with her.

Suddenly, Lila shrieked and pointed over his shoulder. He whipped around.

Someone was in the water.

"Tia?" Rylan leaned over the side to get a better look.

But it was his father's face, beaded with water and fear, that looked back at him.

"Rylan!" Francis paddled through the water viciously, but his efforts did no good. The storm held a strength that Francis could only begin to imagine. "Rylan!" he called again, hand waving over his head.

Francis strained toward them. He was in arm's reach. "Help me," Francis cried. An order.

Rylan's breath stuttered. Time tripped and limped.

Congrats, son. Nemo's dead.

Come on, Rylan. People could be dying.

The tests reanimated themselves around him. The tests that Francis had started giving Rylan when Tia was no longer there to protect him.

Francis had refused to bring Tia home when Rylan found out he was salutatorian because that was second place. That wasn't good enough.

Once, Francis had towed him to the bathroom on a lazy day after school, flooded and plugged the sink, then pushed his son's head underwater to see if Rylan could conquer his panic attacks. He shut the door so Lila didn't hear as she practiced her lines downstairs.

The next month, Francis made Rylan run to school as he drove his Rolls Royce to supervise behind him.

He locked rooms and left hairpins on the floor or emptied the fridge in an attempt to get Rylan to eat the leather from his shoes. *Tests,* Francis called them. Tests that would end when he passed.

But he never passed.

In the corner of the life raft, Lila didn't budge from her seat. Her ashen eyes slid over her husband as if he were another figment of the water. An appendage, already belonging to the sea. Francis didn't turn to her or reach for her. Did he guess she wouldn't save him even if he did?

No, this was Rylan's moment. A test he could finally pass.

Rylan's hand wavered as he held it out. The raft dipped and swayed, keeping the father and son inches out of reach.

Francis howled in frustration. Wind sunk its teeth into the sound, tearing and distorting it.

Francis was laughing as Tia sent Nico over the side of the ship.

He was yelling as his palm connected with Tia's cheek.

Snapping at Rylan every time he failed.

"Power and potential," Francis Cameron had told his son. "That's what I see when I look at the ocean, and it's what I see when I look at you."

Rylan's vision smeared into something grotesque and fragmented—pieces of porcelain, pale purple tentacles, a boy falling overboard in a storm. He'd been trained for this, hadn't he? He'd been trained by Francis to save anyone if he had to. Now was the time to prove himself, right? He counted to ten.

One, two, three, four . . .

"Rylan!" Francis bellowed his name and shook his hand in the air as if Rylan had forgotten about what he must do.

Five, six, seven, eight . . .

"Help me!" Francis commanded in a voice that paled in comparison to the bulleting rain.

Nine . . .

Rylan brought his hand back to the safety of his chest. A calm bubbled up inside him—Rylan's own eye in the storm.

Ten.

"Power and potential, Dad," he said. "You were right."

He sat back in the life raft, hair slicked back against the nape of his neck, and looked away as the storm finished its work.

Beside him, Lila reached out and locked a hand around his wrist. Was this her way of saying she agreed with his decision?

After everything he's done to you, she'd said. Like she knew.

Rylan looked at his mother, really looked at her with her silk-soft skin and her pale, wet hair. She'd always been ghost-like. Had she known about the tests this whole time, hovering at the edges but not revealing herself because she agreed with them? And now she'd let it slip in order to get him to leave Francis behind?

If so, it had worked.

Rylan broke her grip on his wrist with a strength that surprised even him. He pulled away and focused back on the water.

There would be time later to interrogate his mom.

But he only had minutes to save his twin.

If Francis had ended up close to the life raft, so should Tia have, right? Rylan unbuckled his life jacket and hurled it into the sea in the opposite direction of his father. Maybe Tia could find it and hold on. She had to be out there. She had to be alive.

"Tia!"

The Old Eileen had drifted far from them, driven away by the storm. Pirate was alone on that ship, mewling in the dark at being abandoned. Rylan couldn't take any more heartache. He stood, ignoring Lila's yelp as their raft rocked from his movement. He cupped his hands over his mouth and screamed until his voice couldn't scream anymore. The waves might as well have been mountains, their troughs valleys. Soon he couldn't even see his life jacket floating in the water.

Rylan didn't know how long he yelled before his knees gave out. In the corner, Lila curled like a white tulip under the weight of too much dew.

Rylan sat in the puddle of water that had collected in the bottom of the raft. He zipped up the tent with trembling fingers to keep them from flooding. His heart had left his body, making him almost miss the tempo of its beating. The emptiness was somehow worse.

He sat like that until the storm collapsed in on itself and dissipated. He sat until dawn made its appearance, faint and lovely. And only when the sun scattered itself over the placid waves did Rylan accept that who he'd sacrificed to the night would never make up for those that he'd lost.

Chapter 54

Lila Logan Cameron
Call sign: Cassiopeia
Day 11 at Sea

DAWN FRINGED THE HORIZON, the morning of her children's birthday. Lila hadn't spoken since the storm, and neither had her son. They huddled by one another, reliving it all. When the rain stopped hours ago, they had unzipped the orange tent over their heads to let in fresh air, and now the endless expanse of where they were floating became evident. Lila couldn't bear to think of the storm, yet she couldn't tear herself away from the memory of last night. When was the last time she had spoken to her daughter? In the hallway. What was the last thing Tia had said to her?

She didn't know.

And the ship . . . Rylan and Lila had watched helplessly as *The Old Eileen* had been swept farther and farther away, without the fire Lila had envisioned for days. It was salt in the wound: knowing when midnight came and the bomb didn't go off that Alejandro's confession of loyalty to Francis hadn't been faked. He must have put the bag in the bilge so Lila would believe he'd go through with it. Then maybe he'd have found some way around it, convinced her it was too dangerous to get on a raft in a storm. He would play both sides as best he could until he was forced to choose.

And in the end he chose Francis.

Quietly, Lila celebrated his death.

But not half as much as she celebrated Francis's.

Once Lila realized Francis wasn't bringing her home, she had decided she would get there herself. She asked Alejandro to make plans to blow a hole in the ship, something big enough to sink it fast. He had planted a makeshift bomb in the bilges, and Lila's job was to get everyone off of the ship before midnight, before the bomb even went off. She planned for them to be rescued and sensationalized by the media.

Celebrity Shipwreck! Lila Logan Survives Peril at Sea!

With renewed attention on her, her career would resume. They might even make a movie about the sinking. They would arrest Francis for whatever it was he was so desperate to run from, and she could even blame him for *The Old Eileen*'s apparent failing.

She hadn't planned on the storm. Or Alejandro's disloyalty. Or losing her daughter to the sea.

But Rylan was alive. He was gentle and good. He still looked to her for guidance and let her hold him in her arms. He would need her now more than ever, with his father and sister gone.

Lila swallowed the lump in her throat. It was Tia's own fault she'd ended up overboard, right? She was too stubborn, too aggressive. She wouldn't have obeyed her mother to climb into a life raft. She was too hell-bent on fighting.

But to picture her . . . dead . . .

Would the coast guard recover Tia's body? Maybe the media would chalk the incident up to tragedy after all. In a way, Lila would have exactly what she'd wanted: her face on every paper in the country. Even though she hadn't planned for anyone to die, there was nothing, no matter how you spun it, more sensational and newsworthy than death.

Lila's arms were stiff, but she stretched them out anyway and pulled Rylan into her chest. He didn't fight her, limp and unblinking. She stroked his hair and hummed tunelessly. He was going to be okay.

"We'll be rescued," Lila rasped. "We just have to hold on."

Rylan nestled into Lila's embrace, and she shielded his face from the sun's advance.

"What if no one comes?" Rylan's voice cracked.

Lila couldn't think like that. They would be rescued, of course they would be. Once a ship passed them, they could . . . oh, what was it that people did in movies? Fire a flare gun? She knew there were plenty of survival supplies packed on this raft.

She broke her hold on her son to rummage through the raft until she retrieved a canister. Thick, tasteless crackers. Packets of water. Flares, a mirror, and a compass.

"See, lovey? We have everything we need," she told him, but the cheer in her tone fell flat.

She worked to peel open one of the water packets, cursing her French-tipped nails, but the only thing Rylan seemed to be interested in was the little black compass. He picked it up and studied the horizon.

"What is it, my dear?" Lila managed to puncture a hole in the plastic and take a couple greedy gulps of water. She handed it to Rylan, but he didn't take it.

"It's just numbers . . ." Rylan murmured.

"Numbers? Rylan?" Lila touched his shoulder.

Rylan's eyes shuttered, and he began to count. "One, two, three, four . . ."

Lila didn't know what to do. Had he gone mad?

She hugged him to her chest, hoping her embrace would be enough to snap him out of it, but her son counted on.

"Five, six, seven, eight . . ."

"Rylan, darling . . ." Lila detangled his salt-caked hair and willed for him to come to. She couldn't bear to face the sea alone.

"Nine . . ." Rylan's eyes popped open. "One hundred and forty."

"Lovey, I think you skipped a few numbers . . ."

Rylan jolted to his feet, which sent the raft teetering and Lila's stomach to her toes. She grasped the sides of their rickety salvation. "Sit down!"

"One hundred and forty," Rylan told her, as if that meant something. He tapped his finger on the face of the black compass, numbers ringing its perimeter. "That was the heading we were at. Tia told me, she told me days ago that we weren't far from the final destination."

Lila tugged on Rylan's sleeve until he sat again. "How could you know that? He didn't tell any of us where we were going."

Maybe they should have saved Francis.

"No, but Tia found out." Rylan's expression shone with pride. "If we follow the heading, we can make it to the island. Unless a boat comes to pick us up . . . that island is our only chance, Mom."

Their only chance was the mystery island Francis had purchased and plotted to bring them to. After everything they had done to escape their fate, they were just going to claw their way to it? Lila searched every inch of the horizon. They had flares to signal for help. In all of Lila's daydreams about being on this raft, she had never imagined that they simply wouldn't find anyone to rescue them. There had to be a ship nearby, right? There had to be someone who could save them.

But the sky and sea were blank.

They were alone.

As if he could read her mind, Rylan took Lila's hand. "What

choice do we have?" he asked and held out the compass in his palm.

Lila swallowed and wondered if the bitter salt taste of the sea would ever leave her.

"To save ourselves," she said. "Rylan, I'm proud of you. For figuring this out. For doing . . . what you had to do in the storm."

Her sweet, soft son rounded his eyes earnestly. "You know what? Dad would have been proud of me too."

He leaned forward, looking deep into her eyes. "I think I finally passed his test."

Then he smiled, close-lipped, and Lila shivered against the wind as Rylan picked up the paddle to begin.

Chapter 55

Tia Cameron
Call sign: Thimble
Unknown

EVERY BREATH WAS PRECIOUS. She filled her lungs frantically, never knowing which gasp of air would be her last as another wave folded her in black. She spun like a windmill underwater. At one point she struggled for the surface only to find she was actually swimming down. There was no room for panic, no room to call for help. There was only Tia and the sea and the cold eventuality that only one of them would win.

She glimpsed orange soaring wildly in the black. *The life raft.* Tia tried to swim forward. She surged closer one moment, then pinwheeled back the next. It was no use. If she fought this hard for much longer, she would sap her strength and drown.

But she could see them: two little dots on the raft of orange. She could see her mother's silk robe, her brother's dark hair.

And there, in a stretch of black water between her and the raft, was Francis, or at least a form that must be Francis, paddling madly toward them.

A swell brought Tia to a mountainous height, and she saw Rylan's arm stretch out to reach their father.

The swell crested, and Tia went under. She held her breath, and the air in her lungs sent her to the surface again where another wave of water held her up.

Francis was reaching for Rylan's hand.

Again, the ocean sent her down into a bowl rimmed by waves. Tia waited, heart flapping like a luffing sail, until she shot up again, expecting to see three figures huddled on the life raft. Her family intact without her.

But there were only two. Rylan had withdrawn his arm.

The ocean sent Francis spiraling away.

He didn't save him, Tia realized, in awe of her brother.

The last time they'd spoken had been a fight. Tia was still angry, but every part of her was waning, and she didn't want the anger to be the last thing left.

She should have let Rylan say sorry.

She wished he knew she forgave him now.

Tia didn't know how long she battled the storm. Every muscle burned, and her throat seared. Her nose was filled with fire, and she could never rid the salt from her eyes. She wished for a brief moment that she could just die, that it could be over and done with.

Then her hand hit something solid.

She grabbed onto it, not caring if it was a life preserver or a sea monster. She needed something that wasn't liquid. Anything.

It was a life jacket surfing atop a swell. Its buoyancy gave Tia instant relief, and she fumbled to clasp it across her chest. The reprieve allowed her to look around for *The Old Eileen*.

The jagged surface revealed nothing. It could have tossed her miles away and she'd have no idea. Too exhausted to cry, Tia focused on keeping her head above water and wished on the stars for the storm to end.

SALT GLITTERED IN her eyelashes. Her skin grew stiff from dehydration. Light had rendered the angry dark ocean into a calm, silvery mirror that reflected the sunrise. Tia couldn't feel her fingers and toes. A horn blared, and Tia regained her senses.

A boat!

"Help," she tried to say, but her voice crackled. She summoned what little remained of her strength and waved her leaden arms above her head. "Help!" she called again and again until her voice gained power and pierced the quiet air.

If the ship had been a few minutes earlier, it wouldn't have been light enough for them to see her. If the surface had been any rougher, her waving arms wouldn't have made a difference. But the ocean had put her through enough, and the ship changed its course to come get her.

It was a corporate fishing vessel, and the man who helped her aboard still had shaving cream slathered on his lower face and didn't speak English.

"Where's the nearest land?" Tia asked to no avail. She scoured her brain for high-school Spanish. "Um . . . dónde . . . tierra," she said as her hands flailed in the air, "aqui?"

The man gave her a dry towel and some beef jerky. "Tierra?" he asked.

Tia ripped off a piece of the meat with her teeth. "Sí, señor."

"Yo te llevaré allí," the man said with a pat on her back. She could only hope he'd said something along the lines of *Yes, I'll take you somewhere safe.*

The man inputted a destination on his screen, and the little boat motored to life, heading northwest. Northwest . . . That meant Florida!

But what about Rylan in the life raft? She needed to find him, and going to Florida posed a new set of problems. She wasn't some kid taken against her will by her father anymore. She had *killed* someone.

Tia bit off a large bite of jerky to cover up the nasty taste in her mouth. Not just *someone*. She had killed *Nico*. Nico who had helped drown MJ. Nico who had kissed her and touched her while he knew in his soul he was the reason her friend was dead.

And now he was dead.

The man left the screen to go back down below and finish shaving.

When he came back, she gestured to his clean-shaven chin and then to her hair. "Can I use that?" she asked. "Mi pelo . . . uh, apagado."

The man nodded and showed her to the head. She looked through the bathroom drawer and retrieved the razor and a pair of scissors.

She twisted her hair up into a ponytail and began to cut.

THE MAN LET her off in Hallandale, wrapping the remaining jerky in tinfoil and sticking it in her life jacket pocket in farewell. When he was gone, she finished it off and left the life jacket in the nearest dumpster. She kept the raincoat's hood up to protect her bald head from peeling in the sun as she walked for an hour to the nearest homeless shelter. They handed her a toothbrush and fleece blanket at the door. She slept there for three nights.

On the fourth morning, she ate cold scrambled eggs in the mess hall and watched the television. Waiting. Hoping.

There was nothing.

So she left the shelter, Rylan's raincoat knotted around her waist. She shoplifted a turkey sandwich and a pack of cigarettes from the nearest gas station. She walked to the marina and looked out at sea, hands deep in her pockets.

Her fingers closed around a tightly folded piece of paper. Without even pulling it out, she knew what it was: the piece of paper torn from the ship's log. The one with the coordinates to Francis's secret island hideout written in blue ink on the back.

If Rylan and Lila had survived, but they hadn't been rescued, they might have managed to get there. She'd told Rylan the heading they were at.

She turned to walk—to where she wasn't sure—when the sight of a familiar white and teak wood boat caught her eye.

The Old Eileen was tucked between the other sailboats in the marina. Tia's heart clambered into her throat, and she walked toward it, afraid the boat would vanish at any moment and prove to be nothing more than a sailor's mirage.

She wasn't, though. She was real, majestic and tall without so much as a scratch from the night in the storm.

But something was different. Tia paused, noticing the dirty footprints all over the deck, the salt that crusted the railings. No one had taken care of her since docking. She must have been searched by the coast guard when they found her. And yet wasn't it a miracle she was here at all?

"Damn," Tia murmured. Somehow they were both here. Unbroken. Uncaptained.

"Don't have to tell me twice."

Tia jumped. Her first instinct was to turn around and push the person who'd spoken into the harbor. She restrained herself, though, hoping he couldn't hear the blood rush to her head. She glanced over her shoulder at the man. He was old and beer-bellied with strands of fish in his teeth and a Bass Pro Shops cap on his head.

"I found her last night," the man continued. Just *her*. So the ship must have been empty when he found it. "Jus' drifting. Can't understand it. Do you work here in the shipyard?"

He'd given her an easy backstory. "Yeah," she said with a

nod. No need to be specific. Tia offered a cigarette to him and put it between her own lips when he refused.

She would need time, she knew. She would need the man's trust. She would need the coordinates on the paper in her pocket. But most of all, to find Rylan and escape what she'd done, Tia needed the ship.

So she smiled through cigarette smoke, thinking about her family and the sea and how she was now more than ever like Lila's sister, Elaina.

The thing that should have died.

"I'm Lainey."

Chapter 56

Jerry Baugh

IT HAD BEEN one month since Jerry Baugh found *The Old Eileen* empty on the Atlantic. It had been eleven days since Agent Koshida told him his brother was murdered. And it had been twenty-eight minutes since Jerry bought a clip-on tie from Walmart and sat down in the restaurant to meet with Detective Madden.

Madden sat opposite him and ordered a gin and tonic. Jerry scanned the many beers on the menu, then got a club soda.

"So . . ." he said, stirring the carbonated bubbles in his drink.

"So." Madden steepled her hands and leaned in. "Here's what we know."

She reviewed the case in detail: everything from the half-baked meat loaf in the stove to Nico de la Vega's drowned body (still the only body they had managed to recover). She laid out the message in the mirror, the absent life raft, the cat left behind.

"Steve," Jerry interrupted, suppressing a burp from the soda.

"Excuse me?"

"He's not *the cat* anymore. I named him." Jerry shifted in his seat and tried for a smile. It felt strange, so he dropped it. "Steve."

Jerry might have been befuddled by his new sobriety, but he could have sworn that Madden smiled back.

"Anyhow," she pressed on, "this case is going over my team's head at this point. Now that the FBI are involved and all."

Jerry adjusted his tie. He had thought about buying a real one before realizing he didn't own a single shirt with a collar. But this dinner meant something, so he'd done his best with the clip-on and a T-shirt. It was the end of an era, after all. "So that's it, then? You think we'll never know?"

Madden opened her mouth, but their waiter, a perky teenager, came by to get their orders. Jerry asked for salmon, Madden steak. She resumed when the waiter was gone.

"This is a high-profile case, Jerry. It's not just gonna die out. Actually, Will—uh, Agent Koshida—informed me as a courtesy that his people are taking Ernie Carmichael in for interrogation. They think that Cameron's crimes ran deeper than just him, and he had a whole network of friends like Matamoros doing it too, maybe. But as far as the missing people, well . . . We'll just have to see if time decides to tell, right?"

"Guess so." Jerry creased his napkin over and over in his lap. "So that's that, then. We just . . . move on."

Madden nodded.

Jerry's gaze dropped to his lap. He had moved on, at some point, from Steve's death. But with everything churned up again, he wasn't quite sure how to proceed.

"Jerry . . ." Madden said. "I'm not supposed to say this. False hope and whatever. But I want you to rest easy from this whole thing. For Steve. Uh, human Steve."

False hope? Jerry braced himself. "What is it? What do you know?"

"They found another body. And they think it might be Francis Cameron's."

Jerry sat back in his seat. Madden watched as he tried to make sense of the whorls in the table. "I . . . He . . ." Jerry swallowed. "How did he die?"

"Drowned, they think."

Drowned. Jerry didn't know what to think. He didn't know what to do or what to feel until a smile, a real one this time, broke over his face. "Well, goddamn. Sounds like . . . I dunno . . ."

"Justice," Madden said, and she lifted her gin and tonic to him and drank.

They sat in silence until their food was delivered, and they both dug in. The salmon tasted fine, but Jerry could tell it wasn't fresh. Summer was half over, and by November, hurricane season would be through. In four months, he'd be back on the seas cruising in *Sheila 2.0* and eating enough fresh fish to last a lifetime. Until then he'd live at the docks, day-fishing in shallower waters.

"So . . . What, uh, have you been up to besides all that?" Jerry asked.

Madden washed down a bite of steak with some gin. "I've been meaning to tell you, actually. I wanted to wait until Lainey was here, but . . ."

"Yeah, she said she wasn't feeling too good. She's looking after the boats. And Steve. Cat Steve."

"Right." Madden reached for the barbecue sauce. "Well, I, uh, met someone. She was reporting on the case, asked me for an interview, and we went out a couple times. Jennifer Byun."

The name rang a bell. She was the author of that article, one of the first ones that had come out last month. "Oh. Congrats."

"Thanks. And Jenni, well, she invited me to her neighborhood book club."

Jerry set down his fork. The image of the ladies of Cherrywood flooding his old kitchen with strange smells and high-pitched laughter came back to him. He vaguely remembered Ida Graves seated beside Madden on the futon, and how could he forget Sheila shooing him out to the garage just when it was time to serve key lime pie?

"Sounds . . . uh . . ."

"And I wanted to see if you'd like to join," Madden said, meeting his gaze over the rim of her glass.

"Me?" Jerry spat a fish bone from his mouth, then regretted it and covered up the saliva on his plate hastily with his napkin. "I, er . . ."

"For old times' sake," she went on. Almost gentle. "And for new times' as well."

Maybe this wasn't the end of things in all the ways Jerry had thought. Maybe he and Madden would continue to be . . . well, whatever it was that they were. Almost friends.

"I'll, uh, see if I'm busy then," he mumbled, knowing full well he had nothing on his calendar until the end of time. Maybe the ladies at book club would enjoy some strong coffee and fresh-caught fish?

"Good."

Madden finished off her meal. Jerry drank his club soda and tried to think of the last time he'd read a book that wasn't about tying cow hitches and bowline knots. The silence sat more comfortably between them.

"Lainey's invited too," Madden added once their plates were cleared. "Although I'm sure she's got better things to do than—"

"Than go to book clubs with old people?" Jerry grunted.

Madden sniffed. "I'm ten years younger than you. You're the old one, Baugh."

"Ehh." Jerry thumbed through his slim wallet to pay in cash, but Madden waved his money away.

"My treat," she said so grudgingly that he almost forgave her for being so nice.

They paid and left the restaurant behind. Madden got into her Volkswagen and rolled down the window. "Tuesdays at seven. Think about it."

Jerry tapped his temple in a solemn promise and watched the detective drive off down the street. He hooked his fingers in his pockets and walked back to the marina. The sun was setting on Hallandale, showing off the proud masts of the sailboats in the yard.

The Old Eileen was the prettiest of all, ghost white and tall without a speck of damage from the hurricane or otherwise to reveal her haunted interior. It was a shame to sell a ship like this. Jerry hoped Steve (the cat) would be able to accept living in *Sheila 2.0* and that Steve (his brother) wouldn't hate him too hard from the grave for giving up the chance to sail.

Jerry's footsteps fell heavy on the slats of the dock, but he hesitated before climbing the catwalk to the sailboat to check on the cat and on Lainey, who was sick in bed.

Something was off . . .

He studied *The Old Eileen*. She stood tall and shining beneath the moon, a survivor of God knew what, and the old home of the man who'd killed Steve.

Unwind Yachting Co., her life preserver read from the stern. Jerry could see the orange shining from where he stood on the dock.

Safe to sail in any gale!

Eileen wasn't likely to change anytime soon, Jerry thought to himself. So that couldn't be it. He looked around, stumped, until it hit him all at once.

Sheila 2.0 was gone. Her absence looked like a gap in the teeth in the marina's pearly smile. Jerry stared at the vacant space of water. Then he saw the piece of paper weighed to the dock by a brick. He moved the brick and picked up the paper, his heartbeat a distant drum as he read.

> *I didn't mean for things to go this way. I didn't mean to end up liking you so much. Or relating to you. Sometimes I even wished things could stay like this, me working for you on your boats, talking about lost brothers and drinking away bad storms. But there's someone I need to find, and—who knows!—maybe this kick in your ass will be the best thing that ever happened to you. I'm sorry for taking Sheila (though, truly it was time you moved on from her), but now you have no choice. Good-bye, stinkpot! Hello, sailboat! It's time, old man.*
>   *Face your fears.*

A thrill built up in Jerry's stomach unlike anything he'd experienced before. Adrenaline? Fear? Maybe even determination.

He didn't understand fully what had happened, only that fate had forced his hand. And that he wanted to make Lainey and Steve—both Steves—proud.

If it was even from Lainey at all. There was no signature at the bottom of the page, just an object bound by tape. Jerry stared at it, unsure what it meant or if he was even supposed to know. He peeled it back from the paper and held it up to the moonlight that beamed from behind the mast of his sailboat.

It was a thimble.

The Convey

Ernie Carmichael Arrested for Involvement in Cameron Disaster

MIKE GRADY

The disturbing ghost ship turned crime shakedown has more key players than initially imagined. Ernie Carmichael, longtime friend of Francis Cameron and Alejandro Matamoros, has been arrested and charged as an accomplice in Cameron's illicit business practices throughout the years. Carmichael was originally meant to be part of the crew on *The Old Eileen*, but he backed out of the getaway at the last second in the hopes police would not connect him to Cameron's crimes. Cameron, while still officially MIA, is suspected to be dead, leaving no word about the fates of his best friend, first mate, wife, or two teenage children. Only Nicolás de la Vega, Matamoros's nephew and a crew member on *The Old Eileen*, has been officially declared dead now that officials received a family DNA sample to confirm the body's identity. His cause of death is drowning. Authorities have not ruled out foul play.

With the rest of the Camerons and crew likely deceased as well, Carmichael seems poised to become a scapegoat in what looks like will be a long and substantial trial. Longtime fans of Lila Logan Cameron have flocked to post videos and photos on social media of the star in her younger years and to wish for her safe return. Oxbridge Academy has held a candlelight vigil for their two former students after releasing a statement that the Cameron twins, specifically Rylan, were "some of Oxbridge Academy's finest." St. Bernadette's School for Girls stated their prayers remain with the family and the crew, and there is continued hope among those who knew Taliea that she is alive.

With an entire month having gone by since the ship was found empty, investigators say no new information is on the horizon. This leaves the police, the press, and the public alike with only speculation as to what might have happened on those final days aboard *The Old Eileen* and what became of the dark and ill-fated empire that was the Cameron family.

Epilogue

```
Tia Cameron
Call sign: Thimble
One Month After the Storm
```

TIA LAY FLAT on her back on the deck of *Sheila 2.0*. The sun rose around her and stretched itself out in every inch of the sky. It was uninhibited by land, and it used the whole space it was given, baking her watery world in gold.

The trusty old motorboat made an ugly chugging noise as she skipped over the water. Tia had been listening to that sound for days, and she still wasn't used to it, but at least that was a constant. At least with the drone of the motor, she couldn't quite hear the way the waves folded over one another. Even when she managed to catch handfuls of sleep, the engine's sound chased away any nightmares of the storm.

Tia gazed up at the sky, but it was the sea below her that consumed her thoughts. She wondered for the thousandth time if she was riding over shipwrecks and treasures, living monsters and dead. Had she crossed the latitude that held her father's body? What about Alejandro's? MJ's? Nico's?

Was Rylan out here, dead, and she just motored on by without seeing? For all she knew, the only survivors were herself and the white ghost ship she'd left far behind.

Tia had almost stolen *The Old Eileen* on one of the first

nights in the harbor. After she'd introduced herself to Jerry, she'd slipped aboard the ship that night and hidden in the bilges until she thought she was alone. She hadn't been. Jerry had almost seen her, and then all would have been lost.

But it was better this way, stealing *Sheila 2.0*, which was steady and easy to control.

She would find Rylan faster.

Then again, if Rylan were dead, she didn't know what she would do next. That world was an impossible one to occupy, so she dismissed it. In her world, her twin was alive, and she would either find him or be content to search forever.

Above her, the clouds were lined in gold, and the goose bumps that had prickled across her skull dissipated. Her hair was growing back now, dark and thick and stubbly. She itched at it nonstop but was secretly thankful for its return. When the wind blew sharp at night, she had that at least to warm her.

The boat alarm jolted her from her senses. It had the same obnoxious tinniness as *Sheila 2.0*'s engine. Tia got up, groaning, and went to the cockpit where the monitor blinked out its warning. She squinted to see what lay in her path.

Land.

The monitor showed a mile more of ocean and then, there in the middle of it tucked away like a secret, an island shaped rather like a triangle or a teardrop. She was headed right for it. Tia had taped the paper with the coordinates to the dashboard of the cockpit, and it flapped gently in the wind.

Tia sat behind the helm. She sank deep into Jerry's cushioned seat, which smelled faintly of grouper, and took the little wheel in her hands. Was there another world where she ended up with her family alive on this island, where *The Old Eileen* never turned up empty or never turned up at all?

Sheila 2.0 churned doggedly forward until the island became a real thing on the horizon. It grew from a speck to a dot to a blob to a promise. As the boat moved into shallower, greener waters, Tia eased the throttle to a stop.

A brief walk from the shoreline stood a house made almost entirely of glass. It had the sleek style of the most cutting-edge modern architecture with three stories, a slanted roof, and an infinity pool on the second level. Beads of water from the humidity gathered on the massive glass windows, and they caught the sunlight like fine jewels.

Tia dropped anchor and leaped over the side, landing thigh-deep in the water. She couldn't take her eyes off the glass house. How long ago had her father had this built? How had he kept it so secret? And most importantly, could there be anyone inside?

Tia almost admired her father, in that moment. He had accounted for everything.

Everything but her.

Tia walked, trancelike, through the combing waves to the shore and hesitated at the edge of the water. The island seemed suspended and silent. Her heart sank. She had come to an empty home.

Then she saw it. A glimpse of orange in the sea of soft, white sand. Farther down the island, closer to the glass house, a life raft had been dragged up on the shore and abandoned.

The missing life raft from *The Old Eileen*.

Inside the house, a light turned on, and a boy's silhouette was made visible through the wide sheet of silver glass.

Tia broke into a sprint, Rylan's name upon her lips. She tripped in the pillows of sand, laughing and crying as she ran for her brother and left the ocean far behind.

★ ★ ★ ★ ★

Behind the Book

I went to sea in September 2022 with the express purpose of taking a break from writing.

I was in college, burned out, heart-sore, and dreaming frequently about the ocean, which led me to scrap all intentions of studying stage acting in Dublin and instead to wind up on a dock in Civitavecchia, boarding a sailboat for the very first time.

Vela, a 112-foot schooner with six sails, two dinghies, and twenty-six cadet crew including myself became my home for ninety days. Life at sea was a world as close to alien as I will ever get.

We slept in netted bunks that kept us from flying into each other during storms. We took turns cooking in the galley and passing sizzling platters up through a gopher hole. We sang Christmas carols in a thunderstorm, played chanteys on my ukulele, and attended class in the salon as our shipmates chopped onions while wearing scuba masks.

Vela carried us proudly from Rome to Sardinia, from Madeira to the Canaries, across the Atlantic (seventeen days!) and to Dominica and Antigua. On the voyage, I'd been homesick, seasick, awestruck, and inspired. I hadn't dreamed for weeks. My watch team leader told us boat dreams were rare. They happened because they meant something.

My first boat dream was a story I hope I'll write someday soon.

My second boat dream was of the Camerons.

I knew the instant I woke that this was going to be my next novel, and anyone who has ever written a book knows how rare a moment like that can be.

I kept a notebook with me during my three months at sea, detailing every moment that mattered to me. I needed to be able to inhabit the minds of four different people who had four different ways of feeling about life at sea. I wanted there to be a touch of history and mythology to bring the setting alive.

Yet it wasn't until we caught several massive fish in deep waters that the Camerons really crystallized for me. There was a yellow-finned tuna, killed with the same kind of mallet Tia uses in the novel. And there was a sailfish, maybe eight feet long, that had its bill snapped off and kept to make jewelry while the rest of it was thrown back alive. I had never witnessed fishing let alone deep-sea fishing before, and it left me both horrified and mesmerized. I couldn't stop thinking about it. But the image that stuck with me most was not of the fish themselves but of their blood on the white deck and the crewman who quietly hosed it away while most everyone else celebrated at midships.

Replaying it all in my mind later, I knew that I wanted to capture both the twisted nature of the ocean and the even more intricate (and deadly) environment of a family.

This wasn't meant to just be the story of an empty ship or its missing people. It's the story of the kind of person who could beat the fish to death, the person who handed the mallet to someone else, the person who couldn't stand to watch, the person who couldn't look away, and the one who stood back to hose off the blood as everyone else went to feast.

No One Aboard became my love letter to real and storied sea monsters: the ones that swim underwater, and those that sail on top.

Acknowledgments

My profound gratitude and love to all of the following:

Mom, Dad, Pluto—my closest creative confidants, and my lifelong best friends. You are who I write for.

Nathan, who has a matching light in his eyes. Megan, who always picks up. Riona, who would kill for me (and I for her).

My friends who, in making it with me this far (can you believe we've made it this far?), have become family.

Everyone I have ever performed for or alongside, whether it was in a cafechapetorium in Denver, a black box in Sarasota, or one of the venues between San Francisco and Salem.

Ann Rose for finding me and never letting go.

Melanie Fried and the entire team at Graydon House for making my dream my reality, as well as Elita Sidiropoulou and Bora Tekogul for the book's stunning cover design, and Leah Mol for stepping up.

My fellow ferocious Rosebuds—Tom, Alyssa, Cassie, Chelsea, Sydney, Jake, Stan, Amalie, Fish, Emma, Cynthia, Erin, Melissa T, Tammy, Layne, Casper, Richard, Melissa M, Melanie, Stephanie, Bindiya, Heather, Stefany, Charlene, Steph, Celeste, Jennifer, Sara, Caitlin, Renee, Sky, Jessica, Holly, and Ish.

Vela, and everyone who sailed with me in the fall of 2022. Watch Team 2 for letting me butcher retelling *The Odyssey*, the residents of the fo'c'sle for sleeping beside (and on top of) me, and Rachel, Ghost, Zoe, Jac, Skylar, Alison, Calum, Sam, Ash, Matt, Riley, Caro, and Allie for making me feel less alone in the center of the sea.

And finally, you, dear reader. Thank you for lending your precious imagination to this story. This is the beginning.

Discussion Questions

1. *No One Aboard* is told from the perspective of four different characters: Tia, Rylan, Lila, and Jerry. Who did you connect with the most and why? What are the benefits of multiple perspectives in a story like this?

2. How does the ocean atmosphere reflect the journey of the Cameron family? In what ways does the setting affect the mood of the story?

3. In the end, we find out Nico and Alejandro were involved in MJ's death. Is letting someone die the same as killing them? Is Tia's retaliation anything close to justice?

4. Francis Cameron talks a lot about being a self-made man. Does he deserve the life he has? Does he deserve his death?

5. The death of the sailfish gives insight into each character. Who would you be in a similar situation?

6. In the fable of *The Old Eileen*, we learn that a band of sailors attempted to fly to the stars but never returned. What does this tell us about the Camerons, their legacy, and their empty ship?

7. What are the central themes in *No One Aboard*, and how do they manifest through the characters' actions? How does the title reflect these themes?

8. How is the contrast between wealth and personal fulfillment depicted through the narrative?

9. How does the author build suspense and maintain tension within the book?

10. How does the novel's conclusion address the central mystery, and what questions remain unanswered? What do you think happens to Lila and the twins after the end of the novel?